Hidden Secrets

Embrace Change !.

Linda

LINDA RAKOS

Tellwell Talent
www.tellwell.ca

ISBN
978-0-2288-7951-0 (Hardcover)
978-0-2288-7950-3 (Paperback)
978-0-2288-7952-7 (eBook)

PART I

Chapter One

Time passes slowly in hospitals. Glancing at the heart monitor, Kit Bennett noticed that the rhythm was weaker. Her own heart hurt with insufferable sorrow, and she couldn't stop the tears. She knew her grandmother, Lou Kennedy, was on the threshold of death. Kit closed her eyes and wiped her tears. When she felt her grandmother's hand close over hers, Kit leaned forward, and lovingly caressed her grandmother's cheek. The woman had had a hard life and it showed in the deep lines of her face.

In a frail voice, Lou whispered, "I have to tell you something important."

Kit's smile was forced, and deep sadness coated every word, "You need to save your breath. It's too hard for you to talk."

Lou shook her head, "Death is only one thing to be sad over. Regret is another."

"I have never regretted the life I had with you."

Lou could no longer shield her granddaughter from further pain. Her voice faded as she struggled to continue but she was determined, "It's about your mother."

Kit had no desire to dig up painful memories. They had enough to last a lifetime because of her mother, Torrie Kennedy. "You're the only family that Kenzie and I really had."

"There's something you need to know." Kit leaned in closer to concentrate on what her grandmother was saying. "That may not be true. Your father didn't die before you were born." Lou knew what a loaded statement this was. "Your mother lied to you, and she swore me to secrecy. I'm sorry, I was wrong to do that." She braced herself for her granddaughter's reaction.

Kit's reactive anger was intense. Too angry to speak, she allowed the resentment to fester as questions erupted in her mind. Her voice trembled with indignation when she asked the obvious, "Why didn't you tell me?"

Lou's voice became shaky, "It wasn't out of misguided loyalty to your mother. I owed her nothing. We both know she wasn't much of a mother. I didn't want to lose you. I'd already lost Torrie." Lou stopped to take another shallow breath, "Facing death changes things."

Kit stared down at her grandmother in disbelief. For twenty-four years, she believed her father was dead. Her shoulders slumped, wondering how they could have lied.

With all the strength she could muster Lou continued, "Your mother may have died years ago, but I've kept Torrie's keepsakes and journals in the attic. That's where you may find a clue that might help you find your father. What you do with what you find is up to you." With a gesture of resignation, Lou closed her eyes. There was nothing more to say.

Life could be cruel and unfair at times, but this was unbelievable. Kit was numb with shock as a sense of sorrow settled over her. She wondered how Lou had endured keeping such a secret all these years. Closing her own eyes, Kit listened to the monitor counting away her grandmother's life while she reflected on her own.

Tragedy heaped upon tragedy. Death had always seemed to overshadow Kit's life, starting with her mother. Kit used the word lightly, if at all, when thinking about her mother. Torrie had always been a rebellious child growing up, and defiant when she became a parent. Torrie wasn't about to let having a child change her life, so she left Kit for Lou to raise. It was her grandmother who filled the vacated role of mother. Torrie would come and go over the years. When Kit was little, she would spend days looking out the window waiting for her mom to come home. When Torrie did return, Kit would be so excited to see her. Then suddenly she'd be gone. Never a goodbye. Thanks to Lou, Kit understood that it was Torrie who was the problem. The problem would show up unexpectedly, and sporadically, disrupting their lives again and again. Kit was young enough to miss her mother, yet old enough to hate her mother. As Kit grew older, she began to resent Torrie every time she came home. When Kit turned fifteen, Torrie died. That's when their home life became normal. It took Kit years to let go of the hate.

When Kit was eighteen, and attending university, someone new entered her life. The day she met Michael Bennett changed her life. Kit was riding the overcrowded bus home after classes and kept bumping the person behind her with her backpack. When she turned to apologize, she saw an attractive young man with broad shoulders who did justice to his military uniform. Topping off the impressive muscular build was a ruggedly handsome face, and she looked up into the most magnetic blue eyes. Then he smiled, a beautiful heart-stopping smile that made his eyes crinkle at the corners. From that moment on he became her life.

Kit fell in love with Mike. She liked his quietness, his gentleness. His caring nature made him sensitive while being thoughtful, and considerate. Loving him was easy. She felt his love in a thousand ways. Unspoken, but real. His love gave her happiness. It gave meaning to everything else in life. Kit spent hours lost in his arms as they planned their future together and shared their dreams. Kit wanted nothing more than to marry Mike, get their own home, and have children. All Mike wanted was to make her happy and serve his country. He told Kit he always knew his life's purpose was to serve his country. Mike had joined the army the day he turned eighteen. Kit was fiercely proud of him. They knew their love was strong enough to endure the separation should he get deployed.

They were going to wait to get married until after she graduated, but Mike received notice of deployment for active duty overseas just before her final year. They married the following weekend. Their chapel wedding was a small, private ceremony. It was the happiest day of Kit's life. It was the day she began her life with the only man who ever meant anything to her. They may have been young, but they were happy, and excited about their future, which was going to be filled with excitement, adventure, and romance.

Lou beamed as she watched her granddaughter marry the man who had captured her heart. She was proud of Kit, who had chosen an honest, and honorable man for her husband. Someone who would love, and care for Kit and give her everything she needed and deserved. Finally, happiness in her granddaughter's life.

Kit agreed to live with Lou until Mike returned. After Mike left, life returned to what it was before they had married. Even though Mike hadn't been gone long, Kit knew she was missing him. Life was hectic, and she wasn't sleeping well. Feeling tired and listless, Kit hoped she wasn't getting sick.

It was the second morning of being sick to her stomach that Lou addressed the situation. The symptoms Kit had been experiencing recently were just like Torrie's so there was little doubt in Lou's mind when she said, "I think you should stop at the pharmacy on your way home tonight and pick up a pregnancy kit."

That night Lou's belief was confirmed. Once the shock wore off, a smile played around Kit's pale lips as a surge of joy filled her heart. Her hand dropped down to her stomach. Mike's baby. As lousy as she felt, she couldn't stop smiling. Mike was thrilled. They vowed to break the cycle and give their baby a normal childhood filled with love and two parents. Kit and Mike knew they would share something special, unique to both of them. A real family life that would last forever. One can never predict fate. Forever didn't last long. Fate had other plans.

One stormy night in December there was a firm knock on the door. When Lou answered, the taller man spoke, "I'm looking for Mrs. Katherine Bennett."

Kit, who had overheard, was still smiling as she reached the door. She gasped as her eyes darted between the two men in full-dress uniform, and her knees went weak. "I'm Kit Bennett."

The notifying officer cleared his throat. This time his voice was deliberate, and purposeful, "We're sorry to inform you that Petty Officer Michael MacKenzie Bennett was killed yesterday in the line of duty."

Kit cried out as she collapsed in the arms of her grandmother. At the age of twenty she went from wife to war widow.

They gave Mike the military funeral he deserved. Kit stood in front of a snow-covered casket and watched as her husband's body was lowered into the ground. It was the saddest day of her life. Such a tragic time. To have created a child with the man she loved. Something so wondrous and precious, but not having him there to share it with. There would be no tender moments to remember as parents together. Kit wept often. When Kit felt her baby kick it was a reminder that life goes on. "Poor little baby," she cried, as she placed her hands on her rounded stomach. "Your daddy would have loved you so much. I'll love you enough for both of us," she promised. Even though Kit couldn't wait to hold the tiny person growing inside her, her heart ached knowing her baby wouldn't know its father either. Sorrow weighed heavily on her heart until she felt she couldn't bear it. Kit vowed she would never open that part of her heart again.

Life got worse. Due to failing health, Lou had to quit work. Things were different for both of them.

Kit pushed herself through long grueling days of school, and longer nights of loneliness. It would have been easy to slip into a depression, but Kit had been introduced to loss at a young age. She was in her last month of pregnancy, and reality was surfacing. Kit looked down at her growing stomach, recognizing the responsibilities facing her. When she couldn't suppress her feelings of self-doubt, she turned to Lou, "I want to be a good mother."

Accurately reading her granddaughter's fears, Lou tried to comfort Kit, "You're not like Torrie. You're mature, and self-disciplined. You'll always see to your child's welfare even when the odds are against you. You will deal with your responsibilities and fulfill your obligations. I know you'll be a wonderful mother, Kit," she said with true conviction.

Kit prayed her grandmother was right.

Lou forced lightness into her voice, hoping to dispel Kit's gloomy mood, "We'll manage like we always do. Together, we'll get through this, too. You and me, like it has always been."

Kit started to cry. "I don't know what I'd do without you."

Lou gathered Kit in her arms. "I wish there were something that I could say that would ease the pain. Sadly, only time can do that."

It had been a long winter. Kit's baby was due any day. On the first day of spring, the season of new beginnings, and new life, Kit's baby arrived. Kit welcomed her infant daughter with an immediate understanding of Lou's unconditional love for her. Her fears about not having maternal instincts disappeared the moment she held her baby, and she accepted the role naturally. Cuddling her newborn in her arms, she was transfixed by her baby's rosy mouth and tiny fingers. Kit lightly stroked her baby's cheek and kissed her forehead. Her baby girl was tiny, but perfect. "MacKenzie Kennedy Bennett, meet your great-grandmother, the best lady in the world."

Lou giggled, "Let's go with Gram."

"Okay, Gram it is. For short I will call her Kenzie," Kit informed, as she handed her daughter over to Lou to hold.

Lou cuddled Kenzie close and smiled down as her great-granddaughter. "I see a little of Mike in her, and she has Torrie's beautiful green eyes. They sparkle just like Torrie's did."

Kit gave a small, uncertain smile, "I never planned on being a single parent, or to still be living with you. I imagined being happily married and raising this child with the love of my life."

Lou offered no words of comfort. Like always she kept it real. She intentionally held Kit's gaze, "It does no good to brood on what might have been, Life doesn't give us a choice. It's up to you to find your happiness."

Kit smiled down at her infant daughter. "For now, baby girl, you are my happiness." Kenzie would know she was loved, and every day Kit would tell her daughter all about her wonderful dad.

Lou saw it as her responsibility to take care of Kenzie, just like she did with Kit. She felt she had failed Torrie, and because of that Kit had suffered as well. "You know I'll always help you any way I can."

Life moved forward. Kit earned her degree and took a teaching position. Many women raised their children without help. Kit was grateful that she didn't have to. She knew she was lucky to have Lou. She leaned on her grandmother for support, and for strength, especially when she couldn't fill the emptiness she sometimes felt. Kit often cried in her bedroom behind closed doors. Lou often cried in the kitchen. At times, they cried together.

"It's going to be okay," Lou promised.

"Maybe, but not for a long time." Despite all that had happened, Mike's death and the heartache that lingered, Kit always considered the birth of their daughter a blessing. Her baby girl was her reason for living. "Kenzie Bennett, you may not have been planned for, but God works in mysterious ways. You are the best part of your dad that I can ever have." Kit was glad her baby was unaware of the sad circumstances she'd been born into. Kit hoped one day she could explain it to Kenzie, but it sure didn't make sense right now.

Kit pushed the memories away and once again heard the slow beep, beep, beep of the monitor. She sighed heavily, wondering how long she'd been lost in the past. She emptied her mind, unwilling to allow herself to dwell on the unhappy memories that had invaded. She knew how to shut them out and lock them away behind the invisible armor that she had relied on in the past. Kit wiped away her tears as she looked lovingly at her grandmother, grateful for the stability this kind woman had brought to her life.

Before the sun set that night, Lou Kennedy passed away.

*****

Kit had allowed herself to grieve, but now the time had come to pick up the shattered pieces of her life. After existing in a protective numbness, Kit knew it was time to let her grandmother go. It was going to be difficult, but she had no choice. It was strange. The house itself was unchanged but everything was different. Even though Lou was gone, her presence was everywhere. Her latest romance novel was on the side table next to her recliner, her crocheting in the basket below. Kit's eyes welled. She wanted to hear the television that was always too loud or listen to Lou humming in the kitchen as she puttered. The house was too quiet.

Kit's friend had taken Kenzie for the day, and Kit was committed to going through her grandmother's things. She couldn't afford the luxury of wallowing in self-pity. Unconsciously, Kit looked up knowing she had to start in the attic. With grim determination Kit climbed the stairs. The sunlight beaming through the attic window revealed cobwebs hanging from the rafters. The air was stale and hot. Disturbed dust danced in the sunbeams as Kit began to weave her way toward the totes that stored packed memories, and hidden secrets. She dragged a couple of totes over and sat cross-legged in the middle of the floor. In the first box were items saved by Lou. Here were the familiar memories: baby clothes, school pictures, drawings, earned trophies and medals. Another contained photo albums. Looking at a picture of Torrie as a toddler she could see the similarities between her and Kenzie.

Kit's eyes were drawn to the far corner where Mike's personal gear was stacked. The familiar ache came as she knew it would. The loss swept over her, as real as if it had just happened. A sorrow so strong that even the years hadn't diminished it. She missed what they should have had. Sweat ran down her face, mixing in with her tears. She wished that Mike were here to help her get through this. Wiping her tears, she forced herself to pull her scattered thoughts together, and rein in her emotions.

Kit moved on to the totes she guessed were her mother's. She found the journals in the first one she opened. Kit felt her stomach twist. As anxious as she was to read them, she moved to the second tote hoping to find what she was desperately searching for. Inside were the keepsakes that Torrie had collected over the years. At the very bottom in a brown envelope, she found her birth certificate. The walls seemed to close in around her, and for a moment her world stopped. It was time to reveal her mother's betrayal. Her hands shook as she focused her eyes on the print. Above the line for father was the name, William Joseph Calhoun. The full implication of what she found hit her. She had the name of her father. Kit was unable to ignore the hurt and anger. She read the name again, branding it into her memory.

Would she be able to find him? How did she even start? Her mind was bombarded with questions that would have to wait, as she forced her mind away from her disturbing thoughts. She couldn't think about them right now. Kit took the birth certificate, and journals down to her bedroom to read later. Right now, she needed to make the most of her time. Kit started a new tote, placing personal items of Torrie and Lou's inside to be shared with Kenzie when she was older. Torrie may not have been much of a role model, but Kenzie needed to know what an incredible person Lou Kennedy was.

That night, Kit began reading Torrie's journals. Torrie's written words spewed forth a deluge of best forgotten childhood memories. Few were pleasant. Torrie's journal entries were reflective of her mental highs and lows. When she was on a high, they were descriptive, and entertaining. Kit could tell when Torrie began to crash. The entries were less frequent and often depressing. Then there wouldn't be any entries for weeks, even months. She gasped out loud when she found what she was looking for.

What a weekend. Becky and I went to Ellensburg to the rodeo. Love, love, love those cowboys. Easy to hook up and party all night. Got lucky. Roped me a real Canadian cowboy for the night, and he was gorgeous. Partied hard, then left his buddies and walked over to his truck and horse trailer that had sleeping quarters. Perfect. I asked him what BJ was short for. He said his birth name was, William Joseph Calhoun. His family ranched in southern Alberta for generations. When he let my hand go to open the trailer door, I gave him a seductive smile, "Buckle up, cowboy, you're in for a wild ride." I was right.

What a night. I was swept away by BJ Calhoun, but he was just a one-nighter like all the others. I never break my rules. Live for today, never commit to tomorrow. Good looks, good time, goodbye.

Hours passed as Kit turned page after page. Her mother's written words brought back memories she wished she could forget. The ugly truth resurfaced, crumbling her defenses.

I thought I had the stomach flu. Found out today I'm pregnant. Big surprise! I thought I'd been taking my pills. Obviously not. This will give mom something new to bitch about.

Hate being pregnant. Hate living at home. Hate mom's rules. Hate mom!!!

If mom won't let me put the kid up for adoption, she can play the martyr and raise it. I'm not going to let a stupid mistake ruin my life. As soon as I can I'm out of here. I don't mean this house. I mean this God-forsaken town. I might even go to another state.

Emotion overwhelmed Kit. Unbearable pain caused Kit to pause. Taking several deep breaths, she forced herself to continue, even though every word was cutting through her.

My baby is beautiful. One look at her confirmed my belief as to who the father is. She has the same gray eyes as her daddy. The sexy Canadian cowboy didn't shoot blanks. He'll never know. He won't be saddled with a kid any more than I will. No sense ruining his life.

Mom is always riding my ass. I'm sick of hearing that I need to take responsibly for my daughter. God, doesn't she get tired of bitching? I hate being a mother. The biggest mistake I made was not giving my baby up for adoption the day she was born.

Those words hurt Kit more deeply than anything else she had read. It was difficult to breathe. The more Kit read, the more she realized what a pathetic person Torrie was. Not only as a daughter, but as a mother. The message was clear as she read page after page. Torrie neglected her responsibilities for Kit even when she was home. She wasn't about to deal with the duties of raising a child. Kit had to wonder why Torrie even came home.

I'm out of here. I met a guy. Catching the love bus and heading to California. I decide how to live my life. No one is going to tell me what to do, and no kid is going to tie me down.

Kit died a little more inside but continued reading.

Happy birthday, Kitten. I can't believe she's thirteen today. A teenager. I should have been home for Kit's birthday. She must hate me. I hate myself.

Why couldn't Torrie see that every child needs their mother? Kit continued until she had read every journal. Reliving those years, even now, was painful.

I need to go home. I haven't been back for months. I'll have to hitch-hike. I have no money. I have no control over myself. I wish I were dead.

That was the last entry written by Torrie. Kit guessed it was written just months before her death. Every entry was a reminder of Torrie's transient lifestyle, temporary visits, and downhill spirals. Remaining questions would remain unanswered. Kit thought she had buried her feelings deep enough that she could manage this, but she wasn't emotionally prepared for Torrie's continuous cruel words. It wasn't new, and tonight she couldn't make the unbearable pain go away. She relived scenes over and over, and each time she remembered a horrifying new detail. Kit wiped fiercely at her tears with trembling hands as she lay on her bed sobbing. Exhausted, Kit crawled under the covers, and turned off the light. As tired as she was, sleep didn't come quickly. Memory after memory assaulted her bringing with it another flood of emotions. Torrie's words continued to echo in her head. Damn you, Torrie Kennedy. Why couldn't you stay in the past where you belong? Loneliness and grief grabbed hold. Never had she felt so alone.

Kit shifted both her position, and her train of thought. She was at a major crossroad in her life. Now that she had found what she'd been looking for the big question was what was she going to do about it? Her mind was a maze as options whirled. She knew some were too crazy to consider. Or were they? The fact was she had a big decision to make. Did she go looking for her father? At the very least, William Joseph Calhoun had the right to know he had a daughter. What did she want from a stranger? What role did she want him to play in her life? Maybe she would find the answers if she found him. However, a reluctant father could be worse than no father at all. That was a possibility she didn't want to consider.

By daylight Kit knew what she had to do. She had fought her inner battle, and after a great deal of soul-searching, and considerable deliberation, she had chosen her path. She knew she really had only one choice. Even if the odds were insurmountable, she had to try and find her father. This was her chance to put things right and provide Kenzie with a family. She had made a vow to Kenzie the day she was born, and she would never break it. Kenzie was her number one priority, and Kit would do whatever it took to do what was best for her daughter. The responsibility of Kenzie now rested squarely on her shoulders. Although Kit believed this was the right choice, she felt a sense of fear because she had to venture out on her own. There was no Lou. As deeply as she believed in what she had decided, she would have appreciated approval, and support from the person who had been the most important person in her life.

The next few weeks were a blur. Lou Kennedy had lived a simple life. Her will was straightforward, so it was easy to settle her estate. Kit had been surprised at the large life insurance policy Lou had. Thinking back, she realized that was what Lou meant when she said, "I've taken care of you and Kenzie." Thanks to her grandmother Kit didn't have to worry. The house she inherited sold just days after it was listed, Lou's car had sold the week before. Even though it was old, Kit decided to keep the Jeep because it had been Mike's. Kit walked around the empty house. The only thing inside were memories, good and bad. Other than what she packed into the Jeep, the rest of her belongings were now in a rented storage unit. There were times, like now when the loneliness caught up to her, threatening to overwhelm her. Kit lifted her chin. She didn't know what the future would hold, but she was ready to put her past behind her. There were no ties left to cut. No matter what, she would deal with the consequences of her decision. Dare she allow herself to dream, even to hope?

Chapter Two

Kit woke with a start in the early hours of the morning. This had become a familiar pattern since finding the whereabouts of William Joseph Calhoun. Kit recognized how deprived she felt when she discovered he was alive. It reinforced her decision to see if he was her father. If he was, he deserved to know he had a daughter. What Torrie did wasn't fair to either of them. Today was the big day. Kit was leaving Walla Walla with her daughter, and driving to Alberta, Canada. She closed her eyes and prayed for the strength she knew she would need.

Kit had the Jeep stocked with snacks, drinks, Kenzie's favorite blanket, a few toys, and of course Mucky, the stuffed monkey that went everywhere with Kenzie. Her daughter couldn't say monkey when she was little so the name Mucky stuck. Kit buckled Kenzie in her car seat and climbed behind the wheel. After fastening her seat belt Kit sat for a moment. The impact of the path she'd chosen suddenly overwhelmed her. Nothing had ever felt this frightening or more important. She turned the key and pulled away without a backward glance. Her eyes had to be focused on the future. Lou always said that you must have hope and believe in possibilities. Again, Kit had to wonder what was in her future.

The monotonous hours, and endless miles allowed Kit time to think. It also allowed her fears to take over. Was she doing the right thing by chasing a dream? Was she opening herself up to more pain, more disappointment, and more heartache? Possibly. It was a risk she was willing to take. She had nothing to lose. What did she expect from this man if she found him, and he was her father? Trying to be realistic, Kit played the scenario of finding her dad different ways in her head. The more tired she became the worse the scenarios were. What if the man she was going to see wasn't even her dad? Or, even worse, what if he was, and he turned her away. She was unable to rein in her runaway imagination. Kit was aware of fate. You can never predict it, and it can ambush you without warning. Deep down, she still believed this was her only choice. She wiped away the tears that had fallen.

Kit had been driving for hours. Her head throbbed, and her eyes burned with fatigue. Her earlier excitement began to fall by the wayside as she stared at the miles of Interstate ahead. For the hundredth time Kit wondered if she was doing the right thing. She recognized that part of her decision was a result of losing Lou. She was now a single mom who was all alone.

Kenzie began to fuss. She was tired of riding in the car and was hungry. They both were. Daylight was beginning to fade, and Kit didn't want to drive at night. They grabbed a quick meal before checking into a motel. Once Kenzie was settled for the night, Kit became aware of the heavy silence, and the tightness in her chest. Kit missed the familiar: her own room, her grandmother's voice. New thoughts crept in about the man who could be her father. He probably had a family of his own. Would he accept her and Kenzie as an extended family? Worn out, Kit yawned wide, and climbed into bed. Within minutes she, too, was asleep.

The morning sun filtered through the curtains as Kit woke. She lay quietly trying to regain the optimism she felt when she had left Washington. Even though doubts lingered, she was no less determined about her mission when she headed out again. Kit was relieved when they finally crossed into Alberta where golden wheat fields welcomed her. Other areas found cattle grazing alongside the highway. The landscape was ever-changing as she drove west. The flat prairie had transformed to rolling hills that lay at the feet of the majestic Rocky Mountains.

Kit was tired of driving, and her anxiety kicked in because she wasn't sure where she was going. She pulled over to look at her map for the second time. The sunlight was blinding, and it was oppressively hot. She opened her window to let in fresh air. Her face was tense as she consulted the road map.

Kenzie, who had been sleeping, woke up. Kit put down the map and dug around in the tote bag for a fruit bar, and a juice carton. She poked in the straw, and handed it to her daughter, spilling her coffee on the map in the process. Fighting the urge to scream in frustration, Kit gripped the steering wheel with both hands, and laid her forehead against them. She took a deep breath, and squeezed her eyes shut to hold back tears.

A pick-up pulled over in front of her, a young man stepped out, and started toward the Jeep. The red-headed stranger offered a friendly smile as he bent over to talk to her, "Is everything all right?" Dressed in faded wrangler jeans, work shirt, and scuffed boots he was the epitome of a real cowboy. And he smelled like one.

Kit looked up at him with distressed eyes.

Riley's eyes widened a fraction as he gave her a puzzled look, as if he'd seen her before. He knew that was unlikely, since her vehicle had Washington plates. He saw the map on the seat next to her, "Are you lost?"

Kit realized he was staring at her with open curiosity. She stared back, humiliated that she was close to tears. Knowing she was lost, and vulnerable made her willing to trust a stranger. "I'm looking for a ranch owned by the Calhoun family."

"This is your lucky day. I'm Riley Grayson, and that's where I'm headed. I was in town picking up supplies for Will Calhoun. Follow me. Another couple of miles down the road I'll be turning left, and we'll wind our way west. I'll have you there within the hour."

The smile that spread across Kit's face was one of relief. Some of the fatigue disappeared from her eyes, and her uneasiness faded as he walked away.

Riley walked back to his truck thinking again that her face looked familiar. He climbed behind the wheel, signaled as he pulled out, and waved.

Kit did the same and pulled in close behind him and followed as she said a quick prayer of thanks. Her heart had stopped when he said the name, Will Calhoun. In that moment, an unbelievable wave of excitement washed over Kit. Was it possible that she'd soon be meeting her father? Things appeared to be taking a turn for the better. Kit hoped it would last.

An hour later, Riley signaled, and turned off the gravel road, and drove up a long private drive lined with trees on both sides. At the end of the drive was a sprawling ranch house with a triple attached garage. Off to the right in a sheltered clearing was a second dwelling, the original two-story house.

"I think we're here," she muttered to Kenzie, as she drove her Jeep down the private drive. Tears stung Kit's eyes, but now they were tears of relief. Without the stranger's help she would never have found this place. The first part of her ordeal was over. The next part would be far more difficult. Kit swallowed hard and took an anxious breath.

Kit glanced around as they drove slowly past corrals, and outbuildings. Had she not been so blinded by fear, she would have been impressed. She noticed an older man leaning on the rail while a younger man was inside the corral training a horse. She turned her attention away from them, but Kit could feel the curious stares. When Riley pulled over and stopped, Kit did the same. She remained behind the wheel and inhaled deeply to gather her courage.

Will Calhoun set his coffee cup on the counter, and looked out the kitchen window when he heard the vehicles drive in. He was expecting Riley with the supplies, but he didn't recognize the Jeep pulling in behind him.

They all watched as Riley opened the driver door. A young lady stepped out, and quickly opened the back door. Her thick mane of hair fell forward as she pulled out a young child who nestled into her neck. The man on the horse had dismounted and was now leaning on the top rail. The two men at the fence exchanged curious glances. "I wonder who she is?" commented Trace Grayson, the horse trainer, and Riley's older brother.

"She's obviously here for a reason. Something important based on the somber look on her face," was all the older man had to say. Cliff Murphy was a confirmed bachelor, who had called Valley View his home most of his life. He started as a hired hand, but he'd been with them so many years he was more family than employee. He lived year-round in the bunk house that housed part-time wranglers in the busy season.

Will and his wife, Sadie, stepped out on the verandah as Riley led Kit up to the house. Riley took his leave and joined the two men at the corral. The elderly couple greeted Kit with polite smiles. Sadie Calhoun's warm hazel eyes were accented by laugh lines that enhanced the character of her friendly face. There was nothing intimidating about her. Her husband, on the other hand, stood there tall and formidable.

The summer sun, already hot and high, beat down on Kit's pounding head. The butterflies in her stomach had been replaced by sheer panic. This confrontation wouldn't be easy. She forced her legs to move and climb the steps to stand in front of the couple.

Will didn't like strangers showing up unexpectedly. "Can I help you?" he finally said, his voice gruff.

Kit's chin came up. "I'm looking for William Joseph Calhoun." She hoped she didn't sound as frightened as she felt.

"Well, you found him. I'm Will Calhoun. Is there something I can do for you?"

Kit, shocked by the old man's revelation, gathered herself sufficiently to say, "Yes, in fact, there is." Her throat had gone unbearably dry. She swallowed hard. "My name is Kit Bennett, and I believe you are my father."

Will raised a disbelieving eyebrow, "I don't know what you think you know, but I know for sure you aren't my daughter. For God's sake, I'm old enough to be your grandfather."

For a moment, neither Will nor Sadie Calhoun could do more than stare at her. The young woman, with the same dark hair, and gray eyes as their son, gazed at them with troubled eyes. Kit shifted Kenzie to her other hip so she could open her bag. She pulled out her birth certificate. Stuttering, she declared, "My birth mother, Torrie Kennedy, has named you as my birth father." The atmosphere remained unwelcoming. Kit didn't know what would happen next as she stood there terrified and confused.

Will continued to stare at Kit. "I believe it's my son, and namesake, better known as BJ, that you're looking for. I'm sorry to inform you that he's away until tomorrow."

Kit hadn't put any thought into what would happen once she got here. She knew she was in a dilemma, and she struggled to hold back the tears.

Sadie's eyes took in the young woman's pale, pinched features. The elderly woman couldn't ignore the desperation in Kit's tone, and the dark circles under her eyes were clearly visible. Will's eyes narrowed, but before he could say anything, Sadie threw him a silencing look. Sadie reached out, "Welcome to Valley View. I'm Sadie Calhoun, BJ's mother. Come inside so we can figure out what to do."

Kit hesitated, knowing she wasn't welcome. That couldn't matter. She reminded herself that she was here for a reason.

Silently they made their way inside. The house was refreshingly cool, the air-conditioning a welcome relief. It helped to revive Kit. She sat down with Kenzie on her lap while Sadie got them both a glass of water. The kitchen was filled with sunlight, and the delicious smell of homemade baking.

Sadie was impressed that the small child said thank you without a prompt from her mother. It was followed by, "I'm hungry." Sadie asked if it would be okay to give her a cookie.

Kit nodded, "This is my daughter, Kenzie."

Sadie could see the tension in Kit's face. "Are you okay?"

"I'm fine," Kit said wearily, but failed to even convince herself. She took a deep breath hoping it would help. It didn't.

Sadie studied Kit. She could only imagine how hard this was for the poor girl. "Let's worry about tomorrow, tomorrow. We'll deal with things when BJ gets home." The elderly woman's eyes were kind when she said, "You can stay here tonight."

Kit's relief was so overwhelming, that Kit had to close her eyes as the urge to cry swept over her. She never cried, not normally. But, then again, these were hardly normal times. She was relieved because she had no idea where she would have gone. "That's very considerate of you. Your ranch is quite a distance from town. I never thought about what I'd do once I got here." Staying was the obvious solution for today. In a reserved voice, she agreed. She'd stay at least until she'd talked to their son. Her dad?

"Follow me and I'll show you where your rooms are." Kit noticed family pictures as they passed through the living room. The Calhoun home appeared comfortable, and lived in. Sadie turned into a bedroom at the end of a long hallway. "This room connects to a Jack-and-Jill bathroom that leads to another bedroom for your daughter. I'll watch Kenzie while you get whatever you need to bring in. Will can help you."

"That's not necessary. I don't have much. We won't get in your way," Kit said carefully. She kneeled beside her daughter, "I'll be right back, Kenzie. You and Mucky wait here."

"Okay, Mommy." The little girl clutched her monkey tighter.

Sadie took the child's hand, "Come, let's go get another cookie."

While Kit went outside, Sadie returned to the kitchen. Will was seated at the table. Now that they were alone, and Kit was out of earshot, Sadie said the obvious, "Guess there's no doubt who her father is. That girl is the spitting image of BJ. It's going to be an awful shock to him to find out that he not only has a daughter, but a granddaughter as well."

Will leaned back in his chair, "Tongues are sure to wag, and this news will spread like wildfire. I've lived here all my life, and it never fails to surprise me the way word gets around so fast. There are a few folks who are in for some mighty big changes in their lives. They just don't know it yet. Tomorrow is going to be a difficult day."

"No less than today which is far from over. This morning I asked Jenny and Shelby to join us for dinner since BJ won't be home until tomorrow."

As soon as Kit stepped outside, she drew in a deep breath, and took a moment to collect her whirling thoughts. This was not what she had expected. She now had to get through the ordeal of waiting until tomorrow while staying with strangers. Since the Jeep was parked close to the corrals her eyes were drawn to the group of men still gathered. They were all sizing her up, and whispering. Her cheeks reddened. Kit knew she was the unwilling subject of a barrage of gossip. Shading her eyes against the late afternoon sun she stared them down before she opened the back of her Jeep, pulled out a large suitcase, and dropped it to the ground along with a duffle bag, and booster chair.

Refusing to listen to the warning bells, Trace found his legs carrying him toward her. Truth was that her arrival intrigued him.

Kit tensed watching the tall cowboy as he strutted toward her, his stride long and slow. He carried himself with a definite swagger topped off by the arrogance of self-assurance. His denim shirt emphasized his solid muscles, and broad shoulders. Muscles strengthened, and toned by a lifetime of working with horses, and cattle. She could tell he was bold and sure of himself. Some might even say cocky. Kit definitely thought he appeared cocky. The dark stubble covering his strong jaw only emphasized the rugged planes of his face. Her eyes came to rest on his vivid blue eyes. His eyes, Kit noted, were sharp and observant. She squinted a little in the bright sunlight as she looked up at him. Kit maintained eye contact.

Trace's look took in all of her, from her lustrous, auburn hair glowing in the late afternoon sunlight, to her bare legs that looked a mile long in her cutoff shorts. He continued to scrutinize her. Mysterious gray eyes fringed by naturally long lashes glared at him. He didn't know why but a weird feeling pulled at his insides.

Kit had the full impact of those steel-blue eyes. For a moment, her composure slipped. To hide her vulnerability, she stood tall with her hands on her hips. Unable to cope with the rising tide of emotions, Kit's chin jutted out, and her eyes darkened. "What are you staring at?"

That's the moment the light bulb went on. Trace had seen that look more than once on BJ Calhoun's face and he made the connection. She had the Calhoun gray eyes like BJ and Will, incredible eyes that kept challenging him. Murphy was right. He was looking at trouble. Trouble on two long shapely legs stood in front of him, and he had no doubt as to why she was here. Trace believed the unexpected arrival was a single mom looking for a handout. He looked down at her luggage. "Let me help you with that," Trace said with an easy drawl. His smile did not reach his eyes.

Under different circumstances, Kit would have been mesmerized by his voice alone. However, Kit had learned to size people up quickly. For some reason, this man annoyed her, and her dislike for him was instant. "Not necessary. I wouldn't want to take you away from your buddies," she said, keeping her voice even despite his unnerving presence.

Trace's jaw tightened but he continued to linger.

Kit turned away from his intense scrutiny. She grabbed the duffle bag, threw it over her shoulder, and tucked the booster seat under her arm. Her hair tumbled forward as she bent down and grabbed the handle of her suitcase. With her free hand she dragged it behind her as she struggled back to the house. Kit could feel his eyes boring into the back of her head, but she forced herself to hold her head high as she put one foot in front of the other and climbed up the steps. Trembling from the unpleasant exchange, Kit headed into the house. Will and Sadie stopped talking as soon as she entered. Uncomfortable, Kit stood hovering in the doorway.

Will stood up and made a quick exit. Sadie smiled at Kit and invited her to have a seat at the table while she prepared dinner. Will returned just before dinner was ready. Kit was anxious, knowing she would be meeting more strangers.

A brief tap at the door announced the arrival of Jenny Calhoun. A willowy brunette, casually dressed, stepped into the kitchen.

"Where's Shelby?" Will asked.

"Right behind me," Jenny replied, as the door flew open, and her daughter rushed in. She was slender, and graceful like her mother, and a little younger than Kit.

Shelby gave her grandparents a quick hug. Kit was seated at the table next to Kenzie. Shelby smiled at the little girl, "Hello there. Aren't you a cutie?" Her manner was confident, her expression saucy. The long-legged blonde, with the throaty voice was stunning. Her sun-bleached hair was pulled back, and one long braid fell to her waist. Her mega-watt smile lit up the room, and her blue eyes sparkled.

Sadie made quick introductions, "This is Kit Bennett, and her daughter, Kenzie. They came up from Washington to see BJ and are staying here tonight. Kit, this is BJ's wife, Jenny, and their daughter, Shelby. They live in the house next door."

Jenny, who had been staring at Kit, felt a sense of dread. She hated where her mind had taken her, and the last thing she wanted was for anyone to know how unsettled she was. She walked over to the sink to get a glass of water and took a long drink as she tried to gather her crazy thoughts. Who was this young woman and what was she doing here?

Shelby demanded an explanation for Kit's unannounced arrival, "How do you know my dad? Why are you here?"

Will intercepted before Kit could reply, "Kit and her daughter are our guests. She came to see BJ, so for now we will all have to wait for tomorrow." His authoritative tone indicated that this was the end of the interrogation. As head of the family, the others knew that Will Calhoun demanded respect, including to those who were guests in his home.

A challenging sparkle remained in Shelby's eyes, as they shifted back to Kit.

There was no doubt that Jenny and Shelby Calhoun were curious about her being here. Kit knew her presence was causing the uncomfortable atmosphere in the room.

The conversation through dinner was awkward with everyone weighing their words before speaking. Everyone except Shelby. "Where's your daddy, Kenzie?" Shelby suddenly asked, attempting another dig for information. She noticed that Kit didn't wear a wedding ring.

"Daddy is in heaven," Kenzie answered innocently. She had just announced the great tragedy in her short life to strangers. There was dead silence.

Kit's face paled as she tried to keep her composure. She wasn't ready to share any of her life history with these strangers. "Kenzie is finished. If you'll excuse me, I'll go and get her washed up." Needing to compose herself, Kit rose from her chair on wobbly legs, and made her way to the bathroom.

Thankfully, when she returned, Jenny and Shelby had left, and Sadie had just finished cleaning up the kitchen. Will had also made his escape, leaving the two women alone. They chatted until it was time to put Kenzie to bed. Kit tucked Kenzie and Mucky under the covers and crawled up beside her to read her a bedtime story. Kenzie settled with no fuss and nodded off before Kit finished. She kissed her daughter on her forehead and returned to the kitchen.

"Perfect timing, Kit. I made a pot of tea." The two women stayed in the kitchen while Will watched television in the living room.

The conversation was easy flowing, and Kit finally relaxed for the first time all day. It wasn't long before Kit was unable to stifle her yawns.

"Why don't you go to bed," Sadie suggested. "I can see that this has been an exhausting day for you."

"It was. Thank you again for letting us stay tonight." Kit looked in on Kenzie and tucked her and Mucky back under the covers. She watched her daughter sleep for a moment before leaving to take refuge in her room. Once again, exhaustion swept through her, leaving her feeling drained, and lonelier than ever. Once the lights were out, she expected to fall asleep right away. Instead, she was tormented by the image of the tall, dark cowboy. She knew her reaction to his offer of help had been rude, but she was sure she hadn't misread his reaction to her. Forcing his image out of her mind, she knew that the two women weren't happy to see her, either. She worried about tomorrow in case she got the same reaction from the man who by all likelihood was her father.

Chapter Three

Mental and emotional fatigue caused Kit to oversleep. Feeling the warmth of the morning rays through the window she stirred. Remembering where she was, her eyes flew open. She jumped out of bed, and quickly dressed. When she glanced at herself in the mirror, she wasn't surprised at how pale, and drawn she looked. With renewed anxiety, Kit left the room. Today she could be meeting her father.

The aroma of brewed coffee drifted from the kitchen. Sadie smiled in greeting. "How are you feeling?" she asked, noticing Kit still looked exhausted.

"Embarrassed that I overslept, Mrs. Calhoun. Thank you for watching Kenzie. I didn't hear her stir." Kit frowned. Now they probably think I'm a poor mother as well as lazy.

"She was no trouble. Please call us Sadie and Will. Would you like a coffee?"

Kit nodded, still uncomfortable. She bent over to kiss the top of Kenzie's head and smiled. It was a soft smile, a motherly smile. "Good morning, baby girl."

"Hi, Mommy," Kenzie said cheerfully. She turned back and continued to jabber away to Will, who seemed to be listening intently.

Sadie couldn't help but wonder what role Kit's mother played in her daughter's life since her father clearly had never figured in her upbringing. Based on what Kenzie had revealed last night, she guessed that Kit was a single mother. Her own motherly concern kicked in due to the questions she had gathered since yesterday. Her son was in for a real shock.

"Well, sit down, Missy. I don't bite." His face softened with a wry grin that tilted one corner of his mouth.

Kit sat down as ordered. She tried, but failed, to smile. She had to admit that Will Calhoun intimidated her. She accepted the mug of coffee Sadie handed her. "Thank you."

"I'll make you some toast to go with it."

Kit was comforted by the warmth in her voice and felt better. She ventured a glance at Will. Neither of them said anything.

Will broke the silence, "BJ called. He should be home around two."

Kit's stomach flipped. It was only a few more hours, but it had already been a lifetime.

"I'm going down to the barn to talk to Murphy. We're keeping Ginger in the birthing stable. Trace says she's ready to foal any day." Will was glad to make his escape.

After lunch, Kit put Kenzie down. Sadie had already brewed a pot of tea and set out two cups. "You have a beautiful home," Kit said, trying to make conversation.

"We did a major renovation a few years ago. Will wanted an office. I insisted on a full bathroom at the back door, and a large boot room. Now the men can hang their hats and jackets on the hooks there instead of on the back of my kitchen chairs. They can also wash up or shower there when they come in from work instead of traipsing through the house."

While they chatted, Kit caught herself staring at the clock periodically. It seemed to her that the minute hand kept getting stuck between numbers. When they heard BJ's truck pull into the yard. Sadie told Kit to go wait in the living room.

Will and Sadie stood together on the verandah, and watched their son climb out of his truck. His smile was easy, as he waved at his parents. Sadie waved back, then turned, and walked into the house. This was a moment for father and son.

BJ slapped his dad on the back, "How were things while I was gone?"

"Fine, until yesterday. Sit down, son." They sat down in the two wicker rocking chairs.

BJ didn't miss the serious tone in his father's voice. "What's wrong, Dad?"

"We need to talk."

BJ's face drained of color, "That's probably one of the most dreaded expressions in the English language." He sensed that this wouldn't be an enjoyable conversation.

Will's face was expressionless when his eyes fixed on his son. There was no point in beating around the bush, "There's a young lady inside who believes she's your daughter."

"Daughter?" BJ's voice was scarcely above a shocked whisper. It was as if his dad had punched him in his chest and knocked all the wind out of his body.

Will knew his son was digesting what he heard. "The young girl inside looks just like you. Her mother, Torrie Kennedy, named you as the father."

BJ shifted his position, looking uncomfortable and stunned. He felt like a teenager answering to his father for something he did wrong. It seemed an eternity before he could speak. When he did, his defenses kicked in, "Back in my rodeo days there were willing buckle bunnies in every town along the circuit willing to hook up. It was all part of the rodeo life of an unmarried cowboy. I'm not proud to say this, but I sowed my share of wild oats."

"Well, it appears that you now have to reap your harvest and take responsibility."

BJ turned and faced his dad. Seeing the accusatory expression on his father's face, BJ's voice was not only angry but indignant, "I've never had a problem with responsibility."

Will placed a hand on his son's arm. "No, you haven't. You're a good and decent man." Will had no doubt that his son would do the honorable thing for his new family and fulfill his obligations as a father. He also knew that BJ needed a moment to absorb the shock.

BJ closed his eyes, allowing a flashback. Deep emotions flowed through him as little pieces started to surface, and then the past came surging back. Faded images came to life. Lost in thought, BJ recalled the moment he first saw Torrie, the striking redhead with the restless green eyes. Her image was so vivid he began reliving every moment of that night.

He and his life-long friend, Dallas Reed, had been participating in the rodeo circuit all summer. They went wherever the circuit took them, and this weekend they had just finished competing in Ellensburg, Washington. They had both done well and were looking to celebrate. They were in their late teens, single and looking for a good time. In the morning they'd be pulling out and moving on, but tonight they were going to party.

Torrie was up at the bar when BJ walked in with a group of boisterous cowboys. She leaned over to whisper to her friend, and he appreciated her long legs in the tight-fitting jeans. Torrie turned and caught his gaze as he walked by. He merely raised an eyebrow, and moved on with his buddies, providing Torrie with the sight of one of the finest butts she'd ever seen.

Torrie was drawn to BJ. He was tall, dark, and every inch of sexy from his Stetson right down to the well-worn boots. She practically drooled at the sight of him. Torrie was counting on him being her fix for the night. "Dibs on the tall rugged one. Did you see his tight ass? He looks almost as good from the back as he does from the front."

Becky found herself staring at the gorgeous cowboy. "My God, girl. He is sexy."

As soon as the boys sat down Torrie sashayed over to their table. "Hi boys," she drawled, as she focused on BJ with an expression that was downright flirtatious.

BJ had eyes. He was attracted to the cowgirl with the wild mane of hair cascading down her back. She was sexy and seductive, the most desirable female he'd seen in a long time. He knew that women like her flitted from one man to the next and viewed men as objects for their amusement. Some women sent out signals that invited more than a kiss on the cheek. He knew the attraction wasn't one sided. There was immediate chemistry between them.

Torrie's eyes twinkled with amusement, as she gave her long tresses a flip with her hand. "Dance with me," she said, looking directly at BJ.

His buddy, Dallas, elbowed him in the side. BJ didn't mind the ribbing. Dallas was usually the cowboy who made an impression on the buckle bunnies. He was the seasoned hell-raiser, and party boy. BJ set his beer bottle down, and wrapped an arm firmly around Torrie's waist, as he led her onto the sawdust dance floor. Torrie openly flirted with BJ, brushing up against him, and murmuring provocative remarks. She was offering herself to him in every possible way. He knew she was his for the taking. Adolescent urges surged through his veins in anticipation of how the night would end. BJ invited her to join their table.

During a slow dance she whispered against his throat, "Let's get out of here, cowboy."

"Okay, sweetheart." Who could keep a cool head, especially on a hot summer night with an eager body in his arms? She had thrown herself at him all night, and it was time to take what was offered. He readily yielded to temptation in anticipation of what lay ahead. Together, they staggered to his truck with their arms wrapped around each other. Neither had any romantic notions, it was purely physical attraction.

That night with Torrie was a combination of youth and raging hormones. It was everything he expected. And obviously more. BJ shook his head as if to clear it, as he returned to the present. His face was crestfallen when he looked at his dad. Sometimes life was damn difficult, but you man up and deal with it. BJ got up but hesitated before entering the house. He quietly mulled over what he wanted to say before confronting a stranger who might be his daughter. His eyes were troubled as he opened the door.

When BJ entered the kitchen, Sadie placed her hand on her son's shoulder. It hurt her to see her son look so broken. "She's in the living room waiting for you." Sadie turned, and left to go join Will. As soon as she sat down, she started to cry. "He'd never have abandoned her if he'd known."

Will nodded, as he squeezed his wife's hand.

The young woman standing by the window turned to him. She stood there, waiting in silence. He looked at her for a long moment, and he could see the tiny pulse beating in her throat. She was tall, and slender. Not what he expected, since it was Torrie's image that was still in his mind. BJ's gaze passed over her face in a slow search, and he stared at her. There was no doubt in his mind that this was his daughter. The realization temporarily paralyzed him.

Kit studied him just as intently. His face was weathered from sun and wind, and there were light crease lines at the corners of his eyes. His eyes were the same unusual gray color as hers. His jaw was set, his mouth clamped in a hard line. The thick silence between them increased her anxiety. Her short-lived hopes were replaced with newfound fears. It amazed her that he couldn't hear her heart pounding. Kit took a deep breath. She'd come this far. Overriding her fears, she forced herself to take the next step.

BJ's stomach knotted. The real-life image of him walked over until she stood directly in front of him. He simply stared.

It was Kit who broke the silence. In that way, Kit was like her mother, direct and forthright. "My name is Kit Bennett and I believe you knew my mother, Torrie Kennedy."

BJ took the birth certificate she handed him and stared at it. There it was between them. Not an accusation. Not a judgment. Nothing but the bold fact of the matter on the piece of paper he held in his hand. When he spoke, his voice was strained, "This is an unexpected shock."

"Trust me, I felt the same way when I found out." The difference was she was thrilled. "I know this is a bombshell, but I don't believe in keeping a secret like this from the father. You deserved to know the truth just like I did. You can have tests done."

BJ saw that the dates on the certificate coincided with the timeline. His expression was dark and guarded as he gave a nod of acceptance. "There's no need for any tests."

Kit felt a sense of fulfillment. When she set out on this venture, she didn't even know if she would find the right, William Joseph Calhoun. She could hardly breathe. The man in front of her was her father. Joy began to fill her, while tears of happiness gathered in her eyes. This was what she had dreamed about so many times in her world of make believe.

Now that he was real, Kit didn't know what to expect. All she could do was stare at him in wonder. Kit hadn't expected to be welcomed with open arms, but she'd settle for a simple smile from him. Instead, she watched his conflicted features.

A thousand emotions were raging through BJ. His disbelief was suddenly replaced by anger. His feeling of shock turned into resentment, "Why didn't she tell me that I was a father? I had a right to know."

"You had to know my mother longer than one night to understand. She entertained freely, deliberately setting her sights on her prey, and seducing them. She obviously succeeded with you. Let me tell you, she was never a one-man woman. Torrie was considered the any man type. You were merely an evening's entertainment."

BJ was shocked at her bluntness. She seemed so cold and detached. His eyes went hard. "Why did you wait until now to come find me?" he demanded gruffly.

The harshness in his voice stabbed through Kit's heart. She threw out her chin, and bravely stated the facts, "I just found out myself a few months ago. My mother told me you died before I was born. It took me a while to find you since I didn't have much to go on. I also had my own personal business to deal with." Kit's eyes clouded over with sadness.

BJ drew a deep breath trying to collect himself. Those may be the facts. The trouble is facts weren't always enough. Before he could speak Kenzie cried out from the bedroom.

"Excuse me, I have to get my daughter." Kit's face flushed; she hadn't gotten to that part.

BJ hadn't recovered from the first shock. Now the aftershock of finding out he was a grandfather. Talk about the surprise that keeps on giving. This was something else he was going to have to get used to. Up until a few minutes ago his life had been normal. The day had started like any other day. Kit's intrusion in his life was going to upset his whole life, and everyone around him. He felt like a cowboy who'd just been thrown and was waiting to get stomped on. Trying to figure out his feelings, he went over and stood at the window with his back to the room. A dozen questions were racing through his head. He turned when Kit returned with her daughter.

Kit stood in front of him holding her child. BJ could only stare at the little girl. He was shocked at how much she reminded him of Torrie. They had the same dazzling green eyes. The child stared at him as though she was gazing at a familiar face. "Hello there," he said softly, and was pleased with the small smile she gave him.

Kit was grateful when Sadie silently entered the room and took her child.

"Your daughter looks like Torrie." BJ wasn't sure if he really wanted to know, yet had to ask, "Your mother?"

"Torrie died when I was fifteen. She lived a life that was on a collision course that was destined to end in disaster sooner than later. She never accepted the role of mother and was never really in my life. I was raised by my grandmother, Lou Kennedy. Kenzie and I lived with her until her passing a few months ago. I didn't know about you until the day my grandmother died. Torrie made my grandmother keep her secret, but my grandmother confessed on her death bed that you might be alive. I read Torrie's journals and found my birth certificate with your name on it." Kit was silent for a moment and her face revealed a wave of pain. "It wasn't a brave choice to come find you. It was my only choice, not some rash decision made out of loneliness or desperation. Like me, you deserved to know."

"I can't believe you found me," BJ said with a gentleness that surprised Kit.

"It wasn't easy. It took a few weeks of searching." More than once she'd been tempted to give up. Revealing the truth, and finding family spurred her on.

BJ felt it was his turn to explain. "There was no relationship with your mother. We spent the one night together. Our feelings were no more than physical, and we both knew that. I'm surprised she remembered my name. I have to be honest; I only knew your mother as Torrie. I never saw or heard from her again. I have the feeling you've been passing judgment on me before you got here."

Kit looked solemn, even sad. Maybe she had. "Life is too short to carry around anger, and bitterness. However, it does rear its ugly head occasionally." She struggled to even her breathing. "I am angry, but not at you. I'm angry with Torrie. Nothing mattered to her including you and me. You had the right to know you had a daughter. I had the right to know I had a father."

"So, what do you want?" BJ asked suspiciously, still not making one move toward his own child. "Why did you come here?" His expression remained cool, and impersonal.

The question shook Kit. She hadn't really thought about anything beyond telling him he was her father. She forced herself to make eye contact as she exhaled slowly. Boldly holding his gaze, Kit said, "For the record, I didn't come here for a handout, or for someone to take care of me. Not everything is about money." She needed this man to fill the hole in her created long ago by a mother who made her believe she wasn't good enough to warrant love. For the past three years Kit had one priority. Her name was Kenzie. Pain was evident in her voice, "This isn't just about you and me. It's more complicated than that. As you saw, there's a child involved, and I must think about her first. It's amazing what you can do when you're doing it for your child. I have no other family. The only family I had was my grandmother, and as I said she just died. If something happens to me what would happen to my daughter?" Kit looked BJ straight in the eyes. She had to be honest with him, as well as herself. There could be no secrets or lies with their relationship. Her voice was low, "All the way here, I convinced myself I was doing this for Kenzie. In truth, I want to know my dad." Relief swept over Kit. All the worrying, all the speculation was over. She had accomplished what she had set out to do. "I didn't run from my past. I came to find my future. So now you know the truth."

BJ could no longer hold back the anger he'd been struggling with, "The fact that I have another daughter and a granddaughter is a hell of a lot of truth thrown at me unexpectedly." He turned and walked away without another word. There was no doubt that the recent events had left BJ Calhoun reeling.

Once again, Kit felt like an abandoned child.

BJ's parents looked at him with concern when he entered the kitchen, but he was in no mood to talk. Besides that, it was Jenny and Shelby that he needed to talk to. Things had changed. He was just beginning to realize how much. Without so much as a backward glance, he grabbed his hat, and stormed out. His dad was right behind him.

Kit had followed BJ into the kitchen. All her inner strength was needed to hold back the tears that burned her eyes. She was numb from the emotional tailspin she'd just been through. Kit's voice dropped to an agonizing whisper, as she sat down feeling rejected, "Until yesterday I didn't have a father. I didn't know what to expect, but it wasn't this. He just walked away from me." Kit lifted Kenzie onto her lap, grateful that her daughter was unaware of the drama surrounding her. Despite the genuine belief that she had done the right thing, Kit was too emotionally exhausted to cope. Stunned, she sat in despair. She didn't know where this left her. She sat quietly, feeling hopeless and empty. She wanted Lou. "I don't know what to do next."

"Neither does BJ. You both need time to sort this out. Stay here with us, and let's see what the next few days brings."

Kit had risked everything by coming to Alberta. "You have no idea how grateful I am that you, and your husband welcomed me, a stranger, no questions asked," she whispered once she was able to swallow the lump in her throat.

"You may have come here a stranger, but the moment we saw you it was easy to make an educated guess that you were family. You do look a lot like your dad."

Dad! That was still new to her.

Fate had conspired to put all of them in this situation, and none of it was this poor girl's fault. Sadie sensed Kit struggling within herself by the look on her face. Her heart went out to the young woman who felt that she had just been rejected. "We all need time to process this. Is there any reason not to stay?"

Kit shook her head. The Calhouns were her flesh and blood. She hung on to the hope that she would be accepted by her father. "I'll stay," Kit agreed weakly. What choice did she have? She had nowhere to go. She knew she had to build a new life for herself and Kenzie. She hoped it would be here.

Outside, father and son stood for several minutes in silence.

The revelation BJ just received was about the biggest a man could get. Maybe once the shock of having another daughter wore off, he could think more clearly.

Will cast a glance in his son's direction. "Are you all right?" he asked with deep concern.

"No, I'm not," he shouted back. BJ didn't want to get into this right now.

"You have every right to be shocked, and angry. We're all guilty of bad decisions, and youthful indiscretions. In time we learn to live with them. Unfortunately, you don't have that choice. There are two people in there who are going to be part of your life one way or another."

"I don't need any of your philosophy or advice right now. I need to figure out what I'm going to say to Jenny and Shelby." He couldn't delay the inevitable. Shoving his hands into his pockets he headed home.

Jenny was sitting at the kitchen table when he walked in. He knew she had been waiting for him. BJ shot her a nervous glance, "Where's Shelby?"

"She's at the clinic. Do you want to tell me what's going on?" she asked anxiously.

BJ was glad Shelby wasn't home. He would have to face Shelby later, but he was grateful for the reprieve. There was nothing he could do to change what happened years ago, but he was struggling for the right words that were going to change all of their lives. There was nothing to say but the facts. "We need to talk." Oh, God! Those were the same words his dad had used. It really was an ominous statement.

"Is this about Kit and her daughter?" Jenny dared to ask. Her body was tense. She waited through the most unbearable silence for him to continue.

BJ's face flickered with an emotion she didn't recognize. It seemed like an eternity before he spoke, "Kit is my daughter."

Jenny sat motionless as her fears were realized. In her heart she already knew. Watching Kit yesterday was all she had needed, to see the similarities. The familiar facial features, the Calhoun gray eyes. Jenny let out a heavy sigh and waited.

For BJ, the silence was unnerving. "Please believe me when I say, I had no idea until today. It was one night after a rodeo. It was a long time ago. It was in the past," he said in an attempt to defend himself.

"Not anymore. Your carefree past just caught up with you, and she looks just like you."

This wasn't getting any easier. "I swear I never knew about her."

Jenny's resentment surfaced. "That's not the point. This affects all of us, BJ. This is not a simple thing that is going to go away."

"I know. I have some thinking to do," he said desperately.

"You're not the only one." She heard him swear as he slammed the door behind him.

BJ headed toward the barn. Minutes later he was on top of his horse and heading across the meadows. He rode hard, trying to outrun the thoughts racing through his mind. Reaching the familiar rise, BJ slid off his horse, and fastened the reins to a tree branch. Crossing to an often-used rock he sat down and breathed deeply. He felt he hadn't caught his breath since he climbed out of his truck. BJ rested his forearms on his raised knees. In a heartbeat his life had changed dramatically. The longer he sat there, the more real it became. Back at the ranch was a young lady named Kit Bennett, who was his daughter. He had another daughter.

BJ watched the evening sky change colors, aware that tonight it was symbolic. There were changes currently happening in his life. He understood where Kit was coming from. He had no choice either. What was done was done. BJ had to appreciate his daughter's courage to come here. He dug deep to find his own. He rose, patted Zeus on his neck, climbed into the saddle, and headed home. He knew the only way to deal with this was head on.

When BJ returned home Jenny was alone in the kitchen. "Is Shelby back?"

"She's in the living room."

BJ swallowed hard, "Did you say anything to her?"

"It's not my news. But you have to tell her tonight," Jenny said bluntly. She knew telling Shelby would send her child's safe, comfortable world into chaos. Jenny felt like her own world had been upended. Regardless of the shock, it was a fact that everyone needed to deal with.

Looking far from happy, BJ turned and led the way into the living room. He looked at Shelby, and then turned back to Jenny. The look in his eyes was a silent plea for Jenny to help him.

Jenny refused. This was on him.

BJ hung his head. Some battles were lost before they were waged.

Shelby looked up, and again felt the sense of dread she had experienced yesterday at dinner. "Are you going to tell me what's going on around here?" In a voice filled with suspicion, she dared to ask, "This is about Kit and her child, isn't it? Why is she here?"

BJ was shocked at the depth of apprehension on Shelby's face. There was no way to soften the truth. He drew in a deep breath, and cleared his throat, "Kit's my daughter."

Shelby glared at him, not wanting to believe what she just heard.

Seeing the hurt in her eyes, BJ dropped his gaze.

"She's lying." As much as she tried to deny it, Shelby knew it was true.

"There's no doubt that Kit is my daughter. I saw the birth certificate. I didn't know about her until today."

Shelby's face was hard, and unyielding. "I hope your romp in the sheets was worth all of this." The hurt that flashed across her dad's face had no effect on her.

BJ looked over at Jenny hoping she would say something to her daughter. There was only silence.

Shelby dashed out of the room and ran to her bedroom. She slammed the door, the sound vibrating throughout the house.

"I'm sorry, Jenny." He tried to take her in his arms, but she quickly pulled away. BJ dropped his hands to his side.

"This has been a shock for all of us. Put yourself in Shelby's shoes. Kit is your real daughter. Shelby may think she has to take a back seat to a stranger, because she's only a stepdaughter."

"For God's sake you can't be serious. Shelby is my daughter. I adopted her when she was only a baby."

Like him, Jenny needed some time. "We've had to deal with a lot over the years. We will deal with this, too. Give us some time." Head high, she turned and walked away.

They were all reeling from the impact of Torrie Kennedy's lies.

Chapter Four

BJ grabbed his coffee and stepped outside. An uncomfortable feeling weighed on him. Yesterday had been a shocking day followed by a long sleepless night. His eyes were drawn to the main house that now housed his daughter, and granddaughter. The original shock that had overwhelmed him had been replaced by uncertainty. Not that she was his daughter but how to handle the situation in a way that was best for everyone. With a flash of insight, he realized she probably felt just as nervous, and confused as he did. It was time for him to have another talk with Kit. It was mid-morning before BJ had the opportunity to get over to the main house. He was glad that his mom was alone in the kitchen when he arrived. "Where is everyone?"

Sadie hated seeing the anguish on her son's face. She poured them both a coffee and sat down next to him. "Your dad took Kenzie to look at the new kittens, and Kit went for a walk. How are you doing, son? You had a big shock yesterday."

BJ sighed and ran a hand through his hair. The pain in his voice was evident as he confessed, "A thousand emotions raged through me, and anger took the lead. I'm outraged that I've been denied a significant, and irreplaceable part of my life. I never got the chance to be her father, and I don't know anything about my own daughter. I feel like I've been cheated."

It tore at Sadie's heart to see her son like this. "How is Jenny handling this?"

"Better than I expected, but I don't like the icy stares, and silent treatment from Shelby."

"Give them a little time. Everyone has been thrown for a loop."

BJ shook his head. "Shelby won't listen to anything I have to say."

"Shelby's confused, and probably a little scared right now. She needs time to process everything."

"We all do," BJ said with resignation.

"Are you fine if Kit and Kenzie stay with us for a while so everyone can get to know each other? Hopefully, with a little time, it will help everyone accept Kit and her daughter."

"I was hoping you'd say that." BJ's moment of relief was quickly replaced by doubt, "We don't know anything about her though."

"She doesn't know anything about us either. It'll be blind trust on both sides."

"What do I do next?"

"Don't be too quick to judge. Be there for Kit. Be there for both your daughters." She would have gone on, but they were interrupted by a knock at the door. BJ got up and let Trace in.

"Can you get away? Ginger had her foal, a nice little colt. I thought you might want to see him. He's a beauty. I've called Doc and he'll be out in the next day or two."

Sadie looked at her son and nodded. Her smile faded as the two men walked out the door.

BJ's lips were pursed, and his jaw was rigid as they made their way down the steps.

Trace raised a curious eyebrow. He guessed that the conversation in the kitchen had to do with the new arrival. She had definitely stirred up the dust, and it hadn't settled.

BJ fell into step with Trace as they headed to the stables. He knew it was time to fill Trace, and the others in. "I had a surprise visitor yesterday. If you haven't guessed, Kit is my daughter. I had no knowledge of her until she showed up. Kit's mother knew all along that I was the father and chose to keep it a secret."

"Where is her mother?"

"All Kit said was that her mother died when she was fifteen, but she wasn't much of a mother. It was her grandmother who raised her."

Trace had to ask, "Why did she wait until now to tell you?" Trace couldn't help but wonder what she was up to. Why show up now, and what did she want?

"Her mother told Kit that I had died before she was born. Kit's grandmother kept the secret until she was on her death bed. Kit found her birth certificate hidden in the attic. With her grandmother gone, Kit has no other family."

How could a mother be so heartless as to tell her child that her father was dead when he wasn't? In the moment, he felt sorry for Kit. Then he wondered if she was like her mother. Maybe she was looking for someone to take care of her and her kid, now that her grandmother was gone. Or worse, what if she took off, and left her little girl behind?

BJ continued, "Kit said it wasn't some rash decision made out of desperation that brought her here. She said it was about revealing the truth and finding family. She held my gaze and said that she didn't come for a handout or for someone to take care of her."

Trace remained skeptical. He still felt she was a gold digger who followed the rainbow to the Calhoun ranch, but he wisely kept his thoughts to himself.

The two men had just left, and there was another knock on the door. Sadie was a little surprised to see Jenny. She noticed the dark smudges under Jenny's puffy eyes. Jenny looked at her with such despair that Sadie took her into her arms to comfort her.

Jenny immediately broke down, "I need to talk to you." Jenny looked around.

The awkward moment passed when Sadie said, "We're alone."

Jenny's voice cracked with unmistakable emotion, "I'm not coping with this, Sadie. It's bringing back a lot of hurtful memories I had with Dallas. I thought that emotional roller coaster was in my past and would stay there. I thought my old life was behind me after all these years. The arrival of BJ's daughter changed that. It's unfair, but I feel like I've been cheated on."

Sadie regarded Jenny with displeasure, "BJ's not Dallas, and he's still your faithful husband. That hasn't changed."

Sadie's response caught Jenny off-guard. Heat rushed to her face. "I'm sorry. What I said just now wasn't fair. I'm trying to deal with the shock, as well as Shelby's anger. I can't welcome his daughter with open arms. I have my own daughter to deal with. Shelby has always thought of BJ as her dad. With the arrival of his real daughter, it reinforces the fact that he's not her biological dad. Dallas is, and Shelby is only a stepdaughter to BJ."

"Shelby has and always will be a daughter to my son. But BJ has a right to claim this daughter, just as Kit has a right to know her father."

"Why did Kit show up now? What does she want from us?"

Sadie heard Jenny's resentment. "I'm sure we all have preconceived ideas, but they may not be anywhere close to the truth. Right now, the best thing to do is to not judge Kit before we know anything about her. That will take time. She has to be comfortable with us before she'll open up. Only then will we get the answers to our questions. Kit deserves a fair chance."

Jenny nodded. "I'll do my best to be fair, and open-minded. Thanks for listening."

After lunch, BJ went back to the main house. Sadie was sitting out on the verandah quietly rocking away while enjoying a moment of solitude. It had been a trying morning. Looking at her son, she knew it wasn't over. Mother and son spent the next hour in heavy conversation.

"At first I felt like I'd been punched in the chest, and the wind was knocked out of me. I've dealt with the shock, now I need to spend time with Kit. I don't know anything about my own daughter, except the little she spat out in anger."

"Don't judge Kit based on what her mother did to you. Kit isn't her mother so don't put her in the same box. Nor is she accountable for her mother's actions. It wasn't easy for Kit to leave everything familiar and come here. Besides finding you, and telling you the truth, she's concerned for her daughter's welfare. Kit has no other family. She needs us, and we can't let her down. It's time to talk to Kit. Make sure you tell her she can stay with us as long as she wants." Kit deserved a chance to get to know her father, and BJ needed time with his daughter.

BJ remained seated. He was scared to go talk to his own daughter, because she was no more than a stranger. "Do you know where Kit is?"

"I saw her heading over to the corrals. Kenzie's napping so Kit decided to explore."

With Kenzie napping, Kit took the opportunity to look around. A little time to herself was appreciated. She wandered to the back of the house, then ventured further where she came across the creek running through the property. For a few minutes she was content as she appreciated the natural beauty around her. She knew this could easily became a place to escape to. As much as she was enjoying the solitude she didn't stay. Kit decided that she wasn't about to stay hidden away, so before heading back to the house she wandered over to the fenced corrals. She noticed a couple of the hands stop what they were doing to watch her. One poked the other. Obviously, she was still the topic of conversation. Ignoring them, she walked by with her head high. She was hoping that the horses might be out, but to her disappointment the corral was empty. Leaning on the top rail she stared out at the majestic mountains. Out of nowhere, Trace's image came to mind. The man was hard, and rugged like the mountains. She decided he must be good at his job because she couldn't understand why the Calhouns would keep someone with the personality, and manners of a barbarian. With determination, she dismissed the man from her thoughts allowing her mind to change direction. Kit knew her future here was unpredictable. Her courage faltered, and she again questioned her decision to stay. Maybe it would be better for everyone if she just left. To her dismay her eyes filled with tears. So much to consider, and none of it clear. Lost in her thoughts, she was startled when she heard heavy steps approaching.

BJ watched as Kit stood alone looking sad, and vulnerable. He called out her name.

Kit heard but ignored him as she blinked her eyes dry and dabbed at her wet cheeks. She wished he would go away and allow her to have her few moments alone, while trying to deal with the hurting his reaction to her had caused.

BJ stepped closer and placed his hand lightly on her shoulder. After a long disturbing moment, he asked her what was wrong.

Kit sniffed, and shrugged, "Nothing."

"You've been crying."

"So what?" Kit retorted angrily.

It was obvious that she was more than upset. Underlying anger was clear. BJ was uneasy when he asked, "Why are you upset?"

Kit figured if you ask the question, you better be ready for the answer. She decided he deserved to know how she was feeling, even if the truth hurt. She had been devastated after their initial confrontation. Not bothering to mince her words they tumbled out, "I was terrified about coming here. It devasted me when you walked out the door once you realized I was your daughter." Kit had lived a life of broken promises, and shattered dreams, hopes hanging onto a fantasy that always vanished by the reality of life.

BJ hadn't meant to hurt her. "I was reeling from too many shocks in just a few minutes. I'm sorry, Kit. I could have handled that better." A profound sadness swept over BJ. The desperate, searching look in his daughter's eyes was a grim reminder that he had to make her see he wanted to be a father in her life. Perhaps the time had come to say some of the words he'd been avoiding saying. This time he chose his words with care, "If I had known about you, I would have been there for you. I can't begin to understand why your mother did what she did to you. What she did to both of us. Every father deserves the chance to know his child. I can't make up for what happened because of what Torrie did." His voice became heavy with emotion, "I didn't get to watch you grow up, but I do want to get to know you, and watch Kenzie grow up." He wiped the tears from her cheeks. "I don't know what makes you cry, or how to make you laugh." He gently placed his hand over her hand, "I didn't have a choice before. I do now."

It came to her then that she wasn't the only one hurting. "I never did understand Torrie. She had an evil side to her, and at times she seemed to enjoy seeing how much she could hurt someone. Maybe I judged you harshly because of my experiences with Torrie. This hurt me deeply, and I was angry when I found out the truth. I had no one left to take my anger out on so you became the target. It was unfair but I couldn't stop myself. I was so scared. I had no idea what I was about to find. I'm still scared." Kit had revealed her true feelings, but more than that, she had let him see how vulnerable she was.

BJ wasn't upset by her honesty. "You're welcome to stay at the ranch as long as you want."

Kit wanted to tell him how much she wanted to stay, but she hadn't yet worked through her hurt. She was usually reasonable, but she was also stubborn. "My grandmother always kept it real. She said it does no good to brood over what might have been. It's up to us to find our happiness. It's the future I have to worry about, and I don't know what to do."

"The fact is we can't change the past. It's easy to help you out financially, but I can't make up for the lost years." BJ needed to understand her expectations.

Kit had a strong independent streak. Money was not what she wanted from him. Her jaw set in a resolute line. "I don't need your money. I may have to figure out how to cope on my own, but I can, and will, take care of my responsibilities. I've managed to live without you my whole life." Seeing the flash of hurt in his eyes Kit quickly said, "I didn't mean that the way it sounded." She wasn't blaming him. She just wanted him to understand that she'd managed without him and could do it again. "That's not why I came. It's family I need, not money. I have to know there is someone I can count on. The one person I had just died. I feel so alone." Tears wanted to return, but she held them back.

The despondency in her voice pained him. BJ recalled his mother warning him not to be too quick to judge. "I think we both have to take some time, and figure things out. I'm sorry for your loss and your unhappy childhood. I'm sorry about a lot of things. I have made mistakes in my life. You weren't one of them. You're not alone anymore. I will always be there for you." He smiled at her, and her heart turned over.

Pride helped Kit to hold her head high. "Even though it's not easy raising a child on my own, I don't want to become someone's responsibility."

"You're a parent, Kit. Won't you always feel responsible for Kenzie? We're family. If you can't count on family, who can you count on? There's no shame in accepting help."

Understanding what BJ was saying. Kit nodded reluctantly.

Once Kit agreed to stay, and as their conversation progressed, the layers of Kit's anger peeled away, and eased the tension between them. Now that the ice was broken, she felt more confident. "What should I call you?"

"You can call me BJ if that makes you more comfortable, but I would be honored to be called, Dad."

"What do you want Kenzie to call you?"

His expression softened, "Grandpa would be nice."

Kit smiled with approval, "Grandpa, it is. What about Jenny?"

"I'll have to ask her." Neither of them mentioned Shelby. "I'm glad you found us, Kit."

When she chanced to look up at him, she caught him watching her with an expression of acceptance. "Me, too."

They were distracted when Murphy led a mare, and her colt out of the barn. Kit recognized him. He was the old man standing at the corral railing the day she arrived. Both BJ and Kit were grateful for the interruption.

"That's Ginger, and her new newborn, Jasper. He is the first of what we all hope will be a dynasty of prize horses." The mare's chestnut colored coat gleamed in the sunlight.

"She's the prettiest horse I've ever seen, and her foal looks strong, and healthy."

BJ wondered if Kit grew up on a ranch. There was so much he had to learn about his daughter. BJ waved Murphy over.

The old man strolled over on legs bowed from decades in the saddle. As he got closer, Kit studied his wind burned face, the skin leathery, and wrinkled. His gray hair was touching the collar of his shirt, and tufts of gray hair sprung out from his eyebrows. His eyes were clear, and bright under his dusty old cowboy hat.

"Hey, boss." The two horses followed close behind Murphy.

"Cliff Murphy, meet my daughter, Kit."

The old cowboy rubbed his unshaven whiskers, "Reckoned she was from all the gossip flying around here." He extended his hand, "Howdy, Miss Calhoun."

Kit smiled and shook his calloused hand with the tobacco-stained fingers. "Hello, Mr. Murphy. It's Mrs. Bennett, but please call me, Kit."

"Only if you call me, Murphy, like everyone else does."

"Murphy it is."

"And the pipsqueak with you?"

This time Kit smiled freely, "That's my little girl, Kenzie."

BJ slapped Murphy on the shoulder, "I'm a grandpa, Murphy."

"If that don't beat all," he muttered as he walked away.

BJ grinned, and shook his head, "Murphy has been here forever. Although we aren't related, we're the only family he has."

Kit watched the old man disappear into the barn and thought that they had this in common. The Calhouns were her only family now. "Hey,

Ginger," Kit said softly. "How's that pretty baby doing?" Ginger snorted, and tossed her head, but calmed down as Kit continued to talk to her. When the mare dipped her head, Kit scratched her ears.

BJ touched her arm. Kit did not miss the look of regret in his eyes. His voice was husky with emotion, "Every father deserves a chance to know his child. You and I were robbed of too many years, but you and I are not to blame. I'm serious about building a relationship with you. I would like to spend time with you. Would you like to go for a horseback ride in the next day or two, and I'll show you our land?" When Kit nodded, he grinned and left.

Kit knew her life would be changing in many ways if she stayed. Old fears stirred inside her. She knew nothing is ever exactly what you think it will be, but her grandmother always said to have hope, and believe in possibilities.

Returning to the house to relieve Sadie, Kit was drawn by the activity that was now happening in another corral. Trace was astride a young horse. Kit went over and leaned her elbows on the top rail. She had to appreciate the man, who was strong and capable from years of pulling calves, hauling bales and training horses. She stood in silence, taking pleasure in watching the ritual between man and beast. Kit was soon lost in the art of man and animal working the young calf. The horse's head was down, ears back, and everything about his body language told the calf that he was the boss. Each time the calf feinted the horse shifted course, anticipating the calf's every move. The horse was following the cow's lead step for step, proving to be very athletic. Her attention moved back to the rider. She couldn't escape the strange draw to him. Kit quickly left before Trace noticed her. As she walked slowly back to the house, she wondered about this mysterious hired hand.

Chapter Five

Sadie wiped her hands on the dish towel, poured two coffees and joined Kit at the table. Will had already left. "You and BJ spent a lot of time down at the corral yesterday."

"He asked me to stay so we can all get to know each other."

"You can stay here with us for as long as you want. This house has plenty of room. The two of us just rattle around. Besides, you're a Calhoun so it's your home, too."

The elderly Calhouns had welcomed her unconditionally. Kit had to admit it would be the ideal solution for now. "Your neat-as-a-pin house will never be the same. You have seen that Kenzie is a bundle of energy. Peace, and quiet will be a thing of the past. Kenzie isn't always cute and cuddly. She can be mischievous, as well as trying."

"I know the challenges of raising children. Try raising two boys who were as different as night and day. A child's laughter fills the house with pure joy, and a child's arms wrapped around your neck goes right through to your heart. You'll fit in here just fine."

Kit was so moved she found it difficult to speak.

"What's left for you to go back to?"

"Nothing. No home, no job. Nothing other than my personal items, a few pieces of furniture, and our clothes. I gave up everything to come here. There are no ties." Her voice was a mere whisper when she added, "Not anymore." Kit knew that she and Kenzie needed family, and there was a place for them here. She liked these people. She already felt like they were family. Kenzie was a happy well-adjusted child. Staying wouldn't change that. It was Jenny's and Shelby's dislike for her that complicated things. She admitted to herself that that might not change. Worry clouded her expression, as she chose to address her biggest concern with Calhoun directness, "If we stay at Valley View, we're going to be seeing a lot of BJ, and his family. Can they handle that?"

"I told you it was BJ's idea. Family is what unites us. Your dad is a fine man, and a good husband and father. I know he'd like to spend time with you, and it will help you to get to know him. He's hoping that time together will fuse the past and the present."

Kit wanted desperately to be accepted, and build a new life here for herself, and her daughter, but couldn't let go of her worry. "I don't know if that will happen."

"Give it time. We all need to work through this sudden change to our lives."

Kit knew that her life would be changing in many ways if she agreed to stay. Kit sighed. It had already changed. Kit's grandmother had taught her to be willing to take chances, and to fight for what you want. She didn't want to leave. It would be nice to temporarily call Valley View home. Kit's eyes brightened with gratitude, as she nodded.

Sadie wanted to know her granddaughter better. "Why do you call your mom and grandmother by their first names?"

Kit felt Sadie was genuinely interested, not prying, or interrogating her. She knew that a little background was needed for Sadie to understand who she was, and why she was here. Kit took a moment, deciding what to share. "It's not complicated, just unusual. We weren't your conventional family. Lou had just turned forty when I was born. No way was she going to be called Grandma and my mother wanted to be called Torrie. According to Lou, Torrie was always a difficult child, and became rebellious in her early teens. They discovered that she was bipolar. Once diagnosed, Torrie was better, but as soon as she felt better, she'd quit taking her medication. Torrie grew up calling herself a free spirit. In truth she wasn't much more than a party girl. She quit school, left home, came back, left again. One day she came back pregnant and broke. Lou was disappointed, but not surprised. She laid down the law. House rules were strict, and for once Torrie obeyed them. Lou hoped that once Torrie became a mother, she'd settle down, but Torrie wasn't willing to let a child complicate her life or leave her world of parties, and fast living. One of the things about being a parent is to take responsibility for the life you bring into the world. That means every day, whether you liked it or not. Instead, Torrie put her wants first. It was only a few months after I was born that Torrie returned to her old life. Life at home with a baby was a life sentence, so she escaped. Without a moment of guilt, she left me behind to be raised by my grandmother. I did have love, support and caring. Just not from Torrie. That's why I never called her mother. She never was one. She never loved me. I don't think she loved anyone but herself."

Sadie remained silent allowing Kit to continue.

This conversation was opening up old wounds. "It was unfair of Torrie to burden her mother with raising me, but Torrie didn't care. She would get restless, and take off without a word, come back, and leave again. Imagine being forsaken by your mother again, and again. When you're little, you believe that every time she came home, she would stay. As I got older, belief changed to hope. Maybe this time she would love me enough to stay. One day, when I was around ten, she took my hope with her when she left. I think that's when hope was replaced by hate. I realized she wouldn't change. I became quiet, and withdrawn, tormented because my mother always left without saying goodbye. Lou's love couldn't cushion me anymore. I thought it was my fault she left. She didn't love me enough to stay." Kit realized that this was the first time that she'd ever shared these thoughts out loud. She wasn't sure why. Maybe it was because Sadie was so much like Lou but wasn't personally involved.

Sadie's heart went out to Kit who believed she wasn't wanted because she wasn't planned and never had a mother to call her own. She felt her granddaughter's anguish, a young woman whose self-worth had been diminished by her mother's selfishness. Sadie couldn't help but wonder how any mother could forsake her own child.

Kit paused, trying to deal with the unexpected wave of sorrow brought on by the memories. "When Torrie was at home, Lou gave her everything to make her happy, but Torrie was never satisfied. All Lou and Torrie did was fight. It got so I hated it when she came back. The last time she left was when I turned fifteen. A few months later we got the dreaded knock on the door and, as they say, the rest is history. We thought all the drama was buried with Torrie. It was just moved to the attic. Life became normal after Torrie died. Having read Torrie's journals, the last couple of years of her life were rather grim. Torrie bounced around the country, hooking up with anyone who would take care of her and show her a good time. We never knew where she was or who she was with. Torrie lived her life for herself, no one else. That's who the real Torrie Kennedy was." Kit's voice came out more clipped than she intended.

Kit's emotions spilled over. "I remember the day I asked about my father. I wasn't very old, but I never forgot it. Torrie looked at me, an evil look on her face. All she said was, "He's dead." For some reason I wondered if she had lied. I also knew better than to mention him again, to either Torrie or Lou. We all know how that chapter ends so here we are."

Sadie studied her granddaughter with motherly concern as Kit struggled internally.

"It was Lou who taught me things you should learn from your mother. It should be your mother who rocks you to sleep and comforts you when you're upset." Kit's voice was filled with pain, and unchecked tears now ran down her cheeks. For all those years, without a word of complaint, Lou had supported her, and had been there. Until now. Lou was gone.

"Life takes us down different roads. Yours has been a bumpy one, but it has brought you here to us. I'm sure there are many good things ahead for you." Sadie wondered if Kit would open up about Kenzie's dad. "What happened to your husband, Kit?"

A faraway look darkened Kit's eyes. She was comfortable with Sadie, so she felt that she could open up about Mike. A pang of sorrow hit her as it always did when she thought about him. "My husband, Mike, was a military man. I literally bumped into him while we were on a city bus. He was striking in his uniform, but it was his smile that caught my eye. His smile lit up his face, and drew me in. Mike had soulful, intense eyes." Trace has the same kind of eyes, thought Kit, and had to wonder where that came from. The thought caused her to pause for a moment. It startled her how often the man entered her thoughts for no reason.

"Mike was abandoned when he was young and grew up in foster care. As you know, my childhood wasn't great, either. I know illegitimacy no longer has the stigma it used to, but it's still a mark of disgrace to some. Our family lineage, or the lack of it, had no bearing on who we were. It didn't change our love for each other. Mike loved me for who I was.

Our lives were full of promises and surprises. Promises that were snuffed out by ugly surprises. You can never predict fate." Kit took a long pause before continuing, "The military was always Mike's dream. I was still in university when he got called for active duty overseas, so we decided to get married before he left. I found out I was pregnant shortly after Mike was deployed. We were thrilled about having a baby. We swore that our child would be raised by two loving parents. The twisted irony of life," Kit said cynically. "I kissed Mike good-bye, not knowing I would never see him again. Suddenly, my world was turned upside down by another horrible knock on the door. It changed my world. It was the end of my life with Mike, and our hopes and dreams. Mike died before he could be a dad. Kenzie never had the chance to meet her father." Kit looked directly at Sadie, her eyes full of tears, "Thanks to Lou, I was given the chance to find mine."

These memories didn't hurt like Torrie's did but talking about Mike brought back the ache. Mike still lived in her dreams allowing her to remember the way he would make her feel. "What Mike and I had in that short time was special. Mike was a good man. I miss him a lot."

"I'm sorry," Sadie said. "Death is difficult."

"So is life. I was overwhelmed at first. History was repeating itself and I was going to be a single parent like my mother. I desperately needed Lou's help to move forward and get on with my life. I stayed in school. Even though it was difficult to go back, knowing I would have a child to support made me even more determined. After graduating I took a teaching position. Kenzie and I continued to live with Lou, so I was lucky to have a live-in babysitter. Lou, and I set up a routine that worked. Lou always said that no matter how bad things are they always get better. Sometimes, it's a long way to better." Kit choked on her last words.

Sadie still wanted to know more about her granddaughter, but knew it was time to move to another topic, "Is Kit a nickname?" she asked, attempting to lighten the mood.

Kit laughed, "Yes, my birth name is Katherine Grace. Lou loved the old silver screen movies, and ironically this was one thing Lou and Torrie had in common. I think I was named after Katherine Hepburn, and Grace Kelly. Torrie often called me Kitten, which in turn got shortened to Kit. She probably would have preferred a cat instead of a baby." Kit looked over at her daughter, and smiled, "Kenzie's birth name is, MacKenzie Kennedy Bennett. MacKenzie was her dad's middle name. Mike was the love of my life, and this was my way of honoring him. Kennedy is in honor of my grandmother. Family may not have meant anything to Torrie but it's everything to me. That's why I'm here," Kit stated simply.

Kit knew Sadie was still curious, but she had shared enough. Kit had studied the family pictures throughout the house when she was by herself. She was nervous when she asked, "I've told you about my mother, my grandmother, and my husband. Will you tell me about my dad?"

Sadie's smile was gracious. "The Calhoun family is a close family. It always has been. I'm very blessed to have my family around me." Sadie rose, came back with a family picture, and handed it to Kit.

Kit picked out BJ right away. There was another boy standing beside him who was maybe two or three years younger. Kit had to wonder if he was his brother. She recalled Sadie saying they raised two sons.

"There are many memories within these walls, good and bad." Sadie pointed to the younger boy. The older woman's eyes darkened with sorrow. Her voice cracked as her own painful memories surfaced, "There is heartache, and loss in everyone's life. We can't allow it to define us. That's our other son, Danny. He died in a snowmobiling accident when he was fifteen. Every family has their history with tragedy. When someone dies young it really shakes you, and often tests your faith. I can tell you that in time you do heal, and life gets better."

"Will it, Sadie? I keep hoping." Kit knew her arrival here was a shock for everyone, but some were less welcoming than others. Her encounters with Shelby had been met with animosity, and open hostility. It was evident that Shelby didn't want her and Kenzie at Valley View. "You, and Will, and BJ accepted me without reservations. Jenny is trying, but Shelby is another story."

"I'll share something else with you. It may explain why Shelby's so antagonistic toward you. Shelby has the Calhoun name, but BJ isn't her biological father. Shelby is his stepdaughter. BJ married Jenny when Shelby was younger than Kenzie, and he adopted her. Jenny didn't force the role of father on BJ. He took it gladly. He has always considered himself to be Shelby's father, and she calls him dad, but she always knew who her real father was."

Kit's eyes widened in surprise. There was so much she didn't know.

"Shelby's dad, Dallas Reed, was BJ's best friend. Dallas grew up an untamed youth who was strong-willed, and often reckless. He felt he always fell short when he compared himself to BJ. He blamed his parents, believing it was their fault because they were complacent with the minimum basics of life, and couldn't give him the things he wanted. He believed they were failures, and it reflected on him. As he grew older, there were times his actions were too daring. The boy grew up head-strong, and self-centered doing what he wanted without thought to the consequences of his devil-may-care attitude. Their constant companion was Jenny, who loved adventure as much as the two boys. Over the years that friendship grew into love. BJ and Dallas both loved Jenny, and she loved both of them. With Dallas, everything was a competition. In this case Jenny was the prize, and Dallas did everything he could to win her. The boy was very charismatic. In the end, it was Dallas who won Jenny's heart. The innocence of youth overshadowed by illusions. Jenny loved Dallas to distraction and was sure his hell-raising ways would end once they were married. BJ was heartbroken because he was crazy about her, but they still remained the best of friends."

"Both BJ and Dallas competed in amateur rodeos when they were young. They joined the rodeo circuit right out of high school. It was a different lifestyle, one that both Will and I hoped would be short lived. For BJ it was. When he quit, he was ready to settle down, and start taking over running the ranch. BJ hoped that when he quit Dallas would, too. Dallas thrived in the spotlight. The dare-devil cowboy performing for the adoring crowd. He was caught up with the thrill and the fame that came with his success. Dallas always did what he wanted without much thought about the consequences. That didn't change when he and Jenny got married. Right after they were married, Dallas's parents signed the ranch over to him. They pulled up stakes, leaving everything to their son. Dallas wasn't thrilled. He had no interest in being a rancher, so he didn't quit the rodeo like he promised Jenny. We were all sure he'd quit once Shelby was born. Again, Dallas promised he would, but he didn't. Some cowboys don't know when to quit. I'm glad BJ wasn't one of them."

"Dallas's irresponsible lifestyle became a concern for our family. His neglect resulted in the decline of his ranch, and his herd of cattle. The entire ranch was run down, but fence repairs are always necessary. The agreement between our two ranches was that Dallas would maintain the boundary fence between our properties. I know that BJ and Dallas argued about this as well as his neglect to his family."

"We knew Jenny's life was difficult with Dallas gone all the time. I admired Jenny's strength throughout their turbulent marriage. The poor girl knew Dallas didn't honor his vows. When Dallas hurt Jenny, which he often did, it was BJ she turned to. That wasn't fair to BJ. He still loved Jenny, but he had promised Dallas that he would take care of his family when he was away. BJ was always there for Jenny, especially when Dallas was killed at one of the rodeos."

Kit understood about everyone having to deal with loss in their lives. For some it just came sooner. Life could be cruel.

"The heartache following Dallas's death was traumatic, but it was complicated by several factors. Dallas's parents always excused their son's actions and shortfalls. They disowned Jenny, blaming her for their son's death. The year after Dallas died his mother committed suicide. After Peggy's death, Wade left the area. No one heard from him again. On top of everything else, Jenny didn't know the extent of the debt Dallas had accumulated. She had to face the reality of their dire financial circumstances. She was also now on her own. She couldn't handle anything else, emotionally, or financially. Her back was to the wall. She knew she couldn't hang on to the ranch without help. Devastated, Jenny turned to our family, and we were there to help. Not long after Dallas died, BJ married Jenny and adopted Shelby. They took over the Reed Ranch."

"With BJ gone we started hiring part-time wrangles, usually single men who would come and go. We had never hired anyone with a family, but Will and his brother, Buster made an exception when Tom Grayson showed up with his family. Work on a ranch never stops. There are things that must be done every day. Trace and Riley, who were just young boys, mucked stables, hauled bales, pitched hay, and mended fences. They did whatever they could to help. An immediate bond developed between Buster and Trace. Buster soon recognized Trace's deep love for horses. Whenever Trace could he'd spend time down at the stables with Murphy. The boy was an eager student, and Murphy taught him a lot. It wasn't long before Trace began training the horses. He has a natural gift."

Kit had seen for herself Trace's skill with a horse. She realized that there was more between the Calhouns and the Graysons than she realized. Not that it mattered. They had nothing to do with her. It didn't stop her from commenting, "I was surprised to hear that Riley and Trace were brothers. They certainly don't look alike." Trace was much bigger than Riley, taller and broader through the shoulders, and chest. Riley radiated comfortable warmth making him someone you like immediately. Trace, on the other hand, was rigid and aloof.

"Riley looks like his dad. Trace has the Mexican features of his mother. Their dad died when they were young. Like you, we have all lost family. We learn to accept what is and live in the now."

Kit knew this. She had learned this with Mike, and she had learned it a long time ago with Torrie. She was still dealing with her most recent loss.

"All we can do is live for today, let the past go and tomorrow will take care of itself."

That's easier said than done, thought Kit.

"That doesn't mean you forget the past, Kit. Just don't let it keep you from moving forward."

Kit held the older woman's gaze. "That's why I'm here," she said solemnly. "I lived with Lou since the day I was born until the day she died. I not only loved her, but I also liked her as a person, and I respected and admired her. She was a good woman. Things moved along quickly after she was gone. The house sold right away so I had to pack in a hurry. I felt I was packing Lou away, not just her things. It seems like everyone in my family is neatly packed away in a box. Lou, Mike, Torrie. Kenzie is all I have now."

"Not anymore, dear," Sadie said. "Sometimes, life isn't fair, but it does get better. We have more strength than we realize to get through the difficult times."

Kit realized Sadie was a lot like Lou. "Lou was wise and had a lot of sayings that she loved to share. During our hard times she would hug me tight and say that there is always good. Some days you just have to look a little harder." Kit sniffed back her tears. "Sorry, I miss Lou a lot." Overwhelmed by the conversation, Kit stood up, and walked out the door. She needed a moment to herself. It had been an intense morning. Kit wanted time alone to process what Sadie had shared about the Calhouns. What had shocked her the most was what she had learned about Shelby. Obviously, BJ was right, and they all needed time to get to know one another.

No one was around, so Kit wandered down to the corral hoping the horses might be out. She crossed her arms on the top rail, her chin resting on them as she watched the lone horse. Her gaze was focused on the chestnut colt as he pranced freely. He was a magnificent animal. It was evident that he came from good stock. When Kit heard the steady, hollow thud of boot heels approaching she turned, praying that it was anyone but the arrogant cowboy.

BJ went and stood next to her. "You like spending time down here watching the horses. Champ is high spirited, and still needs a lot of training. Trace has been working with him in his spare time." The two-year-old colt picked up his ears and turned his head to find the source of the voices. Champ snorted as if he knew he was the topic of conversation.

Kit wondered again about Trace's strong presence at Valley View, but all thoughts of him disappeared when BJ asked, "Are you ready to go for a ride, and see more of the ranch?"

"Right now?"

BJ nodded.

"I would love to," Kit said with honest enthusiasm. "But everyone seems to forget that I have a child. I don't have the luxury to just take off."

"You seem to forget that you have family that helps." BJ was quick to inform her that he had cleared it with Sadie before he came to find her. "Run in and grab a hat from Ma. See if any of her boots fit you. I'll have Murphy saddle up Blondie for you. Blondie's a fine Palomino mare with a nice disposition, especially with novice riders."

A look of pure joy lit up Kit's face. "Give me two minutes to change," she yelled over her shoulder, excitement shining in her eyes.

When Kit arrived back at the barn, she heard Shelby's voice. She was complaining to her dad, "You could have included me in your plans."

"This was spur of the moment. Besides, these days we never know what you're doing. Your hours at the clinic vary, and if you're not there you're usually off with your friends."

Kit knew that Shelby was jealous, and her whining voice grated on her nerves. She walked into the horse barn, and the smell of fresh straw brought back familiar memories.

BJ and Shelby were standing a couple of stalls over, deep in conversation. When BJ heard Kit, he glanced over and smiled. BJ turned back to Shelby, "By all means join us." It would be good to see his two daughters interact, he thought as he stepped away.

Kit stood in awkward silence waiting for Shelby's verbal attack. She didn't have to wait long. Shelby looked directly at Kit. Her tone became aggressive, "I have to give it to you, Kit. You certainly work fast. I know what you're doing. You obviously came here hoping you'd find a wealthy family to take care of you, and your kid."

"What on earth is your problem?"

"Other than you, nothing." There was uncertainty in Shelby's eyes when she asked, "How long are you planning to stay here at Valley View?"

Kit's gaze never faltered. She was done with this girl's attitude. "As long as I damn well please."

Shelby's voice rose in exasperation, "Don't get too comfortable."

BJ's return cut short their sniping. He had overheard them, but long practice helped him to keep his face impassive. Apparently, they had a few issues to work out. He figured he'd just have to have faith in both of them, and that given time they'd work things out. "I'm glad my two girls have this opportunity to get to know each other better. Isn't that nice?"

"Yes, sir," they said in unison, as they glared at each other.

When BJ stepped away Shelby turned back to Kit, who could tell by the evil delight in Shelby's eyes that she had something else in mind than just a friendly ride. Kit was fully aware that, for now, Shelby had the upper hand. "This isn't over," Shelby promised, as she glared at Kit. "I'll be outside waiting for you with my dad." Her voice had a very territorial ring to it.

Murphy seemed to appear out of the shadows. Kit sighed as she followed him to the next stall where he introduced her to Blondie. The golden Palomino was beautiful, and well-named. Murphy made sure the cinch was tight, and then held the reins. Kit placed her foot firmly in the stirrup and swung easily into the saddle. Murphy's calloused hand closed over hers as he handed her the reins, "Don't guess it's ever as bad as it seems.

Give everyone a little time, including yourself. It's too soon for you all to be judgmental." He turned, and slowly walked away.

Kit reached over the pommel of the saddle, and patted Blondie on her neck. The animal gave a frisky toss of her head in response. Kit managed a small smile as BJ and Shelby pulled alongside. Kit expected to be a little rusty since she hadn't ridden for years, but it was like getting back on a bike. Less than five minutes into the ride it was like she'd never been off a horse. Kit felt exhilarated, and revitalized. It felt good to be back on a horse, and in control. Riding had always brought her joy. She didn't realize how much she'd missed it.

It was a perfect day for riding in the country. Kit took in the sights and sounds of summer. The dry wind carried the scent of the trees and grass, and wispy clouds drifted overhead. When they reached the ridge, they all gazed out. Kit's breath caught as she took in the magnificent view sweeping in all directions. Kit sat deeply engrossed in the unfolding beauty sprawled in front of her, where horses grazed in distant pastures, and cattle in others. She scanned the landscape stretching out on all sides, the rugged mountains a spectacular backdrop to the west. The surrounding beauty could quickly become a part of one's soul, she thought with a strange wistfulness. Her eyes were wide with the wonder of it all as she turned to BJ. "This view is breathtaking. Is all of this your ranch?"

It was Shelby who responded with a nod. For a moment, the old Shelby surfaced, forgetting her anger. She was open, and honest as she spoke, "The view along this valley is spectacular. Hence, the ranch's name Valley View. It's beautiful, and spacious. It's a wonderful place to live. I can't think of another place on earth I'd rather be than here, breathing in the clean mountain air."

BJ pointed to his right. "The ranch one over is Lola Grande, which is owned by Lola Grayson, and her two sons, Trace and Riley."

"I heard Riley was the one who brought you here," Shelby said accusingly.

Kit ignored Shelby's complaint and looked at BJ. "I've seen them both around the ranch. I thought they were hired hands."

BJ shook his head. "Our relationship is too complex to go into right now. The short version is that Valley View, and Lola Grande share some operations jointly. Our main enterprise is cattle. which in itself is a huge enterprise. Trace is the head of the horse operation, while Riley and I manage the cattle. The Graysons are like family." A shadow crossed his face. "There's a lot of history in regard to Lola Grande, and we share more than a boundary fence." He shook his head as if clearing ghosts from the past, and his mood had changed. "This is long enough in the saddle for your first time." They turned from the view and headed back to the ranch.

Shelby had recognized that Kit was far from a novice rider, and she wondered how good she was. She turned her eyes toward Kit, silently challenging her. Shelby began to show off which annoyed Kit. It struck Kit that this was the perfect time to put Shelby in her place. Both horse and rider reacted to the challenge. Having had enough, Kit leaned forward in the saddle, gave Blondie her head, and they took off flying. The two girls were soon racing back to the ranch. Flying over the fields, Kit reveled in the power soaring under her.

Shelby quickly discovered she hadn't given Kit enough credit, as she pulled away.

Back at the ranch, Kit was off Blondie before Shelby rode in. She was feeling ridiculously pleased with herself, and she didn't bother to hide her smirk.

Shelby swung out of the saddle, and stomped over to Kit, "You're a real smart-ass."

"And you're a pain in my ass." Kit stood firm with her feet wide apart. She stared back at Shelby, a smug look on her face. "As you can see, I can ride as good as I can walk. Never underestimate your rival."

Shelby had the grace to blush and stomped off.

BJ, who had just arrived, strolled over. Kit was worried about his reaction to her conduct. A smile tilted one corner of his mouth. "Well, aren't you full of surprises, Kit Bennett. You're an excellent horsewoman. Why didn't you say something?"

Kit laughed at his amazement, while her eyes lit up at his compliment. "Nobody asked. You all assumed I'm just a city girl."

They were both learning new things about each other. "Is there anything else I should know? Or are you just going to keep surprising me?"

Kit knew he was referring to her unexpected arrival. "I spent several summers working at camp. My first year I started working with the horses. I soon became the guide on trail rides. I love to ride, so I took advantage whenever I had the opportunity."

"You're welcome to ride Blondie anytime you like."

"I'm sure I'll be taking you up on that offer. Blondie is a wonderful horse to ride. Thanks for today. It was enjoyable as well as exhilarating." Her eyes twinkled with merriment, "It's been a long time since I had this much fun. Sorry about what just happened with Shelby, but she goaded me one too many times. I don't always play nice," Kit confessed.

BJ laughed. "Don't be sorry. You impressed me on how you handled both Blondie, and Shelby. I never thought I'd see the day that Shelby was at a loss for words. Shelby may have met her match." For the sake of everyone he hoped his daughters would learn to get along.

A shadow came over Kit's face, and some of the excitement faded from her voice, "I'm trying to like Shelby, but she's making it difficult."

"It takes Shelby time to work through her moods so watch out. Give Shelby some time. Overall, she's a good person."

Kit refused to keep her thoughts to herself, "She is self-centered, and rude."

"I think you two might have misjudged each other." Out of the corner of his eye he saw Kit shrug. "Don't you agree?"

"Does what I think really matter?"

"Of course, what you think matters. It's the only way of getting to know you better."

Kit wasn't convinced. "Even if I speak my mind, and it's not what you like to hear?"

"I've managed so far." BJ liked her honesty, though at times it was somewhat unnerving. Nothing more was said as they let the matter drop.

Kit admitted that she had let her temper get the better of her with Shelby. Kit knew she would pay for it sooner than later. A satisfied smile crossed her lips. It was worth it.

Chapter Six

Trace and Murphy were in the barn waiting for the vet who was coming to check Ginger and her new foal.

Shelby stormed in and was in a mood. "I saw dad with his new daughter. Like usual."

"So, you decided to hide out here? Having issues with the new family?"

Shelby gave Trace an impatient look, "Because I have to, I will accept that Kit, and Kenzie are family. In reality, Kit, and I are not sisters, and we definitely are not friends." Her dad may have welcomed his new daughter with open arms, but as far as Shelby was concerned, Kit couldn't leave soon enough. Her voice waivered, "Nothing has been the same since they arrived. Dad is spending all of his time with them. I hate this, Trace. I'm sure that Kit is staying here just to take advantage of my family."

Trace was concerned that Shelby was right. "Even if Kit leaves, it's never going to be the way it was. But I get the feeling she's not going anywhere soon." Kit had found a comfortable place to stay until she got what she wanted.

Shelby's eyes went cold as reality hit. This change in her life could be a permanent one. This was unbelievable. Why couldn't Kit just return to Washington, and stay there? Even though she had been doing everything to make Kit feel unwanted it wasn't working. Shelby hated Kit even more.

Trace was relieved when he heard Doc's truck. He knew Shelby too well. This was far from over, but her continuous drama was getting tiresome.

Kit could see a stranger in the corral with her dad. She joined them when BJ waved her over, happy to be included. Kit's radiant smile faded as Trace walked over with Shelby and joined them. Shelby had obviously been crying on his shoulder, and God only knew what tale she'd spun.

Kit wasn't immune to Trace's probing stares. His penetrating look was boring through her, making her uncomfortable.

Shelby moved next to her dad and tucked her arm through his. He automatically smiled at her. She looked smug as her gaze turned to Kit.

Kit felt a pang of envy, as she watched the affection between father and daughter. She realized she wanted that kind of a relationship with her dad but needed the chance to prove that she was worth it. Kit stepped back from the others feeling like an outsider.

The veterinarian slowly unwound his lanky form from his crouched position beside Jasper. His sandy-colored hair was clipped short, and his hazel eyes gleamed with excitement. He patted Trace on the back. "This foal is a beauty. You have another winner here, Trace. Beautiful lines, healthy and strong."

Kit was dumbfounded to hear these were Trace's horses. Something new to process.

BJ stepped over and stood next to Kit. "Dr. Jim Parker, meet my daughter, Kit Bennett."

"Hello, Doctor. It's a pleasure to meet you." Kit extended her hand, and the tall man shook it as his face brightened.

The vet's gaze remained on Kit, and he experienced an instant tug of attraction. "Call me Doc. I didn't know you had a sister, Shelby." Doc's surprised reaction was as expected.

Deliberately, Shelby lifted her shoulders in a casual shrug, and corrected him. "As Dad said, Kit is his daughter. She is not my sister."

BJ gave Shelby a warning glance. Since Kit's arrival, he'd seen a side of Shelby he didn't like. It was time to have a talk with her.

The vet had a relaxed, and easy manner. If the vet noticed the tension between the two girls, he didn't show it. "Are you here for a visit, Kit?" Doc Parker's sparkling eyes probed without being intrusive. Unlike Trace who continued to hover near her. Watching. Always watching.

Kit was shocked at how cold Shelby's voice was when she said, "She won't be around long. She has no reason to stay."

Kit didn't take kindly to Shelby's comments. The girl was deplorable, turning everything into a personal assault. Kit reminded herself that Valley

View was her home, and she had a right to be here. "I have no definite plans as I just arrived a few days ago." Kit hated the fact that this girl could so easily make her lose her temper and play into her juvenile game. The frustration in her eyes deepened. She had been told that Shelby's behavior was out of character. Kit couldn't excuse it. It had become too personal. At that moment Trace looked her way. He remained silent, but he stared long enough to make Kit uncomfortable. Kit chose to ignore him.

Doc turned back to Trace, "I'll drop by when I do my rounds next week to check on them again. He really is a superb foal."

Trace nodded as he shook the vet's hand, "Thanks for coming out today."

"Don't forget to mark your calendar for our annual barbeque on Labour Day."

"Thanks BJ. Will you still be here, Kit?"

BJ put his arm around Kit. "Of course, she'll be here. The timing is perfect. Kit will get a chance to meet our friends, and neighbors."

And face the curious and nosey. Kit hated being the center of attention.

BJ turned back to Shelby, "You can introduce her to your friends at the same time."

Oh, just dandy, Shelby thought furiously. She didn't reply.

Trace's gaze connected with Kit's, and he drawled, "One never knows. She may leave just as suddenly as she showed up." Hopefully, Kit would take the obvious hint, and leave.

Kit's gaze never faltered. She knew he was baiting her, and she knew she'd have to learn to deal with those around her, no matter how much they irritated her. "If you don't mind," Kit said pointedly to Trace, "I'm perfectly capable of speaking for myself." Kit turned to her dad who had been taking it all in. Showing none of her inner turmoil, Kit smiled, and forced cheerfulness into her voice as she said, "I look forward to your barbeque. It will be a good opportunity to meet others while I'm here." She hoped her smile didn't appear as false as it felt.

Trace had to admire Kit for her spunk.

"Well, Kit, it has been a pleasure meeting you. If I don't see you before, I'll look forward to seeing you then." Doc picked up his bag and turned back to BJ. The two men shook hands and took off in separate directions.

BJ knew it was time to have a talk with Shelby. Now was as good a time as any. He caught up to her as she was heading back to their house. "I want to talk to you."

Shelby tossed him a defiant stare. "Not now, I'm meeting friends," she lied. She was in no mood for a lecture.

BJ gave her no choice when he said, "You can spare a few minutes."

Shelby recognized the Calhoun determination in his set jaw. "Fine."

"What has gotten into you? Your behavior just now was embarrassing. I've had enough with the snide remarks. From now on you will be civil to Kit. We've talked about this before. This is real and it's not going away. That's life. You'll find there are always bumps along the way. Even if Kit leaves it's never going to be the way it was. Kit will always be my daughter. You've been given a sister. You should be grateful instead of acting like a spoiled child."

The stern lecture from her dad only fueled Shelby's anger. There was no way she was going to accept Kit as her sister. Her eyes were cold, and her face took on an expression of hostility, "I'm not about to allow your past dictate my future."

Even though Shelby could be a handful, she'd been raised with good values. BJ had to trust that time would help her figure things out. He just hoped it would be sooner than later. Murphy called him and he left. Disappointment swept through him as he walked away.

Shelby saw Kit heading back to the house. With renewed anger, she quickly caught up to her. Kit tried to leave, but Shelby grabbed her arm, impeding her escape. "Go away, you don't belong here. You can't stay here at the ranch and take advantage of my family."

Anger filled Kit's eyes, "They're my family, too."

"They're just looking out for you out of a sense of duty. Poor Kit. Poor unwanted, Kit. Even your mother didn't want you. I may not have gotten to know my father but at least I know I was wanted."

Kit remained quiet, because under no circumstances could she let Shelby know that her words stung even if it was the truth. Facts were facts. Facts she had faced a long time ago.

Shelby fought dirty, continuing with words that cut deep, "I see there's no father in your daughter's life either. You're no better than your mother was."

Shelby's remarks hurt more than usual. Kit retreated to the house to compose herself.

Meanwhile Trace and Doc were having their own conversation by the vet's truck. "I was surprised when BJ introduced Kit. I didn't know he had another daughter."

"Nor did he until she blew in like a Chinook a few days ago. She has stirred everything up and the dust hasn't settled."

"No husband?"

Trace shook his head, "BJ says she has no other family."

"Kit seems to be a nice young lady."

"That's a matter of opinion," Trace said dryly.

"Did someone of the opposite sex get to you, Trace?" Doc teased.

Trace's face hardly changed expression, but he couldn't deny that for some reason Kit kept getting under his skin. Maybe he wasn't hiding his feelings as well as he thought. "That will be the day that some woman can have any effect on me. She intrigues me, that's all."

"Yeah, right." Doc was enjoying Trace's ill humor. He laughed as he climbed behind the wheel. "I'm looking forward to seeing Kit again. I'm intrigued, too," he added, mocking him.

Trace scowled as the vet's truck pulled away and his farewell honk annoyed him. Doc Parker may be enamored with BJ Calhoun's daughter, but he wasn't.

When Kit returned to the house, Kenzie was bouncing up and down on Will's knee, her blonde curls bouncing wildly. Sadie puttered at the counter preparing dinner. Will pointed to himself and said to Kenzie, "Who am I?"

"Papa."

He pointed over to his wife, "Who is that?"

"GiGi." Kenzie giggled.

Sadie quickly explained, "I know I'm her great-grandmother but, like Lou, I don't think that's what I want to be called. So, we made it simple with GiGi which is short for great-grandmother. I hope you don't mind?"

Kit liked Sadie and Will, but it still felt odd having another family. "No, I don't mind. I'm pleased with it. BJ wants Kenzie to call him, Grandpa."

Although they were happy to hear this, neither of the Calhouns missed the fact that Kit still didn't refer to their son as, Dad. "Words can't express how glad we are to have you here." Sadie had fallen in love with her new family.

Sadie had no idea how much this meant to Kit after her recent encounter with Shelby.

"Can we go see the kitties, Papa?"

Will ruffled Kenzie's hair, "We'll go later."

Kenzie went over and pulled at Will with determination. "I want to go now, Papa."

Will gave in and stood up.

"I hate to admit that my daughter had Lou completely wrapped around her little finger from the moment she was born."

Sadie looked over at her husband, "Like she does her, Papa."

Both women laughed when Will snorted and picked Kenzie up and left.

"It's obvious you're a loving mom in spite of your mother not being there for you." Raising a child alone had to be hard, and it appeared that Kit was doing a good job.

Kit looked down at Kenzie's doll on the floor. "Torrie's fantasy of motherhood was like playing dolls with a beautiful happy baby. That bubble burst quickly."

After Kenzie settled for the night, Kit left Sadie watching television, and stepped outside. Dusk was setting over the mountains. The magnificent sight brought her a special kind of peace.

Will was sitting in one of the rocking chairs, his feet stretched out in front of him. This was the time of the day he loved the most, when the quiet of the night settled over the land allowing those in its universe a chance to rest. The day was done. God willing, he would wake to live another day. "Hello, Missy. Is Kenzie down for the night?"

Kit nodded. "Sleeping like a baby. Am I disturbing you?" When Will shook his head, she sat down next to him. She was glad she had grabbed her sweater as the air was cool. Kit no longer found Will difficult to talk to, "I spent the afternoon with BJ. Will you tell me more about my dad and the Calhouns?"

"What do you want to know?"

Kit was starving for any information about her dad. She was curious about Valley View, and the whole ranching operation. "Everything. Anything," she answered honestly.

Will looked out at the view in front of him. His eyes shifted to the old house where BJ, and his family lived. "Generations of Calhouns have been born and raised in these two houses." His gaze returned to Kit, and he smiled, "Now we have a new generation."

Kit's eyes misted, knowing she'd been accepted as family.

Kit had earned his respect. It took true grit for her to come all this way by herself, not knowing what would be waiting for her. "I may ramble, and get side-tracked, so you can interrupt me if I get carried away. Just remember that you asked. Four generations of Calhouns have dedicated their lives to this ranch. Those who came first bought the sweetest piece of land on the eastern side of the Rockies. They settled here, establishing our future. Land and livestock are what Valley View Ranch is noted for. We are highly respected ranchers who run a first-class cattle business and are known for raising quality beef. Cattle ranching is a life of rebirth, growth, and fulfillment. Ranching keeps a man humble. It's a job you do every day. Days are filled with hard work that isn't always productive, but the rewards make it worth the hardships. You get to watch the sun come up and if you're lucky you get to watch the sun go down."

"Are you and BJ the only Calhouns or are there more?"

Will shifted his position to get comfortable. The older he got the more his joints ached. A shadow crossed Will's face. "Well, little lady, get comfy. The short answer is, yes, but I'll fill you in on a little history, so you understand our family. It will also explain the close relationship that the Calhoun family has with the Grayson family."

Once again Trace's image invaded her thoughts. What was she going to learn about Trace Grayson now? She clasped her hands together and waited.

"My grandfather, Albert Calhoun, was the original homesteader. He followed his dream of freedom to these wide-open spaces. He saw the beauty that lay here in the valley and bought up the land we sit on. When he married my grandmother, Helen, they built the original house that BJ, and his family live in. Four generations have lived in that house."

"I had an older brother. Ben was three years older, and my best friend. He passed away several years ago. Everyone around here knew him as Buster, a childhood nickname that stuck. Buster was the all-star athlete. He was offered scholarships from all over but turned them all down. His love, like mine, was this ranch. Neither one of us wanted any other life than the one we had right here. Buster married his high school sweetheart, Annie Dickson, the summer after graduation. They had only one child, a son whom they named, Joseph, after our dad. When I married Sadie, our parents retired into town, and Buster and I took over managing the homestead. Sadie and I lived with Buster and Annie while we built this house. It was an arrangement of convenience, and fortunately our wives became best friends. Sadie and I had BJ the year after their son was born. Two years later we had another son, Danny. Buster and I both had another generation to pass the ranch down to."

Kit didn't miss the pride in Will's voice.

"Our three boys were inseparable until tragedy struck the year that Joey turned fourteen. It happened the day after he got his learner's license. He begged his mom to let him drive to school. He was excited and wanted to show off. It was early spring, the roads were clear, so his parents agreed. Buster waved as he watched Joey and Annie drive away, an excited young man behind the wheel. That was the day Buster's life changed. A gravel truck failed to stop at the corner stop sign down the road, and T-boned their vehicle. The impact was so hard that both Annie and Joey were pronounced dead on scene. It was a horrible tragedy that affected the whole community. Buster was never the same after that. Their death left him a shell of the man he used to be. He became withdrawn, and he forgot how to laugh. This ranch was his salvation as life moved forward." Will's heart ached as he thought of his own son, Danny. Another young life taken too soon. "Tragedy reared its ugly head again when BJ was seventeen. A group of us went snowmobiling in the mountains. There was another father, and his son that went with us. We all had our own machines. There were no avalanche warnings in the area. It was an area we went to every year, so we were familiar with the runs. No one knows what triggered the avalanche, but Danny and the other boy were buried. It was a recovery mission by the time rescuers were able to find them and dig them out." Will's voice broke, "You know it wasn't your fault, but you still blame yourself. You wonder if you could have done something different. That day I knew the hurt my brother had been going through. I was lucky, I still had Sadie and BJ. Buster had lost his whole family, and never recovered. After our loss I understood my brother better. We became even closer."

Kit turned away hoping that Will didn't see her wipe her eyes.

Will cleared his throat before continuing, "Life was rolling along smoothly, until fate once again stepped in. Buster got cancer. He didn't tell anyone when he was first diagnosed. His cancer was untreatable, and he wasn't given long to live. He didn't say anything until he couldn't hide it anymore. That year was difficult for all of us as we watched a strong, independent man fade away to a mere shadow of himself. Trace, already an old soul, became quiet, and retreated further into himself after Buster died. They were very close. Riley was in his last year of high school and went on to college. The best thing for Riley was when he went away for two years. He developed a new confidence, and a quiet strength. He was able to step out of the shadow of his older brother and find his own path. When he came back from college, Shelby was still the center of his universe. He has been waiting patiently for the girl to grow up and see beyond herself. Your arrival has upset Shelby's world, and we're all waiting to see what happens. Sadly, you're taking the brunt of her actions, but once her world stops reeling you will see a much nicer Shelby."

Kit was taken aback by Will's revelation of Shelby. It was enlightening, and a little surprising. Will called it the way it was and was far more perceptive than she thought. She hoped he was right because right now Kit didn't like Shelby.

"That's our family."

Kit knew he meant the Calhouns and the Graysons.

"I want you to understand that the Graysons are an impressive family. Lola Grayson, Trace, and Riley are honest, trustworthy, ethical people. The Calhouns and the Graysons operate a joint venture with Valley View and Lola Grande. We also have strong personal ties."

This had been an enlightening conversation. Between the conversation with her dad on the ride, and this one, Kit sensed a sadness around Lola Grande, and what had been the Reed Ranch.

"Ranching is more than just our livelihood. It has developed into a business. Our cattle are the product of culling the undesirable over the years. Our bulls are considered to be of superior lineage. The horses we use have been born and trained at the ranch. Trace's area of expertise is with the horses. In time, Riley will become the foreman here at Valley View. Trace is immensely proud of his younger brother, who is capable of taking on this role. We'll see less of Trace as he devotes his time to Lola Grande. We operate the two ranches together, but every year Lola Grande is becoming more independent."

Kit already knew some of this since she had heard it from BJ. What she also heard was the note of respect both men had when talking about the Grayson boys.

"Trace is training several horses right now for cutting. Trace can tell within the early stages if a horse is better suited for the range, or for competition. Or neither. There are colts that have fun chasing something around. It's play, pure and simple. They don't all have the knack to become good at cutting. Once they find out that its work with precision, form, and style, they don't want to do it. Within six to eight months a rider can tell if the horse is suited for ranch life, and it usually takes a minimum of eighteen months of training to prepare a good horse for competition. It takes a man with a lot of patience to train a cutting horse, and Trace is one of the best."

"Does Trace train for both?"

"He does. Trace knows more about training horses than most men I've seen."

Kit couldn't deny that Trace fascinated her. She knew she was too sensitive when it came to Trace. Susceptible might be a better word. The more she learned about him the more confused she became. Kit also wondered why he didn't like her.

Understanding her more than Kit realized, Will covered her hand with his. "Trace is a hard man, often unyielding like the land. He's a loner, and a man who always does his own thing. He isn't exactly the easiest person to get to know. When you do, you'll find that he's someone you can rely on, and trust. Someone who becomes a friend for life." He squeezed her hand before letting go.

For Kit, it had been an incredible evening. She had spent the last few hours completely absorbed in Will's narration. "You love this life, don't you?"

Kit's genuine interest in the ranch had pleased Will. "It's the only life. A cowboy lives to be free and proud of being his own man. Ranching is my life."

The man who at first appeared to be ornery and gruff was quite different once they got to know each other. Will had shared the history of the ranch with colorful stories. She had listened with focused intensity, occasionally pumping Will for more information. Kit could tell that her grandfather loved talking about Valley View. In doing so, she had learned more about Valley View, and those who lived here. She could see the way Will appreciated the land, and how he had passed this on to his son, and the Grayson boys. Learning more about their pasts drew her deeper into their lives. All of them, including Trace Grayson, had earned her respect.

PART II

Chapter Seven

Will's conversation last night with Kit had stirred old memories. He stepped outside, and the early glow in the eastern sky welcomed him. He dropped into one of the wicker chairs with his coffee. He looked over at the old farmhouse knowing that Kit's unexpected arrival would have a powerful impact on all of their lives, just like the Grayson's arrival had. He allowed himself to slip back in time, to the day of their arrival.

It had been a mild winter, but the day dawned cloudy with a cool wind. Will breathed deep and saw his breath as he exhaled. He slowly scanned the landscape, never tiring of the view, especially at this time of the year with the snow-capped mountains that always offered a spectacular backdrop. Last week's Chinook had melted the surrounding snow. The hint of spring was noticeable, and the busy time of the year was just around the corner.

Will waved as Buster approached. Buster went inside, grabbed a coffee, and joined his brother. Buster could tell that Will was in one of his melancholy moods. He sat down in the other rocker, and together they reminisced about days long gone. Buster's gaze drifted back to his house. Even after all this time, he couldn't believe his family was gone. He wandered down his own path of memories. When he finally looked back at his brother, his eyes had that distant look that had become all too familiar. "When someone dies young it really shakes you, but when you lose your whole family, it devastates you. For a while you lose a part of yourself. It tests your faith. Even now there are times that I'm lonely. Sometimes you allow yourself to dream about what might have been, but we learn to accept what is. What does Sadie always say?"

Will chuckled because his wife always had something to say. "Live for today, let the past go, and tomorrow will take care of itself. None of us can forget the past, but you can't let it keep you from moving forward."

Their reminiscing was unexpectedly interrupted when they saw a rusty old pick-up pulling a holiday trailer coming up their private drive. The two men were used to seeing drifters, shiftless men with shiftless lives. They would earn a few dollars and move on. But few came with a family in tow. Will wondered if they were migrant workers looking for work, but it was a little early in the season for that.

Buster looked at Will, "I wonder what this is all about?" He rose to his feet. Buster Calhoun was a tall, powerfully build man. He had a strong face, tanned, and weathered by the outdoors. Will was a mirror image of his brother, but not as tall.

Will got up and stood next to Buster. He didn't like uninvited visitors. Will's gaze missed nothing, so he saw the man's warning glare he gave his family as he climbed out of the truck. Will's eyes narrowed as he looked down at the stranger, while watching every move the man made. There was a little unease in the pit of his stomach as he studied the man.

Tom's manner quickly changed as he stood at the bottom of the steps and nodded politely. "Good morning, gentlemen. I'm Tom Grayson and I'm looking for work. I know it's a bit early for spring labor, but I was hoping you would hire me now, and I could do other work. I have experience, and I'm a good worker." Verbally, the man was smooth, but his manner was bold. Physically, he was a bull of a man. His shoulders were wide and muscled. He was darkly tanned, so he obviously spent time outdoors. His hands were large and calloused, evidence that the man was used to physical labor.

Buster looked past the stranger and studied the passengers in the truck. His gaze rested on the woman in the front seat. Lola Grayson sat with her hands in her lap with her fingers laced together. She looked tired, and the boys in the back were restless. She gave both boys a cautionary glance when they started to fidget. Lola pushed lamely at her disheveled hair with a trembling hand. Lola hadn't missed the look of deliberation that Will had given her husband.

Will wasn't sure if he trusted the drifter. He had met his kind before. The man seemed polite enough, but he appeared to have a restless quality to him. "Why did you leave your last job?" Will demanded, wondering if the man would be honest.

Lola wondered what excuse he'd use this time. She had heard them all.

Tom smiled, "We've been working our way west." And the practiced script began. "Alberta is where we plan to settle. I'm looking to put down roots, and I'm hoping it might be here. I'll earn my keep."

Will was convinced hiring him would be a mistake. This man made him uncomfortable. "We'd want someone for the long haul, not someone who jumps from job to job."

Tom's face darkened, but he controlled himself. "That was a means to an end. As I said, I'm looking to settle here."

Buster was about to say no, but the pleading look in the wife's eyes make him change his mind. Recognizing her look of desperation, he gave Will a swift glance. The silent communication between them was all Will needed. He allowed Buster to take the lead. "We have high standards at Valley View, so there are a couple of hard and fast rules. There is no drinking on the job, and no gambling in the bunkhouse. Our men work hard for their wages, and we don't want them losing their money on a game of chance." An awkward silence followed. Buster saw a flicker in Tom's eyes and guessed this might be a weakness. Their gaze met and held. Whatever his own misgivings might be, Buster nodded to Tom. "We'll give you a chance, but it is only temporary work for now. We pay fair wages, but we expect hard work in return. If you work out, we'll consider keeping you on full-time." Buster was one who usually took his time to think things through before he acted. This was out of character.

"That's great. I've never been afraid of hard work."

This statement was one that Will actually believed, but it didn't ease his concerns. "Our full-time employee, Murphy, lives in the bunk house. The bunk house is for single men, the part-time wrangles that we hire during our busy season."

"That's okay. We've lived in this old trailer for years. We call it home."

"You can start tomorrow. We'll walk over and show you where you can park the trailer. The south side of the bunkhouse will give you some privacy, and there are plug-ins."

Tom nodded. He had promised Lola, and the boys that it would be different for them in Alberta. Hard work was never the issue. This time he needed to make it work.

A look of profound relief crossed Lola Grayson's face as Tom climbed back into the cab.

Buster and Will walked across the yard. Buster kept waiting for Will to say something. He braced himself for his brother's reaction knowing full well that if it was up to Will they wouldn't have hired the drifter.

Will's voice was gruff when he finally spoke, "I was surprised when you hired him. I don't trust that man, and I don't think he'll take orders too well."

"I don't trust him either. We'll keep a real close eye on all of them. We both have misgivings in regard to him. But I feel that the family needs us, and here they will be safe. Let's give it some time and see what happens."

All four family members were standing outside by the trailer as they approached. Will took Tom aside to discuss plans for tomorrow. Buster silently observed the rest of the family. Lola Grayson was a beautiful woman, but she didn't play on her beauty like others. Her beauty was natural. Her black hair was pulled back and twisted in a knot at the nape of her neck. She wore a minimum of make-up and was modestly dressed. The boys clothes were clean, but worn, and both wore baseball caps. The older boy had the Mexican features of his mother. He was dark, and reserved like her, but unlike his dad he had no problem making eye contact. The look in his deep blue eyes was direct, and like his mother's they were guarded. His younger brother, an earnest looking boy, stood next to him. He had the fairer coloring of his father. With his wavy red hair, and mischievous blue eyes, he was boyishly handsome. Buster blinked hard, because at first glance, he reminded him so much of Joey. There was an actual physical catch in Buster's heart. He had to swallow hard before speaking, "Once the trailer is set up, you can let us know if there is anything you need?"

"Thank you, Mr. Calhoun. I'm sure we'll be fine," Lola said politely. Her anxious gaze turned back to Tom, who was talking to Will but watching her. Tom's eyes had narrowed, and his jaw was clenched down hard.

"There is more than one Mr. Calhoun here, so it would be easier if you call me Buster, and my brother is Will."

Though Lola was very polite, her fear of her husband made her unapproachable. Her voice was cool when she spoke, "I can do that, if necessary, but I would like all of the men, including you, to continue to address me as Mrs. Grayson." She pointed to her boys. "Trace is my oldest, and this is Riley."

Will, who had joined them, probed, "Why aren't they in school?"

"As my husband said, we have been working our way west, so I am home schooling them. Our decision to come west was made last summer, so it was the obvious choice." Knowing she was being judged, she became defensive, "I have home schooled them before, and my boys are not behind in their schoolwork." Lola withdrew again. She turned away, but not before Buster saw the fear in her eyes and guessed her husband had put it there.

That night at dinner the Grayson family was the main topic of conversation.

Will was still doubtful about the decision to hire the drifter, but he did agree that the family looked like they might need someone close to oversee what was going on. Their staying in the yard was an ideal solution for now. Will challenged his brother, "You definitely surprised me when you so readily agree to hire him."

"I felt sorry for the family. The wife looked anxious most of the time, especially when she had to talk to us. You terrified the poor woman."

"I don't think it's me that terrifies her. I still think we've hired trouble." There was something odd about this family. He would definitely keep an eye on them, especially the husband. He hoped they hadn't made a mistake.

Based on the two men's discussion, Sadie wasn't sure if Will was over-reacting or if Buster was oblivious. She would go over in the morning to welcome them and see for herself.

The next morning after Tom left with Will, Lola sat down at the kitchen table to enjoy a cup of coffee. Riley was in the bedroom doing his schoolwork, and Trace had left right after his dad did to go explore his new surroundings. The knock on the door startled Lola. Her fears were so ingrained that she was apprehensive opening the door. She was relieved that it wasn't one of the brothers.

Sadie introduced herself, but wasn't invited in. Instead, Lola stepped out, and closed the door behind her. Sadie handed her the fresh baked cinnamon buns.

"Thank you, Mrs. Calhoun, but this wasn't necessary."

Sadie heard the stiffness in Lola's voice. "We're not very formal here at Valley View. Please call me, Sadie. I'm sorry but I don't know your name."

"It's, Lola."

"I came over to welcome you."

"Thank you for the baking. It was kind of you. I know my boys will enjoy them. If you'll excuse me, I'll take them inside."

Sadie was lost in thought as she walked back to the house. If not for the conversation last night, she would have thought that Lola Grayson was rude. The men had been right. Behind Lola's cool facade lay heartache, and secrets. Lola's eyes were so carefully guarded that Sadie wondered what she was hiding.

Lola knew she had appeared rude to Sadie Calhoun, but history had a way of repeating itself. She had been down this road many times, so it was best to remain distant. If she didn't make friends, it didn't hurt as much when they left. Lola's memories carried her back unwillingly, to promises made long ago. Promises broken over and over.

Lola was young and naïve when she met Tom Grayson. He had drifted into town looking for work. He would frequent the restaurant where she worked. At first, Lola though Tom was a handsome devil and was flattered by his attention. Tom easily drew her into his web of illusion, and quickly stripped her of her innocence with his charm. Against her family's wishes, she married Tom in a simple ceremony.

The tenderness Tom showed when he courted her disappeared as soon as they were married. Right after the wedding he shocked her with his announcement, "We're going to head north, and go to Canada. I hear it's a country with lots of opportunity." Lola was forced from her familiar world into a world of harsh reality. Tom's manner became possessive. "Once a woman is married, she becomes her husband's property. You now belong to me, not your parents."

Staring at her husband in disbelief Lola suddenly realized what an evil man he really was. She also knew that the door to her past had been closed.

"Marriage is a practical matter. You have one job, and that's to take care of me, and give me sons." Tom forced her down on the bed, and she felt the bile build in her throat. That was his first forced act of possessiveness that she experienced, but it wasn't the last time she paid the price for her bad judgment.

Lola hated the dire situation she found herself in. It wasn't long before life was utterly unlike what he had promised. She discovered that her husband was a hard-edged man who was addicted to gambling, and whisky. A man who became confrontational when he drank and was unable to control his temper. Her life became a seesaw of hardship, and heartache.

The birth of her two sons gave her the love she needed, but it wasn't always enough. With each betrayal, each disappointment, she lost a little of herself. She recalled the day Tom told her they were coming to Alberta. It was an unpleasant memory. Lola knew better than to argue, but disappointment took over. She felt they were always running away rather than moving forward. Lola guessed they were dodging bill collectors again. Her voice was filled with despair as she questioned the reason for this move.

Her confrontation angered Tom. He grabbed her by the arm and pulled her threateningly close. She could smell the beer on his breath. "It doesn't matter why."

Even though his physical assault startled her, it didn't stop her from retaliating, "I'm tired of moving and having nothing."

"You have a roof over your head, don't you?"

"Yeah, one that leaks that you keep promising to fix." Lola would never forget the day he hauled the trailer home. The smell of stale cigarettes and beer assaulted her the moment she opened the door, and it was filthy. She had scrubbed it clean until her fingers bled. As bad as it was, she did her best to make it a home with the little they had.

"Get off my back, Lola. Pack up instead of bitching." Lola stumbled as he pushed her away. Tom liked to use threats as intimidation, but once in a while, he became physical.

Just then the boys walked in, and Trace saw the fear in his mom's eyes. Trace stepped between his parents.

Tom glared at Trace, "We're leaving first thing in the morning."

Trace had been his dad's whipping post in the past, but over the winter Trace had gotten bigger and stronger. He took a step toward his dad, "Ma deserves better than this. I'm soon old enough to take care of us, and none of us will need you."

Enraged, Tom placed his hand on his son's forearm in anger. The boy was always challenging him these days.

Trace stood his ground as he slapped his dad's hand away. It was at that moment that Trace realized that anger was better than fear. Anger gave a person strength, fear only paralyzed. "Be very clear about this. If you ever lay your hands on any one of us again, you won't live long enough to do it twice."

Tom could tell by Trace's threatening tone that he meant every word. He stormed out of the trailer, slamming the door behind him.

Trace told himself to keep his mouth shut, but the words wouldn't stay down. He turned to his mom, "Why do you stay with him?"

"And go where, Trace? And live on what?" Lola took a calming breath. "We'll be okay, we always are." This was a promise she had made more times than she could remember. Even she didn't believe it anymore. "Your dad heard about a big cattle ranch in Alberta, so we're heading west. It will be a fresh start for all of us."

Trace shrugged his shoulders as he walked away.

Early the next morning everything they owned was packed up. They didn't have much. They'd been living a nomadic lifestyle for years, so made do with the bare necessities.

Tom's mood was not what Lola expected. His voice rose with excitement, "I promise all of you that it's going to be different this time. There will be adventure, and opportunity for everyone. It's beautiful country out west. You'll love it."

The transient lifestyle Lola lived with had taken its toll. Disappointment had chipped away at her spirit year after year, move after move. "We're tired of starting over, Tom. This lifestyle is unfair to the boys. They have no structure in their lives. They are tired of being the new kids. It's time to settle down somewhere, so we can have a real home."

Tom pulled Lola into his arms. "This ranch we're going to will be our dream place." He looked at the boys. "Pile in so we can make some miles."

"Everything will be fine," Lola told her boys. She climbed into the passenger seat and willed herself to believe it. Lola blinked hard and kept her eyes straight ahead as they pulled away. Like a ghost from the past, she heard her mother's parting words the day they drove away, "Camino a la Muerte," which meant road to death. Lola swore she would not cry. As they pulled away, Lola turned her gaze to the side window. Tears blurred her vision.

They had driven for days. Tom turned his head and looked at the boys, "Tomorrow we'll make Alberta. Cattle country."

Lola wished she shared his excitement.

The next day dawned cloudy with a cool wind, but by noon the sky had cleared unveiling the majestic Rocky Mountains. Today, the countryside was ever changing. The boys were impressed with the rolling hills where horses grazed in fenced pastures. Bright white fences defined large homesteads that were surrounded by acres of thick grassland, where large herds of cattle grazed contentedly. Lola relaxed and took in the beauty around her. With the backdrop of the snow-capped mountains in the distance, she felt like Alberta was welcoming them. Tom had been right. She was once again filled with new hope. Maybe this time it would be different. Maybe her ugly memories could be replaced with happy ones. She closed her eyes, crossed her chest, and prayed.

Chapter Eight

Lola Grayson felt that her prayers had been answered. It didn't take the Graysons long to fit in at Valley View, and Tom was being true to his word. It had been impossible to refuse Sadie's friendship. The two women were sitting in Sadie's kitchen sharing a pot of tea. Feeling comfortable, Lola opened up to Sadie, "I was so young and naïve when I met Tom. You've seen how he can turn on the charm. I was quickly drawn into his web. I believed his promises as he pretended to share my dreams. Within weeks after we were married, we headed up to Canada. He wanted to get me as far away from my family as quickly as possible. It was Tom's way of taking control." There was a moment of uncomfortable silence before Lola continued, "I'm sure you're wondering why I stay with him. Tom threatened to find us if I left. He said he would take my boys, and I'd never see them again. There was never a doubt in my mind that he didn't mean it. So, I made the choice to stay because of my boys."

Sadie thought Lola stayed because she was weak. She now realized how wrong she was. Lola stayed because of her deep inner strength. "I don't know what brought you here, but you have found your safe place."

"My sons are my life. I have two wonderful boys but a husband who spent too much time in bars, and often gambled our money away. Since we came here, he hasn't been drinking or gambling. He promised us that this time it would be different. So far, he's kept that promise. The boys, and I really like it here, Sadie. Every day I pray that this is it. A place where I can raise my boys and give them the home life they deserve. I'd hate to have my dreams shattered again. It would hurt me more than usual if we had to leave."

"I hope that doesn't happen. I value you as a friend, and I love your boys."

Lola couldn't always hide her fear. "I worry about Trace. He and Tom rub each other the wrong way. Now that Trace is older, he's more challenging toward his dad. Riley tries to keep the peace or locks himself away. I'm doing the best I can, but it's not always easy."

Sadie was glad that Lola felt that she could share her past, but it caused her concern. She leaned over to take Lola's hand, "Don't ever be afraid to come to any of us if you need our help."

Lola squeezed back in silent agreement. No words were necessary.

Trace was pacing back and forth at the corrals hoping to catch Buster and talk to him. His dad seemed to have settled in at the ranch. Hoping this would be a permanent stay, Trace had a big favor to ask the Calhouns. Trace was nervous. What he wanted to talk to Buster about was very important to him.

Buster strolled over when he saw Trace wave. When the Graysons had first arrived, the boy had seemed moody, and sullen. After getting to know the family better, Buster realized Trace was reserved and complex, more man than boy at too young an age.

Trace got right to the point, "As you know, Riley and I are home schooled. I've already earned all of my required academic credits, but I still need credits to fulfill my Grade Eleven requirements. Mom contacted Foothills Composite High School. and they will allow me to take part in their Work Experience Program. Students can earn credits while working as an employee. I was hoping that you would consider letting me work with the horses. It will give me the opportunity to see if I can learn the skills to become a horse trainer."

Buster smiled to himself. The boy had hardly said two words since he got here, but he knew how to talk when he wanted something. His presentation sounded a little scripted, but he knew the boy was sincere. "Have you had experience with horses?"

"No, but I really want this."

Buster had to admit that the boy had done his research and appeared eager. "I'll talk to Will and Murphy and get back to you tomorrow. If we agree you'll work with Murphy."

An impatient scowl darkened the boy's face as he turned and headed back to the trailer. Trace was hoping Buster would say yes right away.

Buster smiled to himself. Patience was obviously not one of Trace's virtues. The boy would have to learn patience at every level, not just with the animals. Buster sought out Murphy, and quickly filled him in.

The old cowboy rubbed his whiskers, "Does he have any experience with horses?"

"None. Trace is as green as the grass in the pastures." Buster could tell that Murphy was giving it serious thought.

Not much got by Murphy. From what he had seen, he gathered Tom Grayson wasn't much of a father. He decided he was willing to give Trace the opportunity he was looking for, despite his lack of experience. "The boy's young, and I think he might be head strong. But I can see he has a love for horses. He's always at the corrals hoping to see them. The lad needs purpose, so we might as well give him a chance. I don't think either of those boys have had much in their lives."

Buster was more anxious talking to Will because of his brother's continued dislike of Tom. Will's initial silence was unnerving.

It wasn't the boy's request that Will was opposed to. Will wondered if the Grayson family would even be here next week. Tom could pull up stakes like a thief in the night and be gone by morning. Recognizing that it would give Trace purpose while they were here, regardless of the length of time, he agreed.

The next morning Buster saw Trace watching the horses and walked over. "We think your proposal is valid. You will answer to Murphy. He comes across a little gruff, and is a man of few words, but you couldn't have a better trainer. Meet him here tomorrow, eight sharp."

Trace was exuberant when they sat down for supper, and for a change the atmosphere around the table was relaxed. Riley was excited for Trace, but his mind was working. He had to figure out a way to earn money.

As soon as Riley saw Buster in the morning, he approached him with eagerness. Buster suggested that he go talk to Will and Sadie, but Sadie in particular. "She's the boss, if you know what I mean." Every time

Buster looked at Riley he thought of Joey. Watching the boy walk away, he wondered if he had unconsciously pushed Riley away because of this.

After lunch Will and Sadie were sitting on the verandah having coffee. They watched as Riley made his way over. Sadie had taken an immediate liking to the boy. Riley reminded her of a stray dog that wins your heart. You love him, flees and all. "Hi, Riley. What's up?"

Riley took a tentative step forward. The look on the boy's face was heartbreaking for it told a story of its own. His look was too cautious for one so young, his eyes enormous in his thin face. "I would like a job like Trace. Buster said to come and talk to you."

Riley's infectious smile went right to the soft spot in Will's heart. "I don't suppose you know how to run a riding lawn mower, do you? I could use someone to cut the grass around here, and over at Buster's place." Riley's smile left his face as he shook his head. "We have plenty of time to teach you. Do you want the job?"

Riley agreed, but released a heavy sigh, "I was hoping to start working right away."

Will winked at Sadie, "Since Trace will be helping Murphy with the horses how would you like to help me with the cattle? When we drive out to the fields you can ride shotgun so you can check the barbed wire fences to see if any of those dang critters put holes in them, and you can help me with odd jobs around the ranch. There is one important rule though. Your schoolwork has to always come first."

Riley nodded and took off running with boyish keenness.

In the afternoon Buster went over and talked to Lola. If the boys were going to work around the ranch, they needed better footwear. Knowing how proud the woman was, he told her that this was Valley View's requirement for employees under the age of eighteen. Therefore, it was up to the employer to provide them with protective work apparel. He would like to take the boys to town to buy them cowboy boots and a cowboy hat.

Lola agreed, silently accepting the underlying act of charity. She remained outside after he left. Like yesterday, the air was hot and dry, driven by a wind that had no coolness. She knew the temperature in the trailer would continue to climb, and they had no air-conditioning. Another thing that broke down and never got fixed.

The next morning Trace was eager and nervous at the same time. Murphy was standing in front of the barn waiting. "Follow me and we'll get started. Safety with the horses is our first concern, and training horses means understanding them. Once you start to work with them, you'll see that horses have different personalities." They walked over to the first stall. "This youngster is Dusty, and when you start training, he's the one you'll work with." The young colt greeted Trace with a whinny. Trace patted Dusty on the forehead. The foal leaned forward and nudged him. Trace's smile was one of pure joy. Instinctively, Murphy knew it was going to be rewarding training Trace.

Murphy opened the door to the tack room. Methodically, Murphy explained every item, and its purpose. "When anything is used it gets cleaned and put back in its place. That way everyone knows where it is when it's needed."

Trace was quick to realize that Murphy's expectations were high, and his rules were rigid. He thought Murphy sounded a little anal, but it made sense. He listened intently without interruption, but was disappointed when Murphy said, "Your daily morning chores will be mucking the stalls. That means you shovel out manure and soiled bedding from every stall. You will feed and water the horses as well. The feed is over there."

"I thought I was going to learn how to train horses," Trace said in frustration.

"In time you will, but you need to learn everything you can about horses. You have to know what the job is all about before you can do it. It takes intuition, experience, and patience. You have intuition and you'll gain experience. Work on the other."

Trace had the natural arrogance of youth, so was annoyed that both Buster and Murphy implied he lacked patience.

With habitual regularity Trace showed up on time every morning to do his chores without complaining, but all he could think about was working with the horses.

Murphy continued teaching Trace the basics. He explained how to handle the horses, and how to care for them. One thing was very apparent, Murphy knew horses and he loved them. Trace was an avid student, taking in every word. The days passed, one day the same as the other. In the evenings Trace would go see the horses and talk to them.

It was the end of the day when Buster joined Murphy in the barn, "How is Trace doing?"

"The boy is ready. Usually when I train someone the next step would be to have them watch my workout routines, but Trace has been watching me for weeks. There were days I thought I had a second shadow. I didn't tell him that we'll start training Dusty tomorrow. If I had, the poor boy wouldn't sleep tonight. Trace is a good boy, Buster."

That night, mealtime was tense around the Grayson table. Tom was in a mood. The boys had learned long ago that when he was like this, no one talked unless spoken to. Right after supper Tom pushed himself away from the table. "I'm going to town, I need cigarettes."

Lola knew better than to question him, but deep down she knew the old Tom was back. She watched him drive away with a sick feeling in her stomach. Had she let her guard down too soon? Tom wasn't gone long, but later that night Lola saw him come from behind the trailer. She guessed he had a bottle stashed somewhere.

The next morning Murphy was waiting for Trace by the corral fence. "You've been working hard for weeks. Are you ready to start training today?"

Trace nodded. This was what he had been waiting for.

"We still have the morning chores to do. As soon as we're done, we'll head over to the small paddock." The chores were now so familiar that Trace could have done them in his sleep. Murphy patted Trace on the shoulder and followed him into the barn. "I'll give you a hand."

In short time the chores were done, and they were on the way over to the small paddock where Dusty was. Murphy switched back into the role of teacher and explained the four gaits in training a young horse. "This fenced area is where we put the yearlings through their paces. I know I don't have to tell you that the process takes time and patience. Meet me here after lunch and we will start the training in earnest."

After lunch, Buster watched from a distance.

Trace was so excited, but he held it back. He stepped into the paddock, and slowly approached Dusty. He ran his hands gently down Dusty's neck and over his sides, then slowly slipped the bridle on. The whole time Trace spoke softly to the frisky colt. When he was done, he glanced over at Murphy.

"Keep your mind on Dusty. Start by leading him with a simple walk." Murphy knew Trace had no problem when it came to following directions. Now he would observe the boy's attention span, and he wanted to get a clear picture of his confidence level.

Trace's shoulders straightened, and his jaw tightened with determination. He didn't want to disappoint Buster or Murphy. He began leading the horse around by a lead rope, lengthening or shortening the line to change the horse's gait when instructed. He repeatedly led Dusty around the pen. He knew he had a good teacher and was determined to excel as a student.

*****

The weeks passed quickly. As the training continued, Murphy could see the boy's confidence growing. Murphy had quickly recognized Trace as a working protégé. He had been right about Trace being head-strong, but Trace also had a good head on his shoulders. The boy kept impressing Murphy.

Trace squeezed his thighs against the mount. Recognizing the signal, Dusty started walking. Listening to Murphy's slow, and easy voice, Trace began putting the young colt through the paces. Trace looked over when Buster arrived and stood at the rail to watch.

"Keep your mind on what you're doing. It's all about discipline and self-control," Murphy ordered.

Trace focused harder.

"Trust in your horse, and trust in yourself. Always keep your connection with the horse." Throughout the training, Murphy continued to offer words of encouragement. Before Trace knew it, he heard Murphy say, "That's enough for today. When a horse is young you don't want to overdo it. Too much exercise can hurt their joints. We work slowly to make sure we aren't working them too hard."

Trace slowed Dusty's gate to a walk and headed over to the stable to cool him off.

Murphy went over and joined Buster, "Trace is a fast learner."

"I admire your dedication, and patience with the boy. You're doing a great job."

"It's his accomplishment, not mine." Murphy headed to the barn after Buster left. Trace was brushing down Dusty like he'd seen Murphy do. "You've reached a level of skill I'm satisfied with, so tomorrow we advance to a new level. It will involve more work."

Trace grinned, "I'm ready."

Murphy knew he was. He enjoyed his relationship with Trace which had gradually developed into a friendship. "What about Riley? Doesn't he like horses?"

"My brother is completely smitten with Shelby, so he'd rather spend time with her." BJ often brought Shelby along when he came over to Valley View. Riley and Shelby had become good friends. Shelby thought of Riley as her buddy, and Trace was the amused, tolerant, and annoying older brother.

*****

Monday morning the new wranglers were anxious to head out, but the crew was waiting for Tom to show. Will looked at Buster and wondered what was going on as they watched Trace walking toward them. "Where's your dad?"

Trace refused to lie and say that his dad was sick. Instead, he dodged the question saying, "Dad isn't available this morning. Do you think I can go in his place?"

Buster knew that more than anything Trace wanted the experience of being out on the range. Will and Buster exchanged a look and Will nodded.

Will dismounted from Blaze and handed the reins to Trace. "I'll address things here." Both Buster, and Trace knew that Will would also be having words with Tom.

Trace grinned as he hauled his lanky form up into the saddle with ease.

Out on the range, Buster had to admire Trace's easy grace in the saddle. Trace kept his attention on the wranglers and watched the way the cowboys and their horses worked together looking for strays. Trace followed when Buster suddenly turned his horse. They found two strays off in the tall grass.

Trace quickly found that riding a horse while training was a lot different than riding a trained cutting horse. The horse didn't need to be told what to do. When a cow broke away, the horse broke with it. Trace had to learn to go with the movement. Trace soon got the hang of it and quickly became comfortable with the unexpected movements of the horse. He loved riding the quick-moving animal.

While the others were gone Will waited for Tom. Just before noon, Tom finally showed up. It was obvious that Tom had been sleeping off his alcoholic stupor. Will could hardly contain his temper. "Follow me, I need to talk to you." Neither of the Calhoun brothers berated a hire out in the open. Discussions were held behind closed doors.

Tom knew he was in trouble as they headed over to the office. The boss was angry, so he knew he needed to be careful with Will.

Not another word was spoken until Will closed the office door. Will didn't bother to mix words, "Your workday doesn't start at noon, Grayson. You were supposed to head out first thing this morning with the rest of the wranglers. Your no show put everyone behind schedule."

"Why are you taking such a hard stance, Will? It's not like I've done this before."

"What you do in your spare time is your business, but when it affects our business, it matters. When you slack off the others feel they can do it, too. We won't tolerate it."

Tom wanted to keep his job. "I get the message. It won't happen again."

Will didn't believe Tom for a second. "It better not. We have a ranch to run. If you can't do the job, we'll get someone else."

Tom clenched his jaw, and his eyes narrowed. Like usual he became defensive, "There's nothing wrong with my work."

Will bristled. He hated the man's attitude. "No, just your work ethic. Well, since Trace had to fill in for you this morning it looks like you're mucking today."

Tom wasn't thrilled to have to muck stalls. He touched his pocket. At least he would be by himself, so he could take a nip from the flask hidden in his inside pocket. Tom shrugged as he left and swore under his breath.

Will heard and shook his head.

Usually when things didn't go his way, Tom would pull up stakes and leave, but he didn't mind the work here. Lola was happier than she'd been in a long time and the boys had settled in nicely. He had to admit that the Calhouns were fair bosses, even though Will liked to ride his ass. He knew he had to be more careful in the future.

Buster and Will were sitting out on Will's verandah after supper. They waved Trace over. The more they got to know Trace, the more he impressed them. Today, rather than make excuses for his dad, the boy had stepped up like a man and filled in. That counted for a lot to a Calhoun.

Trace sat down on the top step and leaned his back against the post. He had a great deal of respect for these two men. Will said exactly what he thought. Buster was a little more open-minded but reserved. Trace knew that both men were honest and fair. Trace enjoyed listening to the two men talk about a lifestyle they lived and breathed every day.

Trace had impressed Buster out on the range. His skills with a horse came naturally. "You did a good job today considering you had no experience. What we did today was called cutting. It's a work activity that is done as part of the regular work on a ranch. There are many times during the years that we need our horses. Our horses have been trained for cutting, but there are riders out there that pay big dollars for a trained cutting horse for competitions. Cutting expanded beyond the working ranch to equestrian competitions where a horse and a rider work together before a panel of judges. They demonstrate the horse's athleticism, and ability to handle cattle."

This conversation captured Trace's attention and the seed for Caballo Stables was unknowingly planted.

It was late by the time they called it a night. Just as Trace was about to leave Buster said, "Tomorrow I'm picking up my new stud horse, Diego."

"Murphy told me you were getting another horse. We're both excited to see him."

"He's a fine stallion, Trace," Buster said proudly. "Diego is young, and he still needs to be trained. You will be his trainer."

Trace's breath caught, "Are you sure?"

Buster's belief in Trace was based on what he had seen, and Murphy's valued opinion. "With the additional task of training Diego, you will no longer have to do your morning chores. One of the wranglers will take that over for now. When they leave at the end of the season, your dad will take over."

Trace didn't comment, but he knew his dad wouldn't be too happy. Trace was somber walking home. He knew Buster was putting a lot of trust in him with his expensive horse. He also knew that he was capable.

The next morning Trace got up early so he could get his chores done before Buster returned with the new horse. When Trace saw Buster pull in, he was filled with an unexplained rush of excitement. Both Murphy and Trace had been waiting with anticipation. Trace watched silently as Buster unload his horse. Just looking at him, Trace could tell that Diego was a temperamental stallion with undeniable fine lineage. Tossing his head, he whinnied and stomped.

"He's a fine-looking animal, Buster," Murphy acknowledged. The horse truly was a magnificent beast.

The horse's black coat gleamed in the sunlight. Buster patted Diego's thick neck and ran his strong hands over the horse's shoulders. He felt the muscles quiver. "Trace, meet Diego. He is strong with a mind of his own. Put him in the last stall while I move the trailer." It was a profound moment when Buster handed the reins to Trace. The spirit of the horse was clear as he tossed his neck from side to side and pawed the ground.

Murphy chuckled. Both Diego and Trace were head strong. "I reckon you two are pretty fairly matched, so you best let the horse know who's the boss."

Diego was big, strong, and stubborn. Trace pulled hard on Diego's reins, controlling the spirited young stallion. As soon as Trace looked Diego in the eye something changed. There was an immediate connection between man, and horse that was tangible. In the moment it was just the two of them. "Well, Diego, you need to know who the boss is. You can't always have your own way. Your playground is beautiful. Acres of lush grassland with a river running through it. But you have to earn the right to play so let's get started. Come with me and I will show you your new home." Buster and Murphy couldn't stop grinning as Trace led Diego into the stables.

*****

Trace had been training Diego for weeks. Murphy was impressed with both Trace and Diego. He took the time to tell Trace that he was pleased with the progress he was making with the high-spirited horse. Trace appreciated Murphy's praise. Diego was the most stubborn horse Trace had worked with. Diego continuously revealed his heritage and high spirit. Trace gave Murphy one of his cocky smiles. "We're both making progress."

"I know I'm hard on you at times but you're like Diego. There are times you also need to be reined in hard. Sometimes you struggle more than you need to because you refuse to ask anyone for help, but you are making progress."

"I've had a great teacher and mentor. Thanks, Murphy. I'll get Diego so we can start today's training."

Trace was leading Diego out of the barn when Buster showed up. Murphy looked over at his boss, "Trace is a natural with horses, and handles Diego with confidence, and command. You know the boy is in love with that horse," Murphy stated simply.

Buster nodded. "He has been since the day I brought Diego home. The two of them have established an extraordinary bond, some inexplainable, and unbreakable connection." Buster warmly welcomed Trace when he joined them. "You've made considerable progress with Diego, so skip the training this morning. Let's see how he is in the open. You can ride him, and I'll saddle up Trooper. It will be a break for both of us." Buster wanted to see how Trace handled Diego outside the confines of the training pen.

Chapter Nine

The Calhouns liked to reward their employees and celebrate the end of a productive season with an annual barbeque on Labour Day. The Grayson family attended the informal get together along with many of the neighbors. Sadie stood next to Lola, who had been left on her own while Tom mingled. Respecting Lola's reserved nature, she considerately asked, "Would you like me to introduce you to our friends?"

Lola knew from experience it was best to keep to herself. Knowing how possessive Tom was, she didn't want to do anything to antagonize him. Lola smiled at her dear friend, but shook her head, "It's a beautiful day and a wonderful gathering. The boys have met kids their own age. I'm glad to see them enjoying themselves."

"You look sad? Is everything okay?"

"I'm fine, I was just wondering if this was real, and if it is, will it last?" Out of habit Lola kept an eye on Tom, who was displaying his proficient charm with the ladies. Tom still had an overpowering physical appeal and the same charm that had caught her attention. He was also overindulging in the free alcohol provided by the generous hosts. Tom was becoming loud, and from experience Lola knew it wouldn't be long before he'd become obnoxious, and confrontational at any given opportunity. Lola's biggest fear was that he would do something that would cost him his job, but there was nothing she could do. Lola excused herself at her earliest opportunity. It was well after midnight before Tom staggered back to the trailer.

*****

Tom was back to his old habits, and it was worse than it had ever been. He was now drinking every night. Lola hadn't realized he was drinking on the job until she saw him pour a healthy shot of whisky into his coffee thermos. He proceeded to fill the flask he carried in his inside jacket pocket. She was torn by what she had just seen.

It was Friday night and Tom was in an unusually good mood. Lola couldn't swallow the lump of fear in her throat. Odds were he would be going to town after work to drink and find a game of cards in some back room. After supper she followed Tom outside and tried talking to him. Lola made the mistake of grabbing his arm.

Tom pushed her back against the stairs. He was a hard-edged man at the best of times, but lately he was having more violent tendencies.

Buster, who had just come from the bunk house, saw what was happening. Buster usually minded his own business and didn't interfere unless the situation warranted it. Without hesitation he marched over to their trailer, and confronted Tom.

Buster's interference angered Tom, "Mind your own business, Buster. This is between me, and the wife."

"Are you okay, Lola?" Lola nodded, but he saw the fear in her eyes. Buster turned to Tom, "If I ever see you touch your wife, or either of your boys in anger, you may not live to regret it. The only reason you still have your job here is because of your family. This is the last straw, Tom. For your family's sake you better pull yourself together."

Lola and Tom continued arguing after Buster left. "Please don't lose this job, Tom. The boys are happy here. We all are."

Tom lashed out, "Damned if I care. I was looking for a job when I found this one. I can find another." Their argument gave him the excuse he was looking for. He grabbed the keys to the truck and took off for town.

Monday morning Lola was expecting the knock at the door.

"Tom around?" Will asked, even though he guessed the answer.

"He went to town," Lola said evasively. For the last couple of weeks, Tom had gone to town every Friday night.

Will didn't let it go, "I thought he went on Friday?"

Lola hung her head, "He hasn't come home." This was a familiar pattern to Lola. In the past Tom would disappear for days after payday. It was just the first time here. Lola wondered how long he'd be gone this time. This was only one of her concerns. She never knew what kind of mood he'd be in when he got home.

Without a word Will turned and left, digging deep for control with every step he took. When he got back to the main house, Buster was in the kitchen having coffee with Sadie.

One look at his brother, and Buster knew he was upset. "What's going on, Will?"

"I just came from talking to Lola. Tom hasn't been home since Friday night. I don't know what to do, but Tom Grayson has become a problem."

Buster shook his head, "It's a bigger problem than I realized. One of the wranglers told me that Tom carries a flask of whisky with him and is drinking on the job."

This came as no surprise to Will, but he was disappointed for the family. They had already made exceptions for Tom. If he were single, he would have been let go before now, but there was the family to consider. The boys were enrolled in school. Lola had slowly allowed herself to open up to Sadie, and the two women had become friends. Will didn't like what he had to do. "Tom has been challenging us on every level. I'm going to talk to him as soon as he shows up and give him a final warning. We have no other choice."

Buster was concerned, "I hate to think of what will happen to Lola, and those boys, if they leave here."

Sadie knew it was more than that. She got up and gave him an understanding hug, "You have a sentimental streak under that tough exterior, Buster. Riley reminds you of Joey, and you don't want to lose him a second time."

Buster responded without denial, "They are both good boys. Trace is already more man than his dad will ever be."

Before anyone could comment, Will took a phone call. An hour later the two brothers headed over to the trailer.

Hearing voices, Lola looked out. She was surprised to see both Buster and Will making their way to the trailer. Because of the serious expression on their faces, she braced herself. She was sure they were going to tell her that they would have to let Tom go. Lola opened the door before they could knock and invited them in.

Will didn't waste any time with small talk. It wouldn't change the facts. "The police called. Last night, Tom was gambling at one of the known back-room games in town. When Tom lost a big pot, he accused the winner of cheating. A witness said they were both drunk. There was a physical encounter between them. It wasn't their first go round. This time the other guy pulled a knife. Tom didn't have a chance. I'm sorry, Lola, Tom is dead."

After her initial intake of breath, tears sprang to Lola's eyes. Will didn't know if they were tears of grief, or relief. She sat temporarily paralyzed, struggling to compose herself. and sort out her tangled thoughts and emotions. "I don't know what to do."

"Don't worry, Lola. You don't have to do anything today other than tell your boys and be there for them. We'll take you to town tomorrow, and you can deal with things then. Do you want Sadie to come over?"

"I'm fine," she said, but without conviction. Lola had been conditioned to say she was fine whether she was or not. "I'll just wait for my boys." Lola had done a lot of brave things in her life, but that didn't mean she wasn't scared. As she sat alone, one by one her dreams began to unravel. A new realization turned Lola cold. They would have to leave here. All their hopes and dreams were shattered again. She didn't know how they would survive. They were broke, and they were alone. She could almost hear Tom's voice mocking her. Now, his words could no longer hurt her. The man was dead. Besides, she knew she was a lot stronger than her husband ever knew. They would survive, but this would have a huge effect on her boys. When they had settled at Valley View, they found a place that felt like home. Knowing how much they loved it here, it would be hard to leave. She had no idea where they would go. She took a deep breath when she heard them come through the door.

At first, neither of the boys spoke when she told them. Tom had been their father, but he was never much of a dad. Riley was the first to speak, "It's okay, Ma. Now he can't hurt you anymore." He looked at his brother. "He can't hurt anyone."

Lola was surprised to hear these words from her youngest son. He was more aware than she had realized. He leaned over and hugged her, and they both began to cry.

That night before the boys went to bed Lola pulled them close as they sat on the sofa. She managed a weak smile. She'd have to be strong to face the days ahead, and their unknown future. She knew they would be all right, no matter what. "God guided us here with his hand. We have to trust that he has another plan and will guide us again."

*****

Sadie went over to the trailer to see Lola. They sat together at the kitchen table. "What are you planning to do?"

It had been a couple of weeks since Tom's death. The boys were back in school. The necessities, including Tom's funeral had been taken care of. Lola knew it was time to address their future. She struggled to answer, "I don't know."

Her voice had that expressionless tone Sadie had come to recognize. The one that caused Lola to become quiet, and distant whenever Sadie tried to probe. Usually, Sadie was considerate of her conversations with Lola, but today she couldn't stop herself. She was frustrated because she wanted to help her friend but didn't know how. "You're exasperating at times, Lola. When you don't like a question or don't want to answer you just sit there and say nothing."

Lola knew Sadie didn't understand. How could she? "That comes from years of being married to a controlling husband. Sometimes life sucks you in, and before you realize it you've lost a part of yourself that you think you'll never get back."

"Well, Tom's gone, and that's all behind you. I don't mean to be insensitive, but this is a turning point for you, and your boys. Do you have any family you can go home to?"

Lola shook her head, "My father was a strict, authoritarian man who ruled our house like a tyrant. When I married Tom, my family disowned me, saying I had chosen my path. I had also married outside the Catholic Church, and that was unforgivable."

Their eyes met as they clasped hands. Sadie was heartbroken when Lola continued to share. They talked and cried for hours. Sadie knew how much pride this woman had, but she had no idea how much Lola had endured because of her marriage to Tom.

That night Buster, Will, and Sadie were again discussing the Grayson family. Tom's death had affected them as well, and they were concerned for Lola, and the boys. Sadie filled them in about her earlier conversation with Lola. "Lola is terrified but won't admit it. They have nowhere to go. She has no family who can help them. We are the only family she has."

When Buster heard Sadie say this, he quietly shared his plan. He wanted to ask the Graysons to move into his house with him. Lola would be his housekeeper. It was the best solution with the least disruption. Knowing the Graysons were a proud family the Calhouns knew the offer had to be presented tactfully.

Sadie got up and grabbed the coffee pot. "It's interesting, isn't it?" she said as she filled Buster's cup.

"What's that, Sadie?"

"How quickly you get used to having someone in your life."

*****

Lola needed time alone to address the fears that continued to overwhelm her. She wandered down to the creek, found a secluded spot, and sat down. She needed to get a grasp on the events that had abruptly turned their lives upside down. Lola didn't want to leave Valley View. They were settled here, and Sadie had become a real friend. A ray of hope engulfed her. Maybe they could stay. They could continue to live in the trailer, and she could find a job. Then reality hit her. With Tom gone there was no money coming in. How were they going to survive until she could find a job? Who would even hire her? She had never worked because of Tom. She closed her eyes, allowing burning tears to escape.

"Do you mind if I join you?"

Buster's voice startled her. Lola quickly wiped her eyes and retreated behind the mask of composure she usually wore. But she couldn't hide the worry in her dark eyes.

Buster didn't do small talk, so he got right to the point. "I have an offer that I would like to present to you." Lola sat quietly until he was done. "I hope you find my offer favorable." Buster had an overwhelming desire to protect her.

Lola's first reaction was a surge of relief that was followed by a wave of pride. "I don't take charity."

Buster was prepared for her reaction. "This is a working arrangement. You and the boys will move into the house, and you will be my housekeeper. We will fix up a part of the house that will be for you and the boys. After Trace graduates, if he wants, he can become a full-time employee here at the ranch. He would continue to work with Murphy, and the horses." Buster gave Lola one of his rare smiles. "Win, win."

Lola found it difficult to speak. She had never been allowed to make her own decisions. She felt it was necessary to talk to her sons. They were still young, but they needed to have a say. This was something that would affect all of them. From this day forward they would decide things as a family. "I'll get back to you after I talk to Trace and Riley."

After Buster left, Lola found her boys, and presented Buster's offer. "We've all had enough of a transient lifestyle. It's time we were happy, and we're happy here. If you agree we won't have to move, and our days of instability are a thing of the past."

The boys exchanged looks and nodded. The fear of the unknown disappeared from their eyes and was replaced with relief.

Lola knew this would be the perfect solution. A good feeling welled up inside her, as if her life had finally taken a turn for the better. This time they were planning their own future. Lola decided not to wait to let Buster know. She found Buster sitting on his verandah staring out at the mountains. She watched him for a moment, realizing this was a big change for him as well. She went and sat in the chair next to him. "The boys and I have talked, and we would like to continue living here at Valley View. We will move in with you under the conditions you, and I discussed." As soon as Lola agreed she felt safe, secure, and free. "However, you mentioned that I would be going to town to buy groceries and running errands. I must confess that even though I know how to drive, I don't have a driver's license. That was just another way of Tom controlling me and keeping me dependent on him."

Buster knew how dominating Tom had been. This poor woman had been firmly under her husband's control. "That can easily be taken care of. Is there something else bothering you?"

This was more distressing than she realized. "I'm worried about how people will react."

"Why do you care what people might think?" It was no one's business but theirs.

Lola sighed heavily, "I don't care what they say about me. I do care about my boys. I worry they will be teased or bullied. They've had to deal with it all their lives. Being poor. Being the new kids. Having an alcoholic father, and now their mother is moving in with a man she isn't married to." Knowing what Buster was about to say she said, "We know what our arrangement is, but people will twist it."

"Are you changing your mind?"

"No, just feeling guilty because again I can't protect my boys."

"No parent can protect their children from everything." Buster's voice had become distant. Some guilt never left. "We all have difficulties throughout our lives and have to deal with things we can't change. A person has to be open to change and move forward."

Lola responded with resignation, maybe even sadness, underlined by a weariness that made her look older than she really was, "Don't worry, Buster. The boys and I can handle change. I've lived that reality more than once."

By the end of the month, Lola had her Alberta Driver's License, a bank account, and a credit card. She was on her way to becoming a strong independent woman.

Within a few weeks the Grayson family, and Buster had settled into a comfortable routine. The rest of the Calhouns accepted them like extended family. Sadie felt like a second mom to all of them, but Riley held a special place in Sadie's heart. He had since the day she, and Will had hired him as their helper when they first arrived. As for Trace, he loved ranching as much as Buster and Will, so their bond was natural.

Trace believed he was now the head of the Grayson family. He carried such a high level of responsibility at too young an age. He knew that the Calhouns had paid off Tom's gambling debt, and they had also paid for all of the funeral expenses. The Grayson family was proud and had every intention of paying them back.

Lola was right about the gossip. Within weeks the grapevine was busy. The boys soon began hearing nasty remarks about their mom at school.

Over the years Trace had taken the sneers and digs about having the notorious Tom Grayson as their father, but their mom didn't deserve this. Then came the day that he had enough. Trace took care of it in his own way.

When he got home from school, he was sporting one heck of a shiner, and a fat lip.

"What happened?" Lola asked, even though she had a pretty good idea.

"I walked into a door at school. I think it should be okay, now. It just needed a little adjusting."

"Are you having trouble with any other doors?"

"I think the problem with doors has been solved."

Lola smiled to herself. "It's best to take care of some things right away before they can't be fixed. I best get supper started." Lola knew Trace never looked for a fight but was ready to fight if he had to.

The adjustment seemed to do the trick. It was the last of the digs, and snide remarks, at least in his presence.

Lola enjoyed the boys more and more as they let go of their inner fears, and inhibitions. Riley was developing into a confident young man before her eyes. She also realized that she had changed. She thought the woman she'd been before she married Tom was gone forever. Her confidence grew as did the boys.

Buster soon loved the two boys as if they were his own. He respected Lola's position as the parent, but he led by example as he became their mentor. Buster was quick to realize what an incredible woman Lola was. She was brave, smart, and kindhearted.

Chapter Ten

Trace stood at the railing watching Lady graze in the pasture beyond. He knew she was due to foal in the spring. He found it hard to believe that they had been at Valley View almost a year. In reflection, Trace thought this would just be another stop on a well-travelled road. More strangers. More changes. Changes indeed. Little did they know at the time how big the changes would be by moving here. Knowing he intended to be more than a hired hand all of his life, Trace was ready to make a life-changing commitment of his own. The sun had slide down the western sky while he was lost in thought, and as it dropped the wind became colder.

Like most nights, Buster was sitting on the verandah enjoying the solitude the evening often brought. He smiled when Trace joined him. "What's up, Trace? You were staring off into the distance for a long time."

"Can we talk?"

"Sure, let's go inside, though. Now that the sun has dropped that wind has a bite to it."

Trace dug deep for the confidence he needed as he followed. As soon as they were seated Trace said, "I want to start my own business, and I need some help to get started."

Buster, usually a cautious man, knew this was going to be a deep conversation. "Why?" It was a simple, and direct question. He needed to hear the boy's response.

"I'm not afraid of hard work, and I want to be more than somebody's hired hand. I don't mean to offend you, so don't take that the wrong way.

You know how grateful I am for everything all of the Calhouns have done for our family."

Buster decided to be as direct as Trace, "Is all of this because of what people have said about you, and your family since you got here?"

Trace looked Buster in the eye. "If I said no, I would be lying. I want the Grayson name to mean something, but I want my own business because I love horses. I want to train cutting horses, and I know I will be good at it. I want to operate under the name Caballo Stables. I know what I want. I just need to get started. I'm not my dad. I want to put down roots."

"I know you're not your father, Trace. Don't walk around with a chip on your shoulder because of him."

Trace's response carried a thread of anger, "I won't, but I don't have to let my upbringing hold me back. That's in the past. It's my future I'm focusing on."

Buster knew the boy wasn't being arrogant in his beliefs. He had observed Trace many times while he was training, and Murphy often sang his praises. Something Murphy rarely did. Early history with Trace, proved that the boy was unrelenting when he committed himself to something. "How can I help?"

The boy's face lit up with excitement but asking Buster for help was going to be hard on his pride. "The sooner I get started the better, so I want to buy Lady's foal. I will pay a fair price, and after she foals, I will pay you boarding fees as well. If it's a filly, I will breed her, but I know it will be a colt." His deep voice was confident. Trace smiled his cocky smile and Buster believed him. "The problem is that I don't have any money."

Knowing how much pride Trace had, Buster decided to make it easier for him. Trace had a legitimate dream, and he wouldn't make the boy ask for money. "If this is really what you want to do, you and I can arrange a payment plan effective the day Lady foals. After you graduate, we will hire you on full-time as a trainer. We will deduct a portion of your wages every month as payment. Would that work for you?"

There was now a hint of dismay in Trace's voice, "I don't have any money to put down to hold the purchase of Lady's foal. Only my word that I will pay you as quickly as possible. You can trust that when I make a commitment, I honor it. In the meantime, I would like to learn how to train cutting horses. I know what Murphy will expect from me. I am willing to commit if he is. When I want something, I don't consider failure."

"It's already clear that you have committed yourself to your training with Murphy. I'll talk to him, and we can alter your training to focus on the art of cutting. Once you are skilled enough you can train other horses here through your business. When that time comes, together with Will, we will discuss how Valley View will adjust as you establish Caballo Stables."

Trace was now speechless with wonder. He had never been afraid to dream but this was reality. Caballo Stables would be his future.

"I have no doubt that you will succeed in anything you do. We have a deal. You just bought yourself a horse." Buster drew up a promissory note. Once both had signed, they shook hands. Then Buster pulled Trace close and hugged him like a proud father. He couldn't hide his admiration for this young man.

Trace swallowed hard. He couldn't remember his dad ever hugging him.

"Theoretically, you just became a business owner. You will want to register your company name among other things." Buster was looking forward to seeing what Trace was willing to do for himself, and his dream company. He had no double that Trace Grayson, and Caballo Stables would be successful.

Buster had just given Trace the belief in himself that he needed. His dreams would become a reality. He would one day make his mark on something that would stand for generations. "I will be grateful to you for the rest of my life. I'll make you proud. I promise."

"I'm already proud of you, Trace."

*****

Everyone was waiting for Lady to foal. She had been brought in from pasture and was spending her time in one of the paddocks. Trace was as anxious as an expectant father. Work helped to fill the days. This morning he was in the pen training Dusty. Training had taken on a dramatic shift, and the in-depth training intensified as the weeks passed.

Murphy and Buster leaned on the rail, watching with pride. Trace's natural ability and understanding of a horse was something that couldn't be taught. It was pure instinct. Murphy looked at Buster, "Trace is making real progress with a couple of the yearlings. Dusty was a good horse for Trace to start working with and he will make a fine cutting horse."

Buster nodded. "Rumor has it that a couple of ranchers are looking for cutting horses. I'll put the word out that Trace will have Dusty ready by the end of the year."

Murphy winked at Buster. "The boy has what it takes. That combination of arrogance, and steely determination."

They both chuckled. In many ways Trace was still as challenging as a young colt. "You've done a good job with him, Murphy."

Murphy called out to Trace, "Dusty needs a light hand, and a long look at the calf to build his confidence."

Hearing Murphy, Trace nudged the horse with his heals while controlling the big animal with his strong legs, and Dusty responded. This type of teamwork between horse and rider was what had attracted Trace to cutting. The first play the horse made on a calf was a thrill Trace could never describe, even though he felt it every time. It was unexplainable. Man, and animal as much a part of each other, as if they'd been born together. When Dusty snorted, and pawed the ground with restless energy, Trace settled deeper into the saddle, concentrating on the task at hand. Horse and rider, cut and dodged, gaining control that defined the skill level of both. Evidence of the practiced precision, and patience learned from hours of training.

Their attention was drawn away by the expensive truck coming up the drive. Buster groaned out loud when he saw that it was Jackson Beaumont, and his teenage daughter, Olivia. Jackson was an affluent, and ruthless businessman who owned an acreage north of Valley View.

Jackson and Olivia joined Buster at the rails. Jackson, true to form, exaggerated the usual social pleasantries. He hailed Buster as an old friend, "It's been way too long since I've seen you, Buster. How are you and Will doing?" He merely nodded to Murphy.

Being the gentleman he was, Buster welcomed them with a cordial nod. He was more than curious as to their reason for being here but turned his attention back to the action inside the pen. All eyes were now on the gelding, and the cowboy settled on his back.

Trace's concentration wandered when he noticed the daughter. He was only human. The stunning blonde wore form-fitting designer jeans, knee-high boots, and a short leather jacket. Trace's gaze remained fixed on her as if he were hypnotized.

Olivia's attention focused on the rider. She practically drooled as she allowed her gaze to sweep over him. She was captivated by his ruggedness, and hard-toned muscles.

Trace refocused. With a sureness that made it look easy, he let the gelding have his lead. It was up to the horse now.

The overweight middle-aged man turned to Buster to get his attention. "That's a fine-looking horse, you got there, Buster."

And a fine-looking trainer, thought Olivia.

Jackson got right to the point, "I understand that one of your mares is ready to foal. I would like to buy it for my daughter. Olivia's horse is ready to be retired. I would also like your trainer to break it. I hear he does good work."

Jackson's assumptive manner irked Buster. "Well Jackson, you know the saying, "I have good news, and I have bad news." The good news is that Trace can train any of your horses, but the bad news is that Lady's foal is already sold."

Trace had halted his training, curious about the visitors. He crossed his arms, resting them on the horn of the saddle, and fixed his gaze on the daughter from beneath his hat.

Olivia smiled up sweetly with the practiced charm of her father.

"I'll pay you double what your buyer paid." Getting no response from Buster angered Jackson. The man didn't like being refused anything. His eyes narrowed, "I want to know who your buyer is, and I'll make him an offer he can't refuse."

Buster caught Trace's attention and waved him over.

Trace swung his leg over and dismounted with an easy fluid motion. After tugging off his gloves, and stuffing them in his back pocket, he handed the yearling to Murphy. Murphy scowled, irritated by the interruption.

Olivia's eyes trailed down his lanky frame that tapered from wide shoulders to a slim waist. She figured he was about six feet of pure hunk. This was a cowboy.

Trace looked directly at Jackson and touched the brim of his Stetson in greeting.

Buster turned and introduced Trace. "Mr. Beaumont made an offer on Lady's foal. When I told him that it was already sold, he wanted to know who the buyer was."

Jackson's eyes narrowed as he reacted in disbelief, "This upstart is buying your foal?"

Buster didn't like the way the older man looked down his nose at Trace, as if the boy was low life. "Trace Grayson is the owner of Caballo Stables. He trains our horses, and will be training his own, and other horses here. He's one of the best, and we're lucky to have him."

Trace appreciated that this was a bit of an exaggeration, but it was just a matter of time before it was all true.

Seeing Olivia's pout Jackson upped the ante to Trace, "I'll pay you whatever you want." Jackson Beaumont was used to intimidating others with his forcefulness. Trace and Buster looked at each other and communicated silently. The foal was not for sale. When Trace didn't respond, Jackson lost his temper.

Buster was considered by those who knew him, to be an even-tempered man. It surprised everyone when Buster raised his voice as well, "You may think your money can buy anything, but you are mistaken this time. It's best you leave."

As Trace watched the Beaumonts pull away, Trace wasn't sure what he was feeling. He knew that they had just turned down a lot of money.

Knowing Trace was about to say something, Buster snapped, "The foal is yours."

Trace was surprised by Buster's anger.

Buster took a deep breath for control. "Jackson Beaumont is so pretentious that he thinks money can buy anything. He was here on the want of his spoiled daughter. The horses they own are for pleasure, nothing more. Our horses are too good for them."

Tired of the drama, Murphy called Trace back to work.

Trace's mind was still on the Beaumonts. Jackson Beaumont didn't look like a rancher, and Trace said as much to Murphy.

"He's not. He operates his ranch like a hobby farm. He may have one of the best horse facilities in the area, but it's all for show." Murphy actually laughed, "Not getting his own way today had to have burned his big fat ass." Murphy asked Trace a question, but the boy was too preoccupied to pay attention. He poked the boy in the chest, "You became sidetracked by the Beaumonts. When you are training you've got to put yourself in the horse's mind and stay there. You allowed yourself to get distracted just like you are now."

Trace smiled. He knew the crusty old cowboy's bark was worse than his bite. "Come on, Murphy. You're not that old that you can deny that even you noticed how stunning the daughter looked." He grinned again, savoring her image. Despite the rich girl's attitude, he was immediately infatuated with, Olivia Beaumont.

The old man's response was a definite snort, "Mount up so we can get back to work. You think I got nothing better to do than watch you drool over that girl like a puppy." There was no question that Murphy appreciated horses a lot more that he appreciated women.

*****

Burke Benson had been sent to Calgary as the liaison between his father's company in England, and Jackson Beaumont's company in Calgary. Jackson wanted a merger of families as well. Olivia was attracted to Burke, but she wasn't in love with him. His biggest appeal was that he belonged to one of the oldest, and richest families in London. He would continue to provide her with a lifestyle she enjoyed.

Burke was back in London dealing with the final details of the merger. Since Burke would be gone for several months, Olivia decided she needed a diversion. Immediately, Trace Grayson's masculine image came to mind. Summer was here, Burke wasn't. She needed a man so she wouldn't be bored. She laughed. She knew there was no way that Trace would be boring. She had a feeling the gorgeous hunk might even be more than she could handle. She decided it was worth her while to go see the tall, dark, and sexy cowboy. With a feeling of excitement, Olivia headed over to Valley View.

Trace had just finished training when Olivia drove up in her Mini Cooper. Curious, he joined her at the corral railing.

Just seeing Trace again stirred Olivia's desire. This cowboy exuded a masculinity that drew her to him like a magnet. "I want to apologize for my father's behavior when we were here. Daddy knew I wanted Lady's foal, but he handled it all wrong. I'm sorry about that. Are you going to give me a second chance to make a better impression? I'm much more than a pampered daughter. You may be surprised at what I have to offer." The look she gave Trace was a definite challenge.

Trace was immune to her sugary sweetness. With her irresistible charm that she turned on at will, she reminded him of his dad. Yet he couldn't deny his attraction to her. Who was he to ignore a challenge? It might prove interesting.

"My father intimidates most people when they first meet him, but not you?"

"No, not me." Because of his own father. Trace never let anyone intimidate him. Trace knew who he was and had developed a strong sense of self-worth thanks to the Calhouns.

"Let me make it up to you. Come by the ranch on Saturday, and I'll show you around the place. I'm sure you will enjoy seeing our riding arena. We can saddle up and go for a ride. My parents are gone all weekend, so you won't run into Daddy." Olivia had years of practice persuading others to do what she wanted. "See you Saturday?" Her flirtatious smile drew Trace in deeper. Olivia was rewarded with a sexy smile as he agreed.

After she drove away Murphy appeared out of the shadows, "You're playing with fire with that one. Everyone around here knows that her father is set on her marrying his business partner's son. It's what her daddy wants, a merging of business and family."

This revelation meant nothing to Trace, and Murphy's warning fell on deaf ears. Olivia wasn't married yet, and she was the one on the prowl. Life would certainly be a lot more interesting than it had been. All work and no play weren't enough anymore.

"Life is easier if you keep to your own or avoid entanglements with women all together."

Trace looked hard at Murphy and wondered if someone had hurt him deeply. Was that why he had remained a bachelor?

*****

A couple of weeks later Trace took a phone call and was surprised that it was Jackson Beaumont requesting Trace to come over to the ranch. Trace was curious, so he agreed.

There were no pleasantries when Jackson opened the door. "Let's go into my office." Trace silently followed. Jackson sat down at his grand desk and leaned back in his chair. "Sit down," he ordered, as he lit one of his fat cigars he was known for.

Trace refused. He realized that this wasn't going to be a friendly conversation.

"I heard through the grapevine that you're seeing my daughter. I was hoping that her infatuation with you would be short-lived, but for some unknown reason she's attracted to you. All parents have expectations for their children, and mine doesn't include my daughter getting involved with poor white trash, who is out to get whatever he can."

"I don't expect anything. That way I'm not disappointed." Life had taught Trace not to need. He'd seen firsthand how much needing someone could hurt.

Jackson took another run at getting his point across, "I heard your old man was a drunk, and a fighter who got himself killed in a bar fight. I understand you like to fight as well. My daughter is not going to be involved with a hell-raising cowboy."

Trace made no comment. There was no denying the truth. He had no misguided beliefs about the sort of man his father was, but his anger was escalating. When Jackson said cowboy as though it left a foul taste in his mouth, Trace had winced. He remained silent. Temper had never gotten him anywhere, but in trouble.

Jackson snubbed his cigar out in the ashtray, and stated bluntly, "My daughter will be marrying the son of my business partner. Business is business. Olivia deserves to continue to live in the lifestyle she was born into. She doesn't need to be dragged down into yours."

Trace didn't back down. Graysons went down fighting. His words were very controlled, "Being poor isn't a sin."

"Your relationship with the Calhouns may have given you an illusion of entitlement, but you are nothing more than a common laborer."

Jackson Beaumont had sat there as smug as he could be, telling him he wasn't good enough for his daughter, because he was nothing more than a laborer. Trace thought he was done dealing with bullies, and threats. He turned on his heel, and walked out of the room, his past nipping at his heals. The Calhouns were a long-time fixture in the community, who were liked and respected. He was only a Grayson who came from nothing.

The next day Olivia showed up at the ranch. "I heard you met with my father."

"He invited me over, and quickly laid all of his cards on the table. He thinks I'm not good enough for you. He ordered me to leave and not come back."

Olivia gave him a hard look, "You're not going to take him seriously, are you?"

Staring at Olivia with an expression of cold indifference, Trace stated, "Your old man was definitely serious, but I don't take orders from him."

Even though Trace didn't fit into her life, and Olivia had no desire to fit into his, there was something about the arrogant cowboy that fascinated her. Olivia and Trace continued to spend time together throughout the summer.

*****

Buster joined Lola on the verandah. "Mind if I join you?" Despite their age difference, Lola and Buster had established a comfortable friendship. Over time, they had shared bits and pieces of their lives. They enjoyed sitting outside in the evening. Most evenings a cool breeze would blow in off the mountains.

Lola had never had a man as a friend. She smiled fondly as she patted the chair next to her. "I'd love some company. I was just sitting here thinking."

"About what? Or maybe it's none of my business." Buster was always careful not to get too personal.

Lola marveled that a man so forceful, so decisive, could still be shy with her. "I was thinking how much our lives have changed. You've been so good to us. The boys love it here and call this home. Here they feel safe, and secure. Thank you, Buster. I don't know anyone who would have done what you did for us."

Buster, somewhat uncomfortable, changed the subject, "Where are the boys?"

"Will and Sadie went over to BJ's, so they took Riley along. Trace has gone to the city with Olivia."

"That's an odd friendship."

Lola didn't miss much where her sons were concerned. Sometimes she saw things they didn't know they were revealing. Or maybe hadn't realized it yet for themselves. "Trace and Olivia are more than friends, and it is a relationship that could end with Trace getting hurt." There was nothing she could do about it. Some things could be taught. Some had to be learned, sometimes the hard way.

Buster knew Trace wouldn't let anyone take advantage of him, but when the heart was involved, it changed things. He tried to reassure Lola, "Trace will be okay. He's young and expanding his horizons to get a different view. Sometimes the view isn't what you expect, and the beauty disappears at the end of the day."

Their conversation moved on to Riley and his infatuation for Shelby, and her acceptance of his undying attention. Knowing Riley as she did, Lola guessed it might be more than puppy love. That would prove to be an interesting relationship. There were times, like now, when as a parent you just watch them grow, and know you will be there for them.

Buster's life had taken on more meaning now that he had a family living with him. He enjoyed their conversations, especially when Lola shared stories about the boys growing up. Just like him and Will, her sons fought like brothers do, but he knew they would always have each other's back. Every once in a while, he shared his own stories, and his deep inner beliefs. Lola admired him for the fine human being he was.

*****

Olivia and Trace were discussing plans for the weekend. "My parents and I are having a few people over this afternoon. Will you come?"

"You know your dad told me to stay away from you. I wouldn't be welcome."

"Live dangerously," Olivia taunted.

Why not? No one was going to tell him that he wasn't good enough.

When Trace arrived at the ranch, Olivia greeted him with her usual warmth. She put her arm through his and began showing him off to her friends. He was so intensely masculine that the other men paled in comparison, while her female friends fantasized with envy. As they mingled, Trace could see that Olivia thrived on attention.

Trace felt like the outsider he was. Not because he wasn't good enough, but because he didn't measure up financially, or in terms of sophistication like her other friends. He lifted his head high. In time that would change.

Olivia stiffened when she saw her dad approaching, a scowl on his face. "Daddy, you remember Trace. I invited him as my guest. I hope you don't mind?" she said sweetly.

Jackson was more than displeased to see Trace. He was livid. Who the hell did this kid think he was? His reaction had no impact on Trace.

While Trace was being held captive by one of Olivia's girlfriends, Jackson took Olivia inside to his office. He didn't mince words with his daughter, "I don't want you to see that cowboy again. Talk about your friendship with him is getting back to Burke. I want you to end this now."

"I'm old enough to do what I want. I enjoy spending time with Trace." Usually, Olivia could wrap her dad around her little finger. Something in his look told her he was serious. Perhaps it was just as well. Burke would be back soon.

Jackson continued in the forceful way he used when he intended to override any argument, "Men will always be at your disposal. They are either rich or they are poor. You would hate to be poor. I have given you everything you've ever wanted. Well, daughter, it's time to pay the piper. I need this business deal to go through. If you don't marry Burke Benson as planned, I'll disinherit you. Is that clear enough for you?"

Olivia didn't take her father's threat as an empty one.

"I believe this subject is closed. Are we clear on this?" His tone was dismissive.

Olivia enjoyed what her daddy's money could give her too much to defy him. She went over, and gave her father a hug, "As you wish." Olivia wasn't upset by their conversation. She just hated to give up Trace since he'd been such a wonderful distraction.

When Olivia returned to the party it was easy to find Trace. He was surrounded by several young ladies, all vying for his attention. When Trace saw her, he waved, and gave her one of his lazy grins that melted her insides. It had been fun, but she would end it. She wasn't willing to defy her father any more than she was willing to give up her lifestyle. There was no way she would choose a tough cowboy over a gentleman with money. Olivia went over, and slipped her arm though Trace's, "I've been looking for you, but I see I haven't been missed."

Trace was grateful for her arrival. It hadn't taken long for him to realize he didn't have much use for the boring people she called friends. One of her girlfriends had propositioned him in a way that left him feeling uncomfortable. Trace sensed a difference in Olivia. Something had changed, since she had disappeared into the house with her father.

Olivia's face paled when she heard a familiar voice.

"Here she is," Burke Benson said in his crisp English manner, as he walked over to stand next to Olivia. Burke pulled Olivia possessively close, "I should have known right away to look for you where the crowd was gathered."

Olivia wondered how long he'd been here watching her with Trace. She didn't like his unexpected appearance but managed a quick recovery. Olivia smiled, as she leaned in and gave him a kiss. Knowing that Burke would have heard about her time spent with Trace, she played it cool, "What a wonderful surprise, darling. I'd like you to meet my new friend, Trace Grayson. He works for the Calhouns. I was so lonely while you were gone, and he has been kind enough to spend time with me. All of my friends have been busy, and nobody likes being a fifth wheel." This was as good an opportunity as any to sever her relationship with Trace. "Now that you're back, I won't need a distraction."

When Olivia's look lingered on Trace, Burke underwent one of his characteristic mood changes that Olivia had learned to fear. Outwardly, he became very calm and polite, but Olivia knew his jealousy had surfaced. It was something that she had experienced, along with his possessiveness. She hadn't missed the hard glint in Burke's eyes.

Burke shook his head slowly, "You're always full of surprises, my dear." He turned to Trace, his tone dismissive, "Olivia gets herself into trouble when she has too much time on her hands. Now that I'm back she won't be needing others to amuse her. I doubt we'll be seeing each other again as we won't be running in the same circles." He took Olivia by the arm, and practically pulled her away.

Olivia thought how in character Burke was to totally dominate this reunion scene. Without a backward glance, she walked with Burke to a group that included her parents. Jackson Beaumont smirked and tipped his hat to Trace.

Trace had just experienced first-hand how calculating, and malicious Olivia was. The unexpected reality of the end of their relationship was a hard knock, but he'd taken knocks before. Trace took his leave. He wouldn't let this matter to him, though right now it hurt like hell. They may turn their noses up at him now, but things would be different. At that moment, Trace swore that one day he'd be in a position to knock them off their high-and-mighty pedestals. Their ill-bred attitudes only motivated him more.

Chapter Eleven

Life had changed in many ways for Trace. He had formed his own company, bought his first horse, graduated high school, and survived the break-up of a summer romance. He was now a full-time employee. He was working hard with Murphy and learning the art of cutting. Lola had her foal, a beautiful colt he named, Rebel. His dream was coming true. Best of all, he had developed a true friendship with Buster.

At the end of the workday, Buster called Trace into the office. "Sit down, Trace."

Trace wondered what was up.

Buster smiled as he handed the boy the promissory note he signed when he purchased Lady's foal. At the bottom were the words, Paid in Full. "What's next?"

True to form, Trace was open and direct, "Matt and I were talking. His dad is selling a couple of his yearlings. He says there is a filly named Ginger that would be great for breeding. My financial situation is the same as it has always been, but I am the proud owner of my first horse. So, I guess I have collateral."

"You're an honorable man, and an excellent horse trainer. Same terms as last time?"

Gratefully, Trace agreed.

The next day Buster went with Trace to meet Matt and check out the yearlings. A graceful one-year-old with long slender legs flicked her tail and pranced to the fence. Trace took one look at Ginger, and knew he had to have her. Buster braced his foot on the lower rung of the fence. He studied the animal closely, while Trace stroked her long, graceful neck. Trace looked at Buster who nodded. Trace turned to Matt and said he'd take her.

Buster didn't miss the genuine display of pride on Trace's face. He patted Trace on the back, "You bought yourself a fine horse, young man." He went and sat in the truck while Trace and Matt's dad closed the deal.

Will had spent the day helping BJ over at his ranch. Maybe it was because he was tired that his thoughts turned to his brother. Buster seemed to be tired a lot lately and had started taking it easier. It wasn't a bad thing, but it was uncharacteristic. In fact, now that he thought about it, it looked like Buster had lost weight. Will brought his concern up with Sadie during supper, "I know Buster had a doctor's appointment a while back. Last week he went back for another appointment." For a moment, a chilling thought assaulted him. Maybe the last appointment was more than just a follow-up. He prayed there was nothing wrong with his brother.

Sadie tried to ease her husband's concern, "Lola hasn't said anything to me, so it's probably nothing. How did things go over at BJ's?"

"It was a good day, but BJ needs to redo the roof on their house before next winter. I think painting the corral fences will be a good summer job for Shelby and Riley." Will couldn't let his concern go, "Do you think I should say anything to Buster?"

"I guess if it's bothering you, it's best to ask, but try a little discretion. You know how private Buster is. Ssh, he's coming up the steps."

When Sadie invited Buster to join them for coffee, Buster shook his head, and looked at Will. "Can we go talk in the office?" Something definitely wasn't right. Buster was pale, his skin tone ashen, and his look was vacant.

Will exchanged glances with Sadie. He remembered seeing that look years ago. It was the same look Buster had when he told him about Annie and Joey. The feeling of dread spread through his body. Will felt that his brother was going to tell him something he didn't want to hear.

Once they were in the office, Buster closed the door. As soon as they were seated, Buster looked at his brother, and cleared his throat, "I have cancer and it's untreatable. Dr. Layton gave me less than a year to live, but that was a while ago. I've been going downhill quickly the last couple of weeks, so I figured it was time to let everyone know." Buster suddenly looked weary, as if the words he'd spoken had taken all of his energy. The two brothers sat facing each other in agonizing silence. Buster felt sorry for his brother who looked shell-shocked. "I don't want you to be mad that I didn't tell you before now. I didn't tell anyone because I know you all would have started treating me different and wanting me to take it easy. I didn't want that. All that hovering would have been worse than the cancer. But it's getting worse quickly. I'm sure Lola knows something is wrong, but she has been respectful, and hasn't pressed. The boys have both stepped up. They have picked up my slack without saying a word, but Trace keeps looking at me in that uncanny way of his. I couldn't keep this to myself any longer."

Will swore under his breath. He'd been shaken by the news, but he wasn't angry with his brother for not telling him sooner. He probably would have done the same thing. He wished he had a way of dulling his feelings, the raw, agonizing ache within.

"In the beginning I had vague symptoms. When my back hurt, I thought I had strained it, but it kept getting worse. I thought my stomach pain was indigestion, or Lola's cooking."

Both men laughed knowing how offended Lola would be to hear such a statement. It helped to ease the tension in the room.

"Let's get a second opinion."

"I've had all the tests and scans. My cancer was very aggressive. My liver has been taken over by a tumor. It has spread to other organs, as well as my pancreas. Treatment might shrink or slow the growth for a while, but it doesn't cure the cancer. I don't want treatments. I just want to spend my last days here at Valley View."

Will blinked a couple of times, and swallowed hard before he could get the words out, "How long, Buster?"

"I saw the doctor yesterday. He gave me six months at the most, but I don't think I have that long. That said, we have a lot of things we need to talk about."

The two brothers stayed behind closed doors for hours talking about the ranch, the Graysons, and death. Although both Trace and Riley had been pulling Buster's weight around the ranch, it would be good when the new wranglers got there. Buster and Will agreed that if they worked out, they would keep them on full-time. Trace needed to spend his time training the colts, and Riley was graduating this year, and going to college in the fall.

The next morning Buster hung back instead of heading out with Trace. He wanted to talk to Lola alone. As soon as Trace left, Buster turned to Lola, "I know you've been concerned about me, but I wasn't ready to share. I told Will and Sadie last night that I have terminal cancer."

Lola was shocked as she gazed at Buster helplessly, not knowing what to say. A wave of guilt swept through her. She had seen the signs. Over the last few months his face had aged, and his cheeks had hollowed. He no longer had a hearty appetite, even though she had been cooking all his favorites hoping he would gain back the weight he had lost. Deep down she knew he was sick, but she hadn't expected this.

Buster waited a few minutes before he spoke again, "Will you please tell the boys. I will talk to both of them alone when the time is right. Now I need to go and talk to Murphy."

Lola heard the pain in his voice. This wasn't going to be easy for Buster. As soon as he left Lola broke down and sobbed. She had many reasons to cry in her lifetime, but this was the most painful. This news broke her heart. What she felt for Buster was a special kind of love. One that had grown over the years.

Buster headed over to the stables. As expected, Trace was with Murphy. The boy was with him every chance he had. Buster remained in the shadows for a while and listened.

Trace was in the stall with Diego, "I love this horse. You know what it's like, Murphy."

"Aye, I do."

Trace turned at the sound of Buster's footsteps.

Buster patted Trace on the shoulder, "Why don't you take Diego for a run this morning?" Buster wanted to talk to Murphy alone.

"I still have chores to do."

"You've been working hard so take the morning off. Diego could use a good run."

Trace didn't need to be told twice. It was a perfect day for riding in the country. Trace headed out across the grassy plains, anxious to get to the western ridge. The muscular stallion soared across the ground, his long mane flowing behind him. When Trace reached the ridge, he gazed out.

His breath caught like it always did as he took in the magnificent view sweeping in all directions. Trace sat deeply engrossed in the unfolding beauty, and allowed himself to dream, if only for a moment. He wanted a part of this, his own piece of paradise. He patted Diego knowing he could only dream about owning such a magnificent horse, let alone a place of his own. This wasn't his land any more than Diego was his horse. He didn't have any illusions, only dreams. He turned Diego and headed back to Valley View.

Lola was at the sink when Trace walked in. He knew right away that she was crying. Something was wrong.

Riley, who had just come around the corner, looked at his brother and lashed out, "Ma doesn't cry. What did you do to upset her?"

Lola's eyes were bright with tears of concern as she looked at her sons. Her voice was thick with heavy emotion, and tears spilled down her cheeks, "Buster has been sick for a while, but he didn't want any of us to know. He told me this morning that he has terminal cancer and has only a few months to live."

For a moment, her words didn't make any sense. The boys stared at their mother, and then at each other. Nobody said anything. None of them had the words to console the other. Their world was turned upside down again.

*****

As the weeks passed it was difficult watching a strong, independent man fade away to a mere shadow of himself. There were days Buster was quiet, and his distant look was becoming all too familiar. Lola could see how much Trace and Riley were suffering. They all were.

With considerable effort Buster walked outside. He now spent most of his time on the verandah visiting with those who stopped by. The refreshing mountain air, and spectacular scenery was his therapy. His gaze often wandered, looking out at the countryside that he had loved all his life. He sat watching Trace working his horse, Rebel, and he smiled. The boy had come a long way. Buster knew that both Trace and Riley were stepping up to help Will until the new wranglers arrived next week. Spring may be here, but he was in the winter of his existence.

Lola interrupted his thoughts, "Are you okay, Buster. Can I get you something?"

"I don't need anything. You're the best medicine of all. Come sit and read to me."

Lola went inside to get the book she had been reading to him. They had only read a few chapters, and she questioned if Buster would live long enough to hear the end. She tucked his blanket around him and began to read. He gazed toward the distant mountains, an expression of contentment on his face, and closed his eyes. Lola's voice was soothing. It wasn't long, and he was sleeping peacefully. Lola fell into her own silence. Her heart wrenched to see him in this condition. Even knowing he was asleep she stayed with him.

After a while, Buster briefly opened his eyes, "Stay with me, Annie." Buster's periods of confusion were occurring more frequently. This wasn't the first time he had called her Annie. It didn't upset Lola. Instead, she took this as a compliment because she knew how much he loved Annie. What made her sad was the fact that she knew he was nearing the end. Lola knew when the time came, Annie would be waiting for him. When she saw Will coming over from the main house, she straightened her shoulders, and pasted a smile on her face.

As if sensing his brother's presence, Buster opened his eyes. He welcomed his brother, and surprised them by saying, "I want to go for a drive in the country. I want to drive through our land, see our cattle grazing in the meadows, and then stop for a while down by the river."

Will agreed and went to get his truck. When he returned, he helped Buster to stand. It was heart-breaking to see a man who used to be strong, and independent struggle with this disease.

Knowing Will had taken his brother for a drive, Sadie went over to see Lola, and share a pot of tea. She found Lola in the kitchen crying. Lola allowed her release when no one was around. Sadie went over and put her arms around her.

"I'm not good company today," Lola confessed.

Sadie sat down, "That's okay. I know the doctor was here earlier. What did he say?"

"Buster is getting too weak to go up and down the stairs. Dr. Layton said that I need to convince Buster to stay in his room. If he doesn't listen, Buster will have to be in the hospital."

"What did Buster say to that?"

"He said he's not going to take orders from anyone. That Calhoun stubborn streak hasn't weakened, but Buster is getting frailer every day. I told him we could get a bed and set it up down here in the living room, but he is too proud for that. Buster said when the time comes, he wants to be in his room upstairs, and he will make that decision on his own."

"That means more work for you."

Lola nodded. The lines of strain were already beginning to show on her face. "I had the boys take his recliner upstairs last night and set it in front of his window, so he can still look out at the mountains. It might be only a few more days before he's confined to his bedroom."

"You are the most compassionate, amazing woman I've ever known. I'll cook the meals for all of us. After supper Will or I will come sit with Buster and give you a break."

Lola was glad to give back in any way. She would never be able to repay the Calhouns for everything they had done for her family. Her voice broke, "Buster may refuse help because of his pride, but I'm grateful to take it. Thank you."

"What else can we do?"

Lola shook her head, "Nothing for now."

The two ladies embraced, and Sadie left. She could not stop her own tears as she headed home. Buster's death was fast approaching.

When Trace was done for the day, he would sit with Buster. As difficult as it was for Trace, he vowed he would be there for Buster, like he had always been there for him. Trace refused to ask Buster how he was doing. He didn't have to. He could see Buster slowly dying in front of him. Trace would tell him about his day. At times he would share the ongoing drama of the Riley-Shelby saga. It was no secret that Riley was in love with Shelby, and Shelby was enjoying his undying devotion. Being young, she also enjoyed the attention from other boys. Riley understood because she was attractive and fun, so he was patiently biding his time. Trace had to admit that Riley had more patience than he ever would.

Buster was listening to another of Trace's stories when his eyelids closed, and his chin dropped to his chest.

Thinking he was asleep, Trace got up to leave.

"Don't go, Trace."

"You'll be more comfortable in bed, Buster. Come, I'll help you up the stairs."

Buster let out a long despairing sigh. "I'm not going to lie around in my room like some old fart in a nursing home." Buster summoned a smile. "I'm just a little tired, that's all." Once again, he slipped back into a world of his own.

Trace left and made his escape to the stables. Trace was retreating into himself more and more. As always, the horses brought him comfort. He would talk to them, and he didn't always have to be strong.

Seeing her son leave, Lola went out, and woke Buster. He looked pale and lethargic. Lola looked directly into Buster's eyes, "It's time, Buster. Come, I'll help you to your room."

Buster chose to ignore her. The Calhoun stubbornness had kicked in.

"You know what I'm talking about. Doctor's orders."

Buster sighed and promised Lola that starting tomorrow he would stay in his room. He felt bad, knowing it would be even more work for her. He was grateful to have Lola. "I'd like to sit here and watch the sun set."

Lola relented out of compassion. She understood instinctively that he wanted to be alone. She wrapped the blanket tighter around him and left.

Buster sank deeper into his chair. This would be the last time he'd be sitting out here on the verandah. Trace had taken him to the barn to say goodbye to his beloved horses. The hardest goodbyes were yet to come. It would take a different kind of strength to do that, but he had come to terms with it.

Evening settled in, and the last rays of daylight streaked the sky. The sunset over the mountains was a perfect farewell. He sat alone, now just a dark silhouette in the late dusk. For Buster it was more than just the end of a day. Tomorrow he would only be able to rely on memories, but they too were fading like the view in front of him. He wiped at the tears running down his hollow cheeks.

*****

Buster was now confined to bed, or as he referred to it, imprisoned in his room. Lola poured herself a coffee and went upstairs to sit with him. She spent most of her day upstairs. The doctor was coming later in the afternoon, and she was dreading his evaluation. Lola was very aware that Buster was failing fast. He seemed smaller, as if he had shrunk into himself. It was hard watching him grow weaker from one day to the next.

Buster suddenly had a coughing spell. It took a minute before he could catch his breath. "Are you okay, Buster?"

Buster closed his eyes summoning strength. When he opened them, he looked at Lola in frustration, "Who would be, when all a man has left to do is stare at a damned ceiling all day?"

Buster rarely complained, so his present mood worried her. "I'm going downstairs to get your lunch." Buster was staring out the window when she returned with a cup of soup.

Buster glared at her as she approached. "I don't want any damn soup."

His ill-humor had no effect on her, "I can see that you are set on being difficult today."

"I'm not hungry."

Lola sighed; he was never hungry. "I'm not going until this soup is gone."

Buster shared a rare smile and poured it into the basin beside him. "Bye."

Lola released an exhausted sigh. She was trying to do her best in an impossible situation.

"I told you I'm not always going to be pleasant."

"Well, that makes two of us, you old coot."

Buster heard an uncharacteristic trace of anguish. He knew this was hard on her. "You certainly grew a backbone over the last couple of years, young lady."

"I had to with all of you men around me every day."

"It's a good thing, Lola. I know you'll be fine when I'm gone."

Surprising them both, Lola burst into tears. She had been so strong though all of this, but for some reason it was more than she could cope with today.

"It's okay, Lola. I've had a good life. Especially the last few years with you, and the boys. You made these last years better."

"You're the one who made my life better," Lola said, her voice thick with emotion. She had often seen the caring in his eyes. Caring that she had never seen in Tom's eyes.

Buster changed the subject, wanting to erase the sadness in her eyes, "Come sit by me, so I can look at your pretty face. You can read to me."

"You're a silly old fool," she said, as she reached for their book.

*****

Lola was downstairs waiting for the doctor. Will had called him because Buster had declined in the last two days and taken a drastic turn for the worst. As soon as the doctor arrived Lola took him upstairs and left.

Dr. Layton bent over his patient, listened to his heart, and shook his head. Having known Buster for years, it was time to call a spade a spade, "Your time has run out. Do you need anything for the pain?"

Buster shook his head. "I'm just tired." He closed his eyes.

Will had seen the doctor arrive. He went over and joined Lola in the kitchen. They were chatting nervously when Dr. Layton came back downstairs.

"Well, Doc?" Looking at the doctor's face, Will already knew the answer.

The doctor's eyes remained grave. "I'm sorry, Will. It's time for the family to come and say their goodbyes."

Will went back to the house to tell Sadie, and then went to find Murphy. Will found him in the tack room. The look in Will's eyes reflected his inner pain. "Buster is at the end of the trail." Will put his hand on Murphy's shoulder. "Come, I'll take you to him." Will showed Murphy into the room, and then left the two old cowboys alone.

Murphy had no words; he just clasped his friend's hand.

"I'm ready to go, old friend." His voice was labored, and he closed his eyes until his breathing evened out. "You watch out for Trace for me. He still needs guidance. Find Trace and have him come up." It had taken a lot of effort to say the few words he did.

All Murphy could do was nod as he left.

Lola went back up as soon as Murphy left. She brushed Buster's hair back, whispering soothing words while she held a cold cloth to his forehead. She raised Buster's head to help him take a drink.

He took a sip, and laid back down, "I knew you'd be back, Annie."

Lola lay his hands on top of his straightened covers. When Trace came up, she left.

Trace approached the bed quietly. Here lay his best friend, the person who had made him a man. Buster had once been such a strong man. Trace's eyes were dark with grief as he stood at the end of the bed, his hands fisted together so hard that they hurt.

"I'm not sleeping. Come sit down." Buster's face was pinched.

Trace did as he was told. Trace pulled the chair close and took Buster's hand. It felt cold and clammy. There was no spark of life left in Buster's sunken gray eyes.

Buster hated to see the pain in Trace's eyes. "It's okay, Trace, everyone has to die sometime. I'm at peace. I've lived a good life, and thanks to you, and Riley and your mom, the last years gave me a world of happiness. I was a very lonely man."

"Thank you, Buster."

"For what?"

"For giving mom a good life and treating us like your own sons. Words are never enough, Buster." Trace bared his sole as he struggled through what he wanted to say, grateful for having had this man in his life.

No man loved a son more than Buster Calhoun loved Trace. They had a special bond as well as a mutual respect for each other. A deep understanding that didn't always require words. "You've made me proud. Continue being who you are, and always be there for your brother. Find Will and have him come up." Will would be Buster's final farewell. The rest of the family had popped in throughout the day.

Trace left Buster's room but stood leaning against the closed door for a long time struggling to compose himself. After a word with Will, Trace headed over to see Diego.

Will went upstairs and sat down beside his brother. Buster's breathing was labored. The two brothers spoke not a word, but when Buster opened his eyes, they silently said their final farewell. Will remained by the side of the bed. One by one the minutes ticked away into the night. Will was startled when Sadie's hand came to rest on his shoulder. He hadn't heard her come in.

"You're exhausted, Will. Why don't you take a break, and I'll sit with Buster?"

Will shook his head. The last thing he could do for his brother was hold vigil.

Sadie went back downstairs to sit with Lola.

Will sat alone, his mind flipping through old memories. He and Buster wouldn't be making any more together, but he was grateful for all the years they had. When Will looked over, Buster was at peace. All the pain was gone from his face. It was over. Will buried his face in his hands and wept. His brother, and best friend was gone. It was a long time before he rose, and walked out of the room, gently closing the door behind him. When he entered the kitchen, the boys had joined the two women. "Buster's gone."

They all experienced conflicting emotions, each one having to deal with their loss. Lola's biggest concern was for her boys. They may have lost their father several years ago, but this man had been more of a dad to them in the few years that they had lived with him. The loss of their father was nothing compared to this. Lola couldn't comfort her sons; she was dealing with her own pain. Her dear friend was gone.

Trace blinked hard and left. Outside he stood alone. The wind had died down and the night was still. It was like the whole universe was respecting the loss of Buster Calhoun. His life crumbled around him, and Trace began to cry. He hadn't cried when his dad died.

*****

The office was quiet. Everyone was still trying to deal with their loss. Today was the first time they were all together since the funeral. They were gathered for the reading of Buster's will. The presence of all the Graysons had been requested. Buster's lawyer looked at those gathered. "I am truly sorry for your loss," he said, as he handed everyone a sealed envelope. Inside was a letter written by Buster. "Buster wanted to say good-bye to each one of you in his own way. These letters are to be opened in private and only shared if you wish." They sat stone-faced as the lawyer read the will. It was as expected until he said, "To Lola Grayson, I bequeath my share of Valley View, including the house I resided in."

Lola gasped as she put her hand to her throat. "Madre de Dios." She was shocked and outraged by this unexpected inheritance. This made no sense at all. No part of this ranch was hers. It belonged to the Calhouns for generations, and it would stay that way. Her words of disbelief tumbled out, "This is absolutely absurd. I cannot accept this."

"Whether you want to take it or not, Mrs. Grayson, it isn't up to you. This is what Buster wanted." The lawyer continued, "My life insurance policy is to be divided equally between Trace Grayson and Riley Grayson. To Riley, I bequeath my Ford truck. Treat it with respect. To Trace, I bequeath my horse, Diego. He was already yours."

Lola knew Buster loved her sons like his own. The premium on the policy was more than enough to pay for Riley's post education and give Trace money to move forward with his business. This generous offer she understood. Buster wanted to look out for them. This was a means to the future for two young boys, who had experienced more hardships than a great many had in a lifetime.

The reading was over, and everyone started to disperse, taking with them the memory of a decent, hard-working, and honorable man.

Trace headed straight to the stables. He wanted to be alone so he hoped that Murphy wouldn't be there. Both Murphy and BJ were there. Murphy had Diego saddled and handed Trace the reins. Buster had shared his wishes with Murphy, and Murphy knew the boy well enough to know he needed to escape. "Diego is your horse now."

If Trace had ever wanted a horse, it was this one. How many times had he dreamed this? But the intangible price was too high. He lost his best friend to get him. Trace pulled himself up into the saddle. The animal neighed as he accepted his new master. Trace suddenly spurred Diego, and they took off.

BJ and Murphy watched him go. "The lad is hurting."

"Give him time. Every man has to deal with his grief in his own way." BJ was speaking on behalf of all of them.

Like a wounded animal Trace took off. He slapped the reins across the horse's shoulders and galloped toward the ridge that had often brought him peace. To a man like Trace, tears were a private thing. His choked sobs were drowned out by the hoofs of Diego as he flew across the land. Nothing eased the pain. By the time he reached the ridge, his body was trembling. As if knowing his grief, the sun refused to shine. He sat, and watched the black clouds gather, the sky now as turbulent as his mood.

Meanwhile, back at the office, Lola placed her hand on Will's arm. She asked him to stay so they could talk. "Will, I accept, and am grateful for what Buster did for my sons, but Valley View belongs to the Calhoun family. You must understand that I can't accept it."

Will attempted to reassure Lola, "Buster thought of all of you as family. We all do."

"Your brother must have been out of his mind to think I would allow Valley View to be divided this way." As much as she tried, she couldn't understand this.

"First, Buster was as sane as you, and me right to the end. Second, this is what he wanted." He would have gone on, but Lola started to cry. He put his arms around her and wondered where Sadie was. She was much better at handling tears. "The time my brother spent with you, and the boys was the happiest I'd seen him in years. He had been living a sad, and lonely life before you arrived. You, and the boys changed that. His will was not a surprise to me, Lola. Buster and I talked about it the day he told me he was dying."

Lola was frustrated because Will didn't understand. Buster had given them more than a place to live. He had given them a home. They were able to put down permanent roots and plan a future. Lola couldn't change how she felt, it wasn't right. She raised her chin stubbornly, "I said I'm not accepting it." She stormed out of the house and stomped home. Buster's home. Not hers!

"There's no reasoning with that woman," Will muttered, as he entered the kitchen. Will shared their conversation, expecting Sadie to understand. "Why can't she just be grateful, and accept this?"

Sadie heard the frustration in his voice. She also understood Lola's side. "Lola is a very proud woman. Give her a few days, and then have another talk with her." Realizing this was not the time to get into it with Lola, she suggested that they call a Calhoun family meeting. "As we know, Lola can be a very stubborn woman, so be prepared for a battle. Maybe there is an alternate proposal that can be worked out that Lola will accept." Sadie knew there was going to be some challenging days ahead.

Will took Sadie's advice and waited, but now it was time to talk to Lola again. He headed over to the old farmhouse. He couldn't think of it as Buster's or Lola's. That was the problem. Lola answered the door as soon as he knocked. She looked distraught. He now wished he had brought Sadie along. "I have given you time to think about your inheritance, and I understand what you said about wanting Valley View to remain with the Calhouns. I talked to BJ and Jenny. Together, we have come up with a proposal that I hope you will find acceptable. Can you come over to the office after lunch?"

Lola agreed and watched him leave. She'd been struggling for days. She was missing Buster. Her boys were suffering. She wondered how much she could take before she broke down. At lunch time she told the boys about her upcoming meeting with Will. They would have their own meeting after, and she would share everything with them then.

After lunch, Sadie welcomed Lola, took her to the office, and left. Will motioned for her to sit down. She could tell he was as nervous as she was.

"I've talked to the others. We have a proposal that we believe is a reasonable solution to your refusal." Will took the time to explain what would happen. "The end result is that you will own the Reed Ranch in exchange for your willed portion of Valley View, allowing us to keep all of Valley View with the Calhouns."

The concept of the offer made sense. However, there was one major concern that Lola had to address. "How will Jenny and Shelby feel about moving? That is their home."

"The Reed Ranch has many bad memories for Jenny. She is fine with letting it go."

"What about Shelby?" This change would be a significant change.

"Valley View is as much a home to her as her own."

"Will, I know this has been a lot for all of you to deal with, but I need to talk to my boys again." Lola saw the frustration on Will's face.

"Fine. Can we meet here again tomorrow? We do need to know what you want to do. We will have things to work through."

Lola agreed and left. It had been a productive meeting. So was the meeting that followed with the boys. Lola explained the offer in detail and discussed the proposed changes. Both boys were impressed with their mother's ability to explain and rationalize the drastic changes.

Lola and Will met again in the morning. "I still have a couple of things I need to settle with you. If I accept this offer, in a few weeks we will be property owners with all the responsibilities, and frustrations that it will entail. I'm embarrassed to ask, but I have to. Will you help us to get started, and guide us through the initial process? We will gladly pay for your help."

For today, Will just nodded in agreement. The Calhouns would never take payment for helping a neighbor, especially when they were more than friends. They would always be considered as family. "You drive a hard bargain, Lola."

They all knew that Lola had a stubborn side. What they didn't know was that Lola had great business sense. The complicated transaction took days before all the parties came to an agreement. After days of negotiating the Graysons owned the Reed Ranch, and together with the Calhouns they had formed C&G Ranching, a joint venture with the cattle. That night Lola and her sons celebrated. It had been difficult for all of them, but they were confident with the decisions that had been made.

"Can we call our ranch, Lola Grande?" Riley asked sincerely. The boys had talked earlier. Hard work, and heartache was all their father had given their mother. This was their way of honoring their mother for all she had done for them. Her devotion needed to be acknowledged.

Lola nodded, too moved to speak.

Riley looked at his brother. "Do you think she'll always be this agreeable?"

"Hell, no," Trace said, and the boys laughed.

"The ranch will be ours, equal partners between the three of us. I will maintain control with the extra one percent. All of the land, house, buildings, and additional facilities will belong to Lola Grande. C&G Ranching is the partnership between Lola Grande and Valley View, so that is also part of Lola Grande. But Caballo Stables is yours, Trace. This is going to be a lot of work, and as you know the work will never end."

"The Graysons aren't afraid of hard work," Trace said with raw determination. "We'll be the younger version of the Calhoun brothers. Only we are the Grayson brothers. In time our name will mean something like theirs does."

The next morning Will informed Lola, "Trace and I met last night, and he and I have set up a written agreement in regard to Trace's business. We discussed his current employment with Valley View Ranch, and his training other horses here under the umbrella of Caballo Stables."

"I'm pleased that all of this has been addressed. How do we move forward?"

"Delay is pointless once decisions are made. I called my lawyer, and he will have the paperwork drawn up within the next few days. He will have it couriered here so we can review the documents. When that is done, he will come out to the ranch to witness the final signatures."

"Have you addressed the fencing of the portion of the Reed Ranch that you have purchased, even though it will still be used for cattle under C&G Ranching. We need to keep the boundaries clear between us." This was a comment that had more than one meaning.

Will had misjudged Lola again. The woman was tough as nails. "It will be scheduled as soon as our agreement is signed."

Lola finally relaxed, "Thank you for your patience and understanding."

Will choked on his response, "Thank you for giving us back Valley View."

They left the office together and found Sadie in the kitchen. Will excused himself, leaving the two women alone. "It looks like it was an intense meeting," commented Sadie.

"A cup of tea is what I need, as well as a friend to talk to. One who understands how hard this has been. I hope there are no hard feelings?"

Sadie reassured Lola, "After Tom died, and you moved in with Buster, you and the boys became family to all of us. BJ and Jenny are looking forward to moving here to the homestead. The Reed Ranch had sad history because the ghosts of the past continued to linger."

"I miss Buster." His death still weighed heavy on Lola's heart.

Sadie reached over and took Lola's hand. "We all do," she said, her voice revealing her own heartbreak. Despite their age difference, Sadie knew that Buster and Lola had a strong love for each other. "You will finally have a home of your own, Lola," Sadie said with true sincerity.

Sadie was rewarded with a brief smile. "I know that you're trying to make me feel better, and I appreciate it. It still doesn't feel right."

"Buster was blessed to have two wonderful women in his life."

"Annie must have been an amazing woman," Lola said, and she meant it.

"She was," Sadie said, with a remembering smile. "I missed Annie so much when she died. She was my sister-in-law, but we really were more like sisters. It was lonely with her gone. I was surrounded by men day after day. I feel the same about you and now you're leaving."

"I'm just moving up the road. It won't change the friendship we have."

"No, just the fellowship. We've shared a lot over a pot of tea. You are the strongest, most resilient woman I know." Both ladies wiped away tears. What was happening was a big change for them.

Trace was struggling with Buster's passing. Dusk had begun to spread across the land. Standing out on the verandah brought back so many memories. How many times had he and Buster sat together, and talked? It was out here that the beginning of his dreams began. Buster would never see those dreams become reality, but thanks to him his reality would happen sooner. As agreed, the new fencing had been done. Even though the pastureland was still used for the same purpose, part of the old Reed Ranch now belonged to Valley View. The Graysons didn't need all the land for the horses. This was all part of the settlement the Lola had agreed to.

The next few weeks passed in a blur. Both ranches had become a beehive of activity. Sadie helped Lola tackle the old two-story, and together it was cleaned from top to bottom. The households were going to be swapped out on the weekend, and by Sunday night the Reed Ranch would be history. The hardest was packing up Buster's personal items. Lola let Sadie and Will do that. She believed that was private, and personal to the Calhouns. She asked for only one item. She wanted to keep the book that she had been reading to Buster, not because of the story but for the memory. Within the next few days, it all fell into place and the Reed Ranch became Lola Grande.

Chapter Twelve

L ola stood on the front verandah of their home. She looked at her boys with a new light in her eyes. "God guided us here with his hand. This is our home and our land. Lola Grande is our future. Let's go inside." Lola walked slowly from one room to another. She could make changes, move things around, get rid of things, buy new, and she didn't have to ask anyone. They could make this home theirs. Throughout the day, she would pause and look around in disbelief.

It had been an exhausting day, emotionally more than physically. At suppertime, their evening prayer of thanks was very meaningful, and heartfelt. Throughout the meal their moods varied. At times they were overwhelmed with excitement. Other times reality took hold, and they became more somber. They knew they owed Buster so much. That night as Lola lay in bed, a shaft of moonlight illuminated the room, offering a beam of new hope. Her family had begun their life at Lola Grande.

The morning brought with it a sense of reality. The Graysons were now ranchers, whatever that entailed. After breakfast, they walked around their property. "It's too late this year, but next year we'll plant a garden behind the house. It actually looks like there might have been one there at one time."

Trace was anxious to move forward with his dreams, but Buster had taught him well. He had to do his due diligence, and research materials, and suppliers before deciding on what would be the best for his facility. He would need the right pen set-up for the horse training operation. He knew he needed to spend time with Will and BJ, seeking their guidance.

It was times like this that he really missed Buster. His death gave Trace one driving purpose. He wanted to show everyone that Buster's belief in him when he was only seventeen was well-founded.

"The existing buildings are fine for now, so our priority is the horse facility, and the corrals. The horses will continue to be trained at Valley View." Trace knew it would take a lot of physical work, sweat and commitment but he was used to it.

Lola was quick to add, "We need to build a triple garage with a suite on top." She continued quickly, before the boys could react, "I've put a lot of thought into this, and I know we can afford it, since we sold off a good parcel of our land to the Calhouns. When you boys marry, you don't want your mother living with you, and I know that I never want to leave here. This is very personal to me. Here I can let go of the past. It makes sense to do the suited garage at the same time as the horse facility." Lola Grayson had become a smart, and practical woman.

Her confession surprised both boys, but they understood. Their mom had devoted her life at Valley View to Buster and had given up a lot for them. The boys could tell by the tone of her voice that this was important to her. Lola's glance rested on Trace, "Now that we have roots, it's time for you to start thinking about settling down. How come you haven't found a nice girl?"

Trace leaned over, and kissed her cheek, "I'm waiting to find someone as special as you."

Lola smiled. Trace definitely had the Grayson charm.

"If Trace gets married, where am I supposed to live?"

"You and Shelby will be married long before I will."

"Whoever marries first gets the house, the other gets a cot in the barn." They all laughed. "It really is time for you to move on with your life, Trace. I mean beyond Lola Grande, and your horses. When you get thrown from a horse you don't quit riding. Don't let your failed relationship with Olivia prevent you from being open to love."

"I don't have time for romance." For Trace, nothing mattered more than establishing Caballo Stables at Lola Grande. Thanks to Buster's generous bequeath he could start building and bring his horses home sooner.

*****

The next few days were surreal, and at times overwhelming. Their everyday routine was different, and they were all learning to adjust to the changes within themselves, and each other. There were stressful times as they adapted. As well, the Graysons were also preparing for Riley's move to Olds College. He would be starting school next week.

Riley had been withdrawn during the evening meal. Right after dinner he headed outside. He closed the door tight, indicating he wanted to be alone.

Lola sensed there was something bothering her youngest son. "Riley has been awfully quiet the last few days. Do you know what's up?"

Trace had been so busy he hated to admit that he hadn't noticed. "Shelby has probably upset him again."

"This is different. I'm sure it's more than that. Do you think he's worried about going away to school? He hasn't mentioned it lately."

"I'll talk to him, Ma." Despite knowing that his brother wanted to be alone, Trace decided this was as good a time as any. Riley was leaning against the railing staring off into space. "What's up, Riley?"

Riley hesitated before responding, "I've decided not to go to college." One look at Trace, and Riley knew his brother was going to tear into him.

Trace was shocked by Riley's blunt answer, "What are you talking about?"

"You still work at Valley View full-time. Have you forgotten that we have our own ranch to run? You can't do all of this on your own."

Trace made no attempt to hide his irritation, "Don't be stupid. You are going to college."

Riley snapped, "Don't tell me what I have to do. You're not my father."

Trace's mood toward his brother escalated to fury, "Fine, then be a loser like our old man." One look at the hurt on Riley's face made Trace wonder how his father's voice suddenly came out of his mouth. Trace took a deep breath, allowing his anger to escape from his body. "You owe it to both Valley View, and our business venture with the Calhouns to go to school. There was an unwritten agreement that you committed to."

"I also committed to Lola Grande," Riley said, and turned away.

Trace reached out and grabbed Riley by the arm. "What the hell is your problem? Are you seriously trying to piss me off?"

Riley reacted by pushing Trace away. The unexpected force behind the push caused Trace to stumble backwards against the front door.

Hearing their raised voices, and the commotion, Lola went out to see what was going on.

Riley and Trace exchanged dirty looks with each other.

"This is between us brothers." Trace's voice was commanding enough that Lola turned and went back inside. She hoped their disagreement wouldn't get physical. They didn't fight often, but boys would be boys regardless of their age.

Trace's annoyance remained, so he didn't let up, "You have a chance to do something, and now you just want to throw it away. You were always planning on going to college. Thanks to Buster, you don't have to go into debt."

"It's not about the money. We own a ranch. Who is going to help you with all the work around here if I go to school? It's not fair to you."

Trace knew that the right thing was for Riley to go to school even though there would be a lot of work ahead of him, and they couldn't afford to hire help. He was fully aware that he still had his job at Valley View, and he had a new colt to train. He would cope. Trace tried to lighten the conversation, "Ma and I will manage. You might be surprised what we get done if you're not here holding us back." Trace's attempt at humor only caused Riley's scowl to deepen. "It's okay if things around here take longer, including Ma's suite. Neither of us are getting married tomorrow."

"Who would want you, and I have to wait until Shelby grows up. I mean gets older." They both laughed because he was right the first time. It helped to ease the tension.

"You just worry about school. You said that with this education it will help all of us. You work hard at college, and I'll work your ass off when you come home. I'm sorry that I made you mad. I just want more for you. I thought this was what you wanted."

"It is. This program will provide us with unlimited knowledge about the beef industry. Valley View has superior cattle. We need to keep it that way. Cattle ranching keeps evolving. It's important to keep up with the latest science, and trends. Things change in ranching just like they do with everything else. The environmental changes that are happening are ongoing and happening globally. We need to stay current in regard to technology, farm management, and marketing." He looked at Trace, "With what I will be learning, it's not just C&G Ranching that will benefit, but Caballo Stables as well."

Trace was impressed with his brother. He realized that Riley wasn't his little brother anymore, but he'd still been treating him like one. Riley was an intelligent young man who would be an asset to all of them.

Once the issue of school was out of the way, the boys grabbed a couple of beer, and kept talking out on the verandah. And drinking.

Lola headed to bed. Her sons needed this time alone to bond as young men, not as brothers. If they were hung over in the morning, it was on them.

"I envied you growing up. You are always so competent, and capable. I wanted Buster to be proud of me like he was with you."

Trace had never worried about doing the right thing. He just did what needed doing. He had never considered what Riley was feeling. "I'm proud of you. Buster was proud of you, too."

"I know, he told me that in his letter." Up until now no one had talked about what was in their letters. "I always felt that he liked you more than me. I know part of that was because you, and he shared a common interest in horses. The other reason was that I reminded him so much of his son, Joey. He said he was afraid to get too close to me, because it would hurt too much if we left. He said he was sorry, because he didn't realize until later that he was shutting me out."

"He would have given you the moon if you asked for it."

"Buster loved us a lot, didn't he? I loved him more than I did, Dad," Riley confessed.

Trace nodded in agreement. "In my letter, Buster told me that I was a better man than our dad ever was, and not to be afraid to open my heart to others. He said not to give all my love to the horses." Even thinking about it now caused Trace deep sadness. He tried to swallow past the lump in his throat. Both boys were grateful to Buster, because they knew how much he cared. Buster was more of a father than Tom had ever been.

"What do you think he told, Ma?"

"He probably told her how grateful he was that she agreed to stay after Dad died. He would have thanked her for the wonderful care she always gave him, especially at the end. She was happy living with Buster. I know Ma's missing him, too. Get us another beer, and we'll drink to Buster."

Trace grabbed the beer Riley handed him. "Buster and I had a different relationship because I was older when we moved here. I envied the freedom you had to take off with Shelby, and just go and play. It was what it was, and it is what it is."

"You're drunk. I've never known you to be philosophical?"

"I am sorry about earlier."

"I deserved a good talking to."

"You did but I came down on you like dad used to. That was uncalled for. After Buster died, I felt that I had to take on the role of father, instead of brother. I didn't realize you have grown up. I'd rather be your brother anyway. Always remember that we are Graysons. We have enough strength to get through the challenging times."

They continued to talk, and drink, into the early hours of the morning. That night a stronger bond formed between the two brothers. They were becoming like the Calhoun brothers in many ways.

The next morning, both boys were hungover when they got up. Lola smiled as they said no to breakfast. She didn't say a word as she went about her business. If they didn't get any work done today it wouldn't matter. It could wait. Her sons may not have solved all the problems last night, but they strengthened their bond as brothers. She knew if something happened to her, she wouldn't have to worry, because her two boys would take care of each other.

*****

Life settled into a routine after Riley left for college. Lola began taking online courses so she could help Trace with the bookkeeping end of his business, and they could operate Lola Grande independently from Valley View. She was enjoying the new challenge.

Tonight, Lola and Trace were going over to the Calhouns for dinner. Afterwards, Trace was going to discuss his plans with Will and BJ. Trace was looking for their guidance now that he was ready to move forward.

After supper, BJ came over, and joined his dad and Trace in the office. The two men were impressed when they looked at Trace's drawings. They could see that he had put a lot of thought into everything.

Trace appreciated being able to turn to Will and BJ. It helped to have someone to talk to about his plans. Buster always said not to do anything halfway and think long term. Trace knew it would take longer but he was going to have a first-class facility. Trace's voice was charged with excitement, "We will build in two phases. Flexibility is the key, so the original structure will allow for future expansion. Things like the office, bathroom, and birthing stall can be added in phase two. In time we will add an indoor arena. But at the end of phase one, I can bring the horses to Lola Grande and operate Caballo Stables there. For now, we will still have to buy our grain and hay from you."

"That no problem, and you can train your horses here as long as you want."

Now that the topic was on training, BJ said, "Word around the area is that Tyler Lawson, and a couple other ranchers are looking for new horses."

"I've just started to train Champ, but Dusty's ready."

Will couldn't be prouder of Trace. "You do good work, Trace. With you it's both a gift and an art. Caballo Stables will be a successful operation within a couple of years."

Meanwhile, in the kitchen Lola was asking Sadie for advice. Lola had shared her plans about the suite over the garage. Lola wanted to hire a contractor who would be able to build both.

"Andy Shaw did the renovation here at the house, and he also did some of the renovation work in your house. He does larger projects as well. He has a reputation for quality work, and I highly recommend him." Sadie was impressed with Lola. Over the years, she had seen her friend transform from a quiet, withdrawn woman to one who was now assured, and independent. This was a side to Lola she enjoyed seeing. Sadie knew it was Buster more than anyone, who helped Lola to develop the self-confidence she now had.

*****

Lola and Trace were waiting for the arrival of Andy Shaw. He was coming out to Lola Grande so they could meet with him to discuss both the horse facility, and the suited garage. Trace and Lola had already decided that Lola would oversee the project since she would always be on site. She could address any problems right away. Trace was glad that his mother would be taking on a project of her own. It would keep her busy while he was at work, and Riley was away at school.

Trace was outside when Andy arrived. "You will have to deal with the boss," Trace said, as he and Andy entered the kitchen.

"Will he be here today?"

Trace looked at his mom, aware of her displeasure. "My mom is the boss here at Lola Grande. Mom, meet Andy Shaw. Andy, this is my mom, Lola Grayson."

Andy looked bewildered. He had made the mistake of assuming that he would be dealing with men since it was a ranch.

The contractor's assumption was like lighting a match to a fuse. "I may not be what you expected, but I am the boss. I am not an empty-headed female, so I won't be bossed around by you or anyone else if we hire you." Her voice was cold, her eyes colder. Andy Shaw was not what she expected. The huge bear-like man was an imposing figure with his broad chest, and full beard. Without the beard he looked too much like Tom. Lola's negative reaction was a definite result of the past. The scars were deep because of Tom.

Andy knew they had gotten off on the wrong foot. The friction between them was instant.

Lola got right down to business. "The Calhouns recommended you. They said you are honest and do good work. This is a sketch of what I have in mind. I hope you can envision my wants." Lola wanted the garage to compliment the farmhouse as much as possible. Along with the sketch, she had an itemized list of what she wanted inside and out. Lola was hoping that the contractor would be able to make suggestions, and address things that she may have overlooked. "I do not want the quality of work to be builder's grade, and I want a fair quote."

This woman was all business. Andy did a quick scan of the plans and realized at once that she was a detail person. He was impressed but said nothing. Lola Grayson had put him on the defensive. He had to wonder what the son was going to be like to work with.

Trace handed Andy his own rough sketch. "This is not as elaborate as mom's, so I'd like to take you outside, and show you the area where I want to build. We can pace out the footprint of what I want. You can ask me questions as we go."

Outside, Trace explained a few things to Andy, so he would understand his mother better. He hoped it would help their working relationship if there was one. "My mother has sacrificed her whole life for my brother, and me. She's had to deal with a lot in the past, and it's only over the last few years that she has developed a strong sense of worth. Nobody pushes her around anymore. My mother is fearless, capable, and dogged. I thought the Calhouns might have filled you in a little about our history."

Andy shook his head, "They also forgot to mention how curt your mother is."

"It's a defense mechanism. It takes her time to trust somebody, but once she processes things she comes around. Mom is a fair, and honest person. She is also a fearless woman, who can no longer be intimidated. She will be the boss."

Andy liked the young man, and hoped he was right about the mother.

When Trace and Andy were done, Trace went back inside. He stated the obvious, "I was taken aback when I first saw Andy. If he shaved his beard, he would look just like Dad."

Lola agreed, "Unlike your dad, the man doesn't have an ounce of charm. If we hire him, he better understand that I won't be walked on because I'm a woman."

"You weren't very cordial to him. Don't treat him unfairly, because of how he looks. It's not his fault that he reminds you of Dad. He deserves to be given a fair chance going into this. I like the man, and if the Calhouns recommended him he deserves the work if his quote is fair."

Lola stomped away, angry at herself because Trace was right.

*****

Lola updated Trace when they sat down for their evening meal, "Andy Shaw has a quote, and drafted plans for the proposed job. He's coming here tomorrow after lunch." It had been a couple of weeks, and Lola couldn't contain her excitement.

"Do I have to be here to referee?"

"Don't be a smart-ass, Trace. I can handle Andy on my own."

"It's Andy I'm worried about."

"Very funny. If his quote is fair, are you okay if I hire him?"

"I am if you are. He and I can discuss the horse facility later."

The next morning Lola was apprehensive. She was nervous about seeing Andy. She wasn't proud of her behavior the day they met. She greeted him with a courteous smile, and a firm handshake. Lola swallowed hard, "Before we proceed, I owe you an apology. We got off on the wrong foot, and it was my fault. I was discourteous and impolite."

Andy decided to be as direct as she had been, "Will I have to deal with your attitude every day if you hire me?"

"I'd like to say no but I can't promise."

"I still think working for you could be a challenge, but I appreciate your honesty. I will learn to deal with your lack of tact."

Lola started to laugh. "I deserve that. I'll do my best to be reasonable." Andy hadn't backed down, but he wasn't confrontational. Lola felt herself warming up to him.

"I would appreciate the business."

"Let's take a look at what you've got."

Andy popped off the rubber band, unrolled the drawings, and waited.

"I'm impressed," Lola said as she studied the drawings. She noted the details that Andy had added or altered and considered each one carefully. Lola approved of the revisions. When she saw the detailed breakdown of his quote, she had to smile. Andy had obviously picked up on the fact that she would want justification of his prices. If he paid the same kind of attention to his work, she knew he would do a good job. "As you know, I will be overseeing the garage build from start to finish." This project was important to her, and she wanted to be part of the process. "I intend to be involved step by step. I hope that won't be a problem for you?"

Andy grimaced, "As you so emphatically pointed out, you're the boss, Mrs. Grayson."

"I would like to start as soon as possible." Seeing the look on Andy's face, she stopped herself. "I'm sorry, Andy. I'm caught up by the excitement of all of this. When can you start?"

"Permits are required, and they can take up to six weeks. I'll schedule you in for the end of next month. Unless things change, I'll be back then with my crew. I'll have to decide if I need one less because you'll be helping or one extra because you are helping."

To Andy's surprise, Lola laughed. "I'm not intimidated by your growl, and please call me, Lola. It will be wonderful," she added with confidence.

"You can tell Trace that once he has the rest of his details for me, I will finalize his quote within a couple of days."

Trace arrived home just after Andy left. "Did you hire, Andy?"

"I did. I'm confident that he will do a good job." Lola rubbed her hands together. "I can hardly wait to get started."

Trace put his arms around his mom, "I hope Andy is as excited as you are?" He wondered how many times Andy and his mom would butt heads.

*****

Lola was pleased with the work that Andy's crew were doing. Most of the time Lola and Andy worked well together. Andy recognized the focused side of her personality and was no longer bothered by her frankness. He came to realize that she was matter of fact, as opposed to demanding. But there were still times that they butted heads. Today was one of those days.

Lola was tired of the ever-present tradesmen. They had been there for months. Thankfully, the end was in sight.

Andy spotted Lola in worn jeans, and work boots, working on the area around the garage. Lola had earned his respect. "I have those tile samples you wanted. If you can decide today, I can pick them up tomorrow."

They walked over to Andy's truck. Lola didn't like any. She pointed to one, "This is close, but it's too blue. Bring back samples like this, but with gray tones?"

"I'll put off the tilers until next week. This means another delay."

When Lola put her mind to something, nothing was going to stop her. To Lola, the changes justified the delay. "I know that, but that's the way it is. Even with delays, I'm sure there are other things to do." Lola knew Andy was more irritated than usual when he stomped away muttering under his breath. Maybe she was being a little demanding, but there were still times that a man could put her on the defensive. Despite delays like this one, everything was coming together.

Andy was about to leave for the day when Will showed up. He wanted to talk to Trace. "How's it going, Andy?"

"There is no reasoning with that woman," Andy mumbled. "She's stubborn like a mule when she gets something in her head."

Will just smiled. He, too, had dealt with the stubborn side of Lola Grayson.

"It's a good thing that the garage is almost done. Trace and I are going to start his facility next week. She better not be in my face every day with that project." Andy left in a huff.

Will headed over to where Trace was clearing the area where Andy's sub-contractor would start work. Will was worried about all the hours Trace was putting in between the two ranches. He could see the strain on Trace's face. Will got right to the point, and expressed his concerns, "You can't keep up the pace you've been going, especially with the upcoming start of the project with Andy. Don't let your pride get in the way. I know you want to spend more time at Lola Grande. Cole and Lance are going to be kept on full-time. You can start to hand over the reins at Valley View, and they can help you at Lola Grande until Riley's done school."

Trace leaned back against the fence rail. He was bone tired. Lola Grande was a demanding responsibility. At times it was overwhelming because there was always something else to do. Another section of the fence on the north boundary needed to be fixed, but he hadn't gotten to it. Trace rubbed the back of his neck to ease the built-up tension. With Riley gone, his days had often stretched into fifteen-hour workdays. Up until now he'd been able to cope, but Trace knew Will was right. Trace's other issue, a very personal one, was that deep down he felt that once he was done at Valley View, he would be losing another part of Buster.

Will placed a hand on the young man's shoulder. "Buster will be with you every day even if you're not at Valley View."

Trace swallowed his pride and accepted Will's offer.

*****

Riley had finished his two-year program at Olds, and graduated top of his class. He was expected home sometime today. He would be working full-time at Valley View. His focus would be on the business side of the operations of C&G Ranching. Trace would continue training at Valley View for a while longer, but the training was now all through Trace's company, Caballo Stables. Lola was doing the books for Lola Grande, and Caballo Stables. Life was moving forward with positive changes.

Trace had to admit that he was glad that Riley was done school. Now he could devote his time to Lola Grande and focus on the new build. His vision was becoming a reality. Riley's voice broke through Trace's thoughts, as he was cleaning the tack room. Trace turned, thrilled to see his brother. He had missed Riley.

Riley noticed the lines of strain on Trace's face. He knew it had been a long two years for his brother. Now that he was home, he hoped it would make a difference. "I figured you'd be here, so I stopped on the way before heading home."

Trace stood up and stretched out his back. "Was it me or Shelby you wanted to see?"

Riley grinned, "Is she home yet?" While Riley was at Olds College, Shelby was taking courses at NAIT, in Edmonton.

"I think BJ said she's back tomorrow."

"I couldn't wait that long to get home," came the familiar voice that the boys had grown up hearing. The long-legged blonde gave Riley her radiant smile as she ran into his arms.

Riley's heartbeat quickened, and his face lit up. The boy was crazy about this girl.

Shelby couldn't hold back her exciting news, "I talked to Doc Parker. I'm going to start working part-time at his vet clinic next week. I'll be full-time by the end of the summer." Her eyes rested on Riley, "I better head over to the house, and see my folks. Call me later, and we can get together tonight."

Riley nodded. "I better head home, too. I'm sure Ma is waiting. See you later."

PART III

Chapter Thirteen

Will was startled when Kit shook him to get his attention to tell him it was time for lunch. He had spent the whole morning reflecting on the Graysons. He wondered what impact the arrival of Kit Bennett would have on everyone. He was wise enough to know that life could change quickly, and it wasn't always what you expected. Life was always full of surprises.

Will left right after lunch to help BJ at his house, and Sadie headed out to the garden. It had been a trying morning for Kit. Kenzie was in a whiney mood that was less than adorable. Just what I need today, she thought as her head began to pound. When Kenzie suddenly threw her favorite stuffy across the room, Kit lost her patience, "Go and pick Mucky up right now." Kenzie reacted by throwing herself to the floor. This type of behavior was never acceptable, but today it was more than Kit could tolerate. She picked Kenzie up to take her to her room. When she smoothed her daughter's hair back from her forehead it felt hot. Kit noticed Kenzie's cheeks were also flushed.

"Sorry, Mommy." Kenzie nuzzled into her mom, and whimpered, "I want Mucky."

Sadie, who had just come in from outside with a bowl of fresh strawberries, wondered what was going on. She picked Mucky up and handed him to Kenzie. She placed a hand on Kit's shoulder in a comforting gesture.

Kit was touched by how non-judgmental Sadie was. "Kenzie is running a fever, and she says her tummy hurts. I'm sure it's nothing more than a bug, but she's been miserable all morning. Come, baby girl, let's go put you to bed until you feel better." Kit carried her daughter to her room. She changed Kenzie into a fresh nightgown and wiped her face and neck with a cold cloth. "Is that better?" she asked as she sat down next to her daughter.

Kenzie nodded, cuddled Mucky and fell asleep. Kit watched her daughter's chest rise and fall, pulled up the covers, then kissed her flushed cheek. Completely exhausted, Kit walked across the room, sat in the chair by the window, and sighed heavily. Being a single mother was hard enough when everything was going well.

Kit was startled when Will stepped into the room. She had obviously fallen asleep.

"How's our Doodle Bug?" Will asked with worry. Kenzie had stolen the old man's heart.

Kit was touched by his concern. "She is doing better. Her fever broke about an hour ago so she's less restless. I'm sure she'll be back to being a holy terror by tomorrow."

"Why don't you take a break while I sit with her."

With more willpower than strength Kit got up and dragged herself off to the kitchen.

Sadie was at the sink peeling potatoes for supper. "How's Kenzie?"

"She's sleeping soundly. Will is in with her."

Sadie was concerned when Kit dropped heavily into her chair. "How about you? You look like you're sick, too."

Kit thought about denying it, but she didn't have the energy. Her voice filled with dismay, "I do feel a little weak." She didn't confess that she had a pounding headache.

"You need to go to bed, Kit. Kenzie will be fine." Before Kit could refuse, Sadie's voice became firm, "When you're sick you need to rest. Off you go."

Kit didn't argue as she headed to her room. She changed into her pajamas and fell into bed. Her hair fell across her pale cheek as she closed her eyes, aware of nothing other than the fact that her head continued to throb. She drifted off, stirring occasionally. A pattern that lasted throughout the night.

Kit opened her eyes. She lay still for a minute before realizing it was morning. By the time she'd showered and dressed, she was feeling almost human. Kit twisted her hair up and put on a little make-up to give herself some artificial color.

"Are you feeling better this morning, dear?" Sadie asked when Kit entered the kitchen.

Kit nodded, "How's Kenzie?"

"Back to normal. Will and BJ had to pick up supplies, so they decided to take her along. Are you up for coffee, and something to eat?"

"Toast might hit the spot. Are you and Will feeling, okay?"

"We're fine. We aren't run down like you have been."

Kit smiled gratefully when Sadie set the toast in front of her, realizing she was hungry. The ladies were still sitting at the table when Kenzie blew into the kitchen.

Kenzie ran to her mom, "Come, Mommy. I have a new bike." Kenzie tugged at Kit, who let herself be led outside by her excited little girl.

They watched as BJ unloaded a child's pink two-wheel bike that was decked out with streamers, and training wheels.

BJ grinned at his daughter. "Grandpa thought she needed a bike. Next thing will be a horse," he added.

Kit shook her head at that, hoping he was joking. One look at her grandparents, and she knew he was serious. They continued to watch as BJ helped Kenzie onto her bike and held onto the back as she started to pedal.

"Faster, Grandpa," Kenzie said as she giggled with joy.

Tears glistened in Kit's eyes as she looked at Will and Sadie. "He would have been a good dad. I'm glad I have all of you as my family."

That night, Kit was sitting alone on the verandah when BJ strolled over from the other house. "Am I interrupting anything?"

"Your parents are watching television. Kenzie is down for the night, so I made my escape. Kenzie was worn out from all the bike riding. Your granddaughter loves her bike."

BJ closed his eyes, once again overcome by sadness for the loss of years. He had no idea what Kit's life had been like. "I know why you came here, and I'm glad you're staying. Sadly, I don't know much else about my own daughter. I want to know more about you."

Kit hoped that when she and BJ talked, she would learn more about him as well.

BJ took her hand in his and gave her a look filled with regret. "Let's talk about you first. There are so many things I want to know. I need you to fill me in on what you've been doing all these years."

Kit knew what it was like to desperately want something. As anxious as Kit was to know more about him, she appreciated that she was the only one who could tell him about herself. Thanks to Will and Sadie she already knew things about the Calhouns, including her dad. Watching his face, she felt a stab of sympathy for him.

At first their conversation felt awkward. Both unsure of each other. Both afraid of saying too much, or too little.

"When I was growing up, I'd fantasize about having a father. One who would dote on me as daddy's little girl. We'd have father-daughter moments. He would love me no matter what. I know it will take time for you to accept me."

BJ studied her for a moment before answering, "I may still be learning how to deal with this, but I accepted you the minute I realized you were my daughter. Your future is here, Kit. I would like you, and Kenzie to stay for good. This can be your home."

This had to be one of the sweetest moments of Kit's life. Kit nodded, knowing that they could build a relationship while moving forward. He could give her what she wanted, what she needed. "Thank you for offering me an identity I can pass on to my daughter."

"She is my granddaughter. I know you were mainly raised by your grandmother. It must have been exceptionally hard on you to lose her."

"It was, because for the most part she was the only parent figure I knew. She knew it was wrong not to tell me sooner that I might have a dad, but I'm so grateful that she broke her promise to Torrie. Lou did the right thing by telling me. I believe I did, too, by coming here. You deserved to know that you had a daughter, but I put no thought to the impact it would have on your life, and those in it. I'm sorry for that."

BJ spent the next few hours talking to his daughter and catching up on her life, and she on his. As Kit opened up, and shared, BJ interjected with stories of his own.

"I'm curious about your rodeo life since that's where you, and Torrie met."

"Dad said you had asked about my rodeo days."

"Do you miss the rodeo?"

"No. It was exciting at first. I liked being away from home, because the lifestyle was different, and I was young. Reality dulled it quickly. I soon realized it wasn't all thrills and excitement. There was a rodeo in one town, and then we'd drive to the next rodeo town. One town became the same as the last. Most of the time was spent in an arena, fairgrounds, and parking lots. I wasn't really seeing the world. I was just zigzagging across the country. When I left the rodeo circuit, it was because I wanted to. Ranching was my life just like it has been for the generations before me. I didn't know how much I'd missed the ranch until I moved back."

"What was it like being in the rodeo?"

"In truth, it's a dangerous, dirty career, but when you're young all you see is the excitement, and adventure. It was a hard life, a life with little stability, and no roots. It's a contest of strength. and endurance. Man against beast. The men are tough, rugged, and wild like the animals they ride. If you were lucky, things didn't go wrong. When things went wrong it could be deadly."

The look on BJ's face changed, and Kit guessed what was coming.

"Shelby's birth father, Dallas Reed, was my best friend, and we did everything together. We participated in local rodeos, and by high school we were good enough to compete at state levels. We both joined the rodeo circuit full-time right after graduation. I was good, but Dallas was always ahead in points. Dallas, unlike me, had the size, and build of a rodeo cowboy. He was shorter, and compact. He had the potential to be a champion bull rider. There was another big difference between the two of us. Every time I lowered myself onto a bull, I prayed I wouldn't get hurt if I got bucked off. It isn't possible to ride successfully with that kind of fear. Dallas expected to last the eight seconds every time he left the chute. He'd laugh in the face of danger. If he was bucked off, he laughed out of respect to the bull. If he rode the bull, he laughed harder because he knew he won over the bull. The crowd loved him."

"I had never planned on the rodeo as a career, so I quit before I suffered permanent damage to my body. The rodeo, especially bull riding is a young man's sport. Dallas knew what a life of riding could do to a man. It wasn't a question of if a bull rider got injured, but rather when, and how badly. We saw cowboys still in the prime of their lives who were permanently crippled. Even though Dallas knew this, he let the rodeo come first, instead of his family. Dallas was a bad ass cowboy with a fixation for the life of a bull rider. Jenny wanted him to quit, especially once they had Shelby. Every year he promised that it would be his last, but every year he went back. I watched out for Jenny and Shelby while he was gone, just like he had asked. I don't know if he knew that I had never stopped loving his wife."

"What happened to Dallas?"

Another silence as BJ became lost in thought, remembering the day that took his friend's life, and changed his. Not all of those images had faded. They never would. BJ attended the rodeo to support Dallas. Regardless of everything else, he was, and always would be, his best friend. Their friendship was too strong to let their differences prevent them from being there for each other. BJ sat by himself in the bleacher seats, but the stands were full. The hoots and hollers around BJ were deafening. Everyone was clapping and called out encouragement when it was Dallas's turn. BJ found himself experiencing the familiar rush of adrenaline, followed by the buildup of fear. It was a crazy way to make a living.

Dallas waved to the crowd before he climbed over the boards with his cocky confidence. As he lowered his body onto the back of Wild Willie, the crowd went wild. The fans knew what was at stake, and it came down to this last ride. An eight second ride would qualify him for the Calgary Stampede. Wild Willie snorted and shifted direction as soon as Dallas lowered his body. The raging bull thrashed and reared, forcing Dallas to refocus. Dallas nodded his head, and the gate swung open. The crowd went silent.

BJ tensed as he watched the bull hurl forward, and leap in the air trying to dislodge the rider from his back. The bull was spinning in every direction. With head plunged down, he again shifted direction. Dallas was spectacular and rode Wild Willie hard. BJ held his breath for the full eight seconds. It wasn't until the horn blew, and the crowd cheered, that he exhaled. Before Dallas could dismount, Wild Willie bucked him off, and slammed him against the boards. Dallas hit the ground hard and didn't move. The bull wasn't done. Still bucking, the enraged bull charged, and stomped on Dallas before he could be rescued. BJ flinched while he struggled to breathe. It was as if the charging bull had stomped on his own chest. The crowd was quiet as they sat motionless, as motionless as Dallas Reed. No one knew that when Dallas fell, he broke his neck, and could only lay there while Wild Willie stomped his final breath out of him. Dallas's life-long dream was the death of him. BJ rose, his vision blurred. After confirming facts with the officials, BJ left knowing he had to go to Jenny. The burden of telling Jenny lay on him due to a promise made years ago.

Reliving those memories still hurt. BJ took a deep breath before continuing, "One minute a person is here, living and breathing. The next he is gone. It was the internal injuries that killed Dallas, which is just as well. He would have been paralyzed from the neck down. That would have been a living hell for Dallas. Bull riding is an ugly sport that takes too many lives."

A sudden feeling of compassion for Shelby tore through Kit. She was a toddler when she lost her dad in a horrific accident. It touched Kit that BJ was a responsible family man who had stepped into the role as Shelby's father so naturally. Maybe he would do it again with her. Kit could see that Will and Sadie had instilled valued principles in their son. Once again, Kit was reminded of the strong family ties that had been passed down from generation to generation. She may not have had this, but she was going to make sure her daughter would.

BJ had an odd expression on his face. "I looked hard at my life twice. The first time was when I gave up the rodeo. and committed to Valley View, and ranching. The second time was when I committed to Jenny. I married her and adopted Shelby. Both have been life changing in a good way. You did this when you came here. Both our lives are changing again. I'm sure this, too, will be a good thing for both of us."

That's how it began. The intertwining of lives that had been separated so many years ago by a lie. BJ looked up at the black sky. "It's later than I thought."

Despite having a mother who was a poor role model, BJ could see that Kit was a good person, and a caring mother. The endearing smile he gave her was kind and understanding. "You're a good mother. That's only one of the things I admire about you, Kit."

At that, Kit managed a genuine smile. "I try to be. Thanks again for buying Kenzie the bike, Dad."

BJ's heart soared. This was the first time she had called him, Dad. It was a memorable moment. Too moved to speak, BJ only nodded as he got up, and left.

Kit could hear him whistling on his way home. Kit remained outside. In no hurry to go in, she got up, leaned against the rail, and stared into the night sky. She thought she had started out doing this for her daughter, and her dad, but now she knew it was for herself as well.

Chapter Fourteen

K it was sitting and having morning coffee with Will and Sadie while Kenzie sat on the floor playing. "Do you like living here?" Will asked purposely.

Kit still missed Lou, but these two wonderful people made her feel like she was part of a family again. It felt right. "I love it here, but I feel I should be doing something."

"We are in a bit of a dilemma in regard to the office, and we could use a little help. Our bookkeeper fell and broke her hip in May and has decided not to come back to work. We haven't had time to find a replacement and wondered if you could help us out."

"I'll be glad to help out as long as you need me." Kit felt this would give her a chance to build a relationship with them instead of feeling like a house guest.

Will's next statement caused Kit to question her decision. "Besides our family, you'll deal with the Grayson brothers, because Valley View and Lola Grande co-share business operations under the name of C&G Ranching. Riley is the main person you'll be working with, but we'll all be in and out from time to time."

Kit's enthusiasm waned due to the sick feeling in the pit of her stomach as Trace's dark image appeared. "How will they feel about that?"

"They had no problem when Fran was here, so it shouldn't make any difference." Will got up and banged his bad leg against the table leg. "Damn," he swore as his knee buckled.

"Papa said, damn," Kenzie announced, her eyes alight with mischief.

Sadie scowled at her husband, "I told you not to swear in front of the child, Will Calhoun."

Kit picked Kenzie up and put her on her knee. In a stern voice she scolded her daughter, "You know better than that, Kenzie Bennett. Do you want to go to your room?"

Kenzie looked up innocently, "Papa should go to his room?"

"Let's go look at the office," Will stammered, wanting to make his escape.

Kit scanned the room and hoped she didn't look as dazed as she felt. There was clutter everywhere. The fact that the office equipment was the newest technology was the only positive.

Will shook his head, "I'd like to say that it's not as bad as it looks, but it's actually worse. It became too much for Fran, but she never said anything. We didn't realize things had gotten this bad until after she left. Spring is our busiest time, so there's been no time to catch up. Are you sure you want to tackle this?"

"I'm sure," Kit said with conviction. "It is what it is."

"No pressure, but when can you start?"

"There's no time like the present. The sooner I start the sooner it gets done."

"You'll be mainly working with men, so you might hear the occasional cuss word," Will confessed, attempting to make light of his earlier transgression.

"Not to worry, but Kenzie knows better than to say certain words."

Will could see that Kit was a little flustered. "How about GiGi, and I take the Doodle Bug for a ride? It will give you the rest of the morning to check things out."

"I could use a couple of hours in here uninterrupted." Kit knew she had been accepted as family by the Calhouns. She would learn to deal with the Grayson boys.

After Will left, Kit took a deep breath, and let it out. She looked around, grateful for the time to assess the clutter. There was no doubt that this was going to be a challenge. She sat down at the desk and began going through the box of receipts that had piled up for months. A deep male voice broke her concentration. Kit recognized Trace's voice even before she looked up. She hadn't heard him, so she didn't know how long he'd been standing there watching her.

Trace stood in the doorway with his shoulder propped against the door jam. His arms were folded over his broad chest as he glared at her. When he did speak, his voice was deep, and authoritative, "What are you doing sitting at Will's desk going through his papers?"

Kit was locked by his gaze for an annoying moment, before she managed to overcome the hypnotic effect of his steely eyes. Kit felt claustrophobic as his tall muscular frame now stood in front of her.

Trace dropped into the chair across from her. He leaned back and tipped his hat away from his forehead. His manner was easy, and confident. "There was no one in the house so I thought Will might be here. Where is everyone?" He waited, attempting to pry information out of her by sheer intimidation. Getting no response, an angry expression crossed his face. She was getting under his skin. "You haven't answered my question."

Kit refused to let this man intimidate her. "I don't keep track of the activities of everyone around here, but Will and Sadie took Kenzie for a ride, and won't be back until lunchtime."

"So, you decided to snoop around? I would have thought you had enough decency not to start poking your nose where it doesn't belong."

Keeping her voice civil, but cool, Kit said pointedly, "I don't have to explain my actions to you, but Will has asked me to help them out." She returned to the pile of paper hoping that Trace would get the hint.

Kit sounded genuine, but Trace didn't buy it. "Where's BJ?"

Kit bristled at his tone. Keeping her voice even despite his unnerving presence, she replied, "I don't know, but as you can see, he isn't here." Kit turned away, dismissing him. Instead, Trace reached across the desk to grasp her wrist. Kit slapped his hand away. "Keep your hands to yourself, cowboy."

"I'll be keeping my eye on you, Kit. Like a hawk." He rose and left. The threatening words had been spoken quietly, but their impact was loud and clear.

Even though the confrontation had passed, it took Kit several minutes to compose herself. She couldn't figure out why this man was giving her such a hard time.

After supper they all went out and sat on the front verandah. The wind had picked up, and Kit could hear it whistling through the trees. She glanced out at the thunderclouds hanging over the mountains and wondered if it would rain overnight.

Will unexpectedly dropped a bombshell on Kit. "Since you've decided to stay, there's no sense paying for storage. BJ is going to talk to Riley to see if he will pull a stock trailer down to Washington, so you can bring your things here. Kenzie will be fine with us, and you'll only be gone a couple of days."

Kit's heart stopped, and mixed emotions took over. She knew it was the only way of letting go of the past and moving forward with her new family. Accepting this, she realized she had never been away from Kenzie.

*****

The brothers were curious. It wasn't often that a meeting was called. The hair on Trace's neck raised when he saw Kit standing between BJ and Will. BJ got right to the point, "I want to update you on a new development. Fran is recovering nicely, but she won't be coming back to work." He turned and smiled at Kit. "Fortunately, Kit has agreed to step in and help."

Kit took in their reaction. Riley's face was warm, and open. Trace, on the other hand, was wary, and suspicious. He merely raised an eyebrow. His unyielding body did the talking. He didn't like this one bit. Trust had always been an issue with him. The sparks continued between them when they made eye contact. Kit quickly turned her attention back to BJ, who continued with his news. The way BJ spoke about her, and what she would be doing reassured Kit, but she knew she had a lot to prove.

Trace appeared interested in what was being said, but Kit knew better. She was surprised when he spoke, "Welcome, Kit. It looks like you've made yourself at home and slid your way into the family business nicely. It will be interesting to see what other skills you have." On the positive side, Trace thought, this would make it easier for him to keep an eye on her. If she were up to no good, he would soon know it. He still felt that she was a gold digger.

Unconsciously, Kit rubbed her wrist where Trace had grabbed her. Riley walked over to welcome her. His easy manner made her feel better.

She was relieved when Trace, and BJ excused themselves. Will took his leave as well.

Kit and Riley decided they would spend the rest of the morning going over the basics. After that, Kit could delve into things on her own. He addressed the piles of files, "Fran was old school, the computer intimidated her."

They were deep in discussion when Shelby walked in. Seeing Kit, she halted in her tracks. "Gram told me you were in the office, but I didn't know Kit was here with you." Shelby stared at Kit with a piercing gaze, "What are you doing in here?"

It was Riley who replied, "I guess you haven't heard the news yet. Kit is going to be helping us out in the office now that Fran is gone."

Shelby looked at Riley as if she didn't understand English. Her eyes were livid when the realization hit her. Kit had no intention of leaving. Shelby's tone turned cold, "I'm heading home. Will you pick me up at four instead of five? I have an errand to run before we meet the others for dinner. Or has that changed as well in the last few hours?"

Kit was reasonably sure that Shelby was used to getting her own way, so she wasn't surprised when Riley readily agreed.

"This office is looking worse than it ever did," Shelby said, in an icy tone, implying that they were doing nothing more than having a good time.

Kit couldn't resist the opportunity to irritate Shelby even more, "Want to help?"

"Don't be ridiculous." Shelby turned and stormed out.

They laughed, knowing they'd both pay for it later. Kit enjoyed how Riley laughed. Carefree, as if he didn't have a care in the world. In fact, that was his personality. Nothing like his hard-headed brother. How could two brothers be so different?

"Sorry about that. She gets that way on occasion. I'll smooth her ruffled feathers later."

"The girl has attitude. If I let everything Shelby does get to me, she'd drive me crazy. As far as I'm concerned, she is immature, and lives full-time in the world of Shelby."

"She gets to you, huh?"

"Not to worry. I can handle her."

"I know Shelby won't be happy that we'll be spending time together every day. Part of the problem is that she's jealous of you."

"Why would she be jealous? You and I are just working together." Kit looked around at the stacks of paper everywhere. "I have my work cut out for me, Riley. I could use the rest of today to get a handle on what all of this is."

"Okay. I'll go and try to unruffle feathers." They agreed to establish a routine when they returned from Washington. It would give Kit a couple of days to sort through the mound of paperwork. "Wish me luck," he called over his shoulder.

Kit knew he would need it considering he obviously hadn't told Shelby about the trip to Washington. Feathers could fly over that.

*****

Kit was pleased with what she had accomplished in the last couple of days. She looked at the bare surface of the desk knowing it had been a long time since it had seen the light of day. The box of loose receipts had been sorted, and the paid ones had been scanned into computerized files. She was struggling to put a box of old files on the top shelf of the closet while standing on her tip toes. Just as it started to slip, strong hands reached above her.

"Problems, city girl?" Trace's amused voice came from behind her, as he pushed the box forward. She found herself leaning against a solid wall of muscle. Seeing the look on Kit's face he knew he was in for it. Everyone on the ranch called it the "Calhoun look".

"You mean besides you? I am capable of doing things myself. I've lived my whole life without needing a man." Reacting to Trace's quirked eyebrow, Kit blew up. "Do you think every time a light bulb needs replacing, a fuse blows, the faucet drips, or the toilet overflows I sit down and cry waiting for a man to come, and solve my problem? If that were the case, I'd be sitting in the dark knee deep in water."

Trace listened to her rant with amusement. She was a pistol who fired at him every time he offered help. He did a quick survey of the room. In short time, Kit had completely taken over the office. He couldn't believe the transformation. Trace hated to admit that he was impressed. Kit was obviously competent, at least in her organizational skills. "You've been busy."

Kit threw him an exasperated look which he ignored. She wished he'd leave. Not that she feared him. She simply preferred to avoid him. Keeping her voice as even as possible, she glared up at him, "Is there something I can help you with?"

Trace reached into his shirt pocket, pulled out a receipt, and tossed it on the desk.

Kit placed the receipt in the "IN" tray. "You will notice that the shoe box is gone. From now on all invoices and receipts go into the "IN" tray. Efficiency will eliminate extra work. More importantly, it will reduce the chance of something getting lost. I'm trying to set up a routine that will work well for everyone. Now if you'll excuse yourself, as you can see, I have work to do." The man had exhausted her patience and the day had just started.

Trace could do with a little less attitude from her. "Aren't you smug this morning."

"I'm just confident in my abilities. I work hard, and I'm good at what I do." She returned to the file in front of her, an obvious act of dismissal. One that Trace ignored.

"You continually surprise me," he said.

Conflicting emotions raced through Kit. There was a draw to him despite the fact that he continually annoyed her. If only she wasn't so aware of him. This irritated her so she retaliated, "Why? Because I don't throw myself at you?" He was not her type by any stretch of her imagination. Though she could understand why some women might find him attractive, she found him to be arrogant, insufferable, and narrow-minded.

Trace laughed. "You think women throw themselves at me?"

"Don't they?"

He grinned. "Sometimes, but I've been good at dodging them."

The man had the cockiest attitude. "You are either conceited or delusional. I don't know which one. Maybe they changed their minds when they realized how insufferable you are."

"Here I though you found me charming." Trace was beginning to enjoy baiting her.

"You're flattering yourself." Kit had reached the point where she could only think of escape. Needing a minute to compose herself, Kit left on the excuse to refill her coffee mug. She brushed past Riley on the way out the door.

"Kit looked upset. What did you say to her?" Riley demanded to know as he walked in.

"Nothing. Her problem is she has attitude. Everything was working fine until she got here." Things were changing right in front of him, and Trace didn't like change.

"Don't be ridiculous, Trace. The old way of bookkeeping is tedious. Office procedures have been inefficient for a long time. You saw the mess this place was in. Kit's going to be a real asset around here."

As much as Trace hated change, he realized it was something he had no control over. Trace knew if Kit heard Riley singing her praises, she would have given him a smug look.

Riley tried not to be judgmental of his brother, but lately Trace had become impatient, and more irritable than usual. Whatever was bothering his brother, Riley was sure it had to do with the young lady who just stormed out. "You know what your problem is, Trace? You finally met a woman you can't handle. I think you have a thing for BJ's daughter. Anyone with half a brain can see you use every excuse to be at Valley View these days."

Trace became strangely quiet and turned away. From the day Trace met Kit objectivity hadn't been an option. Never had he allowed a woman to get to him like Kit had. Trace glared at Riley as he headed out the door.

Riley laughed. He enjoyed pushing his big brother's buttons.

When Kit returned, she was relieved to see that Trace had left.

Riley apologized for his brother's behavior, "Was Trace giving you a hard time?"

"He was here to submit an invoice and irritate me."

"From the tone of your voice it sounds like he succeeded."

Kit didn't know what Riley was smiling about. Still irritated, she glared at him, too. Riley left, and Kit plunged into her work. Despite Trace, Kit was happy. She enjoyed what she was doing. It filled her day and gave her purpose. She looked over at the avalanche of paperwork that was on the worktable hoping it wouldn't topple over. Piece by piece, she sorted, and filed. It was later than she realized when she checked the time. Deciding to call it a day, and go help Sadie get supper, Kit shut down the computer. She allowed her thoughts to drift as Trace's image invaded her mind. She knew she was too sensitive when it came to Trace. Suddenly Kit knew she wasn't alone. She looked up, and Trace was in the doorway watching her. Kit recalled him saying he was going to keep an eye on her, but this was getting ridiculous. "What do you want now?"

"I thought BJ might be here. Murphy said he was on his way over." There was no reason talking to BJ couldn't wait until later, but he made no move to leave. Trace stroked his jaw before he said, "We need to talk." Kit had been on his mind all day.

"I'm done for the day." This man had already tested the limits of her patience.

The coolness of her response didn't stop him, "I have to admit I was caught off-guard when they hired you."

Trace's distrust was still evident. Besides, what he thought of her was of no importance to her. It was just confusing. "If you listened better, you'd have heard I'm helping out. Nobody hired me. I'm not getting paid to take your abuse so you can leave it at the door."

Trace was impressed that she refused to back down, while putting him in his place. "I want to apologize. I may have misjudged you."

Kit wasn't sure if she'd heard correctly. Was the cowboy apologizing? She questioned his sincerity.

"I can tell that this is important to you," Trace said, as if it was something he was just coming to understand.

His comment eased her anger. "It's the least I can do while Kenzie, and I are staying here. I want my family to know that I am someone they can count on. Having another family is new to me. I need time to get to know them." Kit's expression remained serious. "I can handle your skepticism, even your insults, but I'd rather you give me a chance. It's not fair to judge on preconceived doubts before getting to know someone. I did it with my dad when I got here. Probably with you as well."

Trace decided he needed time to figure Kit out. Past experiences had made him wary, but was he wrong about her?

Just then BJ entered, unaware of the tension between them. Kit got the impression he wanted to talk to Trace alone. She was more than ready to make her escape. "I'll leave you two, and go help Sadie with dinner," she said as she darted past the two men.

Kit was chatting comfortably with Sadie when BJ entered the kitchen with Trace right behind him. Kit's face flushed in annoyance. She had endured enough of him for one day. Kit took a deep breath and looked away to collect herself.

"It sure smells good in here. Is that your famous oven stew I smell, Sadie?"

Sadie nodded, "It's not much, but you're welcome to join us. BJ is staying. Jenny has a dinner meeting." She gave him a warm smile, as if he were welcome anytime.

Trace smiled at her affectionately. His easy smile softened his features. Much nicer than his cocky grin. "You don't have to ask me twice. Mom's gone to the city, and Shelby and Riley have plans."

Sadie smiled and set another place as the two men joined Will at the table.

Kit tried to hide her irritation, but she knew that Trace had read her face.

Trace had hoped that Kit had put the events of earlier behind her, but obviously she hadn't. He wondered what, if anything, he could say or do to get on her good side. He needed to get to know her better to understand who the real Kit Bennett was. Another reason he had agreed to stay for dinner. He sat back and watched.

Kenzie wandered over to Trace and looked him over.

"This is my granddaughter, Kenzie," BJ said proudly.

Trace smiled at the adorable little girl. "Hi there, Kenzie. I'm, Trace." His voice was softer, and friendly.

"Whose daddy are you?" the innocent child asked, unexpectedly.

There was a tense moment before Trace answered, "No one's." Trace liked kids as long as they were somebody else's. He didn't have time for family. He liked being single, and he intended to stay that way. "I'm your Grandpa's friend, and Riley's brother."

"I don't have a brother, or a daddy. You can be my daddy."

This time Trace was speechless. The self-assured cowboy was daunted by a toddler. The idea of that amused Kit to no end, but she was quick to break the uncomfortable silence, "Don't take this personally, cowboy. You aren't my type."

"Are you really a cowboy?" Kenzie asked in awe.

Sadie saw Kit roll her eyes and smiled. She smiled wider when she looked at Trace who still looked a little stunned.

Kit walked over to Kenzie and took her hand. "Let's go wash up for supper."

"Can I have a puppy?" they heard as Kit dragged her away.

The evening meal was more enjoyable than Kit expected. During dinner it was mostly the men who talked. The conversation was all about ranching. BJ didn't always agree with his father, but there was no doubt that he respected him. The same could be said for Trace. The interaction between Trace, and the Calhouns had surprised her. Kit was quick to recognize the strong relationships between the two families. Kit glanced toward Trace to find him studying her.

Trace's face had lost its gaze of indifference. When Kit smiled like she did during dinner she seemed almost innocent. Perhaps he had misjudged her, and underneath all her outward bravado lay a vulnerable young woman. His doubts were slowly fading. "Riley says that you're easy to work with and have a lot of good ideas. He says you've taught him a lot about the new computer program that has been installed thanks to you. He thinks you're brilliant."

A light pink hue rose to her cheeks at this compliment, but she doubted that he knew how much it meant to hear the slight tone of approval in his voice. "As you were told, I do have the job skills. It will take time to learn your operations, but Riley and I are making progress. He's teaching me about operating costs, and budget projections. I find it all very interesting."

"Good girl," Will praised. "How's it going otherwise?"

Kit couldn't resist, "It will get better when everyone starts to accept the necessary changes."

The pointed remark only made Trace smile.

Sadie enjoyed watching the interaction between Kit and Trace. She smiled, recognizing the chemistry between them.

Trace patted his flat stomach as he pushed his empty plate aside and groaned. "I can't move. I'm stuffed."

"No room for dessert? It's homemade apple pie."

"Okay, but just a small piece."

"Ice cream?"

"Of course."

"Me, too, GiGi," Kenzie said.

They sat and lingered over coffee, and dessert. Kit had to admit that she enjoyed the evening despite Trace. Kenzie, who was done, was allowed to leave the table. She began dancing with her monkey. She threw Mucky in the air and missed catching him. Trace's carefree laughter drew Kit's gaze. She shook her head knowing that the man was unaware of what he'd done. This now became a game for Kenzie.

Kit and Sadie began clearing the table.

"I'd offer to help but I know better." There was a hint of a smile in his voice, and Kit saw the corners of his mouth curl in amusement.

Sadie smiled at Trace, believing his offer was sincere, but Kit understood the dig behind his innocent words.

"I better be on my way," Trace said as he pushed himself away from the table. He went over and planted a kiss on Sadie's cheek. "Thanks for dinner. Delicious as always." Trace looked over at Kit and flashed his trademark grin, as he said goodnight. Their eyes met and held.

"No need to hurry off, Trace. How about we retire to the verandah."

BJ looked over his shoulder as the two women cleaned the kitchen. "Ma really likes Kit."

Will patted his son on the back, "Why wouldn't she. Kit's a great gal."

Kit overheard the exchange between father and son and wondered what Trace thought.

Once the kitchen had been tidied, and Kit had settled Kenzie for the night, the two women chatted over tea.

"Well, Trace sure took to Kenzie. They say that a man who loves animals, and children is a man to be trusted."

Kit forced herself to acknowledge Sadie's praise of him. "Oh, I would trust him. I just don't like the man."

Sadie raised her eyebrow in surprise. "Trace? You can't be serious."

"For some unknown reason Trace took a dislike to me, and he has made no effort to hide it."

"Maybe you're imagining it."

Kit shook her head. Even though she had seen a different side of him over dinner, the man still bothered her. "From the first moment I laid eyes on Trace the sparks flew."

Sadie smiled to herself, having seen the sparks for herself.

"So, what's the story behind Trace. Riley is an open book who wears his heart on his sleeve. Trace is impossible to read." Kit didn't know what it was about Trace that irritated and attracted her at the same time. He constantly stirred her emotions, and who knew he'd be so comfortable around a young child. "Tonight, at dinner, I saw a different side of him. He's like Dr. Jekyll, and Mr. Hyde."

"Trace has always been intense."

"I know Riley is infatuated with Shelby. Is there someone in Trace's life?"

"No, even though any number of women would love to be Mrs. Trace Grayson. He's been so focused on Lola Grande that he takes no time to have a personal life. Trace isn't anything like you think. He really is a stand-up guy. He's thoughtful, and hardworking. Both Grayson boys are. Unfortunately, Trace tries to carry the burden of his family alone. He feels that the success of Lola Grande is his responsibility as head of the family. He's also a young man with a lot of distrust because of his past." Sadie left it at that, and Kit refused to pry.

Once Kit heard Trace's truck leave, she stepped outside. Her mind was still on Trace. Seeing him more often over the last few days only made it harder for her to remain detached about her complex feelings toward him. Over dinner, when he was relaxed and friendly to everyone, she saw him in a different light. She'd never known such a disturbing man. It was obvious he could charm any female at any age. She saw that tonight with both Sadie, and Kenzie. The wind picked up, and it cut through the thin jacket she wore. Kit didn't go back inside. Instead, she pulled the collar tighter up around her neck. She looked out at the darkened sky where only a few stars glimmered. She was ready to settle here now that she felt like she belonged. She had to admit she was looking forward to getting away for a couple of days. She was glad it was Riley who was taking her. He was easy going, and she felt comfortable around him. Kit knew she would miss Kenzie, but she could use a break from those devil-blue eyes of Trace Grayson.

Chapter Fifteen

Kit knew it was best to get this out of the way, and she wanted to do it before going to Washington. It was time to pay a visit to Jenny, and there was no time like the present. Kit drew a deep breath as she walked across the yard. Despite her best effort to remain composed, her heart was pounding rapidly when she reached the front door. Summoning all her courage, Kit knocked.

Despite her surprise when she opened the door, Jenny recovered quickly. "BJ must not have known you were coming over. He isn't home."

"I would like to talk to you. May I come in?" Kit asked nervously.

Jenny's expression wasn't exactly friendly as she stepped aside to let Kit in. "Can I offer you something to drink?"

"Whatever you're having will be fine."

Jenny led Kit into the kitchen, poured two coffees, and both ladies sat down at the table.

"I want you to understand why it was so important for me to find my dad. I was desperate when my grandmother died. I have no other family. If something should happen to me, I need to know Kenzie will be taken care of. I didn't have a choice, but to find him. Being a mother, I hope you understand."

Jenny nodded. Compassion replaced the indifference in her eyes.

"Once I got here, I quickly realized that this isn't just about me. I didn't know how that day in the hospital would change so many lives. My actions have changed BJ's life, and everyone else's. I didn't think about the consequences, and for that I am sorry."

Jenny's look remained apprehensive. "Some of us still need time to deal with the shock of your arrival."

"I spent agonizing hours trying to make up my mind about what to do when I found my birth certificate. I was afraid of so many things. I was worried that if I found my father, he wouldn't believe me. Or worse, he'd reject me like my mother did."

Jenny realized it couldn't have been easy for Kit to make her decision. It had taken real courage to come all this way not knowing what would be waiting for her. Then to deal with a bunch of strangers dissecting her every move.

Kit couldn't stop herself from confessing, "The Calhouns, including my dad, have shared a lot about all of you. I know that you experienced a significant loss that resulted in big changes in your life. I'm sorry that Shelby lost her dad, and you your husband. I also know what it's like to lose a husband. My husband, Mike, and I had no chance to be a family. Mike was deployed overseas just months after our wedding. I found out I was pregnant shortly after he left. I was still pregnant when Mike was killed. Kenzie never knew her dad." Tears rimmed Kit's lashes.

This touched Jenny deeply for she did know what it was like to experience heartache, and despair. Her voice quivered with remembered pain, "A life can be taken away from you in a heartbeat. You may learn to live with the hurt, bury it with happier memories, but it's still there." Jenny knew what it was like to be young, pregnant, and lonely. The difference was that Kit was also a widow. "You must have had a hard time coping after your husband's death. I know I did. It's such a shock that at first you don't believe it. Then you have to work through the anger. For me, it was the fact that it didn't have to happen. When Dallas and I got married he promised to quit the rodeo and take over the family ranch. That never happened. My hopes kept vanishing like the dust behind Dallas's truck and trailer every time he pulled away."

Old hurt was evident on Jenny's face as past images returned. Those images reeled her in, and took her back, where she remained caught up in the past. A new rodeo season was starting, and once again Dallas was breaking his promise. The first rodeo of the season was in a couple of days, and he was heading out in the morning. Jenny sat on the end of the bed while Dallas packed. "When are you going to get it through your head that you can't keep running off to one rodeo after another." Jenny knew this would lead to another fight, but now that they had Shelby, she refused to remain silent. She couldn't keep up with the ranching on her own.

Dallas's eyes narrowed as he glared at Jenny. He was tired of her nagging every time he was leaving. "You knew what I was when you married me."

Old hurt caused Jenny's temper to flare, "I did, and I know what you are now. You are a lying, cheating cowboy who has a reputation with the ever-present buckle bunnies. You said you would quit the rodeo when we got married. When I told you I was pregnant you swore you'd quit. But nothing changed. Only the women you keep chasing."

"I told you I've never cheated." Dallas turned away, unable to look her in the eyes.

"A wife has a way of knowing, and if you can lie about one thing, you can lie about another. It's sad the lies we tell each other, and how often. For you, this is just a convenient place to lay your head between rodeos. You need to be here full-time running your ranch. You can't keep expecting BJ to step in for you every time you're gone."

Dallas became defensive, "Is BJ also stepping in, and warming your bed while I'm away?" It was the wrong thing to say. He knew it as soon as he said it. His accusation was another reminder of the shamble of their marriage.

Jenny glared at Dallas, "One cheater in the family is enough."

Dallas was stung by the force of Jenny's words, and the truth of her accusations.

Everything was falling apart around her, including her marriage. "I hate this damn ranch," Jenny said, as she slammed the door on her way out.

"So do I." Dallas continued packing.

Jenny didn't know how long she had been lost in the past. Since Kit's arrival, it was happening too often. "I do understand what you went through. In a different way, I was also a single parent. Dallas had complete disregard for the conventional way of life with commitments. He was off riding bulls and having a great time. He was absent more than he was present, and he had no qualms about leaving. I hated being left alone, being responsible for everything. All Dallas wanted was to live the crazy life of a rodeo cowboy. Nothing else seemed to matter to him. Not the ranch. Not even me. Dallas couldn't give it up. He was addicted to the adrenalin rush the rodeo gave him. He was like an alcoholic who always promises to quit drinking, and the next thing you see is a beer in his hand. Dallas was willing to throw our life away on the rodeo. It was a bigger draw than a haggard wife trying to cope with a colicky baby. Life on the ranch was boring to someone who was used to the thrill, and excitement of the rodeo. I was tired of hearing, "This is the last time." knowing it was a promise he couldn't keep."

Jenny revealed her deeper hurt, "Willing women were always around, so it was easy to enjoy the charms of the ladies they'd meet. The cowboys would move on, leaving nothing behind but memories while dreaming of their next rodeo. Dallas swore he never cheated, but deep down I knew. A wife has a way of knowing." This was the part of the past that still haunted her. The resentment in Jenny turned to bitterness, "Dallas should never have gotten married. He belonged to that different breed of men. To everyone else he was Dallas Reed, famous bull rider. He was a champion, a hometown hero, who had climbed to the top of his game. To me, he was the man who chose riding bulls over his family."

Kit, too, had lived a life of broken promises, and shattered dreams, hopes hanging on a fantasy that always vanished in the reality of life. Kit's thoughts drifted to Torrie, who had also chosen a different life over her family. This was something neither woman would ever understand.

Jenny shook her head as if to escape the visions from her past. "I could never understand why anyone would risk their life again and again on the back of a dangerous animal, whose only goal is to buck you off, and stomp you to death. Dallas reached his ultimate dream. It only cost him his life. I thought my life was over when he died. I was left with a child to raise on my own, and knee deep in debt. BJ had no idea I'd been struggling to keep a roof over our heads, and I was losing the battle. Will and Buster had witnessed the steady devastation of our ranch. It all came out when Dallas died. It was even worse than I thought. It was only a matter of time before the ranch would go into foreclosure. The Calhouns stepped in. I swallowed my pride and let them help. BJ swore to Dallas that he'd take care of us if anything ever happened. He did from the day Dallas died. I already loved BJ, but I didn't know if he still loved me, or was only there out of duty to his best friend. When you're feeling that low you question everything."

Kit drained her coffee, and Jenny got up and filled their cups. It was a positive gesture. "I don't usually open up like this, let alone in such a personal way. Not everyone can understand."

"No, they can't."

"You lose more than the person. For a while you lose a part of yourself, and it can take a long time to find it again. I wouldn't have made it through without BJ's support, and love. We have a solid marriage." As soon as Jenny said it out loud, she knew her, and BJ were going to be okay. Nothing between them had changed. "I hope you find the same happiness one day, Kit." Jenny now felt a kinship she hadn't expected to feel.

Kit was silent for a long moment deciding how to phrase her next question. She still had one more topic to discuss. She decided not to mince words. The direct approach was always the best. "I was taught to deal with people fairly and honestly and in turn you expect them to do the same. Shelby has made it clear that she doesn't want me here. Why does Shelby hate me?" Kit asked, with an intense stare that reminded Jenny so much of BJ.

"Shelby feels threatened by you right now. You're getting the attention she's used to getting, and not just from BJ. The Grayson boys seem to be spending more time at Valley View than at Lola Grande."

Kit went on the defensive, "I'm teaching Riley a new computer program, and Trace despises me just like Shelby does."

"It's more a case of Shelby, and Trace not wanting to like you. You've disrupted their comfortable world. Now they have to learn to deal with a big change. I know this because that's what I'm trying to do. Shelby is strong-willed, spirited, and stubborn like Dallas. A little wild, and very determined. BJ, and I may have given her more freedom than what was always wise, but BJ comes down on her when she really messes up. I know he has spoken to Shelby about her behavior toward you more than once. Right now, she isn't receptive to listening. Fear, and anger are cloaking her good traits. She will come around."

Kit hoped so. She was disappointed that it hadn't already happened. "I know you and I got off to a bad start. I'm not a bad person, Jenny. Please don't treat me like an enemy and give me a chance."

Jenny looked hard at Kit. She was so much like her dad. "I did hate you for coming here and disrupting our lives. As you, and I both know, there's no changing the past. We don't always understand it, we just have to deal with it. This was such an unexpected shock. I would have been less surprised if you said your father was Dallas."

Just then Shelby walked in. "Oh, I didn't realize you had company."

Jenny's gaze turned to Kit, "Family is never company." It was a statement of acceptance.

Shelby glared in anger at both of them, turned, and stormed out.

Jenny sobered quickly. More anger to deal with. "I'm glad you, and I cleared the air. It helps that I understand your actions." Now that she'd gotten to know Kit better, her opinion had changed. Jenny knew it had taken a lot of courage for Kit to come here today. Kit had cleared the air and shown Jenny a strength she hadn't wanted to give Kit credit for having. Kit's honesty, and openness had touched something in Jenny. Recognizing a kindred soul, Jenny knew it was time to bridge the gap. "I would be pleased if you let Kenzie call me Grandma."

"I would be pleased, too," Kit said with gratitude.

They smiled at each other; smiles of understanding. They now had a fragile friendship to build on.

"I better get back to the main house. I don't want to take advantage of Sadie. Kenzie can be a handful."

"Sadie doesn't mind. She loves it."

"Sadie is a wonderful lady. It's like she sees only the good in people."

After leaving the house, Shelby needed a shoulder to cry on. As in the past she drove over to Lola Grande to find Riley. She found him in the barn mucking stalls.

Riley could tell by Shelby's manner that she was in a snit. He steeled himself for whatever crisis brought Shelby here this time. "I know that look. Who are you mad at now?" He was sure he knew the answer.

Shelby's voice shook with anger, "I walked in on my mom, and Kit. They were laughing like old friends. Kit keeps digging her way in deeper."

Riley had always tried to talk Shelby out of her moods, but not today. He was tired of her drama. There was noticeable disappointment in Riley's voice that was not lost on Shelby when he said, "Don't you think it's time to grow up, and quit being so self-centered?" He turned and walked over to the next stall.

Shelby felt the sting of his reprimand and was deeply hurt. Her eyes filled with tears. She trailed after him in shock. Riley had changed. She didn't understand him anymore. "Everything's changing." When she looked up at him, she saw sad resignation in his eyes.

Riley sighed heavily. His entire future had always been planned with Shelby in it. There was no doubt that he loved her, but he was getting a little impatient waiting for her to grow up. The spoiled child attitude was beginning to wear thin. "Maybe you should change, too. It's time to grow up, Shelby. This isn't all about you." Riley went back to work.

Shelby resented the pity she read in his eyes and fled in anger.

*****

Kit and Kenzie were outside in the front yard when Shelby pulled up and slammed her pick-up into park. Kit's stomach plunged when she saw the look on Shelby's face. She braced herself knowing it was impossible to make her escape. Not that she feared Shelby, she simply preferred to avoid her. Especially when everything was spinning in her life right now.

Shelby charged up the sidewalk like a raging bull. "My dad just told me that you, and Riley are going to Washington to get your things so you can move in here with my grandparents." Even though she'd been doing her best to make Kit feel unwelcome, it wasn't working. Why couldn't Kit just return to Washington, and stay there instead of making Valley View her home? "I can't believe your gall. You certainly work fast."

Kit struggled to maintain her control, because of Kenzie's presence. "Look, you've made your position clear. You don't want me here, and you hoped we'd be gone by now. Well, Shelby, you don't always get what you want."

"If you stay, I can cause enough trouble to last you a lifetime."

Kit's own anger flared. She put her hand on Shelby's arm in warning, "I can handle your sass, and I'm not afraid of your threats. What I don't like is the chip on your shoulder. Work on that while I'm gone. If you don't, I may have to knock it off when I get back. I am coming back, and I am staying. Deal with it."

It was a fact, and Shelby knew it. Unfortunately, Kit's staying wasn't the only issue in Shelby's life. She was jealous of Kit's new relationship with Riley. "Women like you are all the same. On the prowl for anyone, attached or not. Stay away from the Grayson boys. Riley Grayson is mine and Trace doesn't like you anymore than I do."

Attracting a man was the last thing Kit wanted.

Without another word, Shelby whirled, and stomped down the steps, wrenched the truck door open, and climbed in. Tires squealed as the truck peeled away.

The frustration in Kit's eyes deepened as she replayed the scene with Shelby. It had been upsetting. She decided to stop fretting about what had just happened and concentrate on her reason for staying. Whether the future was easy or hard, this is where she belonged.

Riley, who had been listening in the kitchen, stepped out as Shelby sped down the road.

Kit guessed he'd overheard their exchange. Her eyes burned with furious tears, but she would not cry.

Riley could see that Kit was shaken. "I was going to come out and help, but it sounded like you were doing fine without me. That was quite the argument."

"It's not an argument when somebody jumps down your throat. It's an attack." Kit closed her eyes for a moment struggling to collect herself. "I hate confrontations. They're extremely upsetting."

"I learned a long time ago to stay out of her way when Shelby gets like that."

"I'm tired of walking on eggshells around Shelby. The princess is pampered and moody." Kit hated moody. She'd lived with it for too long with Torrie.

Riley's face broke into an amused smile. "I see the lady has claws."

"I am a Calhoun," Kit stated proudly.

Whatever was going on between Shelby and Kit was far from over. "Give it some time. I'm sure you two will work this out, and you'll win her over."

Nothing had worked so far, so Kit knew how futile an endeavor that would be. Especially considering Shelby's state of mind. She wished Shelby would grow up already.

"Are you sure you're okay?"

"I'm fine," Kit insisted. She refused to allow Shelby's theatrics affect her.

"Liar," Riley replied easily. "A break from Shelby will do you good. I think we should leave early. Are you fine if we leave at eight? We can push it hard and drive straight through. We will have to take two days to return. It'll take time to load up the trailer, and we'll have to drive slower with a full load. We should also expect a delay at the border."

"I'll be ready. See you tomorrow."

That night at supper, Riley mentioned his trip with Kit. "I'll be gone for the next few days. BJ asked if I would hitch up a stock trailer and take Kit back to Walla Walla to collect her belongings. BJ convinced Kit that it was the only way of letting go of the past and moving forward with her new family. He says that Kit agreed to stay with them until the new year. They want everyone to have time to get to know one another."

"How does Shelby feel about this?"

Riley was realistic about Shelby's shortcomings, but he was getting tired of her drama. "She was livid when she heard. She's behaving like a spoiled brat and wants everyone to hate Kit because she does. Most of us took the time to get to know Kit and like her."

Trace's eyes were indifferent as he ignored the intended shot, "I don't think any of us know the real, Kit Bennett. It certainly didn't take her long to move in?"

"What's with you, Trace? You're no better than Shelby. You decided you didn't like Kit the moment you saw her. Give her a chance, she deserves that much."

From the day Trace met Kit, objectivity hadn't been an option. Never had he allowed a woman to get to him as she had. "Give it a rest, Riley," Trace warned his younger brother, as he headed out the door.

As soon as Trace was gone Riley turned to his mom. "I need your help. Trace needs to be the one to take Kit to Washington."

"You have got to be kidding. Listening to him just now, that's the last thing he will agree to." Looking at the mischievous grin on Riley's face, Lola knew there was a whole lot more to this. "What are you up to, Riley?"

"Sadie says that for some reason, Trace seems to have prejudged Kit in a negative way. You saw it for yourself just now. Sadie wants them to spend some time together without any outside influence. If Trace has to take her, he won't be able to ignore Kit. Maybe once he gets to know her better, he will see what the rest of us see."

"Is Sadie playing matchmaker?"

Riley nodded, "She roped me in as her assistant."

"Did you resist in any way?"

Riley shook his head. "Sadie says they are both clearly attracted to each other, and I agree. I've seen enough sparks fly between the two of them to start a prairie fire. Sadie says that Kit's too stubborn to admit it, and the always cocky cowboy doesn't know what's hit him."

Lola shook her head, "You and Sadie have been spending way too much time together discussing two unsuspecting people, and now you want to set them up? There's no telling what might happen. It could be a miserable trip if they really don't like each other."

Riley was enjoying this. "I'm sure my brother's head is spinning most of the time these days. I've never seen Trace so confused by a woman."

"Well, that would explain his ill-humor lately. I thought it was because he was working too hard."

"You have to convince him that I'm sick. You know that Trace won't believe it for a minute if I tell him. Besides, it will do Trace good to get away for a couple of days. Everyone needs a break now and then."

"You do realize that this could go drastically wrong."

"You have to agree that it will do Trace good to get away. He never stops working, so now he will have to. I know Kit will appreciate a break away from Shelby. She has been deplorable to Kit."

"You can be very persuasive when you want something. Is this girl worth the effort?"

Riley's casual expression became serious. "She's a great girl, mom. You don't need to worry about Kit. I've seen her take on Shelby without backing down, so she can hold her own with Trace."

"She'll have to if Trace agrees to this."

"So, you'll do it?"

They exchanged an amused smile. Lola nodded, and immediately questioned her decision.

Chapter Sixteen

T race exploded when he heard that Riley was sick, and he was expected to take Kit to Washington. He didn't trust his brother, but his mom swore that Riley was too sick to go, so he accepted that he had no choice. He made a couple of calls to rearrange his schedule and headed to Valley View.

As soon as Trace was gone Riley entered the kitchen. "I should probably wait a while before I head over to Valley View, just in case there is a delay in their leaving."

"What? Like Kit refuses to go with Trace."

"As if Trace would let her. She may not go willingly, but he'll persuade her to go one way or another. It's out of our hands now."

Kit woke early due to nervous anxiety. She left her bedroom with her duffle bag and headed to the kitchen. No one was up so she stepped outside. Sorrow was etched on her face as the loneliness of Lou's absence took hold. She may be going back to Walla Walla, but there was no Lou, no home. Nothing. Just keepsakes, and memories to bring back to her life at Valley View. Kit had accepted her new life. The Calhouns were her family. When Kit heard Sadie in the kitchen, she went in. While Sadie prepared breakfast Kit set the table and made coffee.

Will walked in with Kenzie. "Our Doodle Bug says she could eat a bear. Oh, no, she said she's as hungry as a bear." Kenzie giggled, as her Papa placed her in her booster chair. Kit smiled to herself remembering how gruff he had appeared at first.

"Good morning, baby girl," Kit said, kissing Kenzie's neck until she squealed with delight. Kit was subdued during breakfast. Sadie understood, knowing this was a big step for her granddaughter. After breakfast, Kit poured another coffee, excused herself, and went outside to wait for Riley. She was surprised that Riley wasn't there yet. It wasn't like him to be late. Kit almost choked on her coffee when it was Trace's truck that pulled into the yard with the trailer. Her stomach flipped wildly when an unhappy Trace climbed out of the cab. Usually, she couldn't tell anything from his expression, but today there was no doubt that he was annoyed.

Trace had fumed all the way to Valley View. This was the last thing he needed. He had a business to run. He slammed the truck door when he got out. Trace knew he had taken Kit by surprise when he said, "Riley's got the flu, so I'll be taking you instead." His day had not started well. He knew it wasn't about to get any better guessing by the look on Kit's face, and the folded arms across her chest. Classic body language.

Kit wondered if his ill humor was because he had to take her, or because she was coming back. "I can wait until Riley's better."

Kit obviously wanted nothing to do with him. The feeling was mutual, but it didn't change things. Trace's expression hardened, and his harsh voice reflected his aggravation, "That's out of the question. I've already reorganized my schedule, so we are going today. There is no one else so you need my help."

That comment sparked a sharp reaction. Kit couldn't stop her voice from rising, "Let me tell you one thing, Trace Grayson. I don't need any man's help. I didn't ask for help, and if I had a hitch on my Jeep, I could do this myself."

"That's three things." Trace knew he shouldn't tease her, but he liked the way her eyes went from calm to stormy when she got riled.

Kit threw him a dirty look. The fight went out of Kit knowing she was in no position to argue. She did need him. Not once did she factor in the fact that she should be grateful for his help. Kit met Trace's gaze. With as much calm as she could muster, she declared, "I'll do my best to endure the change of plans. I may hate it, but I can be flexible." This trip was going to be difficult enough with the arrogant jerk without starting the day with added tension. She'd already had enough yesterday dealing with Shelby. She didn't feel up to round two today.

How had he ever thought she was vulnerable. "Good. Now that it's settled go say your goodbyes so we can get going. We've already lost time." Trace remained by his truck. He was in no mood for social pleasantries, so he just waved his greeting to Sadie and Will, who had gathered on the verandah with Kenzie.

It took all of Kit's will power not to salute as she climbed up the stairs. "Go say your goodbyes," she mimicked under her breath. She watched him out of the corner of her eye, lounging against the truck, arms and ankles crossed. He was probably congratulating himself on getting his own way. The man irritated her by merely existing. Kit again got the sick feeling that this was going to be a bad trip. She took her time hugging them one by one, thereby, giving herself time to get control of her emotions. She also knew it would annoy Trace.

Trace prayed for patience, something he knew he was short of at the best of times. The sooner they left, the sooner this ordeal would be over. "C'mon, enough with the goodbyes. It's time to hit the road."

That's not what I want to hit. "See you in a couple of days, baby girl. You be good for GiGi and Papa." Although Kenzie looked disappointed at being left behind, she nodded.

Kit's eyes shifted back to Trace, but not before Sadie noticed they had lost their sparkle. Sadie stroked Kit's cheek, "Try to enjoy your time away. Trace may appear intimidating, but he can be interesting, and charming."

Kit huffed under her breath as if to say she'd have to see it to believe it. She intentionally walked slowly to his truck in a show of defiance.

Trace opened the passenger door and waited. He could feel his temper rising. "Are you going to get in, or are you planning on running alongside the truck all the way to Washington?" He felt her eyes throwing daggers at his chest.

"I think I'll live dangerously, and get in. I'm sure I'll live through the ordeal."

"Just get in. There are a lot of miles to drive." His job was clear-cut if she'd just get in the damn truck.

It took effort, but Kit fought the urge to retaliate. With a resigned sigh, Kit climbed in with a combination of annoyance and apprehension.

Trace slammed the door shut. He muttered under his breath as he strode around to the driver side. Trace had other concerns. What if this trip ended up being a waste of time? What if she tired of being a mother, and took off like her own mother? Trace knew he was being a jerk. He wanted to find fault with Kit when there wasn't any reason for it. Kit wasn't like that. He'd seen for himself that Kenzie was her life. Trace eased his large frame behind the wheel and started the engine. He gave Kit a challenging look, as if waiting for her to say something.

Kit, having already fastened her seat belt, sat as stiff as a board. She sat motionless, doing her level best to ignore him, even though the broadness of his chest made the cab feel awfully small. She was painfully aware of his nearness, but she wasn't going to let this arrogant cowboy know how much he affected her.

Kenzie and Sadie waved as they pulled away.

"Well, I best find BJ. He may need my help."

Sadie chuckled, appreciating Riley's willingness to conspire with her. "Riley doesn't have the flu. He'll be here soon."

Will looked at his wife, and caught the gleam in her eyes, "Playing matchmaker, Ma?"

"Maybe a little. For some reason, Trace seems to have prejudged our granddaughter in a negative way. People, and places can bring out sides of a person that you never knew existed. I'm just helping them get to know each other without outside influence."

Will shook his head, "You've seen how they glare at each other. Or are you blinded by your vision of happily ever after? They don't like each other."

Sadie gave Will an insightful look, "Of course, they do. Haven't you noticed the way they keep looking at each other when the other isn't looking? They are clearly attracted to each other. Kit's too frightened to admit it, and I've never seen Trace so confused by a woman. I'm sure his head is spinning."

Will shook his head, "He ignores Kit most of the time."

Sadie laughed, "Now he won't be able to. They have to spend all their time together for the next couple of days. Chemistry works in mysterious ways."

"Interesting morning," Will muttered to himself, as he headed to the barn.

An intense silence fell between Kit and Trace. Kit was aware of the man with every heightened nerve in her body. She stole a glance at his profile as he maneuvered the truck, and trailer out of the drive, and drove down the lane to the main road. Could it be possible that Trace was as apprehensive as she was about this trip?

Trace looked over. Kit looked as apprehensive as he felt. Only the continuous whine of the tires broke the silence. After miles of silence, Trace decided to make the effort. Surely the weather would be a safe subject. Trying to cut through the cold front Kit had erected, Trace attempted a little humor. "Well, it's definitely warmer outside than it is in here."

Kit gave him an icy glare. She turned her head to gaze out the window. It was more to ignore him than to look at the scenery.

"It's going to be a long drive, so why don't we try to make the best of it." Even though Trace didn't think of this as anything more than an unwanted chore, he had decided on the more scenic route. He thought Kit would like to see the mountains up close. "It's a fascinating drive through the Crowsnest Pass, and you'll get to see the Rocky Mountains up close. It's a great way to take in the scenery, as well as seeing for yourself the history of the area. I'm your captive tour guide."

"I'm glad you said captive rather than captivating," Kit countered, with crispness in her voice, to discourage further conversation. To her surprise, Trace filled the close confines of the truck with a howl of laugher.

Kit wasn't prepared for his laughter, which was low and rich. Realizing that she was being difficult, even stubborn, her fairness surfaced.

Trace carried on, "Alberta is a large province. Most of southern Alberta is prairie, rolling grassland broken by deep river valleys like where we ranch. The land is fertile, and the climate is favorable to agriculture. Central Alberta is the parkland region, and northern Alberta has both the forest region, and the gas and oil sands. Alberta is one of the largest oil resources in the world. We also lead Canada in cattle head. There's plenty of land to support large herds of beef cattle. Valley View is only one of many big cattle ranches."

Kit was grateful that the awkward silence was broken. Now that she was relaxed, Kit enjoyed both the countryside, and Trace's commentary. It helped pass the time as his truck chewed up the miles.

Once they turned west, they left the foothills behind, and drove toward the mountains. "We're going to be driving through the town of Frank soon. The town was devastated by a natural disaster in 1903 when eighty-two million tonnes of limestone slid down Turtle Mountain. Ninety seconds of terror caused by a massive rock avalanche that buried the Canadian Pacific Railway line, the coal mine, and part of the town."

As he spoke, they began driving through the rocks that were piled high on both sides of the highway. Kit's mouth gaped open, and her eyes widened in amazement. "This is unbelievable. What caused the mountain to slide?"

"The primary cause was the unstable geological structure of Turtle Mountain, and erosion over time. Scientists later confirmed that coal mining was a secondary contributing factor. In the early 1900's coal was discovered here in the Crowsnest Pass. People came from Europe, the United States, and other parts of Canada to start a new life, all hoping to make a living in the coal mining valley. The town was named after Henry Frank, who co-owned the company that started the mine. Miners noticed the mountain had become increasingly unstable in the months prior to the slide. In the weeks before the disaster, miners felt rumbling from within the mountain. Would you like me to pull over? We can stretch our legs and climb the rocks."

"Do we have the time? I know we got away later than you wanted."

"We could use a break. We'll stop here, and then have lunch down the road by the river. We can see what Sadie has packed in that huge food hamper she sent." Trace pulled over to the shoulder and stepped out.

Immediately, Kit began to climb the pile of rocks, wanting to get a better view. Having reached a spot where she could sit down, Kit looked out at the devastation surrounding her. She had no idea how long she sat in silence, emotionally affected by her surroundings. Sadness and overwhelming loss ripped through her. Time had not diminished the intensity of the event.

Trace understood her silence and sat down next to her without saying a word. There was something different about her. Maybe it was the unguarded, almost vulnerable way she stared into the distance.

Kit forced her attention back to the man beside her. She was unaware of the tears that had formed on her long lashes. "You wake up in the morning expecting your day to be like every other day. In a heartbeat it changes. Just like you make decisions without considering the consequences."

Trace wondered what had happened in her life that could cause her such deep sorrow. He tried to shake off the tug of sympathy for the spitfire who continued to intrigue him. This woman was a total contradiction. She was a hellcat one minute, gentle, and susceptible the next.

Kit's eyes were sad when she turned back to him, "How many lives were lost?"

"At the time of the slide there were around six hundred people living in the town. Because all the bodies were never recovered, there is no exact number. It was estimated around seventy. Too many," he said seriously.

"Were there miners caught in the mine?"

"There were twenty miners working the night shift. Three were outside the mine, and they were killed. The miners underground were trapped. It took thirteen hours to dig themselves out. The Canadian Pacific Railway had the line cleared, and rebuilt within three weeks, but by 1917 it was permanently closed after it became unprofitable."

"Will more of the mountain slide down?" Kit asked, a little nervous.

"The mountain is in a constant state of instability but is continually monitored. Scientists believe that another rockslide will occur at some time, but not of the same magnitude as this one. We should get going, though. We still have a long drive ahead of us." He stood up, reached down, and pulled her up. He continued to hold her hand as they clambered down the rock mass.

Kit struggled with her reaction to Trace, wishing she weren't so moved by his touch. She couldn't deny her physical attraction to him but rationalized it with the fact that it had been a long time since she had spent this much time in the company of such an attractive man. Not to forget that they had spent hours confined in the cab of his truck. The more she got to know him, the less arrogant he seemed. Kit smiled up at him as he opened her door. "Thanks for stopping, and the history lesson. It's a powerful story."

Trace touched his fingers to the brim of his hat. "You're welcome." He let go of her hand and walked to his side of the truck.

The atmosphere between them remained friendlier, allowing him to ask, "Are you originally from Walla Walla?"

Kit hesitated a moment, deciding if she was willing to open up to the man who up until today hadn't trusted her. "Let's make a pact, Trace. If you want to know something about me, you can ask. I might not answer, if I think it's none of your business. In turn, I get to ask you a question. Same rules."

Trace admitted that this trip would give him a much-needed break from everything. He decided to forget the stress he always felt about the ranch, so he agreed to her ridiculous rule. Time would tell where their conversations would take them.

A little surprised at how comfortable she was with him Kit opened up. The words came slowly at first, because she was deciding on what she was willing to share. "I have always lived in Walla Walla, where I was raised by my grandmother. We weren't your typical family. My grandmother had just turned forty when I was born. No way was she going to be called Grandma. She said she was too young, so she had me call her Lou. My birth mother was never around, so there was no mother-daughter relationship. She was adamant about being called, Torrie." Kit shrugged, and blinked hard, "Which was fine, because she didn't deserve to be called, Mother. Torrie continually deserted me from the time I was born until the day she died. Lou, on the other hand, was an incredible, and caring person. Lou was always helping others, and I loved that about her. When you're older, and understand life better, you wonder if she felt like she had to help others because she couldn't help her own daughter. You realize life is never black or white. Life becomes colored with various shades of gray."

Trace was surprised by Kit's insight at such a young age.

"Lou hoped that once her daughter became a mother, she'd settle down. One of the things about being a parent is to take responsibility for the life you bring into the world. That means every day, whether you like it or not. Torrie wasn't willing to let a child complicate her life or leave her world of parties, and fast living. She wasn't going to let a stupid mistake ruin her life. Her words, not mine. Life at home with a baby was a life sentence, so she escaped. Without a moment of guilt, she left me behind to be raised by my grandmother. It was my grandmother that filled the vacated roll of mother. Torrie lived her life for herself, no one else."

Trace's heart hurt for this poor girl. He remained silent wondering if Kit would continue.

Kit continued even though the conversation was opening old wounds. Thanks to Lou, Kit understood that it was Torrie who was the problem. The problem would show up unexpectedly, and sporadically, disturbing their lives again and again. "Torrie would get restless, and take off for months at a time, come back, and leave again. Imagine being forsaken by your mother again, and again. When you're little, you believe that every time she came home, she would stay. When I got older, I thought it was my fault Torrie left. She didn't love me enough to stay." Kit's expression was somber, her eyes anguished.

Trace couldn't help but wonder how any mother could forsake her own child. He studied Kit as she struggled internally.

Deep hurts kept surfacing. "The last time she left was when I turned fifteen. Six months later we got the dreaded knock on the door and, as they say, the rest is history. Life became normal after Torrie died. We thought all the drama was buried with her. It was just moved to the attic. That's where I found Torrie's journals, and my birth certificate. We all know how that chapter ends so here we are."

Trace was appalled. Life could be cruel, and unfair, but this was unbelievable. How could someone be so heartless as to tell her daughter that her father was dead when he wasn't.

"I felt like the bottom had dropped out of my world when my grandmother died. With Lou gone, I had no family left unless what she told me was true. Lou's revelation was my salvation. I spent agonizing hours trying to make up my mind. I was worried that if I found my father, he wouldn't believe me. Or worse, he'd reject me like my mother did. A reluctant father could be worse than no father at all. I had nothing to lose by leaving Walla Walla to go in search of my dad, even though I was terrified about how it might turn out. When the fear set in, I asked myself if I was opening myself up to more pain, more disappointments, and more heartache. What if my dad turned me away?"

Or he was poor instead of a wealthy rancher. Trace was ashamed he even thought this. He was still struggling to let go of his original opinion of Kit. He now knew better. but he had to wonder what role she expected BJ to play in her life. Here she was packing up everything and moving in with grandparents again. Was Kit repeating history?

"This wasn't a decision that came easily. That all scared me, but I couldn't let it stop me. Once I found my dad, I quickly realized that this wasn't just about me. My actions have changed my dad's life, and everyone else's. I didn't think about the consequences. Despite everything, I still believe that I did the right thing. At the very least, my dad deserved to know he had a daughter. It would put things right and provide Kenzie with a family if something happened to me. I didn't have a choice. I made a vow the day Kenzie was born to always love and take care of her. I was willing to do whatever it took to do what was best for my daughter. I know my arrival was a shock to everyone, but some have been less welcoming than others."

Trace felt that this was an intentional shot at him. Neither he, nor Shelby, had accepted her presence at Valley View. Compassion replaced the indifference in his eyes. Kit had shown him a strength, and honesty he hadn't wanted to give her credit for possessing. "Why would your grandmother keep Torrie's secret?"

"That was the first question I asked her. She said that she had already lost her daughter. She didn't want to lose me, and Kenzie. When Lou told me that I might have a dad, I knew it tore her apart. She admitted it was wrong not to tell me sooner. Lou did the right thing by telling me, and I believe I did the right thing by finding my dad and telling him."

All of Kit's sharing caused Trace to question his opinion about her. Here sat a brave young woman who had been willing to face an unknown future alone based on an arduous past. Maybe it really was family, and not money that she wanted. He would try to be open-minded over the next few days while getting to know her better. "Your grandmother sounds like she was a good lady."

Kit's eyes filled with sudden tears. She swallowed the lump that had formed in her throat. "She was a great lady, and I miss her every day. Sadie reminds me so much of Lou." Kit turned to Trace, "Have you been to Walla Walla before?"

Trace smiled knowing she had thrown the conversation back to him, thereby, deflecting further questioning. "No, but I have been to Washington. I delivered a horse to a ranch just outside of Ellensburg."

Kit's smile faded, and a shadow crossed her face. Ellensburg was where BJ met Torrie.

Trace knew something had changed by her pensive expression. Maybe she had things in her past, as he did, that were difficult to talk about. He knew so little about her. "Was this your first time to Canada?"

"Yes. None of my family came north that we know of, but we didn't always know where Torrie was." Over the next few hours Kit continued to share parts of her past, but she wasn't willing to share her life with Mike. She stared wearily at the clock on the dash and let out a tired sigh. It had been a long day of driving. It wasn't the ordeal she had envisioned when they left. In fact, she was surprised at how much she enjoyed the day. When Kit saw the lights of Walla Walla, she became quiet and withdrawn. When they left Alberta, she thought she was coming home. This was no longer home.

Trace was also showing signs of fatigue.

When Trace saw Kit to her room, she placed a hand on his forearm as he was leaving. "I know that I was miserable and appeared ungrateful when we left this morning. I apologize. The day wasn't as bad as I expected. See you in the morning."

Trace merely raised his eyebrow as they parted ways and agreed to meet in the breakfast room at eight. He had a great deal to think about regarding this mystifying woman, since his initial doubts of her were slowly disappearing.

It was late, and Kit was exhausted. She was heavy-hearted as she prepared for bed. Tonight, was the first time she hadn't been there to put Kenzie to bed. She missed tucking her in. "Sweet dreams, baby girl," Kit whispered, as she turned out the light. Unable to contain the emotional turmoil that had been building all day, she cried herself to sleep.

Chapter Seventeen

K it opened her eyes and stared at the ceiling. Today, she was saying her final farewell to her life here. Kit knew she'd have to be strong to face the day ahead. Climbing out of bed, she headed into the bathroom. A hot shower helped relieve her tension but couldn't wash away the dark circles under her troubled eyes.

Trace watched her cross the room to join him at the table. He remembered the day Kit arrived at Valley View. Now that he knew her better, he couldn't help but be impressed with her. She had walked to the house, steps firm, shoulders square, and head held high while everyone stared at her. If she was scared it didn't show. Trace didn't miss the shadows under her eyes. He respected her silence through breakfast knowing it wasn't due to sulking, but apprehension. Today wouldn't be easy for her.

Kit was solemn as Trace pulled up to her storage unit. He opened the trailer door before following Kit. "Where do you want me to start?" he asked as Kit opened the door to the unit. When she didn't answer, he hesitated before asking, "Are you okay?"

Kit tried to answer but was struggling with the reality of letting go. Kit's face paled, and she started trembling. "I just need a moment," she said, while blinking back tears.

Trace didn't miss the open anxiety in her expressive eyes. Behind the facade of bravery, she was crumbling. Trace of all people knew enough to respect the privacy of others. He would give Kit all the time she needed. He remained silent while he jammed his hands into the pockets of his jeans and stepped away.

Kit was sure she'd never felt more alone as she entered the unit. She went over, and sat down in the rocking chair, silently reliving the past. Lou had bought this chair when Torrie had discovered she was pregnant. After Kit was born, it was Lou who had spent hours rocking her precious granddaughter, because her mother was gone. It was the chair that had brought comfort to Kit during her own pregnancy, knowing there would be no father to welcome her baby. Kit wanted her grandmother who had been there for her when Mike died. Lou, who had always been there for her. Unable to choke down the sobs, she buried her face in her hands, and wept as memories assaulted her. She thought she had come to terms with letting go but flashing in and out of her mind were vivid images. Torrie. Mike. Lou. Memories she'd held at bay for a long time stirred inside her. So many memories. Some good, some bad. People didn't last in her life. She'd come to accept that, but she felt like she was saying goodbye to them all over again. She would make a point of rocking her daughter in this chair and tell her all about these people. Kit stopped rocking and wiped her face. It was time to pack up, and trust that she was making the right decision.

Trace was leaning against the trailer waiting. Kit walked over and gazed up at him. She saw a flicker of tenderness in his eyes. It was too much. Her tears returned.

His compassion drew him in. Trace circled his arms around Kit and held her against his chest. He felt the tears through his shirt as he let her cry. He didn't know where all the pain was coming from. Kit Bennett wasn't who he thought she was. She was slowly piercing his exterior shell of distrust.

The hurt wasn't new, but she couldn't make it go away. Kit clung to him unaware of the passing of time. Completely spent, she gazed up at him, tears still glistening in her eyes. She took a deep breath as she pulled away. When Kit looked back at him, she was a little distant. "Let's get busy."

The first few boxes Kit handed Trace were U.S. Army boxes. Trace's expression was both curious, and wary. Once again, Trace realized how little he knew about her.

Kit looked up with haunted eyes, "They belonged to my dead husband."

Hearing her voice crack did something to him. Trace felt like someone had knocked the wind out of him. He absorbed this but was too dumbfounded to comment. He was feeling guilty because he had again prejudged her unfairly.

"You look surprised."

"I assumed you were a single mom, not a widow. I'm sorry."

"More preconceived judgment, Trace?"

Trace knew he deserved that. He was looking at a woman who had obviously known love, and the pain of loss. Now she was facing the challenge of a new life head on. In one single day she had turned his thoughts of her around. Trace had to admire Kit for her incredible inner strength. Trace wished he had been more considerate, and a lot less judgmental.

Without a word, Kit turned, and continued working.

Speechless, he followed suit. He had a lot of questions, but now wasn't the time. He had aways been careful not to get involved, but he needed to know more about this woman.

They worked side by side until the last of Kit's possessions were loaded. These were the last ties to her life here. It was over. Kit looked up at Trace, her eyes vacant. "I thought this would be easier." Kit swallowed the lump in her throat and closed the storage unit door, putting her past here to rest.

Trace had seen how much Kit was grieving. "You have a new family waiting for you. The Calhouns are good people, Kit. You, and your daughter will be fine living with them. Will is like a legend, and BJ is honorable just like his dad. Sadie is like a mom to everyone."

Kit was surprised at the empathy displayed by Trace. "Sadie reminds me so much of Lou, and I know she loves Kenzie to pieces." Her young daughter had so easily transferred her love for Lou to Sadie. Kit climbed into the truck. It was time for a new life.

They pulled away in silence, but Trace saw Kit wipe her eyes before she laid her clasped hands in her lap. Something clenched the pit of his stomach, and his heart began beating a little faster. Trace knew if he let himself, he could care about her.

A few minutes later Kit confessed, "That was hard. It felt like I was packing Lou away again. It seems that everyone in my life is neatly packed away in a box. Lou, Mike, Torrie."

Trace guessed that Mike was her dead husband.

They made Kalispell by late afternoon. Trace decided it was a good place to stop for the night. They could have a relaxing dinner, a comfortable night's sleep, and make Valley View by mid-afternoon, if there were no delays at the border.

After Trace checked them in, he handed Kit her room key. "The clerk said there's a restaurant within walking distance that has excellent food. What do you say?"

"Give me a few minutes."

"I'll be back in twenty."

Kit had just finished freshening up when she heard the knock at the door.

"Ready?"

"Lead the way. I'm starving." Kit's heart pounded as a different kind of hunger, one that had nothing to do with food, surfaced.

"Let's go," he said, taking her arm.

Kit smiled, suddenly feeling a warm glow on the inside as he led her down the block.

The restaurant was quaint, and the hostess welcomed them warmly. Trace's hand came to rest lightly in the small of her back as they followed her to a corner of the dining room that was private, and dimly lit. "She thinks we're a couple." Trace knew his comment would get a rise out of Kit. He wasn't disappointed.

"She does not. You're imagining things."

His eyes twinkled, and a smile lit up his handsome face. "Why else did she put us in this secluded corner?" Trace leaned back, completely at ease. "Would you like a glass of wine?" Knowing Kit was about to decline he quickly added, "No excuse, there's no Kenzie to tend to tonight, and I won't tell her what her mother did."

Even though Trace's potent charm was intoxicating enough, Kit nodded. She decided to relax and enjoy the evening.

While they ate, Trace continued to make Kit feel at ease. The man had irresistible charm. Once Kit relaxed, conversation flowed easily. Kit was seeing a different side of Trace. The hardened cowboy did have some admirable qualities she admitted.

Trace enjoyed seeing Kit like this, her face tension free. He discovered that Kit was intelligent and had a sense of humor to go along with her quick wit. This woman was a total contradiction. She was a hellcat one minute, tender, and susceptible the next. "You intrigue me, Kit. There's more to you than meets the eye." This wasn't a statement of mistrust like she usually heard in his voice.

Kit tilted her head to the side. "My defenses go up when someone doesn't like me."

"I was being cautious."

"You were being judgmental."

There was undeniable truth there. "I've always prided myself on being a good judge of character. I really missed the mark with you. I thought you had come to Valley View so you could hit your dad up for money. The Calhouns are honest, steadfast, and generous so it would have been easy to do that."

"I don't want anything from them but family. I'm not a gold-digger."

It was Trace's turn to feel uncomfortable. "I know you and I got off to a bad start. I was wrong about you. I'm sorry." Kit had won his reluctant admiration.

Kit appreciated that Trace had admitted to having preconceived ideas about her, and that he realized they were unfair, and unjustified. She picked up her wine and took a fortifying sip. "I'm sure Shelby still thinks that. I have tried with Shelby, but she doesn't make it easy."

"I know you two didn't hit it off."

There were few people who irritated Kit as much as Shelby Calhoun. "Shelby has made it clear that she doesn't want me at Valley View. The last thing she said to me was to stay away from you, and Riley."

Trace couldn't stop himself from asking, "What did you say to her?"

Kit had her mother's fiery temper to go along with the Calhoun stubbornness, "I told her she had a chip on her shoulder, and it better be gone by the time I get back, or I'll knock it off. I told her I was coming back to stay, so she needs to learn how to deal with it. I'm not going away. Shelby better figure out how to cope really quick because this is her new reality."

Whatever was going on between Kit, and Shelby was far from over. A slight smile played on Trace's lips. He wondered if Shelby had met her match. "Shelby feels threatened by you. You've disrupted her comfortable world, and she has to learn to adjust to this huge change in her sheltered, privileged life. Give her time."

"Meanwhile, I just turn the other cheek, so she can verbally slap that one?"

"Shelby's mouth gets the better of her. I have a feeling you give as good as you get."

His mocking smile loosened Kit's tongue even more. "I'll have to figure out a way to deal with her when I get back. My life wasn't like Shelby's growing up. I lived in the real world where I grew up fast."

"Yes, compared to you, Shelby has had a very sheltered life with parents who have indulged her."

Kit felt pushed to the limit with Shelby. Her parting words had hurt Kit more than she realized. "My child is involved, and I have to put her first. I didn't have the childhood Shelby did, but I intend to give Kenzie the best things in life I can. I need my new family, even though it includes Shelby. It's unfortunate that your brother is head over heels for the princess."

"For years Riley has said he's going to marry Shelby. He's biding his time waiting for her to grow up."

Kit bit her tongue to stop herself from saying that it could take forever. It was time to get off the subject of Shelby. "What about you, Trace? Is there someone special in your life?"

"I'm not looking for commitment," Trace said bluntly.

The man had basically told her that marriage, and family were not in his future.

Once they moved off the topic of Shelby, Trace found Kit's company pleasurable. He decided to extend the evening and ordered another round of drinks.

It seemed a million years since she'd been young, and carefree. Tonight, Kit decided to relax, and enjoy the moment. Tomorrow she'd return to reality. The soft light fell across Trace's often-rigid features. Kit was suddenly willing to live on the edge. "I've told you about myself. You know why I'm leaving here, and why I'm going back to Valley View. How about telling me something about you for a change?" Both Will, and BJ had shared family history regarding the Calhouns and the Reeds, but very little about the Graysons. There was more to this man that she wanted to know. She took a sip of wine, leaned back, and waited.

Trace took a long drink of beer. Kit had intentionally steered the conversation away from her, and he hadn't missed the veiled challenge in her voice. He wasn't sure if he was ready to share the dark side of his past.

He knew he had misjudged Kit, but trust had to be earned over time. "I don't like to talk about myself. Besides, it's pretty boring." Why dredge up all that pain when he had buried it a long time ago?

"I doubt that." Kit watched him from across the table, refusing to accept his avoidance.

Trace realized Kit wasn't about to give up. He figured he might as well tell her some of his past and get it over with. "Our childhood wasn't normal either. Mom never said why they moved to Canada, but I'm sure by then our dad already had a shady past. We lived a nomadic lifestyle, not always by choice. More than once we were either evicted for non-payment, or we left like thieves in the night. Riley and I grew up knowing what it was like to have nothing. We seldom made friends because we were never in one place long enough. Thank God, we had each other. One day our dad showed up with a holiday trailer that he won in a poker game. That became our home. Trailer life was better in some ways than what we were used to. As least we had a roof over our heads when it was time to sneak away. We towed that old trailer from province to province. We arrived at Valley View unannounced just like you."

This last comment could have held a trace of sarcasm, but Kit detected none.

Trace continued to talk about the painful details of their early unhappy years. Things he rarely shared with anyone. For some reason, he decided to trust her, and he hoped his instincts about her were right. Occasionally, the suffering of those years showed in his eyes. His pain revealed itself in the pauses, the unspoken words. He knew Kit understood the significance of the memories he shared. "Even at a young age I was a challenge to my dad. I hated how he treated our mom. She deserved better. From the time I was little he would whip me, so that I would understand that he was the boss. He made sure no one could see any bruises or marks. If it wasn't physical, it was verbal. He would shout accusations, and utter threats. I was able to protect Riley, but I always had to be on guard. Fortunately, our dad only needed one whipping post. Ma never knew, but Riley did. It was our secret. One we've kept to this day. It would have broken her heart. The outside wounds heal a lot faster than the inside wounds." Talking about his father had caused Trace's eyes to ice over and his jaw tightened. Trace swore he would never tell anyone what he had just shared with Kit. This was something he had buried deep within. But as sure as he knew his own name, he knew Kit would never tell anyone.

Looking into his eyes Kit could see the deep hurt. For the first time in her life, Kit felt someone else's pain deeper than she felt her own. Trace had confided in her, and she would never violate that trust. Everyone had a past. It wasn't always pretty or fair. Trace had Tom in his past. Torrie was in hers. It was impossible to always let the past go. Knowing she may be taking a foolish risk, and he might shut down, Kit dared to ask a very personal question. "Is that why you don't want to get married, and have children? So, you can't let them down? Or have anyone count on you? Guess what, people already count on you, especially Riley. I understand what you're feeling, but we are not our parents. I was afraid I might be like Torrie. If l hadn't released that fear, I wouldn't have Kenzie. No child should have to distrust their own parent, but you shouldn't hold a grudge against a dead man."

"I don't. He's been gone a long time. I just swore I would never follow in his footsteps. My father always said you can't count on anyone. He was right because we sure couldn't count on him. So, my commitment is to Lola Grande." He changed the direction of the conversation, "I don't know what happened, but things changed for the better when we got to Valley View. I must admit that our dad was always a hard worker. Right from the beginning he said that the Calhouns were fair bosses. For a while life was better for all of us. Unfortunately, he couldn't control his addictions for long. His vices literally were the death of him. He was killed over a poker hand in the back room of a bar. The Calhouns were so good to us after our dad died, and things took a dramatic change. Buster took us into his home. From that day on he treated us like family. The rest of the Calhouns were no different. Growing up boys will be boys. Buster was never hard on us, but he always made us accountable for our actions. As much as we hated it, the punishment was always fair. And never physical." Something about his expression changed, and he again closed the door to his past.

Kit recalled Sadie saying Trace was a very private person, so she was surprised that he had shared this much. She studied his features silently and could tell that Trace had put his wall back up. Knowing his love for horses she tried to lighten the somber mood. "I was surprised when I found out that Ginger was your horse. She is a real beauty. Have you ever wanted to be anything other than a rancher?"

"Don't you ever get tired of asking questions?"

"Let's just say I find you fascinating, Mr. Grayson," Kit said with a cheeky grin.

The glint of mischief in her eyes amused him, but his answer was candid, "Being a cowboy is in my blood, city girl. A cowboy lives to be free and is proud being his own man. A wise man once told me that anything you do for love is worth it."

"Buster?"

"I was mad when Buster died." It wasn't until he said it out loud that Trace realized he was still angry, and it was affecting him.

Kit could hear the change in his tone. Kit hated the sadness she saw. Sadness he never meant for her to see. "You miss him."

"All the time. More than anyone, it was Buster who shaped me into the man I am today. Buster gave me the belief in myself that I needed. He taught me to think for myself, and to trust my instincts. If he thought I might be wrong, he would lead me to think in a different way. He wasn't just my mentor; he was my best friend. He was a good man who believed in human decency, and assumed others were just like him."

"Lou always believed that most people when given a choice will do what is right, even when it's hard. It was hard leaving here, Trace. I continue to make hard choices, including staying at Valley View, knowing not everyone wants me there. If you want something bad enough, you don't give in. I've had to change direction in my life more than once. It changed again when my grandmother died, and it took me to Valley View. This is such a different life that I'm living now." Her changed life was still difficult.

"Tell me about your husband, Kit."

A faraway look darkened Kit's eyes. An old ache gripped her, catching her off guard. A pang of sorrow hit her as it always did when she thought about Mike. His memory was so vivid he could have been there with her. Kit took a moment to compose herself.

Misreading her silence Trace said, "You don't have to tell me. I shouldn't have asked. It's none of my business."

Kit didn't object to his request. After all he had shared, she was willing to share more of her own painful past. She smiled, but somehow managed to look twice as sad. "It's okay. Mike was a wonderful man."

"Oh, like me. I kinda grow on you, eh?" he asked, intentionally adding the Canadian "ism" along with his devilish smile.

The tone of his voice told her he was trying to lighten her mood. "I may be the only person not blinded by your charm."

"So, I'm charming too. Be careful. Sweet talk like that may turn my head."

Kit's laughter floated in the air. This man could annoy, and charm her at the same time. She tried not to respond to him when everything inside her urged her to.

"You were getting ready to tell me about your husband." Trace couldn't remember any woman who fascinated him as much as Kit. Her combination of inner strength, and vulnerability intrigued him. Maybe part of his interest was because he still had a lot to learn about her.

Kit took a large sip of her wine. She had accepted that she was willing to share what was very personal to her. No longer surprised at how comfortable she was with Trace she opened up even more. Just like Trace had. "Mike was a military man, and we started dating when I was in university. When he got called for duty, we decided to get married before he left, even though I was still in school. We may have been young, but we were excited about our future. Soon after he left, I found out I was pregnant. I was happy to have something to look forward to while Mike was away. We were going to be a real family. We swore that our child would be raised by two loving parents. Something that neither of us had. I had hoped for a normal life when I married Mike, but once again fate slapped me down. I kissed Mike goodbye, not knowing I would never see him again."

Kit's eyes were solemn when she looked across at Trace. "My world was turned upside down by another fateful knock on the door. You never forget the day itself. You don't wake up knowing that the day will be different. There is no sense of dread as you begin your day the same as you did the day before. It's such a shock at first that you don't believe it. You wonder how you can move forward. You actually wonder if you can. Then you must work through the anger because life again treated you unfair. At the age of twenty I went from wife to war widow. It was the end of my life with Mike, and our hopes, and dreams. You lose more than the person. For a while, you lose part of yourself, and it takes a long time to find it again. You learn to accept that there is heartache, and pain in everyone's life. You can't let it control you."

Kit had been through a loss that had knocked her to her knees. It had taken a long time to recover. She may have lost Mike too soon, but she treasured the fact that he had been in her life. He gave her Kenzie, and wonderful memories. "It felt like my life was over when Mike died, but the arrival of my daughter changed that. My baby girl is my reason for living. Despite all that happened, Mike's death, and the heartache that lingered, I consider the birth of my daughter a blessing. She was the best part of her dad that I could have. Mike was the love of my life. What we had in that short time was special, but our time together was too brief. I choose to remember the happiness we had, rather than the emptiness he left behind."

New emotions flickered in Trace's eyes. He nursed his beer while Kit continued to share.

Kit's eyes were solemn when she looked across at Trace. No longer surprised at how comfortable she was with Trace she opened up even more. "It isn't easy being a widow, and a single mother. I'm not looking for sympathy, just being honest. Sometimes I wish I could have everything that other people have. I miss my husband. In the beginning a stab of jealousy would go through me whenever I saw a family together at the grocery store or playing in the park." Kit felt guilty when she said, "Sometimes I get tired of being both parents, that constant sense of responsibility for everything. That's when I get mad at Mike for leaving me. Then I get mad at myself for being selfish, instead of grateful. My husband left me with such a precious gift." Kit could never regret being a mother. Kenzie gave her so much happiness.

Trace could see the sparkle return to Kit's eyes every time she mentioned Kenzie. Trace had undeniable admiration for Kit. He knew it couldn't be easy raising a child alone.

Kit sighed heavily, "Mike died a hero, but he died before he could become a dad. We had no chance to be a family. Kenzie never had the chance to meet her father." Kit looked directly at Trace, her eyes full of tears. "Thanks to Lou, I was given the chance to find mine." For Kit, reliving those years, even now, was painful. She shook her head to escape the visions from her past. She thought she had buried those feelings deep enough. "I couldn't allow the past to keep me from moving forward. That's why I came to Valley View, and that's why I'm going back." Kit understood that everyone had to deal with loss in their lives. For some it just came sooner. Life could be cruel. She had learned that with Mike, and she had learned it a long time ago with Torrie. She was still dealing with her most recent loss.

"I'm sorry," Trace said. "Death is difficult."

Kim was surprised to see Trace's look of compassion, and it touched her. "So is life. Lou always said that no matter how bad things are they always get better. Sometimes it's a long way to better." Kit choked on her last words. "There are times we like to dream about what might have been. That doesn't change what is, so we have to let the past go." They both knew that was easier said than done.

Trace covered her hand with his and held her gaze, "I'm sorry for all you've been through. This had to have been hard." Hearing her story, he realized that Kit was a woman who was strong enough to handle anything that life threw at her. That didn't mean it made it any easier. Now that he knew what she'd been going through he understood her better and his opinion of her changed drastically. Kit had earned his respect.

Kit was surprised by Trace's look of compassion.

"Life can only beat you up if you let it. I have lost two of the dearest people in the world. Family may not have meant anything to Torrie, but it means everything to me. Nobody's life turns out the way they'd like it to. It's up to us to find our happiness. Life is too short to be unhappy." Kit smiled at Trace, "So here we are, you and I, in a situation neither would have dreamed of, and making the most of it."

Trace was surprised that she could put a smile on her face. She had endured a lot in her young life. She had given him a lot to process, and not just about her. "We should probably get back to the motel. Morning will come early, and we still have a long pull tomorrow." He held her chair as he helped her up.

As soon as she stood up Kit realized she had consumed too much wine. The fresh air would do her good.

Trace smiled as he took her elbow and led her out. When she looped her arm through his, he slowed his stride to match hers. Trace appreciated how much Kit had opened up. They had talked comfortably for hours, but Trace was still curious.

For Kit, the evening had been a welcomed break from motherhood. Walking in the moonlight was the perfect ending to a pleasant evening. When Kit glanced at Trace, she saw a sudden warmth in his eyes that caused her pulse to quicken, and she shivered. Her awareness of him had been present all evening.

Thinking she was cold, Trace took off his jacket, and draped it around her shoulders.

It had been a long time since Kit had strolled with a man by her side. She realized this was just another thing that she missed. Kit smiled her thanks and looked up at the sky. "It seems like the stars are brighter at home."

Trace smiled down at her. He knew she meant Valley View.

Trace had been a perfect gentleman all night. Kit hadn't expected to be so comfortable with him. He had brought her guard down, and she had opened up. So had Trace, and she understood him better. They stopped outside Kit's door. He was standing too close while looking deep into her eyes. She tore her gaze away. "It's late," she said, as she handed him his jacket. It was an obvious signal for him to go, but he lingered.

They stood in silence staring at each other. By getting to know her better, Kit had drawn him in with her openness, and honesty. Trace knew he was beginning to care about this woman. If he denied it, he was only fooling himself. Unwillingly his eyes were drawn to Kit's mouth when she licked her dry lips. She had such a sensual, inviting mouth.

Kit recognized the stirring interest in his eyes but couldn't move away. Trace's mouth moved perilously close to hers, and her lips tingled with anticipation. There sprang between them a heat that had been building since they'd first laid eyes on each other. Trace leaned in, his warm lips barely touching hers. The contact was brief, a mere sweep of his lips over hers. Wanting more, Trace couldn't resist covering her mouth with his.

It felt like the most natural thing in the world to be in Trace's arms. Kit felt herself drifting. The prolonged kiss was intense, exciting, and at the same time terrifying. The wall she'd built around her heart was starting to crack. An intense physical rush of pleasure reminded her that she had lived much too long in a void of nothingness. Her passion was awakened as Trace rekindled the fire. His kiss unlocked the desire she had carefully locked away. It was Kit who broke the embrace, frightened by her own driving need.

Even though Kit tried to hide it, Trace knew she was affected. So was he.

Kit stiffened, torn by indignation, and the most enticing sensation she'd experienced. She was finding it difficult to recover from his kiss. The tug at her heart couldn't be happening. To hide her fear, she pushed against his chest forcing him to release her. Through trembling lips, she managed to stutter, "I'm not one of your casual dates who enjoy lewd kisses at the door."

Trace almost laughed. She had reverted back to the feisty young lady who first showed up at Valley View. Before Kit could retreat inside Trace pulled her back into his arms and pressed his mouth harder onto hers. It wasn't a gentle kiss like last time. This was a taking.

Kit struggled with her reaction. Every inch of her was tingling with desire. Every nerve was alive, wanting more. It felt incredible. She found herself trembling, unsure if it was fear or desire. Either way, it made her push Trace away.

"You can fool yourself by pushing me away, but your eyes tell me something different. You want me, Kit, every bit as much as I want you." Trace let her go and started to walk away. He stopped, returned, and took her back in his arms.

This time the kiss was long, and wonderful, and brought every inch of Kit to life. All of her senses awakened, and her body cried out for more. She wanted him. She hadn't even thought about sex in a long, long time.

"Just reminding myself how sweet your lips are." Trace let her go and lifted the brim of his Stetson with one finger, "You're a hard woman to walk away from. Thanks for the date, city girl." That said, he turned, and walked away.

"It wasn't a date, cowboy," she called out after him. Kit remained where she was standing. She licked her lips as she savored the feel of his lips, the taste of his mouth. Realizing her legs were trembling, Kit went inside, and sat down. It was a long time before her racing heart returned to normal.

Kit changed into her nightshirt and flopped into bed. Although it was emotional leaving Washington, tonight it was other thoughts keeping her awake. As she lay in the strange bed she kept thinking about Trace. Just days ago, she despised the man, but she could no longer lie to herself. Her feelings for him were stronger than simple attraction. Just the memory of his kisses made her heart beat faster. Her response had been natural, and physical. She had kissed him back. Her lips still throbbed from the pressure of his kiss. It had been a long time since her senses had stirred. Hell, they had caught fire. She couldn't confuse physical attraction with love. Wants and needs, very different. Sleep continued to elude her as conflicting emotions confused her. She willed her mind to stop thinking about Trace, but it refused. Groaning, she decided nothing about the man could be good for her as she pummeled the pillow. She knew she'd only end up with a heap of heartache.

Meanwhile in his bed Trace was fairing no better. Sleep was out of the question even though it had been an exhausting day. He closed his eyes and tried to empty his mind. To his surprise a vivid image of Kit appeared. He had been shocked when she told him that she'd been married. Even sadder, she had been expecting when her husband died. He felt guilty knowing how he had judged Kit and had immediately formed the wrong conclusion. Replaying the events of the last two days, he was glad that he'd come. He had been taught a valuable lesson. It was easy to judge someone without knowing little or nothing about them. He knew he had misjudged Kit. This was something that he would have to work on. He recognized that it took incredible courage for Kit to leave here not knowing what her future held. Kit had a high regard for family despite what she told him about her own. It was also clear that she would always put her child first. As she should. He knew with certainty that he was falling for her, and there was nothing he could do about it. Especially now that he had gotten to know more about her. He had always prided himself on his self-control, but this woman had a way of getting to him. There was definitely something there, and he knew she felt it too. He questioned his temporary loss of sanity. He shouldn't have kissed her. It had been such a stupid thing to do. It was a mistake. He grinned. It had felt good. Too good. He had been in a self-imposed female drought. He could no longer ignore the powerful chemistry between them, and he wished she were lying next to him instead of in the room next door. He knew that would never happen. Kit would never entertain a casual relationship. In the limited time he had spent with Kit he knew she would want the full commitment of marriage.

Chapter Eighteen

The sky was just beginning to lighten yet Kit had been awake for hours. She couldn't stop thinking about last night. She couldn't put the blame for last night entirely on Trace. She should have been in control, but she had let her guard down. It wasn't the kiss that disturbed her, it was that she had responded. She rolled onto her back and groaned. Liking it upset and confused her. Along with that came the realization that she was tired of living in a void. Trace had stirred the embers of desire, and she once again felt the longing she had extinguished when Mike died. It was as frightening as it was exciting. Her mind kept recapturing his incredible hot, demanding kisses. For heaven's sake, her body still tingled, and her lips felt bruised. She could no longer pretend it was nothing but a harmless moment of foolishness. Somehow, the man she'd gotten to know last night, and the day before was not the man she thought he was. He was interesting, thoughtful, and a good listener. He was also a man who wanted no commitment with a woman. Especially one with a child. She had to keep Kenzie in the front of her mind, not some tall, suave cowboy. Kit forced her tired body out of bed and headed for the bathroom. Under the spray of the water, she told herself that she had to get her head back on straight. She tried to convince herself that she wasn't immune to Trace's charm because her defenses were down due to the circumstances of her trip. Things would return to the way it was when they were back at Valley View.

When Kit walked into the breakfast room Trace was already seated at a table. His face was pale. Maybe she wasn't the only one who didn't get much sleep last night. She knew their first moments together could be awkward. Hopefully, Trace wouldn't mention the kiss. She shook her head. Why would he? It most likely meant nothing to him.

Trace was already on his second cup of coffee, even though it was just past seven. His restlessness was due to Kit, and her soft femininity beneath her fiery exterior. In the light of a new day, he was angry at himself for losing control last night. Seeing her again made him want her and that also made him angry. He wanted to be done with this whole business and get Kit back to Valley View. "Good morning," he said with false brightness.

Kit nodded her greeting. Just seeing him made her heartbeat quicken. "You all right?" he asked.

"I'm fine," she snapped.

Trace was not slighted. "Not a morning person, Kit?"

"I'm just tired." It would be nice to start the day without a verbal sparring match.

Trace could see Kit hadn't slept well either. Yesterday had brought back a lot of painful memories for both of them. There were dark shadows under her eyes. "What are you tired of?" he teased, trying to lighten her mood.

"You," she said irritably.

Trace smiled to himself. Her response was exactly what he had expected, but he was disappointed that the uptight Kit was back.

The atmosphere remained strained throughout breakfast. Kit was relieved when Trace asked if she was ready to go. She merely nodded. Both were anxious to get home. Without a word passing between them they climbed into his truck.

The tension Kit caused with her silence lengthened with every mile they traveled. Trace finally decided to address the strain between them. "I accept full responsibility for making an ass of myself last night. If I knew kissing you would upset you, I wouldn't have done it. Sorry if I got the wrong impression."

Somewhat relieved, Kit forced a smile, "Let's just put last night behind us. My emotions are in turmoil with leaving Walla Walla." Hopefully, the drive back would give her time to settle herself down, clear her head, and let her everyday world back in. It was time to go back to being a mom. Nothing like a three-year-old to bring you back to reality, and get you grounded.

Both became lost in their private world of thoughts. Trace wanted what they had last night, pleasant conversation in a comfortable atmosphere. They had both opened up, and he hoped he hadn't ruined things by kissing her. Before he finally fell asleep last night, he vowed he wouldn't get romantically involved with her. He was a loner by choice and intended to stay that way. That meant keeping a reasonable distance from her. Trace frowned before remarking, "You're awfully quiet today. Is there something wrong?" He'd been watching her changing expressions while she'd remained deep in thought.

"I was just thinking." Kit had been dealing with conflicting emotions all morning.

"Care to share?"

"No, it has nothing to do with you." Kit knew she was only fooling herself.

Trace looked over, and his killer grin slipped into place. "What!" Trace declared in mock earnest. "I'm not in your thoughts every moment. I must be slipping in the charm department. I guess horses are more easily charmed than women." They both laughed, and it eased the tension between them. "Are you sorry you decided to find your dad?"

"At times," she admitted truthfully.

"Like now?"

"No, but it isn't what I expected. Your dreams never include the unforeseeable hurdles or the negative reaction of others. Do you still think that I'm a gold-digger?"

Trace couldn't forget the look on her face when he said those cruel words. They had learned a lot about each other in the last couple of days. "No. Now I understand why you came, and why you have decided to stay. What else is bothering you."

"My mind is all over the place," Kit confessed. "I'm thinking about the past, as well as my future. I have closed this chapter of my life, and now I'm anxious to start a new one at Valley View." She had resolved to live there; there was no going back. She would make the best of whatever happened next. "It'll be good to get home. I can hardly wait to see Kenzie. I've missed my baby girl." Her softened expression transformed her face.

"You truly like it at Valley View, don't you? You're not just saying it."

"I never say anything I don't mean."

"You said you hated me."

Kit gave him one of her sassy looks, "At the time I did."

Trace was happy to hear the past tense. "You are doing the right thing, Kit. BJ is happy to have you there. All the Calhouns are." Seeing her look change he admitted, "Well, maybe not all." They both knew he meant Shelby. Trace switched topics, "You've done a lot of good work for C&G Ranching. You're efficient, and good at what you do."

Kit was touched by his compliment. "Thank you. It will be good to see everyone and get back to normal."

Trace wondered if things would ever be normal again. Awareness again swept through him, only stronger this time. With every passing day, Kit had continued to amaze him. He may have been drawn to her by her beauty, but she now impressed him with her inner strength, and courage. He cared about her. Was it deeper than that, and he was too stubborn to admit it? It was going to be a long drive if he had to focus on trying to keep his eyes, and thoughts off of Kit. It was impossible not to be aware of her in the confines of the cab of his truck. It would help when they got home where he could keep his distance and refocus on his priorities. Unconsciously, he pressed down on the accelerator.

Kit became introspective. She was committed to a new life in a new country with a new family. Seeing the ranch come into view, Kit's spirits lifted, and her excitement grew. The late afternoon sun shining down on the ranch was welcoming her home, but deep down she knew it was only a temporary home. When they pulled into the yard, the Calhouns were out on the verandah waiting. Kit had missed this family. She turned to Trace, "I'm sorry you were dragged into this, but I want to thank you for everything."

"Don't go reading more into it. Somebody had to do it." He wasn't sure if he was sorry he had done this or not. Moving forward, he knew he had to make better choices regarding her. For that he needed to put distance between them. What happened last night was proof that he couldn't trust himself with her.

Kenzie began jumping up and down, and waving. As soon as Kit was out of the truck Kenzie ran into her mother's arms. Her shriek of delight brought tears to Kit's eyes, and she held Kenzie tight while smothering her with kisses.

Trace climbed up the steps, hugged Sadie, shook Will's hand, and commented on the cast on his foot. "Did you injure your foot kicking Riley in the ass trying to get him to work while I was away?" he teased.

It was Sadie who replied, "He fell the day you left. It's only a hairline fracture, but his foot has to be in a cast for a couple of weeks. Luckily, the only other injuries were a bump on his head, and a bruised ego."

Pain shot through his leg as Will shifted his position. "It hurts like hell."

"You have to use your crutches instead of hopping around."

Will ignored his wife. "It was a stupid fall. I tripped over the hose. It was my own fault."

Trace understood the old man's frustration. "Hopefully, you will have a full recovery. This place can't run without you."

"Better chance if he listens to the doctor and keeps his leg elevated whenever possible," Sadie scolded.

"Like I haven't heard that more than once." It was evident that he was in a foul mood. Will Calhoun suddenly looked old and tired.

Sadie hugged Kit. "I missed you, but I thoroughly enjoyed every minute while you were gone. Come with me." She grabbed Kit by the hand and led her into the house to Kenzie's room.

Kenzie's room had been transformed into a little girl's room. It was decorated in bright colors, pink the most prominent. Kit turned to Sadie in astonishment. "It looks like something out of a magazine, Sadie." This act of permanent acceptance was a wonderful surprise.

Sadie beamed with pride. "I had lots of help from Jenny. I'm glad you like it. It was fun to decorate a little girl's room for a change." It was nice to have Kit back. Sadie had missed her granddaughter.

"How did I get so lucky to have such an amazing family?" Kit turned as Trace stood in the doorway with the rocking chair. She stepped aside to let him enter. Their eyes met, and she recognized that he knew how important the rocker was to her even though she hadn't told him. Kit was so overcome with emotion that she broke into tears. Not because of sad memories, but because she was touched. It had been a long time since anyone had done something special for her. "You knew about this?"

"Sadie filled me in when you went inside to get your duffle bag before we left."

This man was so unpredictable. Trace was not only exciting, and charming, but kind and compassionate.

Jenny came over, and they transformed the family room into Kit's own personal space.

That night it took Kit longer than usual to settle Kenzie for bed. Kenzie wanted to show her everything all over again. Once she was in her pajamas, Kit grabbed Kenzie's blanket, and Mucky, and they went and sat in the familiar rocker. After they had read a bedtime story, Kit talked quietly to her daughter, telling her about Lou until her baby girl fell asleep in her arms. Her gaze lingered on her sleeping daughter, but her thoughts quickly turned to Trace. In her more lucid moments, Kit knew it was best that nothing happened between them. Trace was a complication she didn't need. It was best to nip her feelings for him in the bud, but it might be too late. A week ago, she believed she would have nothing to do with him. Now she couldn't imagine her life without him. Kit sat for a long time thinking things she didn't want to think. Wanting things, she didn't want to want. She closed her eyes. Maybe it was the upheaval of the past few days that had rendered her incapable of dealing with a complicated man like Trace. Defensively, she put up her protective wall.

Kenzie was asleep for the night, and Sadie had gone over to Jenny's to plan the upcoming barbeque. Kit stepped out on the porch.

Will was rocking away contentedly enjoying the stillness of a perfect summer evening. "Come keep me company," Will said, as he shifted to get comfortable. Kit moved an extra chair in front of Will so he could put his leg up. "I wish everyone would stop this fussing. You're as bad as your grandmother."

"If you're going to be cranky, I'm not going to stay. It's up to you."

Will chuckled at her impudence as he rested his foot on the chair. "You sound more, and more like a Calhoun."

Kit leaned over and kissed his cheek before sitting down next to him. She loved being back in the country where it was quiet and peaceful.

Will was obviously frustrated at finding himself temporarily disabled. "Reminds me of when I broke my leg years ago. I had no choice, but to place the burden of the ranch on BJ. He became a man overnight, and he shouldered the responsibility well." Will looked over as BJ was coming up the walk. "Well, speak of the devil, and he shows up."

His son sat down on the step, "I was getting in the way at home. Jenny and Ma are busy finalizing the menu for the barbeque and deciding who will make what."

Kit looked at her dad, "I'm warning you ahead of time. Your dad is a little heavy on the grumpy side."

The old man grinned reluctantly, "Yes, I am, but I'm not too old to still teach you both a thing or two. Same goes for those Grayson boys." He turned to Kit, a teasing glint in his eyes. "Did Trace behave himself, Missy?"

Kit was grateful for the darkness of the evening, knowing the rush of color now warmed her cheeks. "He was nicer than I expected," was all she would confess to.

"Good. The boys were a challenge growing up. Thanks to me, and Buster those Grayson boys are wonderful young men."

Kit enjoyed spending time with the two men. In doing so, she was learning more about each one of the Calhouns as well as the Graysons. She had yet to meet Lola Grayson, so she was intrigued by the mystery lady. Everyone spoke highly of her. Kit had to wonder if anyone could be that nice. She smiled as Lou's image came to mind. The three of them chatted until Sadie returned from next door.

Will reached for his crutches, "I think I'll call it a night. Come on, Ma, help me up."

BJ moved up to the vacated chair and sat next to his daughter.

Once the elderly Calhouns were in the house, Kit turned to her dad, "Your parents are admirable people."

"You and Kenzie have given my parents a whole new world of happiness." Sensing that Kit was feeling a little down, he asked, "Was it hard leaving, Kit?"

"Not as hard as the first time. Thanks to all of you, this time it felt like I was coming home."

They chatted away, but soon Kit was yawning. She was exhausted from getting up so early, so decided to call it a night. She went inside hoping she would have a better sleep. To do that she knew she'd have to dismiss a certain cowboy from her mind.

Chapter Nineteen

Sadie was setting the table for breakfast when BJ entered. "Should I set another plate?"

"No thanks, Ma. I'll just grab a coffee."

They both turned when they heard Will's crutches thumping down the hallway. Sadie groaned, "Here comes, Grumpy."

Will entered the kitchen, flopped down on his chair with a grunt, and leaned his crutches against the wall behind him.

"How're you doing, Dad?"

"I'd be a lot better if I could get rid of these damn crutches."

"You only have to use them for a few more days," Sadie said as she set a cup of coffee in front of him.

"Good morning," Kit said as she entered the kitchen with Kenzie, who immediately climbed up on her Grandpa's knee. "Hi, Dad. What's up?"

"Nothing much. I want Murphy to go into town and pick up an order from the hardware store. I thought he could take Dad along for company. It will get him out of your hair for a couple of hours. Jenny's gone to the city, and Shelby is working full-time with Doc all week."

This news was welcoming to Kit's ears. No unexpected encounters from Shelby. While she was away, Kit had sworn to make every attempt to be nice to Shelby no matter how obnoxious the girl could be. She was glad she wasn't going to be put to the test right away.

Will scowled, "I probably shouldn't go. It looks like if I want any work done around here, I'll have to do it myself. Where is Trace these days? It's like he just up and disappeared."

Nobody commented but Kit wondered the same thing. She couldn't believe that it had been a week since they had returned from Washington. Riley had been in the office helping her every day, but of Trace, she saw nothing. Kit felt an irrational sense of disappointment.

After the men left, Kit went to the office. She looked around with pride, remembering how the office had looked the first time she'd seen it. The extra hours she was putting in were by choice. She knew she had been staying longer hoping to see Trace. Kit smiled when Riley entered. Working with Riley was easy. They were quickly becoming good friends. "What's Caballo Stables? Different things relating to it have popped up a couple of times."

Riley was quick to explain, "With the Calhouns, we make a comfortable living with the cattle, and that is C&G Ranching. They are the mainstay that helped us get Lola Grande on its feet. Even before Lola Grande was ours, Trace started Caballo Stables as his own enterprise. He began breaking, and training horses right out of high school. He now specializes in training horses for cutting. The horse business is Trace's, it is not part of C&G Ranching or Valley View. Trace's hard work is making it a viable operation. In time it will make him independent and offer a good living. Trace has already made a name for himself as a highly respected trainer in western Canada. We no longer have a financial debt to the Calhouns, but we still need their help. Trace works the horses here for now. In time, we will have the facilities at Lola Grande where he will be able to run his own first-rate operation. Lola Grande and Caballo Stables have become Trace's obsession. Between the two of them, he has no time for anything else."

"Like taking time off for an unexpected road trip. Trace was not happy about that."

Riley intentionally ignored Kit's comment, even though he did feel a little guilty.

"This morning, Will questioned Dad about Trace's absence all week."

Riley didn't know what was up with his brother. Maybe it was time to find out. "Will can be very formidable when he gets cranky. His broken foot has really gotten to him."

"It's getting to all of us. We're all trying to stay out of his way. The only person he doesn't snap at is Kenzie."

Riley nodded. "Growing up here, we've seen that side of him."

Kit remained distracted, and her thoughts shifted. She was startled when Riley tapped her on the shoulder.

"Your mind seems to be elsewhere today. Did you create those new files we were talking about?"

Frustrated because her thoughts were still on Trace, Kit's voice was irritable, "When I say I'll do something I do it."

Riley couldn't hide his startled expression.

Between a cantankerous old man, and an absent cowboy, Kit was in a foul mood of her own. She hadn't slept well since she'd left Washington, so she was tired. She was also tired of wrestling with her emotions. The memories of the time spent with Trace refused to leave her. He was on her mind when she went to sleep at night, and again first thing in the morning. She was angry with herself for not having the ability to erase him from her mind.

Kit was relieved when Riley left. She couldn't blame him for leaving early. Her short tempered behavior was due to his brother but he wasn't here to take it out on. Kit exhaled despairingly and got up to get a coffee. Jenny and Sadie were sitting at the kitchen table discussing the upcoming barbeque. Kit sat down, and joined them, welcoming the distraction. Since her return, Kit felt that Jenny was making an effort to get to know her better. Shelby was a different story. It seemed that Shelby's latest ploy was to ignore Kit by staying away. Kit was grateful for that, but it also felt like she was always waiting for an unexpected confrontation.

Kit wasn't the only one who had been replaying the last few days. When confronted with something hard, Trace retreated. Usually all he needed was fresh air, and solitude to clear his head. He had made a point of staying away from Valley View. Trace had hoped that distance would be an effective weapon to counteract this looming attraction. Out of sight, out of mind. Hardly! He may not have seen Kit since returning from Washington, but it didn't mean she wasn't on his mind. If he closed his eyes, he could picture her clearly. Her features were engraved in his brain. He tried to ignore the frustration eating at his gut. He didn't need this. He didn't like it. And he sure as hell didn't understand it. He would not let himself become involved with this woman. She'd want more than he was willing to give.

Trace jumped when Riley slapped him on the back. He was so deep in thought he hadn't heard his brother drive up. He was spending too much time in his head.

"You're a hard man to pin down these days. Will's been asking about you. You've been avoiding everyone since you got back from Wahington. Are you okay, bro?"

Wanting to shift his thoughts away from Kit, Trace went on the attack in an attempt to justify his absence. "There's a lot to take care of at our own ranch since I have your chores to do. I'm working my ass off while you're hustling yours over to Valley View, and spending what I can only hope is productive time in the office with Kit. As you can see there is fence that needs fixing. Lucky, I saw this break, and could repair it before any of the herd escaped. Didn't anyone do anything while I was gone?"

"We were down a man who was away on a road trip. Will broke his foot, and I had the flu," Riley said, with a straight face.

"Well, there's a lot to do. You can get Cole riding fence and checking all the gates. Lance can mow the ditches. The grass is way too high. It should have been cut days ago. If you are going to become the ranch foreman, you need to stay on top of things like this."

"I didn't come out here for a lecture." It suddenly dawned on Riley, "This has to do with Kit, doesn't it? What happened between the two of you while you were away?"

Trace became quiet. His life had been a lot simpler a week ago. "I have been avoiding Valley View because of Kit. She's driving me crazy. I've never met a woman like her. She's feisty and spirited one minute, and vulnerable the next. On one hand she's tough, argumentative, and stubbornly independent. On the other hand, she's genuine, brave, and honest. She has everything a man could possibly want." And more! Who could forget her daughter, Kenzie?

Riley smiled with newfound awareness. "Oh, man, it's worse than I thought. Another Grayson brought to his knees by Cupid's arrow."

There was no more denying the feelings Kit stirred in him. Trace couldn't begin to guess why her? Why now? Lust he understood. It was easy to satisfy and move on. Love, on the other hand, was an emotion that could interfere with a man's judgement, and commitment to goals. Trace had seen the negative effects often enough to want to avoid it. A woman was capable of either consuming a man or smothering him. Trace questioned his new feelings, "How do you know if you're in love?"

"You just know," his younger brother proclaimed. He had fallen in love with Shelby when he was fifteen. She'd been the only one for him ever since.

"When Kit showed up out of the blue, I thought she came here to take advantage of BJ, and the Calhouns. I was wrong about her." While they were away, he had been affected by her story, and everything she'd been through.

"Once you get to know Kit, you realize she's special," Riley said sincerely.

Yes, she was that. She was also a mother. He wasn't cut out for family life. This was part of his past that still haunted Trace. "Women are just too much trouble."

Riley agreed. "And we can't live without them."

Humor was evident in Riley's voice. Trace tossed his brother a dirty look and went back to fixing the fence.

Riley responded with a look of his own. "Maybe you're fixing the wrong fence, Trace."

Trace shook his head. "It's complicated."

"Uncomplicate it. Talk to Kit."

Trace leaned against the fence post. Despite not wanting his brother's unsolicited advice, Riley had opened his eyes to a few truths. He knew he needed to go see Kit. Staying away hadn't solved anything, and he couldn't stay away from Valley View forever. His days had been long, and lonely, accentuated by a feeling of loss. It felt as if something rare had passed him by never to return. He knew he had to try and make things right. The longer he waited the harder it would be. Having made his decision, his dark mood lightened.

*****

Will and Sadie were watching television, and Kenzie was down for the night. Kit waved on her way through and escaped to the front verandah. She listened to the comforting sounds of the night while staring into the gathering darkness. It was good to be back, but her spirits were low. Sitting alone brought the stark reality of her solitary existence. Her thoughts turned to Trace. Apparently, their time together meant nothing. It was simply a brief interlude away from the ranch. So, she'd just forget about it, too. It wasn't like she didn't know up front what kind of a man he was. Kit tried to bury her feelings deeper.

Sadie left Will to join Kit and sat down next to her. She realized Kit had been crying. "What is it, Kit? What's troubling you?" She wasn't the same Kit. The changes were subtle, but they were there. Kit's spontaneous joy had vanished since her trip to Washington.

"Nothing." Seeing Sadie's concerned look, she added, "Really."

When Kit didn't volunteer any more information, Sadie gently asked, "Having second thoughts about moving here?" It couldn't have been easy for Kit to leave Walla Walla.

"No, it's good to be back. I don't know what's wrong with me," Kit declared as her eyes welled. She knew exactly what was wrong, but she wasn't ready to confess that she couldn't sort out her feelings for Trace.

Sadie knew this move was only part of the reason for Kit's state of mind. Sadie believed that Kit's sadness had to do with Trace. She tried probing in a subtle way, "How was your trip?"

Kit smiled but it wasn't her usual bright smile. "It was fine. Trace was a wonderful tour guide on the way down. We drove through the Crowsnest Pass and stopped at Frank Slide. Thanks to our trip, I learned more about him, and realized I had judged him unfairly. He in turn, admitted to having preconceived ideas about me that he realized were unfair, as well as unjustified. So, it was good." Her answer was vague.

"Did something happen? It's odd that Trace hasn't been around for days."

The direct question caught Kit off guard, but she wasn't offended. She knew Sadie was asking out of concern. Whatever her issues with Trace might be, she knew he was a good man. She didn't want Sadie to get the wrong impression. "Not what you're thinking. Trace was a gentleman, but he did kiss me. Other than that, there's nothing much to tell except now I don't know what I feel." All the uncertainty Kit was feeling was revealed in her voice. Kit closed her eyes, fighting the desolation that continued to overwhelm her. She realized it wasn't Trace she was resisting but herself. Her feelings for him scared her to death. Although she was sure Trace was attracted to her, she wondered if his feelings went any deeper. It didn't matter. He wasn't the kind who would tie himself down with a wife and child. He wasn't the marrying kind, and she wouldn't settle for less. She wondered if she'd ever be able to fill the void in her heart caused by one captivating cowboy.

"Don't you think it might be a good idea to find out? It's obvious that you care about him."

Kit looked at Sadie and admitted, "I care but any type of relationship with Trace is on a collision course. He's not interested in anything more than a fling." Well, she had her own rules, including one that didn't allow for short-term pleasure no matter how wonderful it might be.

"Let's assume for the sake of argument that he's probably as miserable as you are. Why else would he be staying away?"

"Who knows why Trace does anything? I told you he's Jekyll and Hyde." Kit rose, and said goodnight, wanting to escape, and take refuge in her room.

✳✳✳✳✳

Kenzie was down for her nap and Will and Sadie had gone to the city for Will's doctor's appointment. Kit poured a glass of iced tea and went outside to enjoy some quiet time. The wind bringing cool air off the mountains was refreshing. Like the clouds overhead, her thoughts drifted aimlessly. It wasn't long, and images of Trace began to wander down what was now a familiar path. Kit had already run the gamut of emotions. Trace had hurt her with his absence. It was as if those moments never mattered to him. So, she'd just forget about them, too. Maybe it was loneliness that was affecting her emotions? She shook her head. She didn't need a man so she wouldn't be alone. Kit sighed; she was tired of trying to analyze her feelings while trying to figure out what she wanted.

When Kit looked out, she wondered if Trace was a figment of her imagination as the man himself approached. She was astonished by the change in him. It looked like he hadn't shaved for a couple of days, and in the bright daylight his face looked drawn. She stared long, and hard at him knowing he wasn't going to disappear merely because she wanted him to. Conflicting emotions since she'd been dying to see him. Kit didn't say anything as she stiffened and crossed her arms over her chest. Unfortunately, her anger was stronger than her compassion.

Trace did not mistake the defensive body language. He sat down anyway. He tipped his hat brim lower to block the afternoon sun. Kit had every right to be mad at him. Trace swallowed hard because he was nervous. He had no idea what to say. There was no explanation or even an excuse for his absence. "How have you been?" he asked lamely.

"I was fine until you got here."

Trace raised an eyebrow, "Wow, that was harsh." He knew from her cool tone this wasn't going to be easy. "I was hoping we could talk."

"Really! Well, I'm busy, and I have no desire to talk to you. I have a lot of work to do now that we're back. Obviously, you've been busy, too."

Hearing the sarcasm in her voice, Trace knew this was going to be more difficult than he thought. He let out a heavy sigh, "I know I deserve this, but will you give me a minute?" His gaze pleaded with her to give him a chance to explain.

Kit could see that he was struggling. Pride kept her silent. She preferred thinking of it as pride, and not stubbornness.

"Hear me out, please."

Her voice remained cool, and her stormy eyes continued to glare at him. "Not right now."

Trace flinched at her tone, "When?"

"When I'm not mad anymore." Temper was so much easier to release when hurt.

Trace laughed. A mistake of course. Laughing at a woman this angry was downright stupid. "That could take forever. You are more stubborn that your father, and grandfather put together."

Kit stared straight ahead while struggling with the fact that he was too close to ignore. He still had the same effect on her.

The trip to Washington had thrown Trace's whole life into turmoil. He had been affected by Kit's story, and how brave she had been with her decisions. Because of what he had learned, this woman mattered. His beckoning eyes were filled with regret, "I try to give a person a chance while getting to know them. I didn't with you. It seems that I keep prejudging you, and I've been wrong every time. But not this time. I don't think I'm wrong about how we feel. We can't ignore the chemistry between us. I want to get to know you better. We can start as friends." Trace had always made it clear in any relationship that he wanted no entanglements. That had been enough until now. He wanted Kit in his life.

Kit swallowed hard, trying to process what he was saying. She felt she was being pulled against her will by her heart strings. Trace had told her more than once he didn't want a relationship with commitment. She had rules, too, including one that didn't allow for short-term pleasure. What were they supposed to do when, even though they wanted each other, they wanted completely different things? Kit had her pride. "If we are going to be friends, I want you to respect my wishes. I'm not interested in any kind of relationship." Kit couldn't deny that she had been attracted to his physical attributes, but since the trip it had become more than physical. She had begun to like Trace, and wanted to get to know him better, too.

Trace nodded, agreeing to this new understanding between them.

"This isn't a game, this is reality. I'm not a teenager anymore. I'm a grown woman, and a mother with responsibilities. I'm a package deal, and Kenzie comes first. It's not just about you, and me." Just then, Kenzie called out. Kit looked at Trace. "Motherhood, always real."

Trace put his hand over Kit's, "Can we give ourselves some time to figure out what's happening between us?"

Trace smiled that captivating smile that made her knees go weak. Kit was frightened by the strong hold he had over her. "I don't know what you really want, Trace."

Trace knew what Kit wanted. This was a woman who wanted forever with a husband, and father. That scared the hell out of him, but not enough to stop him from saying, "I want to know who you are, not who I thought you were. I thought we had begun to do that. Our trip to Washington changed things for me. You're different than the other women I've known, and not because you're a mother."

"We may want the same things, Trace, but I want more than you're willing to give."

So, he wasn't wrong. "The feelings between us took me as much by surprise as it did you. Can we spend some time together?"

Kit swallowed hard, "No strings attached. Just friends?"

"Yes, as friends." It was one thing to say something, and another to mean it. Trace was feeling uneasy when he left. He headed over to the barn.

Murphy was alone in the tack room. "I saw you talking to Kit. Why do you look like you just wrestled a grizzly bear, and lost?"

"Are all women trouble, Murphy?"

"Men understand men. You will never understand women. They are way too much trouble. But then, I've never met a lady like Kit."

"You don't have to sing her praises, Murphy. Riley has already treated me to the full chorus." But he had to agree with Murphy. He'd never met a lady like Kit, either.

Murphy gently placed a hand on Trace's shoulder. "Kit is like Diego, headstrong and proud. Take the time to get to know her like you did, Diego. You have fallen in love with one complex woman."

"I don't love, Kit," Trace lied.

Murphy gave a rare chuckle, "Sure you don't. And grass ain't green."

Chapter Twenty

Today was the annual Labour Day barbeque. This year the Calhouns were celebrating more than a good year for C&G Ranching. The family was celebrating Shelby's graduation and her new job as Doc Parker's veterinary assistant at his clinic. They would also be introducing their new family members.

Sadie and Kit were busy in the kitchen. A rap at the door announced the arrival of Jenny, and Shelby who had their hands loaded down with bowls of salads. Sadie, who was busy filling deviled eggs, motioned toward the fridge with her head, "There's room on the second shelf."

Kit had to ask, "How many people are coming? You have enough food for an army."

"Probably in the count of sixty. It's going to get pretty rowdy around here."

"Oh," Kit said, in a small voice and her stomach turned. Kit was ready to meet new people, accept new experiences, but now she was nervous. The thought of being thrust into the midst of so many strangers suddenly scared her.

The kitchen became a beehive of activity. Both Kit, and Shelby spent the morning helping where needed. Kenzie had been good all morning, but Kit could tell she was getting bored. "Here, you can carry this bag of plastic cups, and we'll go put them on the big table outside." Kit grabbed the plates, and cutlery. As soon as Kenzie was done placing them on the buffet table, she spotted her Papa, and took off running.

Shelby was chatting with Riley, who was busy stacking a pile of firewood. Riley waved Kit over when he saw her.

After engaging in a brief glaring match, Shelby purposely ignored Kit. Shelby had continually given Kit the cold shoulder, so Kit was used to it. "Hi, Riley."

"Looking forward to your first Calhoun shindig? Ready to do a little boot-scootin'? Throw back some cold ones? Rope yourself a cowboy?"

"There will be a lot of eligible cowboys here tonight." Annoyed with the attention Riley kept giving Kit, the baited comment was for him, not Kit.

"And just as many tempting cowgirls," Riley added pointedly, as his gaze turned to Kit.

Shelby wasn't used to Riley's comebacks. Feeling slighted, she left.

"Doesn't her attitude bother you?"

"Eventually, she'll grow up and she'll come around with you, too."

Kit hoped that Riley was right. She'd sworn to try to get along with Shelby, but this was proving to be difficult, since the girl was so stubborn. "You're such a nice guy, Riley." Too nice for Shelby. Kit saw the sadness in his eyes. "There's nothing wrong with being a nice guy," she told him before heading back to the house.

Will and BJ were sitting on the verandah watching the organized bustle of activity. Kit brought out a pitcher of lemonade, and the ladies joined them while they took a break. It was unusually warm for late summer, and the sky was clear. It was going to be a grand day.

Cole and Lance had just finished stringing party lights along the side of the deck, and across the back of the house. Sadie thanked them.

"No problem, Ma'am. We'll be back later for the party."

"Are you bringing dates?" Both boys nodded, and high-fived each other.

Will decided to go find Murphy. He tested his weight as he grabbed his cane.

"Be careful," Sadie called out.

"I know," Will grumbled.

Sadie remarked sympathetically, "He's recovering, but the doctor warned him to slow down. Men don't listen unless you're saying what they want to hear. Will can't keep doing as much as he used to. He knows that BJ is perfectly capable of running the ranch, but it's hard to let go. Despite his age, his will remains strong, so he still thinks he can do everything he used to." The ladies went back inside to address the last-minute tasks.

Kit put Kenzie down for her nap. Before she knew it Kenzie was up and in their way.

"Why don't I take Kenzie outside, and let BJ watch her. Everything is pretty well done for now. You and Jenny can go and get yourselves ready."

Jenny saw the look of anxiety in Kit's eyes. "I'll come back as soon as I'm ready. We can find BJ together." Jenny, and Kit had become friends. Motherhood, widowhood, and inner strength, along with a new understanding, had bonded them.

Kit was grateful. If there was one thing that she hated more than gossip it was being the center of attention.

Sadie also saw Kit's apprehension. She smiled with encouragement, "I want you to relax and have a good time. I'll introduce you to Maggie Walker. She has a little girl who is three. Maggie, and Mitch farm to the south of us. He often helps Trace with the horses. Trace, and Mitch have been solid friends since high school. Off you go, Kit." Sadie shoo-shooed her granddaughter out of the kitchen.

Kit donned a white fringed shirt with a pair of black jeans that hugged her to perfection. She knew she had dressed to impress. Looking in the mirror, she combed her fingers through her silky strands, and smiled. Since having Kenzie she'd denied her sexuality. She looked down and did up one more button on her shirt. Mothers weren't sexy.

Shelby, who was alone in the kitchen when Kit entered, had outdone herself. Her hair was pulled back in a single braid like the day Kit had met her. She had changed into a pair of designer jeans that clung to her lean frame. Her turquoise western shirt was bright and sparkly. Her cowboy boots weren't her everyday boots. The turquoise-flowered boots were the perfect accessory with her outfit. She looked stunning.

Shelby had to admit that Kit looked attractive. Her hair framed her face in soft waves drawing attention to her large gray eyes that sparkled with excitement. Shelby knew that Kit would attract attention. "Trying to compete for the cowboys around here? You know you're just a diversion for the men because you're the new flavor of the month."

Kit had started the day determined to be positive, and not let Shelby get to her. She knew she shouldn't react, but the girl never backed off. "Does that make you yesterday's leftovers?"

BJ entered the kitchen and sensed the tension. He looked at his two daughters with pride, but he knew they had not yet bonded as sisters. "I hope you two are getting along better?" he said, looking directly at Shelby.

"Like best friends," Shelby said sweetly.

Kit rolled her eyes, and retaliated, "All the knives are still in the drawer, but I didn't turn my back on her."

His two daughters were so alike it almost made him laugh. He hoped they would behave themselves today. Shelby stormed out muttering under her breath but neither of them missed her saying, "Stupid bitch."

Kit shook her head at Shelby's immature behavior. She looked up at her dad, "I'll be on my best behavior for the rest of the day."

"I better go rescue Riley. I put him in charge of watching Kenzie while I came to get more ice for the coolers. Friends are starting to arrive, and the beer coolers have been under attack." He grabbed two bags of ice and left.

When Jenny arrived to get her, Kit tried to maintain a show of enthusiasm. Jenny guided her along the path that skirted the house. Even before they rounded the corner Kit heard the loud hum of voices, and boisterous laughter. Groups were scattered across the grounds catching up and exchanging gossip. To Kit, it seemed that the whole county had turned up.

"Well, city girl, aren't you something." Trace was hoping that today would be a perfect opportunity to get to know Kit better. He no longer questioned his feelings for Kit, just his own level of commitment.

Kit turned, recognizing the drawling voice that often played in her head. "Not too bad yourself, cowboy," she said as she gave him a saucy smile. Trace was dressed head to toe in black. She imagined he'd taken less than ten minutes to look ruggedly handsome, while she'd spent an hour dressing so she could look completely casual.

BJ approached the couple and nabbed his daughter. He waved to a couple that had just arrived, anxious to introduce his new daughter. Shelby glared as they walked by. She was sulking because Kit was getting all the attention, and she didn't like it. Kit had caught the eye of many of the young men, and as far as Shelby was concerned, Riley was also paying her too much attention. Shelby was jealous of Kit's relationship with Riley.

Over the next hour Kit met dozens of people. Kit was cordial, kindly answering the same questions over and over. Throughout the afternoon,

Kit also saw a different side of Shelby. The girl was radiant as she greeted guests. It was obvious that Shelby was outgoing, and personable. The lively, likeable young girl everyone said she was. Kit recognized this, and under different circumstances Kit probably would have liked her. Kit hoped that time would change Shelby's negative attitude toward her.

BJ turned to his daughter, "I have to leave you for a while, it's time to start up the grill."

Hoping to make her escape, Kit said, "I'll go and help Sadie."

"Ma told me to tell you that she has everything under control so relax and enjoy yourself. You're off the clock for the rest of the day."

Panic set in as Kit looked around for any familiar face. She smiled with relief as Riley rounded the corner of the house.

Shelby had just brushed him off and he was feeling slighted. Riley knew that she had set the tone for the day because he had teased her earlier. He was used to Shelby's games, but he decided it was time to step up his own game. He wouldn't do anything rash, but he knew if he spent time with Kit, it would make Shelby jealous. He felt a tinge of guilt knowing he would be intentionally using Kit, and she'd take their time together as friendship.

Kit was grateful to see him. "Please stay with me until I find Kenzie."

"I'll stay right by your side, Kit."

"Are you using me, Riley Grayson?" Her eyes were alight with amusement.

Kit was wiser than he realized. "Maybe a little. Your being here has dimmed Shelby's spotlight, so she's being more flirtatious than usual."

Distracted, Shelby was startled when someone pulled her braid.

"Shelby?" Nick Connor did a double take.

"You'd better take a good look, Nick. I'm not little Shelby Calhoun anymore. You haven't been around for a while. I grew up."

"I can see that you have," he agreed, as he ran his gaze over her body from head to toe. Her skinny, tomboy days were gone. She'd grown into a woman. "You're looking super."

"What are you doing here?"

"I ran into Olivia Beaumont, and she invited me along. You know how I love a good party. Who's the stunner with Riley? You two not an item anymore?"

Realizing that others might be thinking the same thing, Shelby's anger toward Riley increased.

Kit's attention was drawn to the loud-mouthed stranger standing next to Shelby. She'd been uncomfortably aware of him staring at her. The man obviously believed he was God's gift to women. She watched as Shelby linked arms with him and pulled him toward her. Kit glared at Shelby knowing full well that her intentions weren't gracious. Kit was relieved when Trace seemed to materialize out of nowhere.

Trace, and Nick glared at each other with mutual dislike. "Why are you here, Connor?" For some reason, this man always rubbed Trace the wrong way.

Nick's gaze lingered on Kit. "I came to meet this pretty little lady."

Trace's mouth tightened.

"Nick Connor, meet Kit Bennett, Dad's long-lost daughter, who just showed up unexpectedly a couple of weeks ago. She's staying with my grandparents."

"Well, I see that beauty runs in the family," Nick said with appreciation, as he ogled Kit. Nick's smile was slow, unmistakably insolent. "All the fellas around here are talking about you."

The hair on Kit's neck stood up. She was appalled by his blatant forwardness. "Did they mention I have a three-year-old daughter?" Kit asked pointedly.

"That scare you off?" Trace challenged.

"Your kid, Trace?" Nick couldn't resist the dig.

Kit was about to answer, but Trace interjected first, "I should be so lucky."

That comment drew Trace further into Kit's heart.

Having recovered, Nick sneered, "Sure cramps a guy's style. I think I'll get me a beer."

Trace was surprised by the sense of protectiveness he felt for Kit. "Stay away from Nick Connor. He's nothing but trouble, and a renowned flirt. Chases anyone in a skirt."

"Good thing I don't wear skirts," Kit replied flippantly.

With those legs you should, thought Trace.

Olivia had crashed the barbeque hoping to see Trace. She looked around at the relaxed gathering. The informal setting was so different from the sophisticated dinners, and pretentious business engagements that made up her social life while she was living in England. Today's barbeque was as she remembered. A lot of food, a lot of mingling, and a lot of people. True to most parties, the men tended to congregate together. Olivia's eyes settled on a group by the bar. Her heart quickened when she saw Trace. In a glance, she took in all of him. Olivia could see that Trace's younger brooding looks had been replaced by newfound confidence. He was as handsome, and dangerous to look at as he had been when she met him. She also knew that Trace was now a rancher, and renowned horse trainer. A lot had changed over the years.

Olivia took a moment to reflect on her own past. She knew she had made a mistake when she married Burke, but she owed it to her dad. During the time Burke had courted her, and until they married, he had showered her with gifts, and pampered her extravagantly. Once the business transaction was completed, things began to change. It was still good in the beginning because everything was new and exciting. Their London apartment was exquisite and luxurious. The staff took excellent care of her, especially in Burke's absence. Olivia lived in luxury, but she often lived there alone. Burke was a workaholic and traveled a lot for business. When he did take her along it was for looks. He wanted to show his clients the image of a happily married man with a beautiful, adoring wife. It didn't take long for Olivia to realize that Burke was extremely jealous. Burke believed he owned her. Olivia's gaze returned to Trace. Olivia recalled seeing a glimmer of Burke's jealousy the summer she spent with Trace while Burke was in London on business. Olivia was bored, so she used Trace to entertain her. She smiled in memory. Trace had been a fascinating summer fling. Things changed and became worse after she married Burke. Well, she wasn't married anymore. And neither was Trace. Not that it would matter.

Olivia had been trying to get Trace's attention all afternoon, but he seemed to be ignoring her. It was evident that BJ's daughter had his unwavering attention. Olivia had heard that Shelby hadn't taken kindly to the unexpected arrival of BJ's real daughter. Why would she, thought Olivia. She couldn't imagine dealing with something that unexpected. When Olivia spotted Shelby, she was surprised at how beautiful she was. Shelby had outdone herself, obviously wanting to overshadow Kit. Olivia smiled in understanding as she approached Shelby. Olivia never hesitated to take advantage of an opportunity.

Trace and Kit were still chatting when Shelby reappeared with Olivia. Kit thought the new arrival should have looked out of place. Olivia was over-dressed in her maxi dress, but accented with fashionable cowboy boots, and a designer denim jacket made it work. The woman was eye-catching. She was sophisticated, pencil thin, and posh. Her platinum blonde hair was cut in a fashion-forward bob.

The look Olivia gave Kit was anything but friendly. Her appraisal of Kit was cool, and she quickly sized Kit up as strikingly wholesome. Ignoring Kit, Olivia greeted Trace with a dazzling smile. She nudged between Kit and Trace, forcing Kit to move over. It was clear that this woman wanted Trace's full attention.

Trace was more annoyed than pleased by Olivia's arrival. He had noticed Olivia when she arrived. It was impossible not to. As enticing as she was to look at, Trace had zero attraction to her anymore. Darkness clouded the cowboy's eyes. Trace recalled the barbeque he, and Olivia had attended together. At the time, he had been infatuated with her, but he had no idea of the strong social status that was expected to be honored. It became evident when she turned on him to obey her father's wishes. That was the last time he had seen Olivia Beaumont. The shadows in his eyes disappeared as they drifted back to Kit.

Olivia could see the cool indifference in his sexy blue eyes. "I haven't seen you even though I've been back for months," she pouted. "My marriage didn't work out, so Burke and I are divorced. I'm living at home for now."

Trace, and Olivia made small talk, doing the cursory catch-up. Kit was relieved to make her escape when Riley waved her over. The tall, dark-haired woman standing next to Riley had to be Lola Grayson.

Riley put his arm around Kit as he made introductions, "Ma, I'd like you to meet Kit Bennett, BJ's daughter. I told you she's a beauty." Riley's eyes were twinkling merrily, knowing that Shelby was within hearing.

Kit blushed knowing full well what Riley was doing, while hoping that his mom wasn't getting the wrong impression.

Lola smiled warmly at Kit, "I've heard so much about you from my boys. I'm pleased to finally meet you."

Trace had managed to make his escape from Olivia and joined them. "Telling Kit about all my good points, Ma?" Trace asked.

Kit was surprised by the tenderness in his voice. When Trace let down his guard, she could see a sensitive side to him that he preferred to keep hidden. Here stood two sons who worshipped their mother. It was evident that this family was close.

"I did. It took all of five seconds. Why not earn some points and get us both a drink?"

"I'll get your usual, Ma. What about you, Kit?"

"Nothing, thanks. I'll get something later. I was on my way to find Kenzie."

Kit studied the Grayson brothers as they headed to the bar. Her eyes lingered on Trace out of habit.

Lola, in turn, studied Kit carefully. She smiled to herself, realizing that Sadie and Riley were right. It was clear that Trace, and Kit were attracted to each other. "My son respects you a lot. He says you're a courageous lady, a hard worker, and a good mom."

Kit smiled, "That was nice of Riley."

Lola shook her head, "It was Trace who said it."

Sadie, who had just arrived with Kenzie, hugged her dear friend. "I'm so glad you came, Lola. Do you mind if I steal Kit away? Mitch and Maggie just arrived." She turned to Kit, "Kenzie will enjoy playing with their daughter, Lucy Rose."

"It was nice to meet you, Mrs. Grayson."

"Please call me, Lola."

Kit smiled as Kenzie started to pull at her hand. More people to meet. She was already starting to forget names, but she knew she wouldn't forget Lola Grayson. She was a striking woman, although reserved.

As soon as Maggie met Kit, she liked her. "Why don't I take Kenzie with us, and we'll go over to the play area. That will free you up to socialize."

"Thank you. Other than the Calhouns and the Graysons, Doc Parker is the only other person I know. I just arrived a few weeks ago and I don't have any friends."

"Well, consider me a friend, because I know we will be. When it's time to eat I'll save you a seat at our table. We can get to know each other better then." Kit nodded in agreement.

Later in the day, when mother and son were by themselves Lola commented on Kit, and Olivia. "There's no comparison between the two women is there?"

Trace's eyes found Kit, who was laughing down at her daughter. "There's a big difference, and her name is, Kenzie."

Lola nodded, and wisely kept her thoughts to herself. She knew from experience that life takes a person down many different roads. None of them knew how much their own arrival at Valley View would change their lives. She looked at Kit and wondered what kind of an impact this young lady would have on their lives. She figured Trace was in for another big change.

Trace and Doc Parker were deep in conversation. Doc glanced over at Kit who was chatting with Maggie. "It's nice to see BJ's daughter enjoying herself. She said this kind of get together is new to her, so it's good to see her laughing, and interacting with everyone. Kit is quite the mystery lady. I'm looking forward to getting to know her better."

Trace gave an expressive shrug, "Go ahead, Doc. Get in line with the rest of the men."

"Are you in that line, Trace?"

Denying his attraction, Trace replied, "Kit, and I are just friends."

"Don't forget I know you, and I've seen you around Kit. It's like you don't even know there are other people around. Like Olivia, who has been vying for your attention all day."

Trace was well aware of that, but he wouldn't use Olivia to get his mind off of Kit. It wouldn't be fair to any of them. Trace quickly reined in his hunger for Kit, and reminded himself what the rules were, but some of his resolute rules seemed to have disappeared.

Doc regarded Trace stoically.

"What?" Trace asked in annoyance.

"You said Kit couldn't get under your skin. I have news for you, Trace. Kit's way, way under your skin. Well, I like the lady, so I'm not about to bow out. I will enjoy spending time today getting to know her better, and we'll see where things go. Game on, partner."

Throughout the day, Trace couldn't stop himself from glancing Kit's way as she mingled. There was something about Kit that drew the young men to her like a magnet. Unaware, his gaze again wandered through the crowd until he spotted Kit chatting away with Doc. He couldn't fault the guy for trying.

Laughter, and music abounded. The party was in full swing, and the mood was infectious. Kit began tapping her foot to the music. Everyone cheered when the music for the Macarena filled the air. Shelby grabbed Riley and looked at Trace who declined. Shelby looked over, daring Kit to join in. Kit chose to ignore her.

"What's the matter, Kit? Afraid you don't fit in here?" Shelby called out.

Trace, who was standing next to her goaded, "Not up to the challenge?"

Kit didn't like being bullied into anything, but she wouldn't mind putting Shelby in her place. Without a word she got up and joined the front line. *There's more to this city girl than you think, sister.* Little did Shelby know that as a camp counselor Kit had learned all the line dances along with the kids. Without a misstep, she stepped into the routine.

The music went from the Macarena to The Electric Slide. The crowd cheered when the next song was Achy Breaky Heart. A few dropped out, including Riley, but both Shelby, and Kit stayed. Step for step, Kit kept up to Shelby right to the end. Having made her point, Kit went, and sat down when it was over.

Trace walked over with two bottles of beer. "You look like you could use this. You're the damndest woman I've ever known," he said with admiration.

Kit wiped her moist brow, and grinned, "That's what they all say." She took a big swig of beer, and then held it up to her flushed cheek. The bottle was cold, the beer refreshing. She took another long drink.

Trace lifted a surprised eyebrow. "I bet you can two-step as well."

Kit nodded. "And polka," she added as she took another swallow of beer.

Jenny, and BJ stood together on the verandah. They smiled at each other, grateful for the brief escape. Their gaze was drawn to Nick Connor who had his arm draped over Shelby's shoulder. BJ expressed his concern, "Shelby's been hanging around with him all day. She's flirting with danger by spending time with that man." BJ experienced a twinge of conscience. He'd been spending less time with Shelby to be with Kit, and Kenzie. He knew this was making Shelby jealous, and rebellious. He understood why Shelby was having difficulty dealing with the recent changes in her life, but maybe it was worse than he realized. Was Shelby rebelling in more ways than one? It was a disturbing thought.

Jenny wasn't concerned. She knew her daughter too well. "Shelby is trying to make Riley jealous. I think Shelby has just realized that Riley is no longer the adoring lap dog who is always there for her. She's no longer the only girl in his universe, and it's Kit of all people that he's spending his time with. Riley, and Kit are just friends, and he enjoys her company. Trace is the one that's smitten." Jenny laughed at the stunned expression on her husband's face. "Are all men obtuse when it comes to love?"

Nick Connor was getting loud, and boisterous. Kit turned to Doc with an uneasy look, "Do you think he'll cause trouble?"

"Nick has a history of creating a scene. He can be a troublemaker but backs down when someone confronts him. But cowboys are cowboys. If the opportunity calls for it, they're all ready to fight. The Grayson boys are no different. BJ has been keeping his eye on all of them."

Kit couldn't see any good coming from physical violence, so she hoped he was right.

Doc gave Kit a warning look, "I'd watch myself around Nick Connor if I were you."

"He's not my type. Not that I'm looking," Kit explained quickly. Intentionally changing the subject, she asked, "How is Shelby doing at work?"

"I knew she'd be great with the animals, but I'm impressed with the way she manages their owners. Shelby has a knack for comforting the anxious owners in a warm, positive manner. She'll be a great asset to the office."

Today, Kit had seen for herself how Shelby was with others. It hurt Kit deeper than she realized that the two of them weren't able to bridge the gap between them. Like always, the friction between them had been evident all day.

Kit was surprised at how fast the day had flown by. Families with younger children had already left, including the Walkers. The lanterns that had been hung earlier now added a warm glow. Kit sighed with contentment as she sat next to Jenny. It had been a nice day. Kenzie leaned against her knees, and Kit could feel the weariness of her slumping body. Kit lifted her onto her lap. "Are you all partied out, baby girl?"

"I'm not tired," Kenzie claimed as she snuggled closer, and let her head droop.

Kit turned to Jenny. "I'm going to take Kenzie back to the house and put her to bed." This gave Kit the opportune excuse to call it a night.

"I'll carry her," Trace said, as he looked down at Kenzie snuggled on Kit's lap.

Kit was unaware that he was standing behind her. He seemed to make it a habit of appearing out of nowhere.

Before Kit could decline, Trace scooped the child up. Kenzie wrapped her arms around his neck and laid her head against his shoulder. He looked down at the angel in his arms and an odd ache stabbed at his heart. Of course, from time to time, he wondered what it might be like to have a family of his own. As he maneuvered through the crowd, he looked over to see Riley grinning at him. Trace glared back.

Watching Trace carry Kenzie, Kit was shaken to the core by the depth of her feelings for him. There were so many facets to this man.

Olivia watched them leave. The day had not gone as planned, but she was a lot like her father. She didn't give up until she got what she wanted, and she wanted Trace Grayson. She took her leave, fully intending to get him back. She had him once, she would have him again. Her life again had purpose. She just wasn't happy about her competition.

It didn't take Kit long to settle Kenzie. She was surprised to see that Trace was still there when she returned to the kitchen. "Kenzie was asleep before her head hit the pillow. She had so much fun today."

"Did you have a good time?"

Kit admitted to Sadie that she had enjoyed herself. Everyone was welcoming to her, and the few uncomfortable questions were easily diverted. "It was a lovely day, Sadie. I'll stay, and help you clean up."

"No, you won't. Go back and have some fun. The old folks had left, and the young ones are ready to party. Besides, Lola is coming up to the house, and we're going to have a quiet visit over a pot of tea. Trace waited for you."

Trace smiled, "I knew you wouldn't come back on your own. Grab your jacket. It gets cooler once the sun goes down. I'll grab mine out of my truck on the way back." With a responding smile, Kit grabbed her jacket.

Those remaining had gathered around the bonfire. A couple of the boys had brought out their guitars. Trace was glad to see that Olivia, and Nick had left. Olivia had made it clear throughout the day that she wanted him.

Someone poked the fire causing the coals to erupt in a fresh burst of flames. Kit's gaze was drawn to Riley, and Shelby who were sitting together on a log holding hands, and kissing. They had obviously made up. Kit looked over at Trace and sighed. "It's hard to remember what it was like to be that young."

"I don't think I was ever that young," Trace said dryly.

Kit knew there was a lot more behind this statement. Maybe in time he would open up again. Kit sighed with contentment as she listened to the music. It was a magical night. But when she yawned for the third time, she knew it was time to call it a night. She stood up to leave.

"I'll walk you to the door," Trace offered softly. He knew he was courting trouble when he made the offer.

Kit nodded, knowing all the while she should have said no.

They walked silently back to the house. Trace followed Kit up the stairs. He made no move to leave. Instead, he reached for a strand of her hair, and let it curl around his finger. When his gaze lingered on her mouth her lips trembled.

Kit remembered what it was like to be kissed by him. She had remembered it every day since her return. Guarding herself against it or not, Kit realized how much Trace got to her. Their attraction seemed to keep growing between them.

Trace drew in a deep breath. He knew without a doubt that he was going to regret this. He also knew he had no choice. Trace wanted her with such burning desire that it scared the hell out of him. In one swift motion, he slipped an arm around her waist, and pulled her close. Kit was too startled to pull away. Trace had intended to keep his promise of no pressure, but her lips were so sensual, so inviting. He lifted her chin and placed a soft kiss on her lips. He tried to keep his kiss gentle, but he remembered too well the fire that blazed beneath her cool exterior. Trace crushed his mouth to hers.

Kit ceased to breath. She had tried to protest, but the truth was she didn't want him to stop. She felt herself tremble as she leaned into him.

She met his lips with passion. They were both breathless when she tore her mouth from his. Kit pushed against his chest and took a step back to gain some distance. She forced herself to remember that regardless of how much she might want him, Trace would not be a constant in their lives. "You really are the most infuriating man I've ever known. I'm not interested in ..."

Trace's lips smothered the rest of her words. His mouth crushed down on hers, a hot, and dangerous thrill.

Kit was serious when he let her go. "This only complicates things."

"Sure, as hell does," Trace said, with a scowl as dark as the night. His voice was shaky.

"This is a mistake."

"For whom?"

Keeping her voice deliberately cool, she informed him, "For both of us." The silence stretched because Trace refused to apologize. Before she could utter a word, his arms locked around her, and he pulled her so close that Kit was incapable of moving.

Trace wasn't a man to break his word. But Kit Bennett had never been a factor before. Up until now, he'd always been a man of self-control. He glanced down at her. "Life is not worth living unless you're willing to take a risk now and then." He kissed her thoroughly. The kiss was possessive, as if he were striking a claim. Trace let her go and left without a backward glance.

Kit watched until he faded into the night. "Damn you, Trace, you don't play fair." Trace was driving her crazy, making her want things she shouldn't be wanting. She knew she loved him, and that admission made her feel hopeless because she had to keep this to herself. Some secrets were best left hidden.

Chapter Twenty-One

Kit's life had settled into a comfortable routine. Over the past few weeks, she had worked diligently in the office, and was now only putting in a few hours once or twice a week. From the beginning, Kit had set out to prove her worth, and she had done that.

"You've done such a good job in the office, Missy. It's starting to look like we may not be able to manage without you."

Kit felt a surge of pride, "Is there anything else I can help with?"

"You've done more than your part to help us get through an unsettling time in the office."

Sadie poured herself a coffee and joined them at the table. "We don't want you to feel like a prisoner here at the ranch. Why don't you drive into Black Diamond? We'll watch Kenzie, and you can walk around the town and check out their unique shops."

"I can't have you look after Kenzie that long."

Sadie's expression was solemn, "Would you do it if it was Lou who had offered?"

Tears welled in Kit's eyes. Her changed life was still difficult at times. "I didn't mean to offend you." She hugged her grandmother, and with a show of genuine enthusiasm Kit accepted the offer.

Kit welcomed the distraction from the ranch. It was a beautiful day to stroll along the sidewalks from one quaint shop to another, browsing at her leisure. She liked the pretty streets, and novel shops. She was peering through a store window when she heard a voice call out. She turned, and her automatic reaction was pleasure at the sight of Doc Parker. Kit gave him a genuine smile, surprised to see a familiar face.

"This is an unexpected pleasure. I'm on lunch break. Care to join me?" Today's chance encounter would give him the perfect opportunity to share Kit's company alone. He was attracted to Kit and looked forward to getting to know her better.

"That would be nice. I was just wondering where to eat." Kit liked the vet. He reminded her of Mike. He was honest, and real, and seemed to have values that matched hers.

"My lucky day," Doc said, as he escorted her into the Black Diamond Hotel. They sat down at a table by the window.

Their waitress came over and dropped off two glasses of water, handed them a menu, and informed them of the special for the day. "I'll be back in a few minutes to take your order."

"What brought you to town today, Kit?"

"I'm trying to get the feel of the area. Sadie said I would enjoy walking around downtown. She was right, so many of the shops have a wonderful selection of treasures."

"This area is home to many talented artists, and musicians, which is why our artistic, and cultural community keeps thriving. Black Diamond is a small town, and we don't mind keeping it that way. We pride ourselves on welcoming visitors."

They chatted comfortably through lunch. Doc was a nice man, and she enjoyed his company. Since Mike died, she hadn't spent much time alone with men.

It came as no surprise when he said, "If you have no plans, how about having dinner with me tomorrow night. The Longview Steakhouse is another local attraction. It sits on a hill, and the beautiful backdrop of the mountains is spectacular."

Kit accepted, knowing she would enjoy an evening out. After she left Doc, doubts surfaced. Kit could tell that Doc was attracted to her. Was she starting something that she wasn't ready for? She was approaching her Jeep when Olivia Beaumont walked out of the store that Kit had parked in front of. Kit groaned. There was no avoiding her.

"Well, hello Kit. Nice to see you again," lied Olivia. "I see you're still visiting."

"I'm not visiting. My daughter and I are living at the main house."

Olivia looked disappointed, and her smile slipped. "I saw you had lunch with Doc Parker. Are you two seeing each other?"

Kit didn't feel like chatting with the woman. Besides, she felt Olivia showed too much interest for being a mere acquaintance. Kit chose not to answer her. "If you'll excuse me, I'm on my way back to the ranch."

Olivia, in turn, chose not to take the hint. "I hope you're not hanging around trying to snag the most eligible bachelor in the county?" Her words dripped ice.

Kit knew that Doc was not only a successful vet, but a wealthy cattle rancher as well. "Doc and I bumped into each other and had lunch together. We're just friends."

"I was talking about Trace Grayson."

Kit almost laughed out loud. Trace had no interest in a permanent relationship.

The look Olivia gave Kit was odd, and her tone changed. With deliberation, she informed Kit, "It might be in your best interest to know that Trace, and I are seeing each other now that I'm back." The lies flowed from her lips with familiar ease. "I should have stayed and married him. Instead, I thought the man I did marry would show me the world. He did, but not for long. I'm glad Trace waited. A smart woman like you should be able to figure out why Trace hasn't married." When Olivia chose to be spiteful, she could do it with practiced skill.

This was news to Kit, so her gaze faltered as she turned, and walked away. Kit had one more errand. She had left the bakery until last. She recalled Sadie saying how much she, and Will enjoyed donuts as a treat. This was Kit's small gesture of thanks.

On the way home Kit replayed the conversation with Olivia. She could still see the smug look on Olivia's face when she recognized the flicker of doubt that had crossed hers. Trace had told her he was not involved with anyone, and she didn't peg him as a liar. She decided to consider the source before judging Trace based on an ex-girlfriend's words. Kit frowned. Maybe things had changed since the barbeque, and Olivia wasn't lying. That, or the woman was intentionally trying to stir up trouble. Kit knew it shouldn't matter either way.

When Kit arrived home, Will was out on the verandah, feet propped up on the rail, and hat lowered over his eyes. In case he was sleeping, Kit walked quietly up the steps.

"Are those donuts I might be smelling?" Will asked without moving.

"Sure are, and they're for after supper. Not before."

"You're a cruel woman, just like your Grandma."

Since Kit was home early, Sadie, and Will decided to drive over to friends for coffee. Everything had been prepared for the evening meal, so Kit decided to spend the afternoon outdoors with Kenzie. A sense of pleasure played on her lips as she watched Kenzie peddle her bike up and down the driveway. Summer had passed so quickly that she realized winter would arrive before she knew it. She wondered what it would be like to experience a Canadian winter.

Kit smiled as Trace headed up the sidewalk. As he approached, her heartbeat quickened. She realized she was feeling too much pleasure in seeing him. Kenzie, also excited to see him, took one hand off her handlebars to wave. As a result, the bike turned unexpectedly. Kenzie veered off the driveway and fell into Sadie's flower garden.

As soon as Kenzie saw the scrape on her knee she screamed out, "I'm broken." She continued screaming while holding her knee.

Quick to react, Trace picked up the child knowing she was more scared than hurt. Kenzie continued screaming until she was in her mother's arms. When Kit dropped a kiss on her golden curls, it filled Trace's chest with an ache he couldn't identify.

Knowing this would require more than a kiss, Kit calmly informed Kenzie, "I think a Band-Aid is what we need to make it better."

Trace winked at Kenzie, "And a cookie, right?"

Kenzie sniffed, "Uh-huh."

As Kit headed inside to get Band-Aids, and a washcloth, she could hear Trace talking to Kenzie. His voice was calm as he soothed her, "That's an awful sad face."

"Mucky fell, too."

When Kit returned, Trace was inspecting both of Mucky's knees. His tender expression took her breath away. This was a sight Kit never expected to see. The man continued to surprise her. Kenzie asked Trace to put the

Band-Aid on her knee. As soon as he was done, he put one on both of Mucky's knees. Kenzie giggled.

Kit looked at the man with the cocky grin and kind heart and was touched and amused at the same time. "Off you go, baby girl. You're not broken any more." They had just finished when Will and Sadie pulled up.

Kenzie showed them her knee and scowled at her Papa. "I fell off my damn bike."

Trace's mouth dropped open while Kit struggled not to laugh. She gave Trace an amused smile, "She sometimes swears like her Papa. We're working on that with both of them."

"Does she have the Calhoun temper, too?"

"Sadly, yes."

Trace wasn't surprised. "She's a sweet kid. You've done a good job with your daughter." Although Trace wasn't admitting it, he'd come to enjoy Kenzie's antics. Seeing them together, mother and child, made him realize that Kit and Kenzie were becoming important to him.

Will approached Trace, "Did you need to talk to me?"

"I dropped off an order for Murphy and popped over before I headed home." He turned to Kit, "I thought maybe we could go for a ride tomorrow if Sadie wouldn't mind keeping an eye on Kenzie." He gave her a devilish smile. That's what friends would do. He was being her friend and respecting her boundaries. He wasn't courting her.

"Sadie is already booked. Doc and I ran into each other this morning in Black Diamond, and we had lunch together. We made plans, and he's taking me to dinner tomorrow night."

Trace had no reason to be upset. Doc had warned him the day of the barbeque. Besides, he had no claim on Kit. His expression remained unchanged with effort. "Are you seeing Doc?"

"What?"

"You know, dating him?" Trace held his breath.

"Like you and me, we are just friends."

The well-aimed reminder cut through him as it was meant to. They had agreed to be just friends, and both maintained the illusion as they fought their attraction to each other.

Will and Sadie excused themselves and went inside. "Do you think Doc is hitting on our granddaughter?"

Sadie nodded as she threw her husband an amused glace. "There's a lot of testosterone around here these days."

Over at the other Calhoun house, a heavy conversation was taking place between mother, and daughter. Jenny looked sharply at Shelby, "Your dad, and I are concerned about your recent behavior, Shelby. Especially to Kit."

Shelby was tired of everyone going on and on about Kit, and her kid. It was like everything now revolved around them. She didn't hold anything back when she said, "I wish Kit and Kenzie would just go away, and everything would go back to the way it was. All Dad cares about is his new family. He just welcomed them with open arms."

"Like BJ did with you," Jenny reminded her gently.

"You don't understand. Dad wants us to be one happy family. Kit isn't really my sister."

"So is BJ not really your dad because he isn't your biological father?"

"That's different."

"Really?" Jenny paused, deciding how to continue.

Shelby gave her mom a hurt look. Her voice waivered, "He is my dad."

"You're right, and he always will be your dad. Fathering or birthing a child isn't what makes a parent. It's being with that child, loving them, and supporting them even through the rough times. If there was any man that fits that description, it's BJ Calhoun. He was the one who raised you. It was BJ who was always there for you and taught you to be fair even when it wasn't easy. He never got to do anything with Kit because he didn't know about her. Kit's not replacing you any more than BJ replaced your dad. He has more than enough love for all of us. He just wants to get to know Kit now that she is a part of his life."

Shelby questioned her mom, "Did you love my dad as much as you love BJ?"

Jenny eyes darkened, "Your dad, and I loved each other with wild passion. It was all fireworks, and thrills in the beginning. Once we were married, I changed as life changed. I accepted the responsibilities that came with change. Your dad didn't, and I saw things that I had overlooked in the beginning. He was selfish, and self-centered. He didn't want the responsibility that came with being a husband, and a father. It may have come in time, but I'll never know. Your dad had his faults. We all do. I always knew that BJ loved me, and I loved him. But I didn't love him like I loved your dad. With your dad it was all about passion. With BJ it's a gentle, patient kind of love. One that is solid, and lasting. We continue to bring out the best in each other. In some ways you're just like Dallas. You're exciting to be around, full of life, and energy. Like Dallas, you live your life on your terms, but that's not always a positive. You don't take into consideration what others are dealing with or how they are feeling. Your determination sometimes makes you inflexible."

"Are you implying that I'm stubborn?"

"No, that's a fact." Jenny hesitated, afraid of saying the wrong thing. Realizing that being honest was more important than hurt feelings at this point, she continued, "That stubbornness is getting in your way. You must accept that there's always going to be change in your life. You will change too. That's what growing up is all about."

Jenny decided her daughter was old enough to know a few hard facts. She proceeded to share some of the painful truths from the past. "You were too young to understand how difficult it was for us when I was married to your dad. If it weren't for the Calhouns, we would have lost our ranch."

What her mother shared shook Shelby. Everything in her life seemed to be in a state of upheaval. Shelby felt helpless. Temper was back in her eyes. "Why are you telling me this now?"

"Because it's important for you to understand. To do that it's necessary to share the past, even the bad." Jenny changed the direction of the conversation. "You keep giving Kit a hard time. How would you feel if I died? Worse yet, what if we were all gone. Me, Dad, your Grandpa, and Grandma. Even the Graysons."

"Why are you doing this?" Shelby cried out in confusion.

"I want you to put yourself in Kit's shoes. That poor girl had a mom who called her a mistake and disowned her at birth to be raised by her grandmother. Kit's mother, who died when she was fifteen, told Kit that her father died before she was born. Even when she found happiness, it was taken from her. Her husband was killed at war before Kenzie was born. Another innocent child growing up without a father. All Kit had was her grandmother, who told Kit on her death bed that her mother had lied, and her dad might be alive. All of Kit's family was gone unless what her grandmother told her was true. Kit needs us, we are her family."

"I didn't know," Shelby whispered.

"That's a poor excuse for your behavior. You have allowed your anger to affect your actions. Do you think it was easy for Kit to come here? Do you think it's easy being here, and trying to fit in? Do you think you're being fair?"

Without another word Shelby flew into her mother's arms. "I've been so miserable."

"I know." Jenny didn't say more. She just held Shelby tight.

*****

Riley knew Trace's bad mood was because Kit was going out with Doc, but it didn't stop him from bugging him. "What's so important that you need to go to Valley View today?"

"It's none of your business."

"Your brother asked you a civil question, Trace. What's with the attitude?"

Riley answered instead, "Kit's going on a date with Doc Parker tonight. He's curious and can't resist spying on them."

Lola couldn't resist poking the bear, "Curiosity killed the cat."

"Hey, Trace, where should we bury the cat?"

Trace was in no mood to be teased. "You're an immature idiot, Riley." Trace could hear them laughing as he stormed out.

On the pretext of business, Trace was in the office with BJ, and Will while Kit was getting ready. Riley, who appeared to be just as curious as his brother, had showed up. Riley couldn't resist opening the can of worms when BJ mentioned Kit's date. Riley slapped his brother on the back, "Does it bother you that Kit is going out with Doc?"

"Not in the least." In truth it bothered him like hell.

Kit was nervous getting ready for her date. She stood in front of her closet deciding what to wear. She pulled out the dress she had bought for Lou's funeral. Fortunately, black was appropriate for any occasion. The dress complimented her willowy figure. She had let her hair air dry allowing it to fall in natural waves to her shoulders. Makeup was usually something she kept to a minimum. Tonight, she put in the extra effort, applying more make-up than usual, making her eyes look mysterious. As a final touch she applied a dark red lipstick. After slipping into a pair of thin strapped sandals she picked up her bottle of perfume and misted herself with the light fragrance. Kit was satisfied with her efforts as she stood in front of the mirror. She knew she looked stunning, but suddenly wondered if she had overdone it. Kit touched the single strand of pearls around her neck. They had belonged to Lou. Kit picked up the framed picture of her grandmother. Kit put the picture back down knowing Lou would approve. It was time to move forward. There was no stopping the butterflies in the pit of her stomach, as she left her bedroom.

The men had just stepped out of the office when Kit walked by. Riley let out a long whistle. Kit blushed and hurried to the kitchen.

Trace was unable to take his eyes off Kit. He'd never seen her look so stunning. Trace wished it were him taking Kit out for a romantic dinner and not Doc Parker. As usual, his face revealed nothing.

Riley had already expressed his approval when he saw Kit. With a twinkle in his eye, and a hint of amusement in his voice, BJ remarked, "My daughter sure looks beautiful. What do you think, Trace?" BJ knew better than to expect an answer.

With a scowl on his face, Trace headed for the back door.

Will winked at BJ as they heard the door slam. "I told you the boy's got it bad."

Doc had arrived and was chatting with Sadie in the kitchen when Kit entered. "You look lovely this evening," he said softly. Kit had taken his breath away.

"Thank you. It isn't often I get the opportunity to dress up. You look very dapper yourself." Kit bent down, and kissed Kenzie on her cheek. "You be good for GiGi."

"Okay. Mommy, you look pretty."

"Thanks, baby girl." Kit accepted Doc's, arm and they left.

Trace was standing at the railing of the corral. He saw Doc say something to Kit as she got into his car, and she laughed in response. Trace was immediately annoyed with himself for the stab of jealousy he was experiencing. He couldn't help but feel a void within as he watched them drive away. Trace headed over to the barn to see Diego. That was the constant in his life that he understood. "She just wants to be friends, and when I try and spend time with her, she tells me she's going out for dinner with Doc Parker. She says they're just friends like we are, but I know that the good old vet wants a whole lot more than just friendship."

Murphy, who was puttering in the tack room, overheard Trace's one-sided conversation with his beloved horse. Normally, he wouldn't interfere, but the poor boy was so blindly in love he couldn't see straight. He went out and joined Trace at the stall. "That's a hell of a hole you've dug for yourself, if you think the two of you can be just friends. You both keep fighting your feelings for each other. It's making you miserable."

"I don't remember asking you what you think, Murphy."

Murphy actually laughed, "No problem, Trace. Glad to help."

"I just need to get a grip and refocus on work. Kit has been too distracting."

"You have been doing a fine job, both at Valley View, and Lola Grande. Buster would be right proud with what you've accomplished, but he'd probably tell you to get on with life in other ways." Murphy turned and went back to the tack room.

Trace scowled. Murphy was a man of few words, and Trace knew he was right. Was he ready to take on another commitment? Trace never expected to want that kind of commitment with anyone, let alone with someone who had a child. Nothing in his early life had taught him anything about being a good father. But there was an emptiness inside him that was almost unbearable. He didn't know what he wanted anymore.

Doc Parker was recognized by the staff, and they were taken to a reserved table next to the window. It was private and secluded. The sun was beginning to set behind the mountains in the distance. The oncoming sunset was spectacular.

"Did you order this view ahead of time?" Kit's voice was breathless with excitement. It was everything he said it would be.

"The view is impressive any time of the year, but absolutely magnificent with snow on the mountains." He hoped she would still be here to see it.

Both decided on the evening special, and red wine. They fell into the same ease, and comfort they had in Black Diamond, so conversation flowed naturally. When Doc reached for the wine bottle and refilled both glasses Kit's mind went back to her dinner with Trace. She couldn't believe how easily Trace always invaded her mind.

Kit's thoughts were interrupted when Doc asked unexpectedly, "I hope you don't take this the wrong way, and you can tell me if I have become too personal. I see you don't wear a wedding ring." He was curious about her past. The more time he spent with Kit the more he liked her, and the more he wanted to know about her.

Needing a moment, Kit took a sip of wine before answering. "There is no ex-husband. Kenzie's father died before she was born." She knew Doc was intrigued, but she wasn't willing to go into specifics like she had with Trace. She wasn't sure why.

Doc recognized that Kit's response was closed. This mysterious lady only intrigued him more. He respectfully changed the subject.

Doc was charming, and funny. Kit enjoyed his company. There was a quiet confidence about him that Kit found refreshing. Nothing like the arrogant cowboy who kept intruding on her thoughts. His body language read relaxed, and comfortable. Over the course of the evening, they found they had many things in common, and the evening passed pleasantly.

The conversation remained casual on the drive home. The porch light was on when they pulled into the driveway. Being the perfect gentleman, Doc walked Kit to the door. "I hope we can do this again soon." Doc leaned in and kissed her. His kiss was tender.

Kit wasn't surprised, but nor was she moved by his kiss. She merely smiled, as she thanked him for a lovely evening.

After he left, Kit remained outside. She didn't want to talk about her evening. She needed time alone to think. When Doc kissed her there was no comparison to the feelings aroused by Trace. Kit recognized how differently she'd reacted to being kissed by two attractive men. One a tender veterinarian, and the other a passionate cowboy. She knew that as nice as Doc Parker was, he paled next to the captivating, Trace Grayson.

Chapter Twenty-Two

With the arrival of fall, most mornings were chilly, but warmed up by mid-morning. Today was an unusually muggy day. Kit, and Kenzie were having lunch at Maggie's ranch. Kit, and Maggie had become good friends.

"I heard that you and Doc dined at the Longview Steakhouse Saturday night." At Kit's questioning look, Maggie said, "Gossip travels quickly in a rural community, and men gossip worse than women. Trace told Matt."

"Not that it's any business of Trace's, but it was just dinner with a friend."

Maggie raised her eyebrow, and her lips twitched.

"Don't let your imagination get carried away, Maggie. I simply enjoyed an evening out. I don't need any complications in my life," Kit added emphatically.

"Doc is a complication?"

"No, Trace is. He is a confusing man to understand." Kit sounded miserable.

Maggie was concerned for her friend, who seemed to be at odds regarding Trace. "Trace is well past the age that most men are married and settled with a family. He might have done so before now if he hadn't dedicated all his time to his work. He doesn't take time to play."

"Well, it looks like he's back in the game. I ran into Olivia Beaumont when I was in Black Diamond. She says they're dating."

"I doubt that. I'm sure it was just an attempt at getting rid of new competition."

"Based on her behavior at the barbecue, and our conversation, she wants Trace back."

"That is unlikely to happen. Olivia broke Trace's heart. She used him and her misleading actions made Trace gun-shy. Her father didn't like Trace because of his lack of breeding. A mere cowboy wasn't good enough for his little girl. Olivia was expected to marry Burke Benson. the son of her father's business partner. She married the suave, and wealthy Englishman. A few months ago, Olivia came back divorced, and if you're right, she wants to pick things up where they left off. Knowing Trace, he won't fall into her trap, again. That woman can be deceitful and catty. Like a cat she landed on her feet after the divorce. Huge settlement. Like a cat she has claws. Be careful, Kit."

"What Trace Grayson does or doesn't do is none of my concern. Just because you're a hopeless romantic who is happily married, do not think that it's for everyone. The last thing I need is a dominating man in my life."

Maggie smiled knowing full well it was Trace Grayson, and not Doc Parker that Kit was referring to. She had seen the sparks flying since the Calhoun barbeque. "So, what are you going to do? Shrivel up, and become an old maid? It's time to accept the fact that you can't hide yourself away on a ranch in the middle of nowhere." Ignoring Kit's scowl, Maggie continued, "Friendship is fine, but what you need is a relationship. I wouldn't have taken you for a coward."

Kit had stopped being a hopeless romantic the day Mike died. That dream now belonged to someone else. She'd had male friends, but never allowed any of them to get too close. As soon as some commitment was expected she quickly moved on. It was easy until now. Was she a coward? Could she find the courage to tell Trace what was in her heart? Kit tucked that question away for later. This had been an intense conversation that she wasn't prepared for.

Will and Sadie were just leaving the house when Kit got home. Will was heading into town for supplies, and Sadie had a few errands of her own. The day had gotten hotter. The late afternoon sun beat down from a clear blue sky, the gentle breeze offering no relief. Knowing Kenzie had to be feeling as hot and sticky as she was, Kit pulled out the wading pool that BJ had bought for her. The Calhouns all tended to spoil Kenzie, but Kit accepted this for now. It was natural. They had missed out on a lot.

Kit wasn't surprised to see Trace's truck pull into the yard. Since the barbeque, Trace had kept his word. They were developing a comfortable friendship. He waved as he stepped out of his truck. Kit sat and watched him saunter over.

Trace noticed that Kit was wearing the same denim shorts and top she had worn the day she had arrived. Today, she was barefoot like her daughter. Kit had bundled her hair on top of her head so it would be cooler. The warm breeze played with the loose strands of hair. He dodged past Kenzie who was splashing away in her pool. "I'm on my way home. I just stopped by to say hi, and see how you were doing," he said as he wiped his brow.

"Kenzie, and I are managing to keep cool. You look hot, Trace." The hose was still lying next to the steps. Trace noticed it as soon as Kit glanced over. Even beneath the shadowed brim of his hat Kit could see the dare. Her eyes sparkled with mischief. Without a second thought she grabbed the hose and opened the nozzle. She aimed and hit his chest dead center. Kit didn't know who was more shocked. Now that his shirt was wet, it clung to his broad chest. It only emphasized the breadth of his shoulders. Kit laughed without a hint of remorse. She shrieked when he unexpectedly lunged for her.

Kit hadn't gotten far before Trace grabbed her around the waist. Kit was giggling uncontrollably as he carried her over to the wading pool. He had lost his hat, and his jet-black hair fell over his eyes. He looked down at Kenzie. "Do you think mommy should have a swim?"

Kenzie clapped her hands. "Yes, yes."

Trace laughed, adoring Kenzie's mischievous smile as he dropped Kit into the pool.

"You are in so much trouble, Trace Grayson," Kit promised as she sat with her bottom in the pool, and her long legs hanging over the edge.

Kenzie was now squealing with delight as she splashed them.

Trace's grin was wide, and his eyes were dancing as he pulled Kit up. This woman did make him laugh and feel more alive.

Kit was still laughing as she went into the house to grab a couple of towels. The pool may have cooled her off, but Trace's touch always brought a different heat to her body. Kit had to admit that his surprise visit made the afternoon more enjoyable.

That night, the thoughts she had tucked away at Maggie's emerged when she climbed into bed. She now enjoyed a comfortable friendship with Trace. That had to be enough. Then she thought of his wonderful kisses and longing took over. Unable to settle, Kit flung the covers aside, and slid out of bed. Hoping a cup of warm milk would help her sleep she crept quietly into the kitchen. With a sinking heart she sat deep in thought. The one person who she could always discuss her problems with was gone.

"Trouble sleeping?" asked a voice from the doorway.

"Sorry. Did I wake you?"

"No. I just want a glass of water." Sadie filled a glass and joined Kit at the table. "What's wrong, Kit? You were sitting here lost in what looked like some deep thoughts. Are you sure you're, okay? You haven't been sleeping well since you got back from Washington."

Kit knew Sadie was waiting for her to say something. Kit remained silent. It wasn't fair to burden her grandmother with her problems.

Sadie persisted, "Does this have anything to do with Trace?"

It was pointless to deny the fact that Trace seemed to have an impact on every aspect of her life. "It's more than Trace. I should never have gone out with Doc. I tried to fool myself that it wasn't a date. We were just friends having dinner." Kit blushed, "He kissed me after our date."

"You like, Doc, don't you?"

"Doc is a nice man who is attractive, and attentive. He's kind, and thoughtful. A decent man in anyone's book."

"But he's not Trace, right?"

Kit ignored her clutch of panic. She was out of her element with Trace. She resorted back to her usual response, "Trace and I are just friends."

"How long are you going to try to convince yourself of that? You've both been denying your feelings."

It was easy to fool others, but not Sadie. The bottom line was she was in love with, Trace. Hopelessly, helplessly, and unwisely. The man was determined to stay single. Therein, lay the biggest problem of all. "Trace doesn't want a relationship with commitment, and I do."

"Who are you to decide what someone else wants?"

"I'm not. Trace has told me that more than once."

"Trace can be a complicated man to understand. At times he's difficult to relate to because he's so private, and he hides his feelings. Since you showed up, he's changed."

"I must be realistic. As a single mom, I have responsibilities." Kit couldn't deny her other fear. "I'd be risking so much if I let myself care."

"It's always a risk caring deeply for another person. It's a risk because there is no guarantee that you won't get your heart broken."

"I know better than anyone that there's no guarantee for happily ever after. I don't need to complicate my life. Right now, I'm happy being a mother. My focus has to be on Kenzie."

"Nobody can deny that you're a good mother, but don't you want to give Kenzie a father? Are you happy now?"

"No." She'd been miserable for days.

"I don't think you're the only one struggling with your feelings."

"How come Trace never got married?"

"For years, his obsession has been Lola Grande, and Caballo Stables. He didn't need anything else, or anyone else. That changed when you arrived. A change that has been for the better. I see a side to him that was missing. His gentleness with Kenzie comes naturally. I hear the yearning in his voice when he talks to you, or about you. I can also tell you're thinking about him all the time. What does your heart tell you?"

Kit looked at Sadie, her eyes wide. "I love that stupid cowboy," she finally choked out. "The first time Trace kissed me it terrified me. I felt truly alive for the first time in years. I'd forgotten how wonderful it felt. The second time terrified me more. It's been so long since anyone made me feel this way. Not since Mike. I know I'm not a teenager anymore, but I need some time to think about things."

The two women were silent for a moment, then Sadie said with a hint of her son's directness, "Four years isn't long enough?"

"What if it's a mistake, Sadie?"

Years of living allowed Sadie to say, "I don't know why a person falls in love with someone. They just do. Falling in love is not in our control. Falling in love with another man takes nothing away from what you had with your husband. Different men, different you. You're in love with Trace, and Trace loves you. He just hasn't gotten around to admitting it yet. Life will pass you by if you don't have the courage to trust your feelings.

I know you have incredible courage, or you wouldn't have come looking for your dad. Life has taught me acceptance, and to live in the moment. I miss our son, Danny. I miss Buster, and Annie, and Joey. I miss them all every day. Some days more than others. I also appreciate every day for what it can bring. The future is full of wonderful surprises. It brought us you and Kenzie."

"I wasn't prepared to feel this kind of love, again."

"If you start locking people out, you end up locking yourself away." Sadie's heart lurched because of a possible realization. "Are you planning on leaving us?"

"No, that's what Torrie would do. I have Calhoun blood running through my veins, and I was raised by a strong, independent lady. Lou always said that life has a way of working things out, so I'll figure it out. I just need time to adjust and accept all the recent changes in my life. In time, I will decide what Kenzie, and I will do, and where we will go. We both need to be here for a while. Is life always so complicated?"

"It doesn't have to be. Maybe it's time to let your heart lead instead of your head. I think Mike would want you to move on with your life."

Kit nodded in understanding. She couldn't erase the past, no more than she could live in it. Mike would be disappointed in her if she didn't move on. That's what they had both done when they got married. They left their unhappy childhoods behind. They planned and dreamed about the happy future they would have despite being young, and inexperienced. Nothing would take away what they had, and life had so much more to offer. She didn't want to end up alone. Sadie had given her a lot to think about.

Sadie reached across the table and closed her hand over Kit's. "I love you, and I want you to be happy. Enough talk for one night. I'm going back to bed."

"Me, too. Thank you, Sadie."

Thanks to their talk, Kit had a good night's sleep after she returned to bed. It was the tantalizing smell of coffee, and bacon that woke her.

Sadie was pouring herself a coffee when Kit entered the kitchen. She smiled down at Kenzie, "Go outside, and get Papa for breakfast." As soon as Kenzie was out of earshot Sadie turned to Kit, "Will and I thought we would take the Doodle Bug to Heritage Park for the day. BJ, and Trace are going to check the herd in the south pasture before heading over to Lola Grande. Riley is meeting with cattlemen in the city. Jenny is gone until Monday, and Shelby, well, she is never around. So, it would just be you, and Murphy."

Kit went over, and hugged Sadie. "You know me so well. Thanks. Good heavens, what will I do with an entire day to myself?"

With the sky clear blue, and the temperature rising, Kit decided it was too nice a day to stay indoors. On her way to the stables. Kit stopped at the corral. Ginger nickered softly, anxious to gain her attention. The beautiful mare had stolen Kit's heart the first day Kit saw her. With gentle fingers, Kit stroked the mare's forehead while she talked softly. Ginger flicked her tail and welcomed the gentle petting. Kit looked over and smiled when Murphy appeared. "I just stopped to say hi to Ginger and Jasper. I'm off to saddle up Blondie. It's a great day for a ride."

"I'll do that for you."

"You don't have to."

Murphy gave her one of his rare smiles. "It's okay, Kit. Gives you a few more minutes with these two."

Anxious to ride, Kit soon headed to the barn where Blondie was waiting. She mounted and headed out. Quick to give Blondie her head, she was soon thundering across the fields. She laughed out loud enjoying the feeling of freedom she always experienced on horseback. She liked the sensation of the wind on her face. When she reached the ridge, Kit leaned forward, and caught her breath. She sat, enjoying the stillness around her. It was like the first time she had seen this view. Kit hadn't realized how deeply the wide-open spaces had settled into her being in the short time she'd been at Valley View. She knew she'd made the right decision coming here. Now she needed to decide how to move forward, knowing they couldn't live at the ranch forever. Although she had agreed to stay until after Christmas, Kit knew that time passes quickly.

That wasn't the only thing weighing on her mind. Kit knew she would never put anything ahead of her daughter, which is why she'd never become involved with someone just to have an affair. Her rules were becoming more difficult to keep. It didn't help when Trace would cross the line and kiss her. She replayed all of Trace's kisses in her head. The man kissed like a dream. The desire he stirred in her was impossible to ignore. Hiding her feelings was a constant struggle.

A warm wind had whipped up from the west by the time Kit returned to the ranch. Kit had enjoyed her ride, but she hadn't been able to outrun her disturbing thoughts. Murphy took Blondie so Kit followed the well-worn trail through the trees. After finding a secluded stretch along the bank, she dropped down. She watched the free-flowing water cascade over the rocks, and foolishly wished that the flowing water would wash away her woes. Kit sighed heavily. She strongly reminded herself that Trace wasn't the marrying kind, and she was a mature adult and mother. She could risk a few bruises on her heart, but she couldn't risk letting her child get hurt. Kit was so deeply absorbed in her thoughts that she had lost track of time. She was startled when she heard Riley approach. "I thought you were in the city."

"My meeting went well so it ended early. I needed to check on some paperwork here at the office. I couldn't believe that no one was around. Murphy guessed you had come down here."

"It's a wonderful place to escape to. I've enjoyed a day to myself. Being around so many people can become overwhelming at times. I spent so many years with just Lou and Kenzie."

"Are you okay with some company?" Kit nodded, so Riley sat down next to her. "You were so deep in thought you didn't even hear me call out. Something bothering you, Kit? Do you need an ear to listen or a shoulder to cry on? I have both."

Kit couldn't help but smile despite her low spirits. "I've talked to Sadie, and it didn't help. She just gave me more to think about."

Riley was observant and understood more than some gave him credit for. He was sure it was Trace that was bothering Kit. "Trace struggles when something is personal, and often withdraws. My brother never considered himself the marrying kind, so now he's all confused inside. He's so crazy about you it's a wonder he gets his boots on the right feet. A man gets a little stupid when it first happens."

Kit laughed out loud. "Riley, you're still mindless when it comes to Shelby."

"I admit I've been in love with that girl for years waiting for her to grow up. Up until now I thought Shelby was just immature, so I kept overlooking her actions. The last few months I've seen a side to her that is concerning. I still love her, but I haven't always liked her behavior. She isn't considering how her behavior is affecting others."

Kit turned to Riley, defeat overtaking her. "I thought Shelby would come around, and we could be friends. I was wrong."

"Come on, Kit. You're the type that's up for any kind of a challenge. Remember, I've seen you take on Shelby more than once. We can't give up on her."

"What's wrong, Riley? Having problems with the princess?"

"Nothing new, but no one can tell Shelby anything lately. She's more hard-headed than she's ever been. You Calhouns are all incredibly stubborn."

"The Grayson boys are no different."

"Shelby and I will work through this. It's Trace I'm worried about. The fool doesn't know how to deal with this. He's afraid of his deep love for you, and your daughter."

"Love shouldn't be this hard."

"It should be simple. A woman loves a man, a man loves a woman. Together you make it work." They looked knowingly at each other. In truth, there was nothing more complicated.

Riley had made her feel better. Kit appreciated the fact that they had such a comfortable friendship. "You're an old soul, Riley. You do realize you're much wiser than, Trace."

"Trace has changed since he met you. He's still trying to figure it all out while he sorts through these new feelings. My brother is head over heels in love with you. He just hasn't worked up the courage to tell you." The question remained, would he ever admit the truth to Kit? Riley's arm went around Kit in a way that was comforting. He held her tight and pressed a light kiss to her temple. Kit leaned in closer feeling a wave of new hope.

Shelby, who had just arrived, was stricken to see Riley, and Kit sitting together. She stood paralyzed in disbelief as the feeling of panic increased. When she saw Riley give Kit a kiss, she felt like she had just lost her best friend to her worst enemy.

Riley rose to leave just in time to see Shelby stomping away and hurried after her. When he caught up to her, he grabbed her arm, "I didn't know you were home. How did you know I was down here?"

"Murphy said he saw you heading down to the creek. I didn't know you were there to be with Kit. I saw you kiss her," she ranted.

"You misread what you saw, and once again you've jumped to conclusions."

"You've changed, Riley."

"And some of us still need to change," he countered back. Shelby turned and ran. Riley refused to chase her. Not this time. The girl needed to think about her actions, and the consequence that went along with her immature behavior.

Chapter Twenty-Three

It had rained during the night, and the weatherman predicted showers later in the evening. Restlessness drove Kit from the house. She climbed in her Jeep and headed out with no destination in mind. Ever since her day trip to Black Diamond last week, and her chance meeting with Olivia Beaumont, she had been troubled. Meeting Olivia unexpectedly had caught Kit by surprise, but not as much as the conversation that followed. It replayed in Kit's mind as she drove down the country road. Before Kit knew it, she was pulling into Lola Grande. Knowing the boys were over at Valley View she was hoping that Lola was home, and they could talk. Kit knocked on the front door, and entered when Lola called her in. "You told me to feel free to drop by anytime. Do you have time for a visit?"

"I just poured myself a coffee." Lola opened the cupboard door and grabbed another cup. Lola could tell that Kit was troubled. "This is a pleasant surprise. What's up?"

Kit wasn't sure how to begin because she wasn't sure how Lola would react to the one thing that was bothering her the most. Kit knew her own feelings were more than attraction in regard to Trace, but he continued to confuse her by his actions.

Lola was wise to Kit's problem, so she bypassed the small talk, "I'll share a little of our history, so you have a better understanding of the Grayson family. After my husband died, our lives changed dramatically. Trace felt he had to take on the role left by his father. He carried such a high level of responsibility at too young an age. He also had his own business to build. Trace was only seventeen when he bought his first horse from the Calhouns. That was the beginning of Trace's dream of Caballo Stables. The Calhoun brothers supported his dreams. Buster and Trace formed a strong friendship because of the horses. Soon afterwards, Buster became terminally ill. Buster's death was hard on everyone but especially Trace. After Buster died, Will and Trace grew closer. I was glad he had Will to turn to. They now have that same rare bond. Lola Grande, and Caballo Stables have become Trace's obsession. He still feels he has to prove himself, both to himself and to others. That kind of commitment didn't leave room for a relationship."

Although Kit already knew some of this, she was grateful that Lola was willing to share. Hopefully, she would learn more about the Grayson boys from their mother.

"Trace and Riley are extremely close as brothers, but Riley felt he didn't always measure up. The best thing for Riley was when he went away to school. He was able to step out of the shadow of his older brother and the magnetic force of Shelby Calhoun. Your arrival has affected that relationship. Shelby's no longer the only girl in his world, and it's you of all people that he's spending time with. Shelby doesn't know how to deal with it. I know you and Riley are just friends, but it will do Shelby good to be taken down a peg or two.".

More than once, Kit had thought about knocking the princess off her lofty perch.

"Since Riley graduated, he is the operational manager of the cattle business, and one day he will be the foreman at Valley View. It's a big responsibility, but he knows he's capable. The two years at college helped him to gain self-confidence that had been overshadowed by his extremely driven brother. Riley tends to easily trust people. Trace on the other hand, makes them earn his trust. If you lose that trust you never want to turn your back on him."

Kit heard the pride in Lola's voice as she talked about her sons. Kit could tell that every member of the Grayson family was proud and honorable. She changed the subject when she dared to ask, "Is Olivia Beaumont in Trace's life? I ran into her last week in Black Diamond. She said that she, and Trace are dating."

Lola smiled to herself. The real reason for Kit's visit finally surfaced. "Olivia is a scheming young lady. Always has been. I'm sure that she was trying to stir up trouble."

"Based on her behavior at the barbecue, and our conversation, she wants Trace back."

"That will never happen. She lost Trace's trust years ago. A few months ago, she came back divorced, and if you're right, she wants to pick things up where they left off. Things changed over the years. We are now landowners. Trace has made a name for himself with his line of horses. He has become a credible businessman, something he wasn't when they were dating. My son would now be acceptable to her father."

Kit could understand why Olivia wanted him back. She wanted him with an intensity that frightened her. "So how come Trace never got married."

"Maybe he was waiting for the right girl to show up." Lola gave Kit an insightful glance, "You don't have to hide your feelings for my son from me, Kit. Both you, and Trace have been denying your feelings. You're in love with Trace, and he is in love with you. He's changed since you arrived. A change that has been for the better. I see a side of my son that was missing. He has never considered himself the marrying kind, so now he's all confused inside. It's a little more complicated because you have a child. I think that the idea of becoming a father scares him. He didn't have much of a role model growing up."

Kit had admitted to herself that she loved Trace, but she had to face another truth. She was afraid of getting hurt again. The people Kit loved always left her, starting with her own mother. It was difficult confessing this to Lola.

Knowing Kit's past, Lola understood. Kit had lost important people in her life and been repeatedly hurt by the person who failed her as a mother. "You're a wonderful mother, but don't you want to give Kenzie a father?"

"There are a lot of single parents out there," Kit said defensively.

"I know. I was one of them. But I had the support of the Calhouns, especially Buster."

Kit remained defensive, "I already have their support. It's not that I'm not receptive to the idea of marriage. Trace doesn't want to be a family man, even though he would make an excellent father."

"Olivia broke Trace's heart. He was young. and it mended, but he put a protective shell around it. I feel you have done that as well. You, my dear, are the person who has broken through that wall, and stole my son's heart. He has been dumbfounded since your arrival. Paths collide in unexpected ways. They brought all of us here. You, and Trace need to be open with your feelings, and see where this path takes you. Whatever happens after that is meant to be. Have faith."

By the time Kit left she was feeling better. Both ladies had allowed themselves to be open and share very personal thoughts and feelings. Kit's visit with Lola had been enlightening. On her drive home Kit reflected on her past. She had been content with her life after Mike died. It was comfortable, and uncomplicated. Then she came here and met the uncompromising Trace Grayson. Kit let out an anguished cry as feelings of guilt surfaced. She had never felt this kind of love with Mike. They were both so young, and innocent, and had so little time together. Kit knew she wanted Trace in her life. Her love for him was real and growing stronger.

After lunch, Kit left Kenzie in the house with her grandparents. Seeing her dad down at the corrals she headed over. Jasper was prancing around, but as soon as Kit joined her dad both Ginger, and Jasper trotted over. BJ and Kit were chatting away when Trace joined them.

"I'm going to saddle up Diego and go for a ride. Care to join me, Kit?"

"I can't take off and leave Kenzie at a moment's notice." Besides, she had spent most of the morning with Lola.

BJ slapped Trace on the back, "I'm sure she'd love to. Kit rides well. Just ask Shelby."

Trace grinned. Murphy had filled him in about the incident with Shelby and Kit.

"Jenny, and I will watch Kenzie for the afternoon. Jenny has wanted her to spend some time with us over at our house."

The clouds that had been threatening earlier had cleared. The leaves were beginning to turn, and Kit knew the changing colors throughout the valley would be spectacular. Temptation won out. "Sure, why not."

"I'll saddle up our horses while you go change."

Minutes later Kit crossed to where the saddled horses waited. Blondie nudged Kit in welcome. Kit mounted in one swift motion.

Diego raised his head and snorted at his owner. The magnificent stallion was spirited like Trace. Trace shoved a foot into the stirrup, and with easy cowboy grace he swung up into the saddle. Trace waited for Kit to pull alongside.

Kit wondered where they were going. "Thanks for the invite. It has turned out to be a gorgeous day. How long do these summerlike days last?"

"One never knows. You've seen for yourself how the weather can change in a minute, but we are experiencing a splendid fall with warmer than normal conditions."

They rode leisurely and chatted like old friends. Kit was reminded of the trip they took together to Washington and smiled knowing how much had changed between them. They had established a sound, and safe friendship despite their strong feeling for each other.

Trace topped a gentle bluff and reined in Diego. The horses, side by side, were as quiet as their riders. They sat looking out at the land, letting the silence encompass them. There it was, lying low in the wide valley between the lower ridges of the mountains. Lola Grande. Trace looked out over the land he could call his own. Usually when he rode out here, he was alone, and there was nothing else to look at but the vastness of the land. Today, his gaze took in Kit. She looked as beautiful as the countryside around them.

Kit appreciated the panoramic view. Leaves had already begun to fall, carpeting the landscape like a patchwork quilt. She was unaware that they had crossed over to Lola Grande land. "This view is spectacular. I've never seen anything so beautiful."

"Neither have I," he said, continuing to look at Kit. Trace twisted in his saddle and motioned to the natural beauty in front of them. A sense of pride filled his voice, "Kit, this is Lola Grande. This is our heritage, our roots. Lola Grande is the Grayson dream coming to life."

Sudden tears sprang to her eyes. Kit knew she had been honored. Now, stronger than ever, came the feeling that life was full of possibilities.

They gazed out over the pastureland below where horses grazed freely on acres of fine Alberta grassland. The land was the perfect spot for raising horses. The breathtaking beauty gave Kit a thrill. A peace like none she'd known settled over her. A peace derived from the timelessness of the land, and view around her. "How can a person ever get tired of this? Nature at its best. It draws you in, and spoils you for anything else." She took a few deep breaths, enjoying the stillness surrounding her.

"You feel it, too," Trace said softly.

Kit nodded. She could see how much he loved this land that fulfilled his dreams. She swallowed the lump in her throat. She closed her eyes in understanding. How many times had she sat at the window waiting for her mom, while dreaming that she had a dad who loved her, and wanted her? And would never leave her. Now, here she was at Valley View, and her dreams had come true. She looked over at Trace. Dare she allow herself to dream again?

"When we moved here, I'd ride out here. This has always been my place of refuge. Back then it was the Reed Ranch. I wanted my own land, and I knew that somehow, I would get it. I never once dreamed that this would become ours." Trace knew, and loved every acre spread out in front of him. The disappointments, and the hard work were worth it. He hadn't saved the ranch on his own. All three Graysons had pulled together at different times for the good of all of them. They had weathered the hardships of the last several years. For Trace, there was nowhere else, or anything else that mattered. He looked at Kit. Until now.

"Ranching gets in your blood and becomes your life. It takes a certain kind of man to make ranching work. Will Calhoun is a true rancher. Physically, his body might be less than what it was, but his inner will has never diminished. He passed that on to BJ. The Calhouns are legends in these parts and are highly respected. Riley, and I strive to live up to their standards, and honor Buster's memory. Riley is like them, but my love has always been the horses." His gaze returned to the horses that grazed in the lower pasture. "Nothing can beat the satisfaction of watching horses run wild and free. Simple pleasures in life."

Trace's expression was relaxed. He never doubted that he was following his true calling. He knew they couldn't have done it without the Calhouns, who had been there for them since the day they had arrived at Valley View. "I'm boarding and training our horses at Valley View while we build our training facilities at Lola Grande. Our financial debt to the Calhouns is paid off. We are now investing money into our business. In time, we will build an indoor arena, but that won't be for a few years. When that is done, it will be a top-quality facility at every level. When we first got to Lola

Grande, Riley, and I wanted Mom to have her dream house. She vetoed that, saying it wasn't practical because the house was fine the way it was. We all started to laugh. We arrived here in a holiday trailer with a roof that leaked. That was our home for years. Mom said there were other priorities. Under her cool exterior lies a stubborn, and strong businesswoman. It was because of our mom that we have our ranch, and that's why it's named after her. Riley, and I wanted to honor her by recognizing the sacrifices she made for us while married to our dad." Trace's usual reserved look was replaced with a look of pride. With every word he spoke, his love for the land, his ranch, and his family came through.

Trace remained nostalgic, "We grew up living hand to mouth because our father drifted from one job to another. That all changed when we arrived at Valley View. Life was better here. Dad wanted to prove himself in the beginning. For a short period of time, life was stable, and we could hope again. Those were the carefree days before dad resorted back to bad habits."

Kit had seen vulnerability in him when they were in Washington. It was when he had opened the door to his past. Today, he was again sharing, and that vulnerability was back. "There is no doubt that you, and Riley had harsh childhoods. You also had a lot of responsibility at a young age. My grandmother said it builds strength of character. You, and I know it does but it's not always easy."

Kit's response stirred up old feelings. Out here he could usually forget all that, but today the ghosts from the past had pushed their way through. His face grew somber as memories he didn't want to recall took over. "I told you that our father liked horses and women."

Kit's eyebrow raised thinking that Trace did, too.

Trace read her expressive gesture correctly. "I do, too, but not in the same way. Tom Grayson gambled on the horses and chased the skirts. He never wanted to be tied down by anyone or anything. He'd take off for days leaving us behind. When he was broke, he'd show up again. No explanation, no excuses. When he was absent, I'd step in to do his work so that he wouldn't lose his job or wages. I did it for Mom, and Riley." Kit wasn't surprised when Trace said, "I never want to be like my father."

"I understand. I never want to be like Torrie, and I'm not." Kit knew Trace hadn't told her everything, but more than he intended. Years of hatred. Such a burden to carry for so long. She hated the sadness she saw. Maybe someday he'd figure it all out. She wished she could help him.

"After our dad died it got better. For our mom, too, even though he left us with unpaid debts. Riley, and I both worked after school, and summers to pay it off. It wasn't all bad. We discovered that this was a way of life that we both wanted. I fell in love with the horses. The animals themselves. They are magnificent beasts. I love the challenge of training them without breaking their spirit." Trace turned to Kit, "The Graysons are a proud family. We have earned back the respectability that our father lost. This is our land, and our heritage begins here."

Trace had a far-off look in his eyes as he drifted in thought. He'd taken every action and made every decision with the single-minded intention of establishing Caballo Sables, and Lola Grande. It had been his focus. He suddenly questioned himself. Had it all become so important to him that he had closed his heart to everything else. He closed his eyes for a moment, surprised to discover how easy it was to picture Kit as part of the future. A home, a wife, children. A growing sense of excitement of new possibilities. Before now it wasn't possible. "I wanted to bring you here so you would understand. This is Lola Grande, the place that matters most in my life. My reason for living, for breathing. Until recently, I thought it was all I needed."

A comfortable silence settled between them as they continued to gaze out at the valley below. The thick humid air grew heavier with the scent of rain. Sheets of rain now obscured the mountains to the west. They continued to sit in silence watching the light show as lightning bolts zigzagged across the faraway hilltops. The wind suddenly picked up, the temperature dropped, and a deep rumble sounded in the distance. Kit turned her uneasy gaze to Trace, "It looks like the bottom is going to fall out of the sky any minute, and it's coming our way."

"It's been closing in faster than I thought. We'll never make it to either of the ranches. With luck, I think we can make the horse shelter." Turning away from the rim, they took off. No words passed between them. Kit followed as Trace veered Diego to the shelter. They raced the storm and lost. The heavy, dark clouds opened as another fork of lightning split the sky. Trace came to a stop and slid down from his saddle. As soon as Kit dismounted, he grabbed her bridle, and pulled both horses in closer to protect them. "I thought it would hold off, but it blew in so fast. Let's hope it's a quick storm." His strong arms reached out and pulled her against his chest as the wind and the rain whipped around them.

Kit was very conscious of their physical closeness as she felt the heat of his body through his soaked shirt. She snuggled closer to draw from his warmth. She looked up, and for a split second her gaze locked with his. Trace's lips dropped to her mouth and pressed to hers. This time she didn't resist. Instead, she wrapped her arms around his neck. It felt so right. She closed her eyes and kissed him back. Trace felt her surrender and deepened his kiss.

Kit knew what she was doing as she revealed her deep feelings to him. She was going to follow her heart. She might end up getting her heart broken, but she was willing to take the risk. Now it was up to Trace to decide what he was going to do.

Trace gently lifted her chin, "I see your face in my mind all day, and you haunt my dreams at night. I don't want to be just friends."

"I think you crossed that line a couple of times."

The storm was short lived. Trace kissed her forehead, then her lips before letting go. "I think it's safe to head home." Trace pointed to the rainbow, "Ma says rainbows are a reminder to continue through the dark times. It provides us with hope."

With a new understanding between them, they remounted, and headed back to Valley View. Thunder again rumbled in a darkening sky when they arrived at the ranch. "I'll head home before those approaching clouds burst. See you tomorrow."

Kit was deep in thought as she headed over to her dads to get Kenzie. Like the lightning that had darted across the sky earlier. Kit's mind darted from Trace to Mike. With Mike, it had taken love, and time to soften the hard, bitter edge of a tough brooding street kid. She'd seen him struggle emotionally before becoming comfortable in their relationship. For both her and Trace, the trust had to come first. Their love for each was beginning to flourish. Looking out, her gaze lingered on the rainbow arcing across the sky, providing her with new hope. Since finding her dad, she'd begun to believe all things were possible.

Chapter Twenty-Four

Kenzie was playing with her Barbie dolls on the verandah while Kit sat in the rocker reading. Shelby was inside talking to Sadie, and as usual, Kit had been intentionally excluded. Kit sighed. Surely by now Shelby could make an effort.

Kit looked up when the door opened, and Shelby walked out. "Gramps wants to see you in the office for a minute."

Kenzie was playing so nicely that Kit hated to disturb her. Dare she ask Shelby to watch her? The request was out before Kit had a chance to think twice.

Every once in a while, Shelby's inner good surfaced. Her eyes softened as she gazed at Kenzie. She really was a sweet little girl. "Sure."

A flicker of hope followed Kit inside.

Shelby was sitting on the steps chatting away on her phone when Kit returned twenty minutes later. "Where's Kenzie."

"I thought she went inside," Shelby said, without apology.

Kit's mother intuition caused her stomach to turn, and her heart to stop. She called out for Kenzie and waited. Kit called again, only louder. Both Sadie and Will rushed out of the house. BJ, and Trace were coming up the drive. "Kenzie is gone."

Shelby's heart thundered in her chest as her face paled. She could hear the desperation in Kit's voice, and she knew this was her fault.

Trace turned to the others and began giving orders, "We need to split up. Look everywhere, inside every building, and in every place a little girl can hide. BJ, why don't you go over to your house, and see if she wandered over there to see Jenny. I'll check the barn and see if Murphy has seen her." Trace's voice was grave, his expression visibly worried.

Trace had taken control, but Will didn't miss the fear in his eyes. He'd never known Trace to be afraid of anything, but one little girl changed that. Sadie left to check the house while Will headed around back toward the creek.

When Trace pulled Kit into his arms, he could feel her trembling. He spoke softly trying to calm her, but his own voice was tight, "If any of the boys find her, they'll bring her back to the house, so you need to be here. We'll find her, Kit." Trace hated the sense of helplessness he felt as he headed to the barn. Inside, the light was dim. He halted, waiting for his eyes to adjust so he could look around the shadowy interior. An expression of intense relief spread over Trace's face when he heard jabbering. Thank God she'd come to the barn, and not down to the creek. He found Kenzie in the shadows of the last stall with the kittens. Something stirred within him as he stood silently watching her. When had this little girl penetrated his defenses, and stolen his heart? Choked up, he swallowed hard before speaking, "Hi, Kenzie."

An impish grin covered the little girl's face as she clutched her favorite kitten to her chest. "I came all by myself to play with the kitties. I'm a big girl. Papa said so."

Trace dropped to his knees and picked up one of the other kittens and began scratching his belly. "You are a big girl and getting bigger every day. Right now, your mommy is missing you because she doesn't know where you are. Let's go back to the house." Trace was overtaken by a new desire, one that quickly expanded into a yearning for a family of his own. He was tired of fighting it. He loved Kit, and her precious daughter and wanted them as his family. There, he finally admitted it. The big question was, what was he going to do about it? Was he even cut out for fatherhood? Then Kenzie smiled at him and squeezed his hand. He smiled as his heart answered. Her simple gesture erased all of his doubts. For years, he believed he was meant to be alone. Now he realized how lonely that would be. Trace picked Kenzie up and tossed her onto his shoulders. She squealed with delight.

The tears Kit fought came when she saw them. With a cry of relief Kit flew off the steps and began heaping kisses on her daughter's sweet face.

As Trace surrendered the little girl, it felt as though some vital part of him was being torn from him.

"Hi, Mommy. I was playing with the kitties." Unaware of the fear she had caused, Kenzie squirmed in her mother's tight grip.

Over Kenzie's head Kit's gaze connected with Trace's. "Thank you."

Trace smiled back. Until Kit, until Kenzie, he had been able to convince himself that Lola Grande was enough. Without a word, Trace turned, and walked away. He needed time alone to process these new feelings. He had never wanted the responsibility that came with a family. Besides, he already had more responsibility than one man needed. Everything had changed over the last few months including himself, but was he ready to make an even bigger change? Out of nowhere the words in Buster's letter appeared vividly in Trace's mind. *Trust in yourself, and don't give all of your love to the horses. Don't be afraid to open yourself up to others.*

Trace's departure left Shelby alone with Kit. Shelby wiped away her own tears. "I'm sorry, Kit. This was my fault."

"It could have happened to anyone, including me." There was no ill-will in Kit's voice.

Kit's act of forgiveness, with no hint of blame, crushed Shelby's attitude. Shelby's voice was small and the crack in it was real, "I've been mean to you so many times, but I never wished harm on either of you. All I wanted was for you to go away. You were taking my dad's attention away from me. It had always been me my whole life, and he always had time for me. I didn't like the attention he was giving to you, and Kenzie." Shelby hung her head as she revealed the real truth, "I was afraid he would love you more than me because you were his real daughter."

Shelby spoke with such genuine regret that Kit couldn't help but feel sorry for her. "We'll put this behind us, but you and I need to talk."

Shelby was nervous, not knowing what to expect.

Kit decided it was time to share a few facts of her own. "You were able to have all the time with your dad growing up. I know that on paper he is your stepdad, but in reality, he is your dad. Every day. All day. You were able to have wonderful times with your dad growing up. Mine were all make believe. Now those dreams are coming true. It wasn't easy for me to come here, and try to fit in. It has been difficult dealing with your spitefulness, and dig-in-attitude to get rid of me. You haven't taken into consideration what others are dealing with, or how they are feeling. It would be easier on everyone if you'd let your animosity toward me go. I admit that I haven't always been nice either. You bring the worst out in me. Even though it hurt, I was impressed with your deep commitment to your personal cause to get rid of me. That is real Calhoun determination."

"You are a Calhoun, too."

Although a lot had been left unsaid, it had been a profound morning for both of them. A little girl brought down the wall that had existed between the two girls.

Shelby headed home. She needed to talk to her dad. She found him in the kitchen.

BJ looked up with a happy smile, "I heard Trace found Kenzie in the barn."

Shelby nodded her head, "I didn't mean for this to happen."

"Nobody is blaming you."

"Not even Kit. We had a long talk before I came home. She forgave me when I told her how sorry I was. Not just about today, but how I've treated Kit since she arrived. I'm sorry, Dad." Shelby hated herself for the way she'd been behaving. She'd been so single-minded that she'd forgotten the values she'd been raised on. Confessing was hard for Shelby, but she continued, "Kit's arrival was such a big shock. My world was rocked. As usual, I made it all about me. I was hurt so I allowed it to overshadow everything. I know my behavior was immature. I hung on to my resentment out of stubbornness."

That made BJ smile. Shelby never admitted fault. BJ watched as Shelby continued to struggle. BJ's guilt surfaced, wondering how he could have handled things differently. He took Shelby into his arms, "I love your mother more than I though was possible to love a woman. When she became part of my life, she brought a beautiful baby girl. I was proud to claim you as my daughter, and I'm proud to have you as my daughter now. But I have another daughter who I am trying to get to know. It has been taking time away from you, but it doesn't mean that I love you less. I thought you knew that."

"Until Kit arrived, I never felt insecure or jealous. Things even changed between me, and Riley. I always thought Riley would wait for me. Then

Kit showed up, and she seemed to be taking him away." Shelby's eyes remained dismal, "Why is growing up so hard at times?"

"It can be difficult at any age. We just learn how to cope better with age, and experience. I know you hate to admit when you're wrong, hate advice even more. You are independent, and strongly believe in yourself. A positive trait when used properly. I can't believe how lucky I am to have two wonderful daughters."

*****

Kit's feelings were mixed when she saw Trace drive up the next day. She had endured a troubled night questioning his actions. Yesterday had been an emotional day on several levels. Kit had been so frightened when Kenzie was missing, and she had been incredibly hurt when Trace disappeared just as suddenly. She didn't understand his absence. Fear clutched at her heart. Had she started to read too much into his actions? No. She knew Trace was an honorable man. Kit watched him, the strong man she had come to rely on.

Trace's face was solemn when he walked over and sat down. Even now he was unable to forget the raw panic that had grabbed him when Kenzie was missing. There was no way he could forget the terror in Kit's eyes when she looked at him. He realized that Kit, and Kenzie had become as important to him as breathing. He was ready to surrender. He was ready to let the past go. It was the future that mattered.

Trace decided to be candid, "I'm sure you've been wondering why I took off yesterday. I needed time alone to think. For the past few years everyone knows I had one priority. Everything in my life related to and revolved around Lola Grande. There were so many responsibilities. Paying off our debt. Reviving our ranch. Making the Grayson name mean something. Establishing Caballo Stables was my way of making my mark. Lola Grande, and Caballo Stables were all I needed until now. When Kenzie was missing, it scared the hell out of me. I was glad that I was there for you. I realized I want to always be here for you, and Kenzie. I hadn't counted on this new sense of responsibility for someone, rather than something. There are still things to accomplish like making Caballo Stables a successful independent business. But now I have another vision. I need you, and your daughter in my life for it to be complete. A thriving ranch means nothing without someone to share it with. I'm in love with you, Kit." That confession was exciting, and terrifying at the same time. "I want to be your husband, and a father to your daughter. I want us to be a family. I want to have more family with you. I want to grow old with you surrounded by our children and their children. I want a lifetime with you. I don't have a lot to offer, not nearly as much as you deserve."

Kit smiled as she gently touched his cheek, "You said you love me, and Kenzie. That's all I need. What's in our hearts is more important than anything else. Love is the essence of what life is made of. Not pride, not parents, not one person alone. You never know life's path, or what your future has in store. All you need is the courage to move forward."

"You realize that I have no idea what it takes to be a good dad."

"I didn't know how to be a mom. I was afraid I might not be a good mother because of my own mother. I found out that it comes naturally. You love them, and they sneak their way into your heart before you can blink."

Trace nodded, "Kenzie has already done that. I don't want to end up treating Kenzie the way our dad treated us."

Kit finally understood. It wasn't being a father that scared Trace. It was the type of father he might be. "You could never be like your dad, Trace. You learned from Buster, and Will, and BJ. All strong, honorable, and fair men. I don't question that you will love my daughter as your own." Kit was as sure of this as she was about her love for this man.

"What if I make mistakes."

"I've made my own, and there will be more. There are days that I'm scared. Parenting is not only a big responsibility, but it something you do every day. Like ranching, it becomes part of who you are. Lou always said that if what you do is out of love, it can't be wrong."

Trace realized that Kit was right. The Calhouns were positive role models. He'd learned so much about how a real family lives by watching them. He took Kit in his arms and kissed her with such tenderness that her eyes teared. "I can no longer imagine my life without you. I love you with my whole being. I went to Calgary today. That's why I wasn't here earlier." Trace had always been a man of action once he made a decision. He reached into his pocket as he went down on one knee. "I love you, Kit Bennett. Will you do me the honor of becoming my wife? I need you in my life to make it complete."

Kit was willing to reach out and embrace her future. A future with Trace at Lola Grande. "Yes, I'll marry you. I love you, too."

Trace was sure his sigh of relief echoed through the surrounding mountains. "I would like to get married as soon as possible. Ma will want a big wedding. You've been married before, so maybe you don't want a big wedding?"

Kit took Trace's hands in hers, "This may not be my first wedding, but it's my first wedding to you. I want my dad to walk me down the aisle like every little girl dreams. But this isn't all about me. What do you want?"

"I want the world to hear me say, "I do." I want to start adoption proceedings as soon as possible. I want Kenzie to be my daughter. I would like her to call me, Dad."

After sharing their exciting news with both Calhoun families, Kit and Trace returned to the verandah. "I'm heading home to tell my family. I hope Ma can handle the shock." Trace wasn't sure if his feet even touched the ground before he climbed into his truck. He couldn't wipe the grin off his face all the way home. Trace managed to wait until they were sitting down for supper before he blurted out, "Ma, what could be better than a Calhoun barbeque?" Not waiting for an answer, he continued, "How about a Calhoun and Grayson wedding?"

Lola looked over at Riley, who looked as dumbfounded as she did.

"Kit and I got engaged today. You ladies can plan everything, just tell Riley, and me when to show up. You will be my best man, won't you, Riley?"

Riley's grin was as wide as his brother's as he agreed.

Lola had a million questions but knew she wouldn't get anything more out of Trace. She would be going to Valley View first thing tomorrow.

*****

A few weeks had passed since Trace's surprise announcement. Trace and Kit had decided on the simplicity of an outdoor spring wedding. Spring was symbolic to both. It was the season of life, and new beginnings. They wanted to get married at Valley View for sentimental reasons. That was where their paths brought them together. It would also serve as a tribute to the Calhouns. It would be an afternoon wedding with the majestic Rocky Mountains as a backdrop. If the weather didn't cooperate, the ceremony could easily be moved inside to the Quonset, which would be set up for the reception and dance. The Calhouns were quick to inform Kit that ranchers had a community of their own, and it was an established practice to invite friends, and neighbors to share in the day of celebration. Kit knew that having everyone there supporting them would make the day special. This was going to be a wedding that every little girl dreamed of. Best of all, her dad would be walking her down the aisle. After the wedding reception, they would then go home to Lola Grande as the Grayson family.

Kit and Shelby were out on the verandah at Lola Grande waiting for Jenny to arrive so they could discuss the plans for the wedding. Sadie was already inside with Lola. Kit looked over at Shelby. Family was the most important thing in Kit's life. It was time to establish a new bond. Kit gently laid her hand on Shelby's arm, "I have something to ask you before we head in. I would like you to be my maid of honor?"

Kit's request surprised Shelby. Her voice was small and the wonder in it was real, "Why would you want me after how I've acted toward you?"

"It's time to start over as sisters, without anger getting in the way."

"Thank you. I would like to stand up with you on your wedding day." Shelby had finally reached a new level of maturity.

Both girls were grateful for the arrival of Jenny. They went in and joined the other ladies. They gathered around the table as Lola unwrapped a faded and tattered box. Lola was beaming with pleasure, and she hoped that what was inside would be received with pleasure. It could be the "something old" for Kit. Inside was Lola's bridal veil. "Tom didn't allow me to bring much with me when we left after the wedding, but I insisted that this would stay with me wherever I went. It was my mother's veil that she passed on to me when I married. It has travelled from Mexico to the United States, and across Canada. I always dreamed that one day I would pass it on to a future daughter-in-law."

Kit accepted the intricately woven lace veil with tears in her eyes. "Lola, this is so delicate, and beautiful. I would be more than honored to wear it."

Plans were made knowing the day was fast approaching. "I hope everything goes well," Sadie said to Lola.

Kit smiled at them, "There is no need to stress. At the end of the day, I will be married to the man I love. Whatever goes wrong will never matter."

It was late afternoon by the time the ladies left. Kit stayed behind. Kit, and Lola still had things to discuss. Lola was glad to have the opportunity to have a few words alone with Kit. "Lola Grande will be your home. The boys, and I never had much to call our own, so we appreciated everything that BJ, and Jenny left when they moved to Valley View. Our history was different, and so is your future. I want you to make the house yours. I have taken what I want and have moved into my suite. Pack up the things you don't want, and we'll give them to Good Will. Make this home yours, and Trace's, and Kenzie's." Lola remembered the day she moved in, and the feeling of stepping into somebody else's life. In time, she made it her own. She wanted Kit to feel she could do the same, without guilt or hesitation.

Kit appreciated Lola's thoughtfulness.

"As a mother, you always imagine your children growing up, getting married, and having children of their own. My husband promised me he would give me the world. In a way he did. Tom gave me my two sons. Trace, and Riley are my world."

Kit could understand. "All I wanted was a family when I came here."

Lola smiled, "And you got two. I just wanted a home, and I got a ranch."

Chapter Twenty-Five

There was a raw wind sweeping down from the high country and the temperature had dropped. Spring storms in Alberta could be severe. Trace figured they might be in for one before the day was over. He cast a glance skyward. Slate gray clouds remained low on the mountains.

Trace was fully operational at Lola Grande. He already had two new yearlings booked in for spring. All his horses had been moved over. Even though phase two was still on hold, he was satisfied. The lack of funding to proceed right now didn't alter his final vision.

Trace wanted to fit in a training session with Champ before the weather turned. Champ was his own colt, one of the first sired by Rebel. He was a beauty, strong, and agile with wonderful lines. Trace was anxious to put the skittish colt through the paces when a stranger's truck pulled up. He watched as a seasoned cowboy stepped out. Trace dropped the reins over the railing and walked over. "Is there something I can do for you?"

"Afternoon. I'm looking for Trace Grayson."

"You found him."

"I'm Brody Maddox."

Trace recognized the name. Brody Maddox was well known in the professional cutting horse circuit.

"One of my buddies got his last horse from Valley View. He was a strong yearling named, Dusty. Do you know the horse?"

"I trained him, but I now operate Caballo Stables here at Lola Grande."

"I'm looking for a new horse. I've heard your name floating around the arenas for the last few years. I came to see what you've got."

Trace had earned his reputation. It had taken commitment, and sheer determination to get where he was. His hard work had paid off. "This is my own colt, Champ. I introduced him to a few calves last week. He's a quick learner. I was just about to have a training session with him." Trace had high expectations for all of his horses.

"He's a magnificent looking horse. Do you mind if I stay and watch?"

With Trace's permission, Brody watched in appreciation. Trace had great hands, and exact skills. Brody admired the horse's ability to shift direction, anticipating the calf's every move. Brody could see Trace's gentle, and patient technique with Champ. As a result, it was obvious that Champ was both a quiet, and responsive horse.

When Trace was finished, he joined Brody at the railing. Brody could see why Trace Grayson had the reputation of being one of the best trainers in the industry. "It's obvious that you have worked a lot of hours with Champ. When will he be ready for competition?"

"It usually takes me twelve to eighteen months of concentrated training before a horse is ready for competition. I have been training Champ for over a year, but he still needs a few more months of training with the calves."

"I don't want to lose out on this opportunity, so if I buy him now, will you board him, and continue with his training?"

"Of course, for an additional monthly fee."

"No problem. My brother, Grady has a new colt. He's looking for a trainer. I'll pass your name on to him."

"Thanks, I appreciate referrals." With great pride, Trace shook the hand of Brody Maddox, Champ's new owner.

"If Champ lives up to his name, I'm sure you'll be getting a lot more business. He really is a fine specimen." Brody climbed into his pick-up and pulled away.

The price Trace accepted was staggering, but it was still difficult to turn the reins of one of his horses over to someone else. Trace didn't think it would get any easier. He knew the sale of Champ meant prestige, and recognition for Caballo Stables. More important, it meant substantial revenue. Dreams were again becoming a reality. He had paid his dues and was now reaping the rewards. Trace pulled up the collar of his jacket as he headed back to the barn. The weather had worsened as the cold front from the north continued to blow in.

*****

Trace loved operating at Lola Grande, but he had to admit he missed the daily interaction with the others at Valley View. It was only a few weeks until the wedding. Kit was in the house with Lola reviewing the wedding check list. Everything was coming together. Trace knew there would be last minute things to do the closer the big day came. He headed over to the new corrals. There were still everyday things that needed to be done.

Trace groaned out loud when he saw the bright red sports car coming up the drive, knowing it had to be Olivia. "A pick-up never was your style, was it?" Trace commented as she climbed out. She was dressed too causally for Trace's likes, with her braless breasts almost falling out of her skimpy top, and her cut off denim shorts barely covering the cheeks of her butt. He was sure Olivia thought she looked sexy. Trace thought she looked cheap.

"No, I still prefer a fancy sports car." Olivia was disappointed at the unwelcoming look on Trace's face. Her sole purpose for being here was another attempt to get him back. Olivia gave Trace one of her best sultry looks, "I feel bad for the way things ended between us. I made a mistake. Can we try again?"

"You're not the only one who made a mistake. I stepped out of my class. I was a poor horse wrangler who didn't fit in with the kind of crowd you ran with."

"We've both changed and grown up over the years. We can get back what we had."

"Why would I?"

"You don't want what we had back then?"

"No, it became toxic."

Olivia didn't miss the hard glint in his eyes, or the firm set of his jaw. "Daddy wanted me to marry Burke."

"You had no problem making your choice."

"My marriage to Burke was horrible. I soon found myself in a volatile marriage. When it became physical, I told my dad, hoping he would support me, and talk to Burke. Instead, every time I was upset, Daddy would suggest I take a holiday with my mom. That's when I had a better understanding of my mom's lonely life. My dad said he couldn't afford a scandal. It would be bad for business. So, I stayed for Daddy's sake, and maintained the facade of being happily married." Looking for sympathy, and attempting to draw Trace in, she continued, "The night before I left, Burke and I attended another business dinner. When we got home, I knew he was in one of his jealous moods. I had talked to one of the male guests too much. I tried explaining that it was his business associate who kept coming on to me. He called me a liar, and he hit me. It wasn't just a slap, and it wasn't only once. After he left for work the next day, I packed a bag, and flew home. I refused to be a victim. When my dad saw my beaten face, he helped me file divorce papers. I never saw Burke again."

The defeated tone in Olivia's voice affected Trace. He understood the effects of abuse. Olivia had been given all the luxuries, but she had paid for them in other ways. It didn't change the way he felt about her. "So now you want to move on to someone else, and see if that works out better? Anyone will do?"

Olivia placed her hands on his rock-solid chest. "You're not anyone, Trace. You still fascinate me. Don't play hard to get to teach me a lesson. We were just kids back then."

Before she could go any further, Trace grabbed both of her wrists, forcing her arms away. "We're not kids any more. I'm not interested in playing your game, Olivia."

Olivia stared him down. "You've changed. I remember when you were willing to challenge life and defy anyone to make a point. You're even more serious than you used to be. Did I hurt you that much? Were you in love with me, Trace?"

"I thought I was, but I was young and unsophisticated. Sadly, I believed you loved me, too. Instead, you were amusing yourself until Burke returned. Over time, I realized it was only teenage infatuation, and physical attraction."

"I still have that attraction." Olivia pushed her body up against him and wrapped her arms around his neck.

Trace tensed with discomfort, "You're still seeing what you want to see. The old Trace who wasn't afraid to stand up to your dad and was easily manipulated by your charms. It doesn't work anymore. You're right. I have changed, and that's thanks to Kit. I have a whole new life, and I've moved on. Kit and I are engaged."

Olivia was shocked by his announcement. "Well, you're not married yet."

"I'm not in the running, Olivia. What I have with Kit is different. She makes me happy. She brought out the side of me I thought I had lost." His tone, his voice, the light in his eyes said it all. He loved Kit Bennett.

This was not at all what Olivia expected. "You'll never be anything more than a cowboy." Olivia could still be haughty and bad-tempered when things didn't go her way.

Trace didn't react. Olivia no longer had the power to hurt him.

Kit had spent all morning discussing plans with Lola. Wanting to finalize a few details with Trace she decided to see if he was around. When she stepped out of the house, she spotted Olivia at the paddock with her arms intimately wrapped around Trace's neck. The way the blonde was clinging to Trace got under Kit's skin. Kit knew she could ignore it or address it. There was no choice once the Calhoun temper kicked in. Eyes blazing, she marched toward the entwined couple.

Seeing Kit approaching out of the corner of her eye, Olivia pulled Trace's head down, and kissed him before he could push her away.

"I'm done talking, Olivia. Go home. I have a ranch to run." He didn't have time to listen to her marital failure, and jealous ranting.

Unaware of Kit's approach, Trace headed into the barn. Olivia hung back. For Olivia, power was a heady thing. Especially the power to hurt. Jackson had taught her well. "Trace, and I were just reminiscing over days past. We both miss what we had."

Olivia's blatant lie made Kit's blood boil. Kit's words were clear and slow, as though she was addressing a blonde bimbo, "I'm not asking you to keep your hands off Trace. I'm telling you." There was no mistaking the warning in her tone.

Olivia didn't heed Kit's warning. "Trace regrets our breakup. Being the gentleman he is, he doesn't know how to break if off with you. Why not make it easy for him? Take your brat with you and go back to where you came from."

"I don't know what fantasy world you live in, Olivia, but it's time you get out of ours." Kit turned and went back to the house to calm down.

Trace had heard the commotion. After Olivia left, he joined Kit.

Kit was still fuming, "Olivia is obsessed with getting back together with you. She thinks if she pours on the charm, she can convince you to take her back."

Trace started to smirk, "I've never had two beautiful women fight over me before."

"I suppose that does wonders for your ego."

Trace laughed, "My ego doesn't need inflating."

"That woman better stay the hell away from you. She is conniving, and deceitful, and her lies flow with ease."

"Her showing up today took me back. It gave me a chance to take those old feelings and look at them hard. When I did, I knew I never loved Olivia. I was eighteen, and drawn into an uncomfortable environment, but was too stubborn to admit I didn't belong. I had more hormones than good sense. I was infatuated with this beautiful girl who represented all the glamour, and excitement a young man could dream about. Looking back, I used her as well. I knew she wasn't my type, but I wanted to see how rich folks lived. I was a simple cowboy when I met her. I still am and I'm proud of it. Olivia's family had money, and class. I was skilled labor. Two different worlds. Her parents, especially her dad, objected to our dating because I wasn't good enough. It amused Olivia to rebel, and she stroked my ego. When Olivia dumped me, she dumped me hard. It took me a long time to get over her betrayal. That's why I was so defensive when you arrived. When I heard that she was divorced and back home, it didn't matter to me. It didn't matter to me then; it doesn't matter now. You are the only woman I want to share my life with."

Kit's jealousy was erased by Trace's honesty. She knew her temper had gotten the better of her.

"Now that I'm a businessman, and landowner I've moved up the class ladder. I have made the Grayson name mean something. I no longer have to prove anything to the Beaumonts or anyone else. Lola Grande is my future, and that future will include you, and Kenzie."

*****

Trace and Kit were standing at the railing watching Jasper romp when they saw the vehicle coming up the drive. Trace could not believe the gall of the Beaumonts. He thought that after the confrontation Olivia had with Kit, and the fact that he said he wanted nothing to do with her that she'd accept reality. "Doesn't she ever give up?"

Kit was very aware of Jackson Beaumont's social position, but his reputation hadn't prepared her for the real man. The man looked much older than his years. He was stooped over, and walked with a cane.

With his celebrated charm he took Kit's hand, "I'm so glad to meet you, Miss Calhoun. I see that Trace has good taste in women, as well as horses."

"It's Mrs. Bennett," Kit corrected. Neither Kit, nor Olivia pretended social politeness. In truth, neither one was pleased to see the other. Olivia would have preferred her to leave, but Kit remained by Trace's side. It was an unspoken, but unmistakable act of ownership.

"That foal is a beauty, Trace. I want to buy him for Olivia, and have you train him. I'll pay you whatever you want." Jackson was still doing everything he could to make his little girl happy. But it wasn't the horse that Olivia wanted. It was Trace.

Trace was tired of the Beaumonts. He gave Jackson a blistering stare, "Don't waste your time or mine. My horse is not for sale, and there are training facilities closer to your ranch."

"You're the best and nothing is too good for my little girl. I know you and I had our differences, but I'm sure we can overlook them. Olivia wants that horse so name your price."

Olivia moved closer to Trace, "You know it would be good for your reputation. My father's well known for his fine stock. This would add credibility to your business." Realizing her words were having no effect on Trace, Olivia pulled Trace aside. Her look became deliberate, "Trace, think about this realistically, my father is a very powerful man. He will roll over you if he doesn't get his way."

Trace could see Jackson in Olivia's eyes. Trace thought back to when they had dated. She had always played on her irresistible charm like her daddy. Today, he saw her true character. When she couldn't have her way, she turned ugly just like her dad. "He can try."

Trace turned back to Jackson and stared him down. He had never been intimidated by this man. "I can't be bought, and threats don't work.

There was a time you said I wasn't good enough for your daughter. Well, Jackson, my horses are too good for your daughter."

The poor man looked like he might burst a blood vessel. "You wait just a damn minute. You're just saying no because of our past." Getting no response, contempt curled the man's lips, "You obviously haven't lived here long enough to know how powerful I am. You cross me, and you'll be sorry. I promise you that."

Today, Trace was calling the shots. It gave him great pleasure to say, "I think a wealthy, and hard-nosed businessman once told me that business is business. Right, Jackson? I have made my position clear. I'm telling you for the last time. I'll not do business with either one of you."

Jackson's temper was vile when lost, "This isn't over, Grayson. You don't know the kind of enemy you made today. You will regret this." Jackson Beaumont had a way of going after people who defied him with retribution.

Trace stared him down and took a step forward. "Stay away from me and my property."

Kit had watched all of this in silence and was relieved when they left. She had no doubt that buying Jasper was just Olivia's way of having an excuse to spend time with Trace. Kit couldn't refrain from saying, "Can he really hurt you?"

"That fat, cigar-smoking bastard thinks he can intimidate me with threats. It didn't work with my own dad. It sure as hell won't work now. I don't care about the money. Diego, and Rebel's stud fees alone will carry us this year, and Ginger is ready to foal." Trace held her by the shoulders, "Buster taught me many lessons before he died. When I started Caballo Stables he told me to never settle. It may take longer, but it will be worth it. The day I have to do business with a man like Jackson Beaumont is the day I close the doors to my business."

"I agree, but there are times you could utilize some people skills."

Trace snapped back, "I don't have any."

"I know, that's why you need me."

Laughing, Trace pulled her close, and kissed her soundly. "That's not why I need you." Trace wiped his brow with his shirt sleeve, "I could use a beer."

"Me, too. I really hate confrontations." They headed over to the house arm in arm.

Once they were seated, Kit decided to address something that was troubling her. "I have something to ask you, and I hope it won't offend you. Is it the lack of cash flow that is holding you back from doing phase two right away?"

"You are upset that I turned down Jackson's offer?"

"No, I support your decision. I'm proud of your moral standards. This has nothing to do with that."

Trace's brow furrowed. "Yes, if I had the money the expansion for the rest of the facility could be done by the end of the year and I'd renovate the barn right away. That's where I would have the birthing stall, and an office. My ultimate dream is to then build an indoor arena so I can train year-round, but I refuse to go into debt." Trace looked over and could tell by the serious expression on Kit's face that she had something on her mind.

"Please hear me out before you say anything." Kit, who usually approached things in a direct manner, employed a different tactic. "Are you expecting me to take the Grayson name when we are married?"

Not expecting this, Trace was surprised, "I assumed you would. Don't you want to?"

Kit, pleased with his response, baited him further, "I will be honored to take the Grayson name. When I do, that makes me a Grayson, right?"

"Yeah," he said with hesitation. He didn't know where she was going with this.

"And as a Grayson, I become part of Lola Grande?"

"Of course."

"Good. Then I can contribute financially if I choose. Right?"

Pride wouldn't allow him to answer. Trace knew right away he was going to lose a battle. "We'll talk about it later. I have to get back to work."

Kit put her hand on his arm, "You will always have work to get back to, but that excuse won't work this time. My grandmother left me with a sizeable inheritance, and I have already set up a trust fund for Kenzie. We can use my money and start phase two right away, and also build the indoor arena. I want to do this, Trace."

"Look, Kit, I can't let you do that."

"Trace Grayson, don't you know by now that you can't tell me what I can, and cannot do? I don't need your approval. This is what I want to do."

Trace was trying desperately to swallow his pride. Kit was an unbelievable woman. He had been so judgmental when she arrived, and she still continued to amaze him with her generous actions. "You do realize that you just chip away until you get your own way."

"When we marry, we commit to each other. We are in this together. So, there's nothing left to discuss, is there?"

Trace was an independent man, but he knew she was right. Being a man, he wouldn't admit it. "You are an exasperating woman, Kit Bennett."

Kit knew she had won. "I thought you had work to do. You can't sit around here all day and I have to go in and finish up details for the wedding."

"You're the most stubborn woman I've met. Makes me wonder what our children will be like." Trace took his leave.

Kit hadn't missed the glint of admiration in his eyes. Kit loved Trace's strong qualities, but along with her own Calhoun stubbornness there was no doubt that there would be many head-butting matches. Kit smiled and went back into the house.

Chapter Twenty-Six

The sun was barely up, and the air, though chilly, was pure in the way only country air can be. Trace had ridden out to the ridge, wanting to be alone before tomorrow's big day. It was a time for reflection. The familiar sounds of nature surrounded Trace as he sat on Diego and gazed out at the vastness of the land in front of him, recalling the day Lola Grande become theirs. His mother had taken the hand of both her sons, "God guided us here with his hand. This ranch is our legacy. It is our destiny." From that day forward, Trace had only one priority. He wanted to make the Grayson name mean something and make their mark on the land. It had consumed him, but Trace had no regrets. This was the place that meant so many things to Trace. This was where he had allowed himself to dream, to grieve, and dream again. The ridge had brought him comfort when Buster died. This was where he finally admitted his feelings for Kit.

Kit had opened his heart to new dreams. Trace smiled. From the day they met, she was a distraction he couldn't ignore. His life changed the day he met Kit and tomorrow he was marrying the fiery spitfire. There was no denying that after tomorrow things would be very different. He didn't question his decision, just the challenges that would follow. He wouldn't be going down that road alone, and Kit was the most courageous woman he had ever met. Trace smiled in anticipation to begin his shared life with Kit, and Kenzie.

Trace looked up thinking of Buster. Trace missed his friend, his mentor. The man had been such a positive role model. Trace had idolized him. He no longer felt the anger at his loss, just the unfairness of Buster's death. A good man taken too soon. A wonderful man who had taken the Grayson family in without reservation and raised him and Riley as his own. The man who loved and treated their mother with the kind of respect she deserved. Trace touched his pocket. Inside was the letter from Buster. It would be with him again tomorrow. Buster Calhoun would be at the wedding.

Trace had ridden out here because there were still some things in his past that he needed to come to terms with. Kit had told him that he shouldn't hold a grudge against a dead man. Kit was right. He didn't want to bring anger into their marriage. Trace decided to let go of the hatred he had carried for too long toward his dad. He was ready to leave it on the ridge. Just like the sadness of the Reed Ranch was no more, the sadness of his past would be no more. It was time to push the ghosts back into the past where they belonged. He knew he couldn't erase the past, and he couldn't let it stop him from moving forward.

Back at Valley View, Kit was also being introspective. She had gathered her memories and reflected on the journey that brought her to Valley View. She was soon lost in thought, thinking of Mike, and their time together. The day that Kit met Michael Bennett had changed her life. Mike was the first man who ever meant anything to her, and she fell in love with him. They were young, innocent, and excited about discovering the depth of love within a relationship. Their days were filled with excitement, adventure, and romance. His love gave meaning to everything in her life. What they had in their short time together was special. Kit treasured the fact that he had been in her life.

When Mike died, Kit had vowed never to open up that part of her heart again. She smiled. She hadn't met Trace Grayson. She had no control over Mike's death, but she had control over her future. Once again, she would dream and plan a future with the man she loved. Kit's mind drifted between Mike and Trace. Mike had lived in her dreams allowing her to remember the way he could make her feel. Trace woke her up and brought that part of her back to life. Trace could be tender. She'd seen it with Kenzie, and of course with his beloved horses. But he was cowboy tough. Once Trace made his mind up about something, or someone, he was as unmovable as the Rocky Mountains. Her love for Trace was all-consuming.

It may have been Mike with whom she discovered love, but it was Trace who reignited the embers, and fueled her desire to marry again.

Kit was ready to leave the past behind. The heartache, the broken dreams, and struggles had all been part of the journey. Tomorrow was the beginning of a new journey. Like Trace, she released her feelings toward Torrie through a conscious act of forgiveness. That bitterness was now replaced with sadness for the shallow life her mother had lived. Torrie had never experienced the joy that having a family could bring. Kit's father had helped ease the pain of her past. Tomorrow, he would proudly walk her down the aisle. Childhood dreams coming true. She would always encourage Kenzie to believe in herself and follow her dreams.

Kit wished that Lou were here to see how happy she was. She knew Lou would approve of Trace. Kenzie already loved Trace. She could hardly wait to call him Daddy. Kenzie thought she was a special little girl because she would have two dads. One in heaven, and one here. Kit smiled when Kenzie said that maybe this daddy would buy her a puppy. Life was full of so many possibilities. Kit felt blessed.

*****

Kit woke feeling rested and filled with peace. She lay in bed, listening to the murmur of excitement that moved throughout the house. Today was her wedding day. Kit was excited, knowing that together with Trace they were moving forward and becoming a family. Slipping from bed, she headed to the kitchen.

Sadie started to cry the minute she saw Kit, "I'm going to miss you and Kenzie."

Kit went and hugged her. This woman had welcomed them with open arms the day they showed up at Valley View. Sadie hadn't replaced Lou; she filled a vacancy. She had continued giving Kit and Kenzie the unconditional love they needed. "I'm going to miss you, too."

Valley View became a beehive of activity inside, and out as everyone tended to last minute details for the upcoming ceremony. All of a sudden it was time to get ready. Kit was overflowing with happiness as she dressed. Shelby had been there to help her, but once she was ready, she asked Shelby to leave so she could have a few moments alone. Kit studied her reflection in the mirror. For a brief moment, tears misted her eyes as she thought of both Mike, and Lou. She knew they were here in spirit. It was also her last day here at Valley View. She wasn't sad, rather reflective. This had been her haven in her transition from her past to her future. Her thoughts were interrupted by a knock on her door. BJ entered and they smiled at each other. This was a special day for both of them.

"You are a beautiful bride, Kit. You look radiant and happy."

"I am, Dad." Happier than she had ever dreamed she could be. Kit was filled with excitement as they left to join her bridal party.

Mother Nature had worked her magic. Thin white clouds drifted like ribbons in a sapphire blue sky. The gentle breeze in the trees whispered promises of hope. A sunny glow crept across the land, encircling those present with a warm embrace.

A tranquil calm surrounded Kit. She smiled down at Kenzie who looked like an angel in pink ruffles. "It's time, baby girl. You can spread the petals as you walk up to Trace. Remember to walk slow. Shelby will follow you, and Grampa, and I will be right behind Shelby."

Kenzie beamed as she tossed the petals as she walked down the aisle. At the front, Trace waited, and proudly took her hand so she could stand beside him. Shelby proceeded up the aisle where Riley stood next to Trace.

The music changed, and the first chords of the "Wedding March" began. "That's our cue, daughter." BJ crooked his arm, and Kit took it. "Are you ready?"

Kit was glowing, "I have dreamt of this day so many times I can't believe it's real. Yes, I'm ready."

Kit turned her attention to the man standing spellbound under the trellis. The men had built the trellis that was decorated with white curtains that were pulled back by green foliage and bright flowers from Sadie's garden. No man had ever looked as her the way Trace was looking at her.

Kit was a vision as her veil flowed behind her like a cascading waterfall. Kit felt like she was floating in a beautiful dream as she walked down the aisle with her dad.

Trace stood waiting for her, his familiar grin curving his lips. He continued to stare at her, astonished again by the miracle that this beautiful woman was going to be his wife.

When Kit reached the front, she took the other hand of her daughter. The three of them stood together as the bride, and groom exchanged their meaningful vows. After they exchanged rings, Trace reached into his pocket, and pulled out a ring for Kenzie. He vowed to love her and be her proud dad from this day forward. They walked back down the aisle as husband and wife, father and daughter, family. There was hardly a dry eye as they walked past their guests.

Over the next couple of hours, the bride and groom posed for pictures, and mingled. All too soon, it was time to gather inside for the reception. The cool breeze that had picked up late in the day had kept the Quonset cool for the reception.

At the end of dinner, the toasts began. Trace shifted uncomfortably when it was time for Riley's. He was a little nervous, not knowing what Riley was going to say. Riley grinned at his brother and paused for effect. He spoke with true sincerity, closing with, "Kit and Trace, may you always be as happy as you are today. May God bless you with a long life together." Riley looked over at Shelby. "Today unites the Calhouns and the Graysons as family. Trace may have started a trend." Shelby blushed, knowing she wanted this, too.

Trace, moved by Riley's toast, was glad to have Kit by his side as he responded. "Kit, and I would like to thank everyone for coming today and sharing our joy." He smiled down at Kenzie. "I remember the day that I met Kenzie. She asked me whose daddy I was. When I said that I was nobody's daddy she said I could be hers. Words that were innocently put out to the universe and fell on God's ears. God just didn't know how much work that would be." He picked Kenzie up and kissed her on the cheek. "To us, Kit. You me, Kenzie and hopefully more children. We are the first generation of Lola Grande. I will do my best to make you happy every day of your life."

"And I'll do my best to let you." Everyone laughed.

The music began for the first dance. Trace smiled at Kit. "You are a vision to behold," he said, taking her hand. "You took my breath away when you were coming down the aisle." When the music started for the second dance, Trace took Kenzie into his arms, and danced her around the dance floor. His smile never left his face. Kit watched with tears in her eyes.

The festivities continued. Trace grabbed Kit's hand and pulled her away. "Come with me, I want to show you your wedding gift." They snuck away and headed over to the corral where Ginger grazed with a huge bow around her neck. "You fell in love with Ginger before you fell in love with me. It was the appropriate gift for you."

The beautiful mare had stolen Kit's heart the first day Kit saw her. With gentle fingers she stroked the mare's forehead. Ginger flicked her tail as she accepted the gentle petting. "Trace, we can't keep every horse you have."

Trace took Kit into his arms, "It will be hard to let them go but I will always have you."

"Thank you, Trace," Kit said softly.

Trace leaned in to kiss her. "I love you, city girl."

"It's Kit Grayson, cowboy. Mrs. Kit Grayson." It sounded so right.

Trace gently put his arm around his wife, the love of his life, and kissed her tenderly. It was time to move forward with his family. "Let's go get our daughter and go home." Home to Lola Grande where future generations would be raised.